GURPS

MW01580902

Traveller®

Science Fiction Adventure in the Far Future

SECOND EDITION

By LOREN WISEMAN

Based on the award-winning Traveller science-fiction universe by MARC MILLER

Spaceship Design and Combat System by DAVID PULVER

Character Templates by SEAN PUNCH

Additional Material and Assistance by M.J. DOUGHERTY, NEIL FRIER, WILLIAM H. KEITH, JR., J. ANDREW KEITH, DAVID NILSEN, DAVID SUMMERS, AND AERRON WINSOR

Edited by JACK ELMY, STEVE JACKSON, AND GENE SEABOLT

Illustrated by YESSE AMERICA, KURT BRUGEL, ROB CASWELL, JESSE DEGRAFF, LANGDON FOSS, GLENN GRANT, MARCUS KIM, DANIEL LUNSFORD, ALAN NUNIS, TOM PETERS, AND LANCE WINKEL

GURPS System Design ∎ STEVE JACKSON
Managing Editor ∎ ALAIN H. DAWSON
GURPS Line Editor ∎ SEAN PUNCH
GURPS Traveller Line Editor ∎ LOREN WISEMAN
Production ∎ JACK ELMY AND GENE SEABOLT
Production Assistance ∎ ALEX FERNANDEZ AND J. ZAUDER
Print Buying ∎ RUSSELL GODWIN
Art Direction ∎ ALAIN H. DAWSON and LOREN WISEMAN
GURPS Errata Coordinator ∎ MICHAEL BOWMAN
Sales Manager ∎ ROSS JEPSON

Playtesters: Andy Akins, John H. Bogan, Jr., Rob Day, Robert Eaglestone, Steven Hudson, David Pulver, Hans Rancke, Brett Slocum, and David Summers and his Star Captains. Special thanks to Onno Meyer and all the other second-edition contributors.

ISBN 1-55634-408-2

1 2 3 4 5 6 7 8 9 10

STEVE JACKSON GAMES

Contents

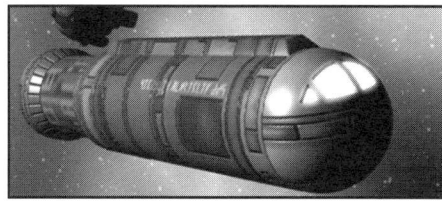

About GURPS

Steve Jackson Games is committed to full support of the **GURPS** system. Our address is SJ Games, Box 18957, Austin, TX 78760. Please include a self-addressed, stamped envelope (SASE) any time you write us! Resources now available include:

Pyramid (**www.sjgames.com/pyramid**). Our online magazine includes new rules and articles for **GURPS**. It also covers all the hobby's top games – **AD&D, Traveller, World of Darkness, Call of Cthulhu, Shadowrun** and many more – and other SJ Games releases like **In Nomine, INWO, Car Wars, Toon, Ogre Miniatures** and more. And *Pyramid* subscribers also have access to playtest files online, to see (and comment on) new books before they're released.

New supplements and adventures. **GURPS** continues to grow, and we'll be happy to let you know what's new. A current catalog is available for an SASE. Or check out our Web site (below).

Errata. Everyone makes mistakes, including us – but we do our best to fix our errors. Up-to-date errata sheets for all **GURPS** releases, including this book, are always available from SJ Games; be sure to include an SASE with your request. Or download them from the Web – see below.

Q&A. We do our best to answer any game question accompanied by an SASE.

Gamer input. We value your comments. We will consider them, not only for new products, but also when we update this book on later printings!

Internet. Visit us on the World Wide Web at **www.sjgames.com** for an online catalog, errata and updates, and hundreds of pages of information. The home page for **GURPS Traveller** is located at **www.sjgames.com/gurps/traveller**. We also have conferences on Compuserve and America Online. **GURPS** has its own Usenet group, too: rec.games.frp.gurps.

Much of the online discussion of **GURPS** happens on GURPSnet. To join, send mail to majordomo@io.com with "subscribe GURPSnet-L" in the body, or point your World Wide Web browser to: **www.io.com/GURPSnet/www**.

Page References

See *GURPS Compendium I*, p. 181 for a list of abbreviations for **GURPS** titles. Any page reference that begins with a B refers to **GURPS Basic Set**, *Third Edition, Revised*; e.g., p. B144 refers to page 144 of *Basic Set*. CI refers to *Compendium I*, CII to *Compendium II*, S to *Space*, Second Edition, T:AI to *Traveller: Alien Races 1*, T:FT to *Traveller: Far Trader*, UT to *Ultra-Tech*, UTT to *Ultra-Tech 2*, and VE to *Vehicles*.

INTRODUCTION

Traveller was first published by Game Designers' Workshop in 1977, and was one of the first science-fiction roleplaying games (indeed, one of the first roleplaying games of any sort). With one of the most extensive backgrounds of *any* RPG, *Traveller* quickly attracted many loyal fans (some of whom were inspired to add to the background themselves) and rapidly grew to became the standard against which other SF roleplaying games were measured. The broad scope of the game's milieu has given thousands a canvas upon which to paint, in broad strokes or fine, a universe all their own, but still one they could share with others. It is, after all, a big universe.

Traveller went through several editions over the years, and quite a few changes were incorporated along the way. One of those was the Rebellion. In the 1116th year of the Third Imperium, Emperor Strephon was assassinated by a power-seeking rival, and the Imperium split into several warring factions, shaking the very foundations of the game . . . and bringing conflict and excitement to languishing campaigns.

As fascinating as the Rebellion was, there existed a desire in the minds of many for the whole thing to have never happened! (GDW once parodied this sentiment in an April Fool's Day issue of *Challenge* magazine, wherein we described Strephon's assassin awakening to discover Strephon in the shower.) Over the years, GDW was approached by several outside authors, all with the idea for a sourcebook where Strephon lived and the Rebellion never happened – in essence, an alternate timeline for *Traveller*. GDW never followed up on these proposals for various reasons. This same idea, however, is what Steve Jackson Games has undertaken: an alternate timeline, a parallel universe, if you will, where Strephon, the 43rd Emperor of the Third Imperium, lives. This is not to say that all is well with the universe. A story without conflict is not a very good story. So, expect things to happen in this universe . . . changes *will* occur.

There is another reason for **GURPS Traveller**. Many of the original books that detail the history and background of the Third Imperium are long out of print. In this work, new players and referees can have access to the same information as 20-year collectors. Enjoy.

A number of individuals have contributed suggestions and ideas for this book. A few have gone above and beyond the call of duty. Thanks (in great profusion, and in no particular order) to Sean Punch (aka Dr. Kromm), David Pulver, Brett Slocum, and David Summers, as well as the **GURPS** Brain Trust, the **GURPS Traveller** Impromptu Cabal (you know who you are), and the *Traveller* Mailing List.

Lastly, the author would like to pay tribute to those giants whose shoulders have served him so very well. *Traveller* is, was, and always will be a collective creation, and I don't have space to even mention, let alone properly honor, all of the people whose talents and imaginations have contributed to the game. Thanks.

– *Loren Wiseman*

ABOUT THE AUTHOR

Loren Wiseman was one of the founding partners of GDW, Inc., original publisher of *Traveller,* and spent over 20 years there as a game designer, developer, typesetter, and editor. After GDW closed, Loren freelanced for a time, and then came to SJ Games, where he is the art director and *Traveller* line editor and expert-in-residence.

THE TRAVELLER NEWS SERVICE

For many years a feature of the *Journal of the Travellers' Aid Society*, **TNS** chronicled the ongoing life and times of the Imperium. Loren Wiseman is once again writing **TNS** as the alternate history of the Third Imperium develops. It is updated regularly; read it online at **www.sjgames. com/gurps/traveller/news.html**. "Back issues" of *TNS* are also online.

The SJ Games *Traveller* page has links to the *Traveller* Web Ring, and thus links to most of the major *Traveller*-oriented web sites that exist. For information on subscribing to the *Traveller* Mailing List, contact rwm@mpgn.com.

The universe of the Third Imperium is similar to our own in two respects: the laws of physics, and the players' own society. These aspects will serve as familiar reference points from which to explore the universe of *Traveller.*

The *Traveller* universe is an extension of our own, projected into the far future. As such, the laws of physics still apply – with a few exceptions necessary to the game. Jump drives, maneuver drives, and contragrav technology all violate one or more physical laws (at least as we currently understand them), yet they are major facets of *Traveller,* and will require some suspension of disbelief. Along the way a few aspects of other sciences will be ignored as well, all in the interest of a good, fun game. In general, however, players can count on physics to work for them in the *Traveller* universe as it does in their own.

From a societal standpoint, the basic culture more or less resembles that of present-day Terra (with a few more technological gadgets). This is intentional: Players are from this culture, and it makes it easier for them to relate to the characters they play. Another reason is to heighten the contrast between Imperial society and the more unusual societies the characters will encounter in their travels. As its name implies, *Traveller* is about traveling. Many exciting things can be done on a single world, in a single city, but eventually most characters move to other worlds and encounter alien cultures. To paraphrase Han Solo, they're going to see a lot of strange stuff . . .

Only a Dream

"I dreamt of horrors last night. The emperor murdered, the Imperium shattered into a half-dozen feuding shards – and over it all, some hideous, bestial face, all wires and pulleys and gears, swallowing the stars themselves, one by one, until the sky was completely, totally black. I am not usually given to nightmares, and normally I forget what I dream within minutes of awakening, but for some reason, this particular dream stayed with me hours later, and I vividly recall every detail."

*– personal journal of
Prince Varian Paulo Alkhalikoi,
Entry for 133-1116*

THE IMPERIUM

The Third Imperium (usually called "The Imperium" for short) is a far-flung interstellar community encompassing more than 11,000 worlds within a region approximately 700 parsecs across. It has ruled its territory for 11 centuries and looks to continue for many more. The present emperor, Strephon, is the 43rd person to hold the title and will soon celebrate the golden jubilee of his coronation.

Three factors are worth mentioning in any brief survey of the Imperium: culture, travel time, and feudalism.

Culture

The dominant cultural tradition found within the Imperium is that of the Vilani, the branch of Humaniti that established the First Imperium. Second most widespread, and considerably intermixed with Vilani culture, is that of the Solomani: humans from Terra who overwhelmed the First Imperium and established the Second. These two cultures (or more properly, a blend of them) serve as the baseline culture of *Traveller,* and it is from this baseline that variant and divergent groups are measured.

Note: This chapter provides the players with a general history of the universe in which their characters find themselves. Consider it a briefing document on what the average character knows about the *Traveller* universe, and as such it should be freely available to the players.

Pelican
Nebula

Vargr Extents

• Lair
(Vargr Home World)

• Zhodane
(Zhodani Home World)

Zhodani Consulate

• Regina

Vland
(Vilani Home World) •

• Antares

**Spinward
Marches**

• Deneb

Corridor

Human Client States

SPINWARD

**Vanguard
Reaches**

**The
Beyond**

**Reft
Sector**

Capital
•

The Imperium

Aslan Colonies

• Reference

Great Rift

J-5 Route

**The Old
Expanses**

**Dark
Nebula**

**Solomani
Rim**
• Terra
(Solomani Home World

Aslan Hierate

Kuzu •
(Aslan Home World)

**Solomani
Sphere**

Aslan
Client States

• Canopus

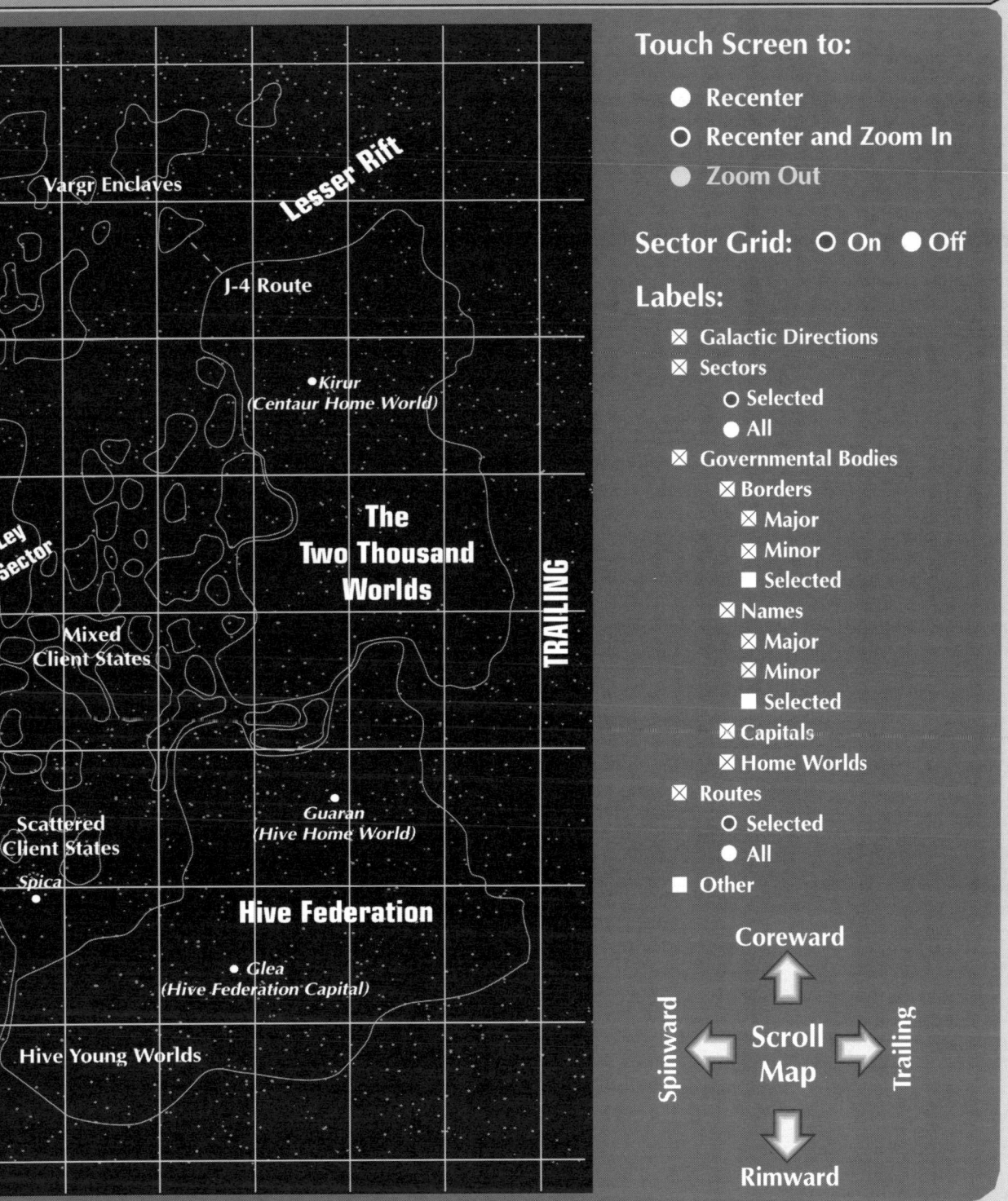

Vargr Enclaves

Lesser Rift

J-4 Route

Ley Sector

•Kirur
(Centaur Home World)

The
Two Thousand
Worlds

TRAILING

Mixed
Client States

Scattered
Client States

Spica

Guaran
(Hive Home World)

Hive Federation

• Glea
(Hive Federation Capital)

Hive Young Worlds

Touch Screen to:

● Recenter
○ Recenter and Zoom In
● Zoom Out

Sector Grid: ○ On ● Off

Labels:

⊠ Galactic Directions
⊠ Sectors
  ○ Selected
  ● All
⊠ Governmental Bodies
  ⊠ Borders
    ⊠ Major
    ⊠ Minor
    ■ Selected
  ⊠ Names
    ⊠ Major
    ⊠ Minor
    ■ Selected
  ⊠ Capitals
  ⊠ Home Worlds
⊠ Routes
  ○ Selected
  ● All
■ Other

Coreward

Spinward   Scroll
             Map   Trailing

Rimward

In a Nutshell . . .

In the not too distant future, Humans invent a means of faster-than-light travel. They have previously been exploring and exploiting the solar system in small, in-system spacecraft, and have established economic and scientific colonies and other outposts here and there. After a few years of exploration, an expedition to Barnard's Star encounters other Human beings, and a mystery that will not be solved for many centuries: How did they get there? Did Humanity originate on Earth, or was it planted there eons ago by a force or forces unknown?

The Terrans had encountered the outskirts of a vast interstellar empire populated mostly by Humans who called themselves Vilani (with quite a few non-Human intelligences represented as well). The Vilani were in a state of slow decline after ruling space for centuries. Almost instantly, conflict broke out, and against all odds, the Terrans conquered the Vilani Empire (later called the First Imperium) and managed to postpone its collapse for a few centuries. Humans from Earth become known as Solomani, and found themselves masters of a gigantic empire incorporating thousands of worlds. Scattered among these worlds were groups of non-Human intelligences, but there were a bewildering number of worlds populated by Humans. Some were identical to Terrans, some vastly different, but all were clearly connected by a common ancestry, and were clearly in a superior position vis-a-vis the non-Humans.

After a few centuries of Solomani rule (which the Terrans called the Rule of Man, the Vilani called the Ramshackle Empire, and historians call the Second Empire), the light of interstellar civilization was extinguished, and the 1,000-year period known as the Long Night begins. It was a time of political and economic chaos, during which many worlds completely lost their technological base, and all worlds lost the capability of interstellar flight.

Continued on next page . . .

The Imperium is *diverse*. A vast number of cultures, both human and alien, constitute its citizenry. With rare exceptions, each world in the Imperium chooses its own government, its own laws (within certain limits), and its own customs, behaviors, and fashions. As a result, nearly any society imaginable either exists within the Imperium or once did, and interstellar travelers will encounter things undreamed of by their planet-bound brethren.

The most widespread group with which the characters will likely interact is the interstellar community of starship crews. Equally widespread are the people who interact with *them*: officials, technicians, cargo brokers, clerks, bartenders, and the myriad hangers-on at starports who perpetually try to gain something from travelers.

Travel Time

Interstellar government over an area as large as that of the Imperium is a significant problem, which, at first, seems insurmountable. Vast distances, long travel times, and communication lags all conspire against a functioning, efficient system which can meet the population's needs. According to history this is nothing new: Around the first century Rome ruled all of Europe, and in the 16th century Spain ruled much of the New World, with travel times of up to a year between the seat of government and the new territories. In fact, through most of history, timely governmental communication, with both a rapid dispatch of instructions and an equally rapid response, has been more a dream than a reality.

The Imperium has come upon two solutions, which together lessen the problem of distance: the Xboat network and feudalism.

The Xboat Network: Like a living body, with its network of veins and arteries, the Imperium is crisscrossed by Xboat routes, or links, devoted entirely to the carriage of messages for official, commercial, and private purposes.

The express boat (commonly known as "Xboat") is a small, fast ship comprising a pilot's compartment, data banks, and jump drives. The fit is so tight that the tiny ships don't even have maneuver drives. Each is capable of jump-4 (four parsecs in a week); it jumps, relaying its messages to the station on arrival. It then waits to be picked up by a specialized vessel known as an Xboat tender, refueled, and sent on its way to the next station en route. The local station on a world accepts messages, encodes them, and transmits them to a station at the edge of the stellar system. The network works like the Pony Express, with messages always moving at top speed. Transfer time for the messages from one Xboat to another can be as short as 10 minutes, and is rarely more than an hour.

Ultimately, the little Xboats make their way to one of the many Imperial Way Stations scattered throughout the Imperium's subsectors. There they are refitted, overhauled, and refurbished, only to be sent on their way again.

The Xboat network puts the edge of the Imperium about 44 weeks out from Core/Capital; that represents a savings of better than 75% of normal travel time. And still the Imperium is straining under the effects of distance.

Feudalism

The vast distances separating stellar systems make individual responsibility and authority very important. The Imperium is divided into 20 sectors, each about 32-by-40 parsecs. Each sector is divided into 16 subsectors (8-by-10 parsecs). A subsector contains perhaps 30 or more systems, each with at least one star, worlds, and satellites.

Worlds and star systems are free to govern themselves pretty much as they desire, provided ultimate sovereignty over external affairs is accorded the Imperium. Interstellar government begins at the subsector level, on one world designated the subsector capital. The subsector capital is ruled by a high-ranking noble selected by higher levels of government. This figure, normally called a duke (technically a sector duke, but even in official documents the shorter title has come into vogue) has a free hand in government, and is subject only to broad guidelines from his superiors. At the same time, the duke owes fealty to the higher levels of government, ultimately to the emperor himself. The feudal approach depends greatly on a sense of honor, one cultivated by the hereditary aristocracy. This sense of honor is very strong within the Imperium; it has proven essential to the survival of such a far-flung community. The system has worked for a very long time.

WE ARE NOT ALONE

The known interstellar community encompasses thousands of worlds, many of them inhabited, and not all by Humaniti. The number of intelligent life-forms that has been contacted is quite high: within the Imperium itself, more than 100. When regions beyond the Imperial boundaries are included, the total number rises to well over 400.

Major and Minor Races: A superficial classification system for the various intelligent races has been created, based on empirical evidence and to some extent on tradition. In general, the dominant races of known space are those which have achieved faster-than-light travel by themselves, rather than receiving it through contact with starfaring civilizations. These dominant races are called major races; all others are called minor races. Thus, the term major race has become attached to a single technical development regardless of other merit. A somewhat sound reason backs this concept: Races that developed FTL rapidly expanded into space, spreading their influence across the stars. Slower races were contacted before they had a chance to discover the FTL secret and emerged into a universe already controlled by the major races. Indeed, the shock of being found by a superior race (often superior only in their knowledge of FTL technology) may demoralize that race as a whole, causing them to reluctantly accept a secondary role in interstellar society. The classification scheme is, of course, simplistic, but the major races tend to perpetuate it since it works to their advantage.

In a Nutshell . . .

[Continued]

Recovery was slow, but some worlds finally clawed their way back up the ladder of civilization. Gradually, as interstellar travel was rediscovered, star systems coalesced into larger interstellar states, and these began to grow. Finally, over 1,100 years ago, on a world named Sylea, a Human named Cleon Zhunastu converted the multi-world Sylean Federation into the Third Imperium.

It is now the 1120th year of that Third Imperium, and Cleon's 42nd successor now rules an empire larger and more advanced than either that preceded it. The Third Imperium is not alone. Other interstellar governments stand on its boundaries as neighbors, allies, enemies, partners, and competitors.

Some think that the Third Imperium has also grown too large, and is headed for collapse, but others believe it will adapt itself to changing conditions and continue ever stronger.

And the answer to the riddle as to where did Humaniti originate? In 1120, it is known that all Humans in the universe descend from groups removed from Terra more than 100 millennia in the past, and carried to dozens of worlds by an unknown agency. Who was this agency? Who scattered Humaniti throughout the galaxy, and why? For every answer, it seems, there is another question.

THE SIX RACES

Similar to the major/minor race division is the concept of the Six Races. The origin of the term is uncertain, but it appears independently in Aslan, Vargr, and Centaur sources. There is some disagreement as to the proper identification of the Six, but most commentators agree that all must be major races. The most common definition was once Aslan, Centaurs, Hive, Vargr, Zhodani, and Imperials (both Solomani and Vilani). The confirmation (in 790, Imperial date) of multiple worlds inhabited by the Droyne, and of archeological evidence that they possessed FTL travel before the entry of any of the modern dominant races into space, gave new weight to the Six Races concept. With the inclusion of the Droyne, Humaniti could be neatly categorized as one race, with six truly distinct races now included: Aslan, Centaurs, Droyne, Hive, Humans, and Vargr.

Aslan are roughly Human-sized and are descended from four-limbed, upright, bipedal carnivore/pouncer stock. The earliest Terran explorers saw in them a vague resemblance to the Terran lion, and they have been described (by Terrans, at least, and by some others) as lion-like ever since, although there is very little true similarity. They are native to their own biosphere, and no more related to a lion than they are to an eggplant. See full profile in *GURPS Traveller Alien Races 2*.

Centaurs (they call themselves the K'kree) are among the most massive of the major races, and are the only examples of the major races descended from herbivores. K'kree are conservative, gregarious with their own kind (to the point of distress if isolated), and claustrophobic. These characteristics derive from their evolutionary origins as herd animals. See *GURPS Traveller Alien Races 2*.

Droyne are a small race, both in stature and in dominion, with only limited settlements on a small number of worlds. The history of their evolution is a puzzle, as their home world is not known with certainty. The Droyne have no empires, and actually rule only a few worlds. In some few cases, they possess the technology to produce sophisticated machinery, including jump drives and starships, but they seem content to stay on their own worlds.

Humaniti (old spelling: Humanity) is a special case. Originally evolved on Terra, Humans were disseminated over nearly 50 worlds about 300,000 years ago by an unknown agency. These various examples of Humaniti then independently developed. Unlike non-Human races, individual Human races are classified as major or minor. Three Human races (the Solomani of Terra, the Vilani of the First Imperium, and the Zhodani far to spinward) are major races. The nearly 50 other races of Humaniti are all minor. The Zhodani are profiled in *GURPS Traveller Alien Races 1*.

Vargr are an intelligent race genetically manipulated from carnivore/chaser stock by the same Ancients who disseminated Humaniti to the stars. Vargr have long suffered from an inability to organize themselves (to any degree or for any length of time) beyond the star-system level, and their empires tend to rise and fall with regularity. Vargr have an intense racial pride, and are easily insulted. They are prone to enter into fights without regard for possible consequences. Refer to *GURPS Traveller Alien Races 1* for a complete profile.

Hivers (a Human term applied to them – their own name for themselves has no spoken equivalent) are the most obviously alien of the major races: They are descended from omnivore gatherer/scavenger stock, and are unique in that they attained a form of agriculture before they became sentient. They exhibit a six-fold radial symmetry. The body has an internal skeleton consisting of a series of rings supporting the limbs, while a fused carapace protects the brain and internal organs. Hivers themselves are highly individualistic (the term "hive" is an early misconception) while driven by curiosity, parental instinct, and a desire to maintain the unity and uniformity of their race both within and outside their Federation.

CAMPAIGNS

A wide variety of campaigns are possible in the *Traveller* setting. Some of those discussed in *GURPS Space* pp. 4-6 are of particular interest, and are expanded on below:

SELLING THE MOON – WHOLESALE

Mercantile wheeling and dealing was designed into the original *Traveller* games, and remains one of, if not *the* most, popular pursuits for characters. The *Beowulf* mentioned on the original game box was a free trader, intended as a rough analog to the tramp steamers of the late 19th and early 20th century – a small merchant ship, eking out a living transporting cargo and passengers from world to world.

This sort of campaign works best in frontier regions where there are not a lot of established trading companies already working the trade routes for all they are worth, or in areas where the big guys have suffered a temporary setback that allows the little guys (the PCs) to get a foothold. On the other hand, once the PCs' starship line gets big enough, it can expand into other, more settled regions and come into conflict with the established companies. Merchant campaigns can blend into other types as well. Trade wars between rival spaceship lines can spark small wars where mercenaries are needed. Industrial espionage is as dangerous and as lucrative as the other variety. Merchant princes with enough cash can become powerful political forces.

The Game Master must work out the economies of the worlds in fair detail, figuring out what it is that one world wants that another (reasonably nearby) world has in abundance. *GURPS Traveller Far Trader* provides all the tools and tips needed to work up a mercantile campaign's setting.

MERCENARIES – TRAVEL TO DISTANT WORLDS, MEET EXOTIC BEINGS . . . AND KILL THEM

Of about equal popularity in the original *Traveller* games was the mercenary-based campaign, where the PCs were soldiers for hire. The background was set up so that the Imperium tolerated a fair number of low-intensity, localized wars, provided they never got to be a threat to the wider order. The Imperium would step in when things threatened to destabilize a whole region, but otherwise left things pretty much alone. Local governments or other groups hire mercenary units to fight other groups and other units. Players can be a small, elite strike force, or the senior officers of a larger company- or battalion-sized force. Individual specialists might be hired by units in need of a sniper, perhaps, or a demolitions engineer.

The Game Master must be willing to conduct a great many firefights and out-and-out battles (this is a wonderful type of campaign for people who are also military miniatures players). The players must be willing to start over again as new characters more often than in other types of campaigns (soldiering is not the safest of occupations). This is not a campaign type for people who have no interest in weapons and things military.

GURPS Traveller Star Mercs provides additional insight into the organization, conduct, and equipment of mercenaries in the Imperium.

Reflections of a Grognard

"There's nothing like a good war to ruin the merc trade. You get a lot of enthusiastic amateurs who think they know what they are doing because they managed to survive basic training, and who got hooked on the adrenaline when they finally see action. The problem is that they have not yet acquired sufficient instincts for self-preservation, which means that they are more likely to get themselves killed. This, in and of itself, is not necessarily a bad thing, but they have a tendency to take us grognards with them by accident."

– Captain Yunara N. "Jinks" Giancana,
Imperial Marines, ret.

Good Guys
and Bad Guys

The original *Traveller* was occasionally criticized (or lampooned) because many of the early adventures required or encouraged the characters to engage in some form of illegal activity (smuggling, breaking and entering, piracy, etc.) or acts of questionable morality (mercenary actions, espionage, state-sanctioned assassination). There were several reasons for this, but the main one was that these were the kinds of adventures people seemed most interested in. They were the type most often submitted, and were the most commonly encountered at conventions.

There is considerable pleasure to be had in vicarious law breaking. Most people are law-abiding, non-violent, and pretty much socialized, but it can be entertaining to imagine ourselves as otherwise. This is not the place to go into "bad guys" as heroes, but the character is well established in books and movies: Robin Hood, Frank and Jesse James, the Ringo Kid (as played by John Wayne), Bonnie and Clyde (as played by Warren Beatty and Faye Dunaway), Butch and Sundance (Paul Newman and Robert Redford) and several blockbusters' worth of smugglers, con-men, and "rebels against the empire" (or Earth Force as the case may be). *Traveller* was not alone in encouraging rule-bending heroes, but perhaps we went a little overboard in the early days.

As gamers became more sophisticated, they began to see the entertainment value in activities other than the criminal ones, and later versions of *Traveller* became more sophisticated.

POLITICS, DIPLOMACY, AND ESPIONAGE

For Game Masters and players who are interested in politics and complex governmental interactions (or for those who just want to play spies), the Third Imperium presents a broad canvas upon which to paint a campaign of political action and diplomatic intrigue.

For example, frontier campaigns are possible where the players interact with the many political entities along the borders of the Imperium. The Imperium also has client states, governments that are not part of the Imperium for whatever reason, as well as large neighboring governments that must be interacted with. Politics *within* the Imperium can be the subject of long and interesting campaigns, too. PCs could become involved in complex court intrigues at the Imperial palace, or at one or more of the archducal or ducal courts. Private and public scandals, blackmail, plot and counterplot – all offer rich veins of adventuring ore to be mined. Why, one could stumble across a plot to kill the emperor and overthrow the empire!

Of course, espionage and diplomacy often go hand in hand. How many delicate diplomatic negotiations depend on one vital piece of information that tips the scales one way or the other? How many embassies have been embarrassed by spy scandals? Small actions can have large repercussions, and one or two well-placed people can change the course of an entire empire.

Be warned, political campaigns require even more work on the part of the GM than military or economic ones, and they are not for everyone.

LAWBREAKERS AND LAW ENFORCERS

The *Traveller* setting is well suited to this type of campaign. Any number of "less-than-legal" professions, such as smuggler, interplanetary cat-burglar, pirate, and world-hopping grifter, are open to players who wish to experience an illicit vocation without actually becoming a blight on society. Conversely, they may prefer to play the law enforcers whose job it is to serve and protect the Imperium from such scofflaws. Another possibility involves the characters being thrust by circumstance to one side of the law or the other. For instance, the details of the economic grind may tempt otherwise law-abiding merchants into smuggling or piracy as a means of getting the ledger back into the black. This sort of campaign can easily blend into a mercantile or political one.

REBELS AGAINST THE EMPIRE

Taking a page from another book, the players may want to try to overthrow the Third Imperium! There are those who feel that the oligarchs that presently rule have lost touch with the best interests of the people and that the Imperium must become more responsive to its citizens' demands – *or else!* A rebellion requires leaders, soldiers, spies, and financiers – all pursuits that can provide many exciting adventures.

STRANGE NEW WORLDS

There is little room left for exploring "where no one has gone before" in the year 1120 of the Imperium. Things are pretty much explored (in a geographic sense, anyway – there is still much to learn, otherwise). Campaigns can be set in previous years, however, when exploration and settlement of new worlds was a common endeavor – the history of the *Traveller* universe has many such eras ripe for exploitation. With a little work, a creative GM could devise a campaign set, for instance, in the first century of the current Imperium. No matter the period, *GURPS Traveller First In* will enhance an exploration campaign.

CHAPTER TWO

Details of a Universe

This chapter discusses the details of the *Traveller* universe, and serves more as a Game Master briefing than a players' guide. Most of the information in this chapter was designed to be given out during a game session, as part of a character's background knowledge or as a result of their research. Some sections are intended for GMs only, and are clearly marked as such.

FTL TRAVEL – THE JUMP DRIVE

The key to the stars is the jump drive. Without it, the space between the stars takes years, even lifetimes, to cross; with it, starships travel parsec distances in a matter of days. The development of a jump drive marks the beginning of interstellar travel for any race, including Humaniti.

A jump drive is both fast and simple. With one, it is possible to move from *here* to *there* (where both places are at least 100 diameters out from any large masses) in a period of about a week. The time in transit is independent of the distance traveled, which makes this system practical for interstellar travel, but for little else. The distance traveled with the jump drive depends on the drive in use – from 1 to 6 parsecs, with greater distances as yet unavailable. In point of fact, the current theory of jump drive actually precludes greater jump distances (these can occasionally occur by accident, but the destination is totally uncontrollable). See p. 44 and p. 157 for more about jump drives.

Another central fact of interstellar travel is that no method of information transfer faster than jump drives has been invented. Ships can carry messages, but radio still lags at mere light speed. Communication is always restricted to the speed of interstellar transportation. The very fastest ships have jump-6 . . . so news and commerce never travel more than 6 parsecs per week, and usually more slowly than that.

GOVERNMENT

It is often said that the Imperium rules the space between worlds and leaves the dirt to the worlds themselves, but that is (as with most sayings) a simplification. In point of fact, the Imperium governs all things it chooses to govern, which includes the space between the worlds within its boundaries, but also includes many worlds themselves, and a great many places besides. The Imperium controls and/or regulates:

- All interstellar commerce and relations within its boundaries.
- Any planetary commerce and relations that affect the control and/or regulation of the above.
- Anything that constitutes a threat to the stability or security of the Imperium as a whole or in part.
- Any planetary or near-planetary bodies necessary to control and/or regulate the above.

The Metric System

The original *Traveller* used – and in its present edition, still uses – the metric system of measurements. This was done to give the game a scientific basis, as well as a more international aspect and appeal. *GURPS* uses the imperial system of weights and measures in its American editions, but metric in its overseas translations (German, Spanish, etc.). *GURPS Traveller* will use the imperial system, for compatibility with other *GURPS* products.

Game Masters who wish to preserve the overall scientific feel of the original may make use of the metric system with the author's blessing, and a conversion table is provided herewith (please note that "imperial" on this table denotes the system of measurement used in the United States, and not that of the *Traveller* Imperium). The first column gives a "quick-and-dirty" conversion value, good enough for most gaming purposes, and the second gives a more precise value.

Imperial	Game Metric	Real Metric
1 foot (ft)	30 cm	30.48 cm
1 yd (yd)	1 meter	0.914 meter
1 mile (mi)	1.5 km	1.609 km
1 inch (in)	2.5 cm	2.54 cm
1 pound (lb)	0.5 kg	0.453 kg
1 ton (tn)	1 metric ton	0.907 metric tons
1 long ton (tn)	1 metric ton	1.02 metric tons
1 gallon (gal)	4 liters	3.785 liters
1 quart (qt)	1 liter	0.946 liters
1 ounce (oz)	30 grams	31.103 grams
1 cubic inch (ci)	16 cubic cm	16.387 cubic cm
1 cubic yard (cy)	0.75 cubic m	0.765 cubic m

Temperatures: To convert degrees Fahrenheit to degrees Celsius, subtract 32 from the Fahrenheit reading and multiply by 5/9. Note that -40 degrees is the same on both scales.

Nanotechnology

Physicist Richard Feynman first suggested the notion of atom-by-atom manipulation of matter in the late 1950s in his talk *There's Plenty of Room at the Bottom*. But it wasn't until the 1981 book *The Engines of Creation* that author K. Eric Drexler gave the notion a name and outlined the possibilities. This is not the place to go into a complete essay on the subject, but it is a good place to explain why *Traveller* does not directly incorporate most of the possibilities represented by *micro electrical-mechanical systems* (MEMS).

Drexler's basic concept was that individual molecules (or even individual atoms) could be manipulated by microscopic machines, in any way that the laws of physics allowed. Cars, buildings, spaceships, whatever, could be grown out of whatever material was desired. MEMS could disassemble an object into its component atoms, and reassemble them as something completely different. Given enough atoms of the right sort, it would be theoretically possible to fabricate anything on the spot, the only restrictions being the energy needed for the job and enough atoms of the proper elements being present. A cloud of MEMS (the so-called "smart fog" of science-fiction stories) could grow a seven-course meal right in front of the diners, including the table, chairs, plates, tablecloth, utensils, and water in the fingerbowls. The leftovers (including the table, the plates, and so on) could be converted into a recliner couch for the diners to nap on after the meal is eaten. Furthermore, the MEMS could conceivably build other MEMS, so the technology of replication would be self-replicating. Infections could be dealt with by disassembling the infectious bacteria, injuries healed by rebuilding the tissues at a molecular level, surgery accomplished by a horde of microscopic repair robots that grow new heart valves or replacement limbs.

Continued on next page . . .

GMG '98

If this sounds vague and open to interpretation, it is. If it sounds undemocratic, it is. It does make for a relatively quiet and profitable climate for the empire as a whole, however.

It could be said that all Imperial government is military government, because the ultimate threat the Imperium can hold over anyone's head (literally and figuratively) is military. The Imperial Navy, the Imperial Marines, and (to a lesser extent) the Imperial Army are the "big stick" behind all Imperial control. However, the Imperium has vast economic, technological, and political resources that can be brought to bear as well, and these are not inconsequential.

RELIGION IN THE THIRD IMPERIUM

Religion is a touchy subject, even in roleplaying games, and especially where existing religions are concerned. There is no doubt that religion can be a major factor in RPGs. It can motivate adventurers, and provide a source of both conflict and unity among characters. On the other hand, religion is a highly charged topic and many players may not like to see their religion "trivialized" in game form.

Also, religion poses a number of questions for those wishing to include it in their games: Will any current religion still exist in the *Traveller* universe thousands of years from now? How will the discovery of non-Human intelligent life change Human religions (i.e., can non-Humans have souls)? Will aliens be welcomed into Human religions (and vice versa)? What new religions and offshoots of existing religions will form? How will advances in technology change religion? No quick or simple answers present themselves to many of these questions. It is left up to individual Game Masters to decide what is best for their campaigns (and players).

A Chronology of the Traveller Universe

Dates in the distant past are approximate (the margin of error varies). Dates after 0 Imperial are accurate to within a year unless otherwise noted.

Imperial	Vilani	Solomani	Event
-310,000	233,000 P.I.	305,000 B.C.	Ancients arise on Droyne home world.
-300,000	226,000 P.I.	295,000 B.C.	Humans transplanted to various worlds throughout known space.
-290,000	218,000 P.I.	285,000 B.C.	Final war destroys Ancient civilization.
-20,000	12,000 P.I.	15,000 B.C.	Ancients' warbots on Vland run down. Vilani cultural development begins.
-15,000	8500 P.I.	10,500 B.C.	Solomani cultural development begins during the retreat of the last major glaciation.
-11,000	5300 P.I.	6500 B.C.	Flowering of Vilani culture.
-10,011	4547 P.I.	5491 B.C.	First Vilani space explorations. Approximate date of development of agriculture on Terra.
-9400	4081 P.I.	4880 B.C.	Vilani sublight interstellar colonization.
-9310	4013 P.I.	4790 B.C.	Vilani discover non-Vilani Human civilization.
-9235	3955 P.I.	4715 B.C.	Vilani invent jump-1 drive.
-7071	2304 P.I.	2551 B.C.	Egyptian civilization on Earth constructs the Great Pyramids.
-6731	2046 P.I.	2211 B.C.	First Psionic Games. Zhodani calendar begins.
-6720	1351 P.I.	1300 B.C.	Shang Dynasty rules China on Terra.
-5430	1054 P.I.	910 B.C.	Vilani invent jump-2 drive.
-5415	1043 P.I.	895 B.C.	Zhodani develop jump drive.
-5400	1032 P.I.	880 B.C.	Vilani Consolidation Wars begin.
-4698	496 P.I.	178 B.C.	Hivers develop inferior jump drive.
-4520	361 P.I.	1 A.D.	Solomani dating system begins.
-4404	272 P.I.	117 A.D.	Vega absorbed by Vilani. Dacians absorbed by Roman Empire on Terra.
-4305	197 P.I.	216 A.D.	Unification of K'kree homeworld.
-4212	126 P.I.	309 A.D.	Hivers invent standard jump drive. China in the midst of the "Three Kingdoms" era on Terra.
-4142	72 P.I.	379 A.D.	K'kree invent jump drive.

Nanotechnology

[Continued]

MEMS also present a dark side: They could be used as weapons. An enemy could be converted to a pool of constituent atoms by a cloud of microscopic attack machines. Since these attack MEMS could be self-replicating, it would only be necessary to send one in the attack force. The only defense would be other MEMS. The whole situation would be beyond the individual's direct control, and would somewhat resemble chemical/biological warfare – you just have to hope that your defensive MEMS remain superior to the attacker's offensive MEMS.

A good roleplaying game could be designed incorporating nanotech, but that game would not be *Traveller*. If goods can be made to order on the spot, there will be no need for trade, which is one of the primary sources of adventure in the *Traveller* universe. (Indeed, much of what we know about supply-and-demand economics will cease to be relevant.) There would be no mercenary adventures: Why use armies to invade when you need only introduce a few self-replicating attack MEMS to the enemy world? After every living thing is dismantled to its component atoms, you send in your colonists and their MEMS grow their infrastructure.

In *Traveller,* nanotechnology can be assumed to be present at a low level. It forms the basis of certain medical devices (more and more as TL rises), and is probably the means by which much high-tech manufacturing takes place. If we assume that MEMS are very, very expensive, and are not self-replicating (for whatever reason), we have the basis for excluding much of Drexler's nanotechnology from *Traveller*. Imperial research stations (q.v.) are probably experimenting with nanotech, and GMs who wish to put their victims . . . er . . . players through a "nanites gone wild" scenario can look to these places for justification. Individual GMs, however, are free to make nanotechnology as widespread as they like (*GURPS Robots* and the two *Ultra-Tech* books contain the relevant rules; indeed, the discussion of the Safetech technology path on pp. UTT9 pretty much describes how to set up the *Traveller* universe).

Cybertechnology

Prosthetics to replace damaged or defective body parts are common throughout the Imperium (where technology permits). Prosthetics that enhance performance beyond Human norms are viewed as scandalous in most of the Imperium (especially those which do not resemble the body part replaced), and are illegal in many places because of their obvious potential for criminal abuse (many worlds still harbor what used to be called a "Frankenstein complex"). Most of the larger passenger starship lines require passengers with any prosthetics to register them before boarding (even some normal prosthetic replacements can interfere with ship systems – or so it is claimed). Free traders, of course, are not always so picky. As a rule, the more an implant outwardly resembles its biological prototype, the less likely its user is to be hassled. An artificial hand covered in synthetic skin would be acceptable; a chainsaw would not.

Another potential problem is if someone accumulates too high a proportion of cyberware in their body, they may be classified as a robot, and subjected to regulations which restrict robot-carried weaponry. Robots are considered nonsentient beings in the Imperium and do not have the same rights as more meat-oriented citizens. *GURPS Robots* explores the line between man and machine.

Imperial technology is fully up to the manufacture of body enhancements, and many Imperial Research Stations are undoubtedly secret factories for the manufacture of cyber implants for use by Imperial intelligence agencies. Megacorporations are also capable of making such devices, and undoubtedly do so more often than they care to admit publicly.

Note that neural interfaces to computers are not forbidden by most worlds, but most such implants are designed to allow read-only access to public information databases (and they do not always work equally well everywhere).

Biotechnology

The Vilani, for reasons explained elsewhere (see p. 75), were very backward in certain of the biological sciences. The Solomani, however, have made great advances in geneering (genetic engineering), especially cloning. The Solomani have genetically altered several Terran lifeforms to bring them up to sentience, including dolphins and simians (gibbons and orangutans). While genetic alteration of Humans is frowned upon by most cultures of the Imperium, it has been known to occur (the minor races known as the Iziri and Wuan, for example). There are persistent rumors of extra-Imperial Solomani plots to geneer some horrible bioweapon and unleash it upon the Imperium.

Continued on next page . . .

IMPERIAL	VILANI	SOLOMANI	EVENT
-4045	1 V.I.	476 A.D.	Consolidation Wars end. Ziru Sirka (First, or Vilani, Imperium) founded. Vilani calendar begins.
-4000	35 V.I.	521 A.D.	Vilani cease exploration.
-3810	180 V.I.	711 A.D.	Vargr invent jump drive. Maya civilization at its height on Terra.
-3500	416 V.I.	1021 A.D.	First (Vilani) Imperium reaches greatest extent.
-2562	1136 V.I.	1959 A.D.	Solomani space exploration begins.
-2460	1209 V.I.	2061 A.D.	Solomani bases throughout solar system.
-2431	1231 V.I.	2090 A.D.	Solomani invent jump drive.
-2424	1237 V.I.	2097 A.D.	Solomani visit Barnard's Star.
-2424	1237 V.I.	2097 A.D.	First contact between Solomani and Vilani.
-2408	1249 V.I.	2113 A.D.	First Interstellar War begins.
-2398	1256 V.I.	2123 A.D.	Establishment of Terran Confederation.
-2235	1380 V.I.	2286 A.D.	Nth Interstellar War begins.
-2219	1393 V.I.	2302 A.D.	Nth Interstellar War ends.
-2204	1404 V.I.	2317 A.D.	Terran Confederation ends. The Rule of Man (Second Imperium) begins.
-2190	1415 V.I.	2331 A.D.	Aslan First World War.
-2160	1438 V.I.	2361 A.D.	Aslan Nuclear War.
-2136	1456 V.I.	2385 A.D.	First Aslan space explorations.
-2083	1496 V.I.	2438 A.D.	Beginning of Aslan calendar.
-2045	1525 V.I.	2476 A.D.	First contact between K'kree and Hivers.
-2029	1537 V.I.	2492 A.D.	Hiver/K'kree War begins.
-2023	1542 V.I.	2498 A.D.	Hive Federation established in current form.
-2018	1546 V.I.	2503 A.D.	Hiver manipulation of K'kree worlds begins.
-2013	1550 V.I.	2508 A.D.	Hiver/K'kree War ends with complete withdrawal of K'kree forces from Hive space.

IMPERIAL	VILANI	SOLOMANI	EVENT
-2000	1560 V.I.	2521 A.D.	First contact between Zhodani and Vilani traders.
-1999	1560 V.I.	2522 A.D.	Aslan develop jump drive.
-1980	1575 V.I.	2541 A.D.	First Aslan/Human contact.
-1802	1711 V.I.	2719 A.D.	First Human/Hiver contact.
-1776	1730 V.I.	2745 A.D.	Collapse of the Rule of Man. Long Night begins.
-1690	1796 V.I.	2831 A.D.	Terran Mercantile Community established.
-1526	1921 V.I.	2995 A.D.	Interstellar trade ceases. Long Night deepens.
-1511	1932 V.I.	3010 A.D.	Solomani traders contact Darrians.
-1118	2232 V.I.	3403 A.D.	First Aslan Border War begins.
-1110	2238 V.I.	3411 A.D.	Old Earth Union established.
-1000	2322 V.I.	3521 A.D.	Zhodani Consulate reaches present size.
-924	2380 V.I.	3597 A.D.	Darrians reach TL13. Darrian sun destabilized.
-650	2589 V.I.	3871 A.D.	Sylean Federation established.
-200	2932 V.I.	4321 A.D.	First Human/K'kree contact.

Cybertechnology
[Continued]

Several worlds within the Imperium have created what are effectively minor races through manipulation of their genetic code. Often this was to adapt them to conditions on a specific world to make colonization easier; sometimes the rationale was more unusual. It is uncommon for these geneered minor races to be found more than a few parsecs from their homeworld in any significant numbers.

Some worlds take a different view, and biotechnological limitation regulations are not an uncommon feature of many local planetary law codes. The only Imperial regulations deal with identity: No person may change their genetic makeup with the intent to commit a crime or to defraud, and all present and past genetic codes must be noted in the Imperial identity document (see p. 40).

As with other cutting-edge technologies, Imperial Research Stations and megacorporations are the best ways to bring biotechnological aspects to the game. See *GURPS Bio-Tech* for ideas.

IY 404: First Shudusham Conference on Robotics

GMG '99

IMPERIAL	VILANI	SOLOMANI	EVENT
-110	3001 V.I.	4411 A.D.	Shudusham Concords.
-30	3062 V.I.	4491 A.D.	Cleon's campaign begins.
0	3084 V.I.	4524 A.D.	Third Imperium established. Imperial dating system begins.
50	3123 V.I.	4571 A.D.	First Zhodani contact with Imperial traders.
60	3130 V.I.	4582 A.D.	Colonization of Spinward Marches begins.
76	3142 V.I.	4597 A.D.	Pacification Campaigns begin.
114	3171 V.I.	4635 A.D.	Solomani Hypothesis proposed.
120	3176 V.I.	4641 A.D.	Pacification Campaigns end.
148	3197 V.I.	4669 A.D.	Imperial Interstellar Scout Service recontacts Darrians.
210	3245 V.I.	4731 A.D.	Vargr Corridor Campaigns begin.
348	3350 V.I.	4869 A.D.	Vargr Corridor Campaigns end.
380	3374 V.I.	4901 A.D.	Peace of Ftahalr. Imperial/Aslan border established.
404	3392 V.I.	4925 A.D.	First Shudusham Robotics Conference results in the Shudusham Accords regulating artificial intelligence and cybertechnology.
420	3405 V.I.	4941 A.D.	First Survey of Imperium completed.
426	3409 V.I.	4947 A.D.	Easter Concordat established.
588	3533 V.I.	5109 A.D.	Terra incorporated into Third Imperium.
589	3533 V.I.	5110 A.D.	First Frontier War begins.
604	3545 V.I.	5125 A.D.	First Frontier War ends. Civil War begins.
615	3553 V.I.	5136 A.D.	Second Frontier War begins.
620	3557 V.I.	5141 A.D.	Second Frontier War ends.
622	3559 V.I.	5143 A.D.	Civil War ends.
624	3560 V.I.	5145 A.D.	Xboat system established.
679	3602 V.I.	5200 A.D.	Solomani power broken at court.
704	3621 V.I.	5225 A.D.	Solomani Autonomous Region created.
799	3694 V.I.	5320 A.D.	Crisis of '99.
800	3694 V.I.	5321 A.D.	Psionic Suppressions begin.
826	3714 V.I.	5347 A.D.	Psionic Suppressions end.
871	3748 V.I.	5392 A.D.	Solomani Confederation established.
940	3801 V.I.	5461 A.D.	Solomani/Imperial friction increases.
950	3908 V.I.	5471 A.D.	Solomani Autonomous Region dissolved by Margaret.

Robots and Artificial Intelligence

Vilani conservatism and a prejudice against excessive experimental technology means that true artificial intelligence (self-awareness) is fairly rare throughout the Imperium, although robots are widespread in many areas. It is possible to program a robot to act Human, and to act fairly intelligent, but Imperial technology has stopped short of manufacturing artificial self-aware intelligences. As with nanotech, however, Imperial research stations *may* be working on the problem, unbeknownst to the public. Rumors of the development of a self-aware machine have circulated for many years.

Robots are considered non-sentient beings in the Imperium (at least under current laws) and are covered by a number of restrictions on their technology such as the Shudusham Accords (see p. 59), which ban robot-carried weaponry. Later laws have decreed that mechanical or artificial constructs are not eligible for Imperial citizenship (see *Cybertechnology*, p. 16, for some repercussions to PCs).

Machine intelligences could make their way into a game, and GMs can introduce them as plot devices (and all the more effectively, as players won't be expecting them). See *GURPS Robots* for ideas.

IMPERIAL	VILANI	SOLOMANI	EVENT
979	3831 V.I.	5500 A.D.	Third Frontier War begins.
986	3836 V.I.	5507 A.D.	Third Frontier War ends.
990	3839 V.I.	5511 A.D.	Solomani Rim War begins.
1002	3848 V.I.	5523 A.D.	Siege of Terra. Solomani Rim War ends.
1005	3851 V.I.	5526 A.D.	Solomani Home Guard created.
1040	3877 V.I.	5561 A.D.	Destruction of Phoenix Project begins.
1045	3881 V.I.	5566 A.D.	Destruction of Phoenix Project ends.
1065	3896 V.I.	5586 A.D.	Second Survey of Imperium completed.
1082	3909 V.I.	5603 A.D.	False War (Fourth Frontier War) begins.
1084	3911 V.I.	5605 A.D.	False War (Fourth Frontier War) ends.
1107	3928 V.I.	5628 A.D.	Fifth Frontier War begins.
1110	3931 V.I.	5631 A.D.	Fifth Frontier War ends.

LIBRARY DATA

"Library data" is a general term used to describe the information available from a typical computer using its library program. It represents the information generally available to player characters, and tends to be over-general and over-simplified. Game Masters may alter or add to Library Data as they see fit for their individual campaign purposes. Various entries later in this book supply additional details for use by GMs, and should be read only by them.

A

AAB: The abbreviation for *Argushiigi Admegulasha Bilanidin,* which in Vilani means the "Vilani Repository of All Knowledge." The AAB is a major scientific institution located on the world of Vland and its extensive facilities include a vast museum, a library, and several research centers and publishing houses. The term is also applied (by non-Vilani) to any extensive museum or library of Vilani origin.

AMBER ZONE: Part of a system used by the Imperial Interstellar Scout Service (q.v.) and the Travellers' Aid Society (p. 35) for classification of a nation, world, or system. An Amber Zone classification indicates a need for caution in contacts with the entity so classified. The Amber Zone classification may indicate chaos, upheaval, or xenophobia in local business, politics, society, or culture, or it may be applied for other reasons. Travelers should exercise caution.

See also *Red Zone, Travel Zone.*

ANCIENTS: The name assigned by scholars to a highly intelligent race which gained prominence 300,000 to 400,000 years ago. Most of what is known about the Ancients has been gleaned from archeological excavations of Ancient sites: the remains of cities, bases, outposts, and settlements of the Ancients. Scientific dating techniques have established that a "Final War" spanning a 2,000-year period destroyed virtually all of the Ancients at that time.

The Information Age?

Players in *Traveller* expect information to be available to them in massive quantities. Computers are commonplace, right? Everything is interconnected, right? I can get any bit of data I need, right? An early review of *Traveller* remarked that the game was unique in that good play was primarily rewarded more in knowledge of the game universe than in experience or money, and was thus a departure from every other game then on the market.

However, the information age presents several problems to *Traveller* GMs, not the least of which is the perceived need to generate the gigantic amounts of data the players feel their characters deserve. Players being players, they want the full floorplans of every building (down to the secret ventilator duct leading into the room they need to sneak into), manufacturer's schematics of the alarm system (hopefully detailing that it does not cover the aforementioned ventilator grill), and a schedule of the security guards, including when the fat one goes out for doughnuts and leaves the ventilator duct unguarded. Unfortunately for everyone involved, this sort of information makes it difficult to surprise the players, and pretty much guarantees a dull game for the players and a frustrating one for the GM.

The solution is to try to design scenarios where having all the information is not necessary – don't let the database drive the adventure. Players should recognize that it is impossible *for them* to know everything their characters know, and should not overload the GM with demands for data.

Planetary Statistics

The library data contains several planets with *Traveller* statistics. Since these don't precisely translate to *GURPS* stats, the original data has been preserved to let individual GMs fine-tune their conversion with the charts on p. 123.

The stats consist of eight digits. In sequence, these represent: starport size, planet size, atmosphere type, hydrographic percentage, population, government, law level, and (after the hyphen) tech level.

The letters A through F represent the numbers 10 through 15, in sequence; i.e., A is 10, B is 11, etc.

Why the Ancients?

Why the Ancients? *Traveller*'s designers wanted a large, decadent interstellar empire for the Terrans to encounter and conquer. This concept was first outlined in the board game *Imperium*. In this game, forces of Earth (one player) encounter a backwater province of a much larger empire. The governor of the province (the other player) must convince the uncaring central government of the true threat to the borders, fending off Terrans and battling incompetent bureaucrats for a budget at the same time.

Traveller players will recognize this situation as the period known as the Interstellar Wars (pp. 33, 51). In *Traveller*, the empire that the Terrans encountered was to be Human. Humans evolved on Earth, so the only viable option for their lengthy existence on other worlds was for them to have moved there from Earth. In the absence of a star-faring civilization on Earth before recorded history (something the designers ruled out), Humans must have been transplanted by some other agency, and that agency was called the Ancients. Our version is as good as any, and better than most.

The influence of the Ancients is broadly felt in the universe. The vast majority of scholars now believe that the Ancients transported Humans from Terra to many worlds, where their descendants became the Vilani and the Zhodani, as well as the 47 known minor Human races. The Vargr have been shown (through genetic testing) to be descendants of genetically manipulated Terran canines (apparently, the canine stock was acquired at the same time as the Humans were taken from Terra). Ancient artifacts which have been discovered show a very high level of technology, and an equally high degree of sophistication; such artifacts often reveal previously uninvented or unexploited technologies.

The Ancients were responsible for several major features within the region now occupied by the Imperium. Their warfare resulted in the large proportion of asteroid belts throughout explored space, and there is evidence they created the multi-world rosette at Tireen (Knaeleng 2910, in the Vargr Extents). Scattered, empty cities (most severely damaged by battle) stand as evidence of their wars; most, however, are restricted areas under investigation by the Imperium and not open to the public. One notable exception is the world known as Antiquity (Corridor 0816). The Antiquity Ancients site is open to tourists; its fascinating museum displays many wondrous and mystifying artifacts, many of which are still in working condition. See p. 21.

See also *Humaniti, Solomani Hypothesis, Vargr.*

Andory (Spinward Marches/Five Sisters 0236 C695735-9): Prime candidate for the Droyne homeworld. Discovered in 802 and placed under interdiction (Red Travel Zone) by Imperial Interstellar Scout Service.

See also *Droyne.*

Anglic: The official language of the Third Imperium. A distant descendent of Terran English, Anglic was the language of the Rule of Man (-2294 to -1776). Anglic remained a common interstellar language for trade and commerce during the Long Night (q.v.). Its widespread use on the original worlds of the Third Imperium made it the natural language when the Imperium was established.

On many worlds, Anglic is only a second language used for system traffic control, commercial operations, and interstellar communications. Anglic is sometimes called Galanglic (for Galactic Anglic).

The Imperium has not been able to prevent the emergence of a wide variety of Anglic dialects. Interstellar communications, holocrystals, and recordings help to spread a uniform pronunciation of Anglic throughout the entire Imperium. Within the Imperium, any Anglic speaker can understand almost any other speaker, but isolated communities on worlds with limited contact with the interstellar trade lanes shift their speech patterns to form dialects. In addition, broad areas within the Imperium have established their own pronunciation patterns; accepted dialects include Rim (which includes Terra), Core (the central region of the Imperium), Riftian (the spinward frontiers), and Transform (the Antares region). Other minor variants exist, and are left to Game Masters to detail as they see fit.

Antares: Trailing region of the Third Imperium. The name Antares is applied to a variety of places at the trailing fringe of the Imperium. Antares is a domain of the Imperium, a sector within that domain, and the capital of that sector (in addition to the star of that name).

Antares, Domain of: A Domain of the Third Imperium, consisting of the Lishun, Antares, Mendan, and Amdukan sectors.

Antares, League of: The League of Antares (although it does not include the Antares system) is an autonomous region within the Imperium. The worlds were originally pressed into the Imperium during the Antarean Pacification Campaign. The worlds were occupied by the Julian Protectorate during the Julian War. When regained for the Imperium at the end of that war, the peace terms included a mandate that the League of Antares be given limited autonomy for control of trade, commerce, and internal affairs.

The autonomy of the League of Antares served as a model for the later establishment of the Solomani Autonomous Region (see p. 60).

Antebellum: Literally, before the war (from the ancient Terran language Latin). General historical term referring to the period within the Imperium before the Civil War, specifically the years 210 to 604.

The antebellum period was characterized by expansion of the Imperium with large-scale colonization efforts, integration of numerous regions into Imperial society, and an overall mood of growth and exploration. With the end of the antebellum period, the Imperium turned more attention inward and devoted resources to internal development and consolidation.

Artifact: Any manufactured object. The term artifact is commonly used to refer to any object, item, or group of related items produced by the Ancients.

Antiquity (Corridor/Ian 0806 A223420-C): One of the best preserved Ancient sites in existence. Discovered in 385, the site is unique in that many parts of it are still operational. The biggest problem faced by researchers has been figuring out what things did and how they worked. Many items are still a mystery.

Aslan: The Aslan are a race of intelligent beings with an established interstellar empire spinward and rimward of the Imperium; in addition, large numbers have settled within the Imperium.

Aslan are roughly Human-sized, averaging 6 feet in height and weighing about 200 lbs. They are descended from four-limbed, upright, bipedal carnivore/pouncer stock originally adapted to a solitary arboreal existence.

The earliest Terran explorers saw in them a vague resemblance to the Terran lion, and they have been described (by Terrans) as lion-like or feline ever since, although there is very little biological similarity. The derivation of the word Aslan is unknown. There are two sexes, male and female. Externally, the male is most easily distinguished by his larger size and prominent mane. Females outnumber males by 3-to-1.

Aslan have a single highly specialized dewclaw at the distal end of each thumb which folds back jackknife-fashion into a horny covering along the ventral surface of each thumb and palm.

A vast Aslan-dominated empire (the Aslan Hierate) lies far to rimward, but Aslan themselves have ranged well beyond its borders, with many settling within the Imperium and attaining full status as citizens. As citizens, they subordinate themselves to Imperial authority, although they have remained culturally separated from Human society. Aslan serve in the Imperial armed forces, achieve nobility, pay taxes, and run businesses just as other citizens do.

Aslan

The origin of the word "Aslan" has two facets: that of the real world, and that of the fictional milieu of *Traveller.* Strangely enough, both are the same. "Aslan" is the name of the lion/Christ figure in C. S. Lewis' *Chronicles of Narnia.* "Aslan" means "lion" in several Turkic languages. Whether Marc Miller took the name from the novels or from a Turkish dictionary is something that none of us can remember clearly. It is not important, since Lewis drew his inspiration from a similar source, so the roots all lead back to the same tree.

In game terms, it has been pointed out that the first Humans to make contact with the Aslan must have been descended from Turkic speakers. This minor fact can speak volumes about the people who left Earth to settle space.

The notation that "the derivation of the word 'Aslan' is unknown" merely means that it was unknown to the compilers of the AAB. Scholars on Terra certainly have a better notion where the word came from, but the compilers of the AAB evidently didn't consult them. The PCs will run into contradictory information quite often in their adventures. Sometimes it will be minor and unimportant to the grand scheme of things; sometimes it will be of vital concern.

Aliens

There is a tendency to imbue alien creatures with the characteristics of the animals they most closely resemble on Earth. Show a SF gamer a drawing of a scaled quadruped and the name "lizard" is certain to be applied, with all that implies: forked tongues, egg-laying reproduction, and a tendency to bask on warm rocks after eating. It is worth remembering that scales and egg-laying do not go hand in hand, nor do fur, milk, and live birth. Aliens arose on other worlds, through different evolutionary pathways, and simply because they resemble Earth creatures superficially, they do not share other characteristics. Droyne are not lizards. Aslan are not cats. K'kree are not horses.

Aslan Society: An individual Aslan is usually a member of a family of two to 12 individuals under a patriarchal leader. Several families will combine into a pride with one family dominant. A number of prides form a clan, again with a top pride. Aside from military organizations and the ruling council (within the Hierate), the clan is the highest social and political organization among the Aslan.

A deep-seated territorial instinct causes the Aslan to have an inordinate (from a Human standpoint) concern with land. For male Aslan, owning land is a major goal in life. An Aslan's stature is determined by the amount of land he (or her husband) controls, or by the amount of land owned by any higher lord whom the Aslan serves as vassal. The lowest classes of Aslan society are landless, and provide the farmers, laborers, craftsmen, and factory workers. A holder of a large territory will often grant authority over it to vassals (usually sons, brothers, or male relatives by marriage) who administer the land in his name.

The sexes have very different roles in Aslan society. Males (in all but the lowest classes) are concerned mostly with military operations, acquisition of territory, and political affairs. Females are concerned with trade, industry, and the accumulation of knowledge. Upper-class males have little conception of money and are largely incapable of functioning in a technological society without aid, so they are thus seldom encountered without the supervision and/or assistance of a wife, mother, or other female relative or employer.

For instance, a typical Aslan mercenary unit will be organized by a wealthy married female, who will then assign its operation, for a share of the proceeds, to an unmarried female relative. The battle commander and most of the troops will be unmarried males (many of them also relatives) hired with the promise of land grants (and the opportunity to gain honor and reputation in combat). Staff, operations, supply, and intelligence officers will generally be female.

The clawed, deadly nature of any combat between primitive Aslan led to a rigid, ritualized pattern of behavior designed to reduce conflict. To this day Aslan are very polite, and while most have learned to be patient with non-Aslan, accidental fights still occur. Disputes between individuals are handled by the patriarchs; disputes between families are handled by the pride leader; disputes between prides are handled by the clan leader.

See *GURPS Traveller Alien Races 2* for more information.

Aslan Calendar: The Aslan calendar is based on the period of Kuzu (the Aslan homeworld) around *Tyeyo*, its star. The Aslan *ftahea* (year) is 319.98 standard days in length.

See also *Aslan Border Wars, Aslan Hierate, Kuzu.*

Aslan Border Wars (-1118 to 380): Series of conflicts between various Aslan clans and Human systems as the Aslan expanded toward already settled Human territory. The Aslan achieved jump drive late (-1999) and proceeded to expand into the available territory in their region of space. Contacts along their trailing border necessarily resulted in friction with the Human systems in that region.

Because the Long Night was already well under way by the time the Aslan encountered Humans, no central Human government existed to resist Aslan attacks. Since there was no united Aslan authority either, the sides were fairly matched, and numerous small wars erupted between Aslan clans and Human splinter states, with alliances constantly forming and dissolving.

The border between Human and Aslan space remained relatively constant, with a few systems changing hands after each war. At this time some clans also launched raids into the interior of the former Imperial domains, where they conquered and settled worlds as much as 40 parsecs beyond the border.

Once the Third Imperium expanded into the region (circa 200), its superior organization and technology gradually put an end to the Aslan threat. The final treaties, known as the Peace of *Ftahalr*, were negotiated with all the major clans. They established a buffer zone about 30 parsecs wide between the Imperial border and the region of Aslan control. There has been no war since then (380), although the Solomani have violated portions of the zone and incorporated it into their boundaries.

See also *Aslan, Aslan Hierate*.

Aslan Hierate: Interstellar, multisector government of the many Aslan clans. Aslan society centers on the clan. Within the Hierate, the family structure of the Aslan and the governmental structure are the same. The highest governmental functions are performed by a council of 29 clan leaders chosen from among the most powerful clans.

"The 29" (as they are called) have quasi-religious status and represent the essential unity of the Aslan race. To be chosen as one of the 29 is the highest honor to which any Aslan can aspire. The 29 meet continually on Kuzu to adjudicate interclan disputes and decide matters of group policy. No member of the 29 speaks for the Hierate as a whole, nor (for that matter) does the whole 29.

There are no Hierate military forces – each clan has its own, and they rarely act in concert with those of other clans. The Hierate itself can call upon military forces only insofar as the clans themselves agree to provide such forces (and a clan can provide forces only insofar as its constituent families provide them). Even the minor forces conveying the 29's decisions are actually under the control of individual clan leaders.

See also *Aslan, Aslan Border Wars, Kuzu*.

Astrography: The science of mapping interstellar space. Basic to any science of mapping is a coordinate system. The scientific system used by the Imperium is fairly technical, and not used by ordinary citizens.

In ordinary discourse, a world is referred to by its name, sector, and subsector. For example, the homeworld of Archduke Norris is Regina (Spinward Marches/Regina) – that is, the world Regina in the Spinward Marches sector's Regina subsector.

B

Barracks Emperors: Collective term describing the succession of emperors springing from military backgrounds (and usually seizing the throne by force) during the Civil War (q.v.).

See *Emperors of the Flag*.

"Behind the Claw": A slang term used by inhabitants of the Spinward Marches, Deneb, and Trojan Reach sectors to refer to these areas. The term derives from a supposed resemblance between a claw and the Great Rift, as seen on maps of the Imperium. Inhabitants of this region feel a certain pride in this designation, and it is used to imply that they share a camaraderie and common interest. The name was once used as the title of a popular news magazine with a circulation encompassing the three sectors named above. The term is rarely used by inhabitants of other areas of the Imperium. The entire area "behind the claw" is now part of the Domain of Deneb, under the rule of Archduke Norris of Regina.

See **GURPS Traveller Behind the Claw** for more information.

The Year of the Four Emperors

The notion of the Barracks Emperors is loosely drawn from the history of the Roman Empire, specifically the unfortunate year 69, the "Year of the Four Emperors." This single year saw the reigns of four emperors: Galba (who succeeded the infamous Nero), Otho, Vitellius, and Vespasian (who ruled until 79).

The 18-year period of the Barracks Emperors saw a similar wave of chaos and civil war sweep the Third Imperium. One year saw five different emperors occupying (or claiming) the Iridium Throne, and one two-year period had no emperor at all, demonstrating that military and governmental talents do not always overlap.

Belt Mining: The process of extracting useful minerals and other substances from asteroids. Asteroids fall into three basic categories, each of which is different in nature and value.

Nickel-iron asteroids are reasonably dense sources of metal, mostly sought after by local ship-building concerns for use as planetoid starship hulls.

Carbonaceous asteroids are the most common and have the lowest value in most marketplaces. These stony chunks are most useful in systems where space colonies and large stations can make use of the variety of useful elements – carbon, hydrogen, oxygen, and so on – that can be extracted from them.

Ice chunks are made up of various frozen volatiles, including methane, water, and the like. These "dirty snowballs" are a source of hydrogen fuel and hence support an entire specialty of "ice miners." In systems where gas giants cannot be mined for one reason or another, a starport or space station may pay reasonably good money for ice chunks, though they will never make a belter rich.

None of these three categories of asteroid is particularly valuable, and few belters ever make a fortune strictly from discovering and mining any of these. Other, more valuable resources are to be found. Many asteroids, most particularly nickel-iron rocks, contain varying amounts of the valuable minerals – platinum, iridium, and so forth, and sometimes radioactives. Occasionally an asteroid will be discovered with an unusual configuration that makes it valuable for scientific or even aesthetic purposes. And, finally, there are artifacts, which take in the entire gamut from the flotsam of a week-old wreck to a trove left by the Ancients, and which vary in value accordingly.

Belter: Strictly speaking, one who practices the profession of asteroid prospector and miner, usually working alone or with a small number of partners. Loosely, any resident of an asteroid belt (including citizens of civilized belts such as Glisten, some of whom have never been in a spaceship).

Brzk: Archduke of Antares, a Vargr. Brzk's great (to the eighth) grandfather, Admiral Soegz (q.v.), was a loyal supporter of Arbellatra in the final years of the Civil War.

Capital

The reason the Imperial capital world is named "Capital" is mere circumstance. On the first rough map of the Imperium, we labeled one of the worlds "capital" with every intention of coming up with a "real" name later on. Various names were suggested, but none seemed suitable. Finally, more by default than anything else, we left it "Capital."

There is ample historical precedent for this sort of thing. When the Roman republic annexed Macedonia, it split the kingdom into three provinces, named (in Latin, of course), Macedonia One, Macedonia Two, and Macedonia Three. It must be assumed that a similar lack of inspiration plagued Cleon I when he chose to rename his capital planet.

Capital (Core/Capital 2118 A586A98-F): Central world of the Imperium and seat of government since its founding. Situated in the center of the Imperium, Capital's position has given it prime importance as a communications hub, a cultural center, and an industrial focus. See *Sylea,* p. 66.

Centaurs: Common name applied to the K'kree, because of their resemblance to mythical Terran creatures. See *K'kree.*

Chirper: A minor race native to many worlds in and outside the Imperium, named for the sharp bird-like chirp which characterizes their speech. Chirpers are omnivore/gatherers weighing roughly 55 pounds. Living in small groups with limited social organization, they gather fruits and berries. They supplement their diets with occasional small animals, which they catch and kill with crude tools.

Chirper intelligence is at the low end of the scale and ranges from a few points above animal levels to a few points below the average for Humans.

It is well understood by scientists, though of little interest to most citizens of the Imperium, that Chirpers are genetically identical to Droyne (see sidebar, p. 29.) Nevertheless, Chirpers are recognized by Imperial authorities as intelligent, and as such, they enjoy the protections and responsibilities of intelligent species within the Imperium. Most Chirpers live in established reservations with only limited interchange with Humans.

Church of the Chosen Ones: A fanatical Vargr sect which believes that the Ancients not only "invented" the Vargr race by genetic manipulation of Terran carnivores, but that the Ancients also returned to the Vargr several times and improved the race to the point that it could take its rightful place as the leader of this part of the galaxy. Some Church members even believe that the Ancients will return again to bring this about. The Church has waned in influence since its founding 200 years ago, but it still has followers on many worlds. See pp. T:AI83-84.

Ciencia Iphegenia: (b. 1088) Grand Princess of the Imperium, daughter of Emperor Strephon and Empress Iolanthe. As heir to the Iridium Throne, Grand Princess Ciencia Iphegenia was educated from birth to eventually assume the mantle of authority for the Imperium. Her early fascination with the sciences prompted an extensive interest in the Imperial Interstellar Scout Service, which considers her its patron and staunch supporter at court.

As yet unmarried, Grand Princess Iphegenia is the subject of a great deal of speculation as to when and whom she will choose to wed.

Civil War (604 to 622): Fought between various factions within the Imperium for control of the bureaucracy. It had its origins in the strain on communications within the Imperium caused by the long lag times dictated by the very size of the Imperium. To cite one cause, however, would be simplistic. The diverse backgrounds of the many constituents of the Imperium had its effects, as did rivalry for power by major naval and military commanders and a lessening in the Imperium's expansionist tendencies.

The spark which started the Civil War came from the First Frontier War (589 to 604) in the Spinward Marches. Communication lags and a lack of preparedness forced the Marches to conduct most of the war on its own with little additional help or support from the Imperium. Grand Admiral of the Marches Olav hault-Plankwell forced the war to an end and found solid support for a new government. Advancing on Capital with his war fleet, he forced an audience with Empress Jacqueline I, supposedly for recognition of his war effort. In the course of the meeting in 606, he personally murdered the Empress, and then proclaimed himself Emperor by right of fleet control. The ensuing power struggle lasted through 18 years and 18 emperors.

The Civil War strife was of two varieties: fringe battles for power bases and central battles for power in the Core. The fringe battles were fought throughout the Imperium as rival factions recruited forces. Once any power bloc built up enough strength to make a victory seem possible, the forces were moved to the Core and used to either seize power or to wrest it away from someone else.

But there was also a cheaper, easier route open to many. The dynastic crisis of 244 had produced a precedent for the assassination of the emperor if he or she overstepped the bounds of legitimate activity. The concept was introduced

"It'll be at least eight hours before this ice storm blows itself out. After that we can start digging – maybe another eight hours to dig the Wayward out of the drifts."

Darryn glanced out at the pine forest slowly being buried by several yards of snow, then turned to the engineer . . . who, as usual, was covered in grease and held his oversized mug of coffee in both hands.

"What are the captain's chances, SB?"

The engineer stared at his coffee mug and read the logo, which proclaimed "I Love Regina." He said, "Out there, in that? Poor. Out there, in that, if the bears find him? Zero."

"Damn. He still owes me another 600 credits from that craps game on Trifuge."

Both men knew what the astrogator meant. They stared out of the Wayward's view screen at the frozen forest and driving snow, hoping to see the familiar figure of their captain.

■ ■ ■

The captain was remembering Trifuge, too. "You'd think I would have learned I'm a lousy gambler. But no, I had to come out in this." He aimed his pistol carefully.

The beast had a head the size of a man's body, weighed down by a thick plate of leathery armor. Its two eyes gleamed with an evil green light as it advanced on the stocky little captain. Then the pistol fired and one of the eyes became a mess of green and running red.

The Debarre bear staggered back from the hollow the captain had crawled into and roared its pain and hatred at the wounded man.

With frozen hands the Wayward's captain raised the pistol again, desperately fighting the shivering that spoiled his aim. Three rounds left in the clip, hands too frozen to reload. He stilled the shivers by an effort of will.

In this storm he wasn't going to get far. But the bear was staying here for good.

Once again gunshots rang out throughout Debarre's frozen woods, but this time no roar followed them.

The captain pulled his inadequate coat around his shoulders, struggled to read his locator, and dragged himself back into the storm.

Roman Roots

As with so much of *Traveller,* the concept of a client state was drawn from history – specifically, the Roman Empire. To gain a stable frontier without the expense of conquest, Rome would install a friendly monarch in a small border state, and secure loyalty by subsidies, bribes, trade guarantees, or taking the monarch's children hostage. The hostages would be educated in Rome, as Romans, and would eventually succeed their parents as rulers. After a couple of generations, the rulers were Romans in all but name. *Traveller* incorporates a version of this same concept, using a series of allied states to act as buffers between major interstellar entities.

Interested GMs might find plot ideas for Imperial politics in *GURPS Rome*.

to legitimize the elimination of Cleon the Mad and was never intended for any other purpose. Nevertheless, in the turmoil of the Civil War, assassination was introduced and accepted, at least by those utilizing the technique, as a way of promoting a succession in government.

The line of emperors during the Civil War came mostly from naval officers, and they are collectively called the Emperors of the Flag. Of these 18, seven were assassinated, 10 were killed in battle, and one survived: Arbellatra.

During the course of the Civil War, the Outworld Coalition (of Zhodani and Vargr) saw that their defeat in the First Frontier War at the hands of Olav need not be permanent. They attacked again in the Second Frontier War (615 to 620). Their defeat in that war had greater effects than they would know. Grand Admiral Arbellatra managed the meager forces of the Imperium against the Coalition and managed to force a second defeat.

Arbellatra's strategy after the war was (like Olav) to march on the Capital and seize power. She, however, did not make the mistake of seizing the throne. Instead, she defeated the putative emperor and then took possession of power, holding it in trust for a rightful successor. She held the post of regent for seven years while mounting a search for a member of Jacqueline's family to take the throne.

The stability she brought made an impression on the Moot and succeeded in establishing a broad power base. Ultimately, the Moot approached her to take the throne herself, which was probably in her mind all along.

With the end of the two Frontier Wars and the Civil War, the Imperium entered a period of renewed expansion and consolidation. The express boat system was established to enhance government, commercial, and private communications; the Solomani influence in the Imperium was lessened and replaced with a more cosmopolitan policy; renewed efforts at interior development of existing Imperial territories provided a new focus for the nobles of the Moot.

See also *First Frontier War, Moot, Outworld Coalition, Second Frontier War.*

Client State: An independent political unit which has elected (or had forced upon it) the patronage of a larger political unit. This relationship is generally mutually beneficial and is essentially commercial in nature. That is, the political or defensive ties which may be part of any patron-client relationship are ultimately intended to promote trade between the two.

Confederation: Group of independent states, worlds, or systems united for specified purposes while generally retaining more freedom of action than the members of a federation. Also a league or alliance (especially of princes, nations, states, worlds, or systems).

Corridor: Imperial sector containing 267 systems dramatically split by the Great Rift; 69 systems lie rimward of the Rift and 149 systems form the coreward third of the sector.

Corridor is named for its role connecting old, well-established Vland Sector with the frontier sectors Deneb and the Spinward Marches. The name Corridor dates from about 140 and has displaced the old Vilani name (Eneri, rough translation: "star salad") for the sector.

Coyns: Of the rare artifacts recovered from Ancient sites, the most common are coyns, small disks of metal engraved with various symbols. Their specific purpose is unknown. They may have served as money, jewelry, psionic focuses, or something completely different.

Original coyns have been found in various precious metals such as gold, silver, platinum, iridium, monadium, and even uranium. Sets range in size from six to 38 pieces, and are considered desirable to museums throughout the Imperium. Each coyn has a scrap value of Cr400 (if gold); to a museum, the value is closer to Cr4,000.

Copies of sets of coyns are made of aluminum, lead, or zinc and are more frequently encountered in the hands of unscrupulous merchants or traders. Such fake coyns have a value of about Cr2 each.

Crisis of '99: Albert Croale, in his book *Almost Disaster,* presents a hypothesis that the Third Frontier War (979 to 986) occurred two centuries too late. After reviewing the progress of events in the spinward reaches of the Imperium from the antebellum period to the late seventh century, Croale then analyzes the rise of the Psionics Institutes, their growing public acceptance, and their spreading power. Finally, he presents that a straight projection of events would predict a resurgence of the Outworld Coalition, increased hostilities, and finally, a Third Frontier War.

Instead, his hypothesis as stated in his book indicates that the Psionic Suppressions (800 to 826 and beyond) were a massive manipulation of the population of the Imperium, a form of psychohistory, intended to eliminate the power of the Institutes. War preparations were continuing, and the Imperium made representations of strength (in 799) to the Coalition. It backed down. But the psychohistory project went wrong and resulted in wholesale rejection of psionics within the Imperium, to the point that even the government had difficulty in using the science of psionics for its official purposes.

Currency, Imperial: The basic unit of legal tender in the Imperium is the Imperial credit. Individual worlds may issue their own currencies, and those currencies may or may not be acceptable on other worlds. Similarly, corporations and megacorporations may issue scrip, and its acceptance outside of the corporate environment varies.

Imperial credits are accepted everywhere in the Imperium and in many locations outside of it. The standard abbreviation is Cr, placed before the amount. In Solomani-influenced areas, it is not unusual to see the $ sign used.

Imperial credits are almost impossible to counterfeit because of their unique method of manufacture. Plastic fibers are combined under high temperature and pressure and extruded as a rectangular bundle of great length. The different colored fibers form the pattern of the bill. The bills are not printed; their characters and design are created by the mixture of fibers used. The bundle is sliced to paper thinness, and a 14-digit alphanumeric (letter/number combination) is added for uniqueness. Bills are issued in Cr10, Cr20, Cr50, Cr100, Cr500, Cr1,000, and Cr10,000 denominations. Plastic coins, manufactured in a similar manner in various shapes, are issued in Cr0.25, Cr0.5, Cr1, and Cr5 denominations. Coinage in precious metals is limited to special commemoratives and collectors' editions.

Imperial credits can be bulky in large quantities. Bills measure 3 by 5 inches; 1,000 bills stand 2 inches high and weigh 1 pound.

Other forms of money are common, both in Imperial credits and the currencies issued by worlds and large corporations. Checks, credit/debit systems (involving cards or other mechanisms), smart cards, and electronic systems of various sorts are all in use on various worlds. Interstellar exchanges of large amounts of money are accomplished by bank drafts and other financial instruments. These are essentially "checks" written from one large bank to another and involve extensive security procedures to prevent fraud.

Repeated efforts to remove "paper" money from Imperial finances have all been thwarted by coalitions of various political and free-trade interests.

Jesedipere (Spinward Marches/Aramis) 132/1120

Jesedipere downport's Joy Street is famous throughout the Aramis subsector for its bars, gambling dens, and other dives, but nothing could prepare me for the dirt, cramped streets, and overpowering smell of Vargr restaurants. It's even worse when you're out of cash and your home is a disused garbage can at the corner of Marquis Way and Extent Street.

I had been on Jesedipere for three weeks, since I used up my last credits getting back into the Imperium on board a Vargr trader after my job as a belter in the Thoelgling Empire failed to pay.

My papers show that I'm a pretty good engineer, but at Jesedipere no one seemed to be interested. Then my luck changed during one of Jesedipere's frequent rainstorms. I had waited amid the mud and street-scum to see if any new ships were landing at the pads.

I couldn't believe it as it came through the misty clouds. The battered hull gleamed in the rain, her old red and silver paint varnished by moisture to shine like new in the gray light. It was the legendary **March Harrier** *– the subsized merchant that humbled Tukera. This was my chance to get a ride in a legend!*

Even if the legend looked like it was held together by gum and good faith.

Faldor (Spinward Marches/ District 268) 68/1120

Ahead lay the statue of Queen Nabalus III, the first worldwide ruler of Faldor. It rose 45' above the swampy terrain which passed as a park in Faldor's capital, Amballus. It was constructed out of millions of tiny animal bones. It was, however, a very detailed statue, and I had to admit Otarri bone sculpture was impressive.

At the base of the statue stood my welcoming party, a group of Otarri. Otarri are the natural race of Faldor. Many Humans call them Lung-Fish – they still resemble their swamp-dwelling amphibian ancestors.

The leading Otarri walked forward, his tail sliding in the mud behind him, a red headband marking him as a young male. In good Galanglic he stated that he was Ctariis of House Atoliis and that I was Darryn of the Scouts, which led me to ask him how he knew. It was of course my Ileshian black uniform, a mark of my military job and my belief in Virasa.

Looking pleased with himself – then again, with their upturned mouths Otarri always looked pleased – Ctariis stated that my friends of the Space Craft Wayward *were waiting at the house of Atolis to welcome me to Faldor.*

Darmine: Cultural region in the Zarushagar sector. Darmine had a separate but submerged cultural identity within the First Imperium and happily threw off that domination when the First Imperium fell. Allowed to flourish by the Rule of Man, the community of worlds survived the Long Night with little harm other than to its technology level.

Darmine was the primary focus of the Ilelish Pacification Campaign (76 to 120).

Darrian Confederation: Group of worlds in the Darrian subsector settled by Humans from Darrian (Spinward Marches/Darrian 0627 A463955-G) during the period -1137 to -927. The current capital is Mire (Spinward Marches/Darrian 0527 A665A95-B).

The Darrian Confederation contains 18 worlds within the same subsector and has a population of 17.19 billion. Darrians are Humans who developed independently on Darrian. Some Solomani blood is evident from Solomani traders who encountered Darrian in -1511 and provided them with sufficient technology to explore their subsector.

The Darrian Confederation is a client state of the Imperium. It has had long-standing conflicts with the Sword Worlds (q.v.).

See *Humans.*

Darrians: Minor Human race in the Spinward Marches, dominant race of the Darrian Confederation (q.v.). See *GURPS Traveller Behind the Claw*.

Deneb: Imperial sector containing 385 systems lying beyond the Great Rift; named for the sector's brightest star, Deneb.

Deneb sector was sporadically settled by both Vilani and Vargr during the latter years of the First Imperium, but major development of the sector only took place after Third Imperium Scout Service explorations located major resource worlds in quantity. Industrial worlds that exploited those resources soon created trade routes and commercial ties that linked the Imperial core with the Spinward Marches.

Deneb sector is primarily Imperial. The Imperial border runs just within the coreward edge of the sector, and scattered Vargr systems (as well as non-aligned systems and client states) lie beyond the border.

Deneb is part of the Domain of Deneb, a region loyal to the Imperium under the leadership of Archduke Norris. See *GURPS Traveller Behind the Claw*.

Deneb, Domain of: A domain of the Third Imperium, consisting of the Spinward Marches, Deneb, Trojan Reach, and Reft sectors.

Directions, Galactic: North, south, east, and west are insufficient for referring to directions within the galaxy. Instead, the following conventions are used when referring to direction:

Toward the galactic core (toward Capital from Terra) is coreward; away from it, in the direction of the rim, is rimward. In the direction in which the galaxy is rotating (toward the Spinward Marches from Vland) is spinward, and the other direction is trailing.

These directions are in widespread use in describing Imperial features and businesses. For example, the Spinward Marches is a sector at the extreme spinward fringe of the Imperium; Rimward Lines is an important interstellar transport company.

Domain: Group of four sectors within the Imperium under the general control and direction of an archduke.

Droyne: Intelligent major race inhabiting scattered worlds within an area slightly larger than the region of the current Third Imperium. The Droyne are a small race derived from winged herbivorous gatherers. They vary in size depending on caste, but generally stand 3 feet tall (large workers and warriors can be larger than Humans). The history of their evolution remains a puzzle because their home world is not known with certainty.

Droyne society is divided into rigid castes determined when an individual reaches adolescence. The six castes of the Droyne all serve different functions within Droyne society. Although identical at the time of caste selection, caste members develop pronounced physical and mental differences by maturity. Different genetic programs are awakened by differences in diet and environment among the various castes. Young leaders, for instance, experience a nearly 30% increase in brain size in the first year after casting, drones develop sexual organs, and so on. The following are descriptions and definitions of the castes:

Worker: Manual labor and mundane ordinary activity are the province of the worker. Workers are not too smart and are temperamentally suited to contentment with ordinary labor and subservient tasks.

Droyne and Chirpers

Chirpers (see p. 24) are uncasted Droyne, which is to say they are a primitive version of the Droyne. As such they are less interesting in game terms, and it is for this reason that they have never been a serious contender for PC status. (In 20 years, I have never seen anyone seriously propose a Chirper character.)

The fact that Chirpers and Droyne are the same is readily verified by close xenological examination, and proven beyond doubt by DNA analysis. It is also a matter of common knowledge, although it is not something that most people really care about. It is one of those boring facts they fill extra spaces in newspapers with – squib-fodder.

Consider, however, the following facts:

■ An unknown agency spread Humans throughout a vast area of space, vaster than the borders of the current Imperium. These Humans take many forms, and are known collectively as Humaniti.

■ It has been proven that all of the various races of Humaniti are descended from the inhabitants of a single world, and that world is Terra in the Solomani Rim sector. Since the Terrans are known to have been stone-age primitives when they were distributed throughout known space, it follows that another intelligence was responsible.

■ It has been proven that the Vargr are also descended from a Terran life form, and they too were transplanted over a large area (although not as widely scattered as Humaniti).

And one final fact: When you look at Droyne and Chirpers together, they are almost as widespread as Humaniti.

Continued on next page . . .

A logical conclusion from these facts is that the unknown agency which took Humaniti and Vargr from Terra also took the Droyne from somewhere. The Droyne homeworld has never been located – is that homeworld Terra? Are the Droyne descended from some Terran life form, either directly like Humaniti or through geneering, like the Vargr?

Most scientific authorities dismiss this notion. The Droyne biochemistry differs too radically from all known Terran organisms for them to be related. But some people ask: Are the Droyne the last surviving vestige of a totally different form of life, one that developed, flourished, and then vanished from the face of Terra before the current Terran life-forms developed? There have been several mass extinctions on Terra over the years – did one wipe out all life completely? And did a small vestige of that life survive because they were transported elsewhere by beings unknown?

GMG '98

The Alternate Dulinor

In the original background history of *Traveller*, Archduke Dulinor played a more substantial role: He assassinated the emperor (or at least he *thought* he had) and threw the Imperium into chaos. In the alternate universe depicted in *GURPS Traveller*, Dulinor himself is killed and the rebellion never comes to pass.

In the original timeline, Dulinor had actually killed a double, used on special occasions where the emperor had to be in two places at once. The reason Strephon was away from Capital remains the same in both universes, and will be revealed over the course of several books in the *GURPS Traveller* series.

Warrior: Trained for combat and possessing comparatively well-developed muscles and reflexes, the warrior is the security troop, the soldier, the marine, and the policeman of the Droyne culture. They are common in frontier bases, and less numerous in civilized areas.

Drone: Drones have a variety of purposes in Droyne society. They perform a reproductive role which makes them both fathers and mothers to Droyne young, and they have a role in the ceremonies which determine caste for maturing young. In addition, drones compose a sort of middle-management caste, which is responsible for many of the routine functions in business, trade, and administration.

Technician: This caste is the science-oriented portion of Droyne society, and is concerned with both research and practical implementation of technology.

Sport: Although the caste system of the Droyne is rather rigid, the sport is the deliberately accepted exception to caste structure. Sports are special individuals who cross caste lines to become individual scouts, messengers, representatives, hunters, and prospectors, and to take other occupations that require individual initiative or separation from Droyne society for long periods of time. Sports are the most commonly encountered Droyne away from a Droyne world.

Leader: Leaders are required to manage and direct society. They are ultimately responsible for everything that the Droyne as a whole do.

Society: There is little individual freedom in Droyne society, and as a result, society and government join into one concept. Workers work. Leaders lead. All of society is dedicated to continuing the existence that provides all members with food, shelter, and the other amenities that make life enjoyable. In addition, there is little discord in Droyne society when things are running smoothly, as each member of society has its own function to perform. Only when disaster happens is the group forced to strain.

A typical Droyne group consists of a variety of Droyne from the different castes. There will be many workers, a few drones and leaders, and technicians and warriors based on current needs. Each group will also have several sports, although they may not be present; instead they may be occupied with their own solitary tasks.

This is not to say that Droyne are mindless. Leaders are quite capable and responsible; warriors have strategic and tactical sense; technicians are inventive and clever. But all accept the central group as the purpose of their lives, and work for its benefit above their own.

Dulinor (1066-1116): Dulinor Astrin Ilethian, former archduke of Ilelish, killed in 1116 when the gig in which he was a passenger exploded mysteriously while taking him to Capital for an audience with Emperor Strephon. It is, of course, unusual and alarming when one of the Imperium's ranking nobles dies in a "mysterious explosion," especially before an Imperial audience. In the absence of any concrete evidence, three general theories circulate:

■ The explosion was an accident.
■ The explosion was intentional, and Dulinor was the target.
■ The explosion was intentional, and some other passenger was the target.

Of these, the second is the most widely held. A number of conspiracy theories have sprouted over who would want Dulinor dead and why, and a small library could be filled with books about the incident. The final report of the Imperial Navy's investigation into the explosion was issued on 004-1117, and reported that there was insufficient evidence for any firm conclusion.

Why is this important to the campaign? See the sidebar. It may safely be concluded that there is more to Dulinor's death than the Navy will ever admit, and perhaps more than it will ever learn.

E

Emperors of the Flag: During the Civil War period (604 to 622), the Imperium was in the hands of a series of naval officers of flag (admiral) rank. These 18 emperors achieved the throne through assassination, fleet action, political maneuvers, and general mayhem. The year 619 particularly saw five emperors serve on the throne, none of them for more than three months.

The succession of Emperors of the Flag began with the seizure of the throne by Olav hault-Plankwell in 604, which precipitated the Civil War. It ended with the naming of Arbellatra as regent of the Imperium by the Moot in 622.

See also *Civil War*.

Express Boats: Rapid communication ships which are designed to make optimum use of jump technology in communicating information within the Imperium. Because the Imperium is so large, ordinary communication must depend on ships traveling along established trade routes, making Regina nearly four years out from the Imperial Core given routine jump lengths and layovers.

The express boat (abbreviated Xboat) system, established originally in 624 and expanded to cover the entire Imperium by 718, cuts this communication time by more than 75%. Selected locations along major trade routes are established as sites for Xboat stations (see p. 78), which are orbital facilities that service and refuel the Xboats on their communications runs.

As an Xboat arrives in a system, it beams its recorded data to the Xboat station, which then retransmits it to an Xboat standing by for a jump outsystem. Time between jumps is almost always less than four hours and has been recorded at less than seven minutes, making the speed of communication nearly the speed of jump (since Xboats carry jump-4 drives, this is basically four parsecs per week). In practice, this speed is reduced by the fact that trade routes do not follow straight lines and that not all jumps are made at jump-4. Nonetheless, the system achieves approximately jump-2.6 per week.

Emperors of the Third Imperium

Emperor	Reign
Cleon I	0-53
Cleon II (aka Cleon the Weak)	53-54
Artemsus	54-166
Martin I	166-195
Martin II	195-244
Cleon III (aka Cleon the Mad)	244-245
Porfiria	245-326
Anguistus	326-365
Martin III	365-456
Martin V	456-457
Nicholle	457-475
Cleon IV	475-555
Jerome	555-582
Jaqueline I	582-604
Olav	604-609
Ramon I	609
Constantus	609-610
Nicolai	610-612
George	612-613
Interregnum	613-615
Cleon V	615-618
Joseph	618
Donald	618
Emdiri	618-619
Catharine	619
Ramon II	619
Jaqueline II	619
Usuti	619-620
Marava	620
Ivan	620-621
Martin VI	621
Gustus	621-622
Arbellatra (regent)	622-629
Arbellatra (empress)	629-666
Zhakirov	666-688
Margaret I	688-736
Paulo I	736-767
Tomutov I	767-768
Paula II	768-836
Tomutova II	836-908
Margaret II	908-945
Styryx	945-989
Gavin	989-1031
Paulo III	1031-1071
Strephon	1071-present

Wars and Rumors of Wars

The various Frontier Wars fought between the Zhodani and the Third Imperium take their inspiration partly from the series of "brushfire wars" in the last half of the 20th century between the Eastern bloc (consisting of the Soviet Union and its allies) and the Western bloc (the United States and its allies). Another source of inspiration was the series of wars in the 18th century between Prussia under Frederick the Great and the rest of Europe (with a few exceptions).

Our purpose was to create a history of tension and conflict along a border area between two large political entities, and thus set the stage for the widest possible range of political, economic, and military adventures.

F

False War (1082 to 1084): The short, fourth war in the series of Frontier Wars between the Third Imperium and the Zhodani Consulate.

See *Fourth Frontier War.*

Federation: Group of states, worlds, or systems, each internally independent, joined into a union to which has been surrendered certain rights and responsibilities, most generally having to do with foreign affairs.

Fifth Frontier War (1107 to 1110): Latest in the series of continuing wars between the Zhodani and the Imperium. Following several years of unrest and provocation, Zhodani forces attacked across the Imperial borders while previously placed guerrillas on selected Imperial worlds began uprisings. Vargr and Sword World forces allied with the Zhodani also participated in the attacks.

The armistice, signed in 1110, resulted in the loss of no worlds to the hostiles and returned to the *ante bellum* status quo.

First Frontier War (589 to 604): The first of the modern border clashes between the Imperium and the Zhodani, which sparked the beginning of a continuing antipathy between the two major lines of Humaniti.

At the conclusion of the war, Olav hault-Plankwell drove to the Imperial core with his war fleet and took the reins of government, dispatching Empress Jacqueline and thus beginning the Civil War and the reign of its Barracks Emperors.

First Imperium (-4045 to -2204): The first major interstellar civilization, politically and culturally dominated by Humans originating on Vland. The jump drive was invented on Vland in -9235. Immediately the Vilani discovered a number of interfertile and technologically primitive Human races on worlds within 60 parsecs. These were gradually brought to a high-technology state with Vilani help and assimilated into a loose interstellar community bound by trade and common culture.

Eventually, the client races themselves explored beyond the local sphere, contacting and trading with still more races. These new races gained their technology without being assimilated into Vilani culture. The resulting increase in cultural friction eventually triggered a series of wars beginning about -5400.

In response to the threat, Vland began tightening its control of its trade sphere, finally organizing it into a centralized state in -5273. This marked the beginnings of the First Imperium, although there was as yet no emperor. During the 1,000-year period of the Consolidation Wars, Vland conquered and absorbed its enemies until no civilized states remained on its borders (except for a portion of the Vargr Extents, isolated from the Imperium by the Great Rift).

The last war ended in -4045, and the Vilani declared the establishment of an interstellar empire to govern all Vilani territory. Known as the Grand Empire of Stars or Ziru Sirka, Vilani dating begins at this point. With no exterior threats, the Ziru Sirka lasted for nearly 1,200 years; at its height, which was attained soon after the end of the wars, the First Imperium contained 27 sectors and more than 15,000 worlds.

The cost of maintaining centralized control over this vast expanse was cultural rigidity. Exploration had ceased with the beginning of the wars; now scientific research slowed to a halt and the beginnings of a hereditary caste system began to emerge. Civilization declined.

As long as no exterior threat surfaced, the Grand Empire was safe; but gradually technology leaked across the borders, despite all efforts. New interstellar states arose, and the Imperium could no longer afford to absorb them. Gradually, the Imperium lost territory along its coreward and trailing marches. Then, in -2422, the Imperium was contacted along its rimward border by the Terrans, who had recently emerged into space. Terran expansionism led to a series of interstellar wars, which ultimately resulted in Terran conquest of the Imperium in -2204 and the founding of the Rule of Man.

First Interstellar War (-2408 to -2400): The first military engagement between the Vilani of the First Imperium and the Solomani of the Terran Confederation. This began an on-again, off-again series of wars between the two major Human races, which ended in the defeat of the Imperium and the ascendance of the Solomani.

See *Nth Interstellar War.*

Fourth Frontier War (1082 to 1084): Also known as the False War, this was a short, inconclusive war fought primarily in the Jewell subsector of the Spinward Marches between the Imperium and the Zhodani Consulate. Initial assaults by the Zhodani against the Jewell and Regina subsectors stalled at the borders. Its final battle, the Battle of Two Suns (1084), was waged in the vicinity of Yres and Menorb and resulted in Imperial victory. The armistice was signed before instructions for the conduct of the war were received from Capital.

A Concise History of Ziru Sirka, Part I

Prepared for Solomani readers by the Vilani Historical Documents Subcommittee, Kasiiga University Press, Ishimaga, Vland, 001-1116.

The Vilani name for their Imperium was *Ziru Sirka* – the Grand Empire of Stars. They were able to create their great empire for one basic reason: They reached the stars first.

Early History

The Vilani first explored space in about 5500 B.C. by the Solomani calender. They ventured out into their own star system (from their homeworld, Vland) in a region of space about 300 parsecs closer to the galactic core than Terra. They visited every world and moon in their system, colonized a few, and put scientific bases on the rest over the course of a century.

By 5300 B.C. the Vilani had reached a point culturally and technologically where they were ready to reach for the stars. They launched sublight interstellar colonization missions aimed at the nearest stars. Tauri, a mere 2.17 light-years away, was the first system visited, but several more were explored in rapid succession. Over the course of the next 500 years, the Vilani created a small interstellar community of six systems, each with its own colonies and scientific stations.

Continued on next page . . .

A Concise History of Ziru Sirka, Part I

[Continued]

The first Vilani contact with intelligence took place in 4789 B.C. when an expedition to the nearby system of Tahaver discovered a race of aquatic mantas with a non-technological culture. The mantas, although intelligent, were easily dominated by the Vilani, and over several hundred years became a servitor (some say slave) race, assigned to fish-herding and kelp-gathering in Tahaver's vast seas. This first contact with an intelligent race set the tone for future contacts between the Vilani and other intelligent beings: The Vilani seemed naturally suited to rule and exploit others.

The dramatic key to the expansion of the Vilani was their invention of the jump drive in about 4714 B.C. A research team working on the outer fringes of the Vland system created the first working prototype and demonstrated its effects with a harrowing jump to the nearby Tauri system. The Vilani now had the key to interstellar travel.

Luck also had a hand in the future of Vland. The elementary jump drive which the Vilani invented was capable of transporting a starship across the vast interstellar distances at a speed of about 170 times light speed – a full parsec in about a week. The range of that elementary jump-1 drive was limited to a single parsec as well, given that early ships couldn't carry fuel for multiple jumps. Since the average distance between stars is closer to 2 parsecs, the first ships of most Major Races were greatly restricted as to which stars could be their destinations.

Vland, however, is one world in an immense chain of star systems, each of which lies within 1 parsec of the next – the Vilani Main. This Vilani Main became the highway over which Vilani ships traveled. Within 10 years, starships had been built and sent to every system within 20 parsecs. By 4400 B.C., the Vilani sphere had reached about 10 parsecs in diameter.

Galanglic: See *Anglic*.

Gas Giant: A large planet with an extensive atmosphere of hydrogen and hydrogen compounds. Starships can fuel themselves by diving into this atmosphere and skimming hydrogen from this atmosphere. Jupiter, in the Sol system, is an example of a gas giant.

Gateway, Domain of: A domain of the Third Imperium, consisting of the Ley, Glimmerdrift Reaches, Gateway, and Crucis Margin sectors.

General Shipyards: The largest starship manufacturer in Regina Subsector, with yards at Regina, Efate, and Pixie. Originally a military contractor, General no longer produces ships for military use; instead it concentrates on the more lucrative commercial market. The yard at Regina is capable of producing ships up to 5,000 tons, while the subsidiary yards at Pixie and Efate are limited to 600 tons, and devote most of their attention to annual maintenance.

Glea (Centrax/Glea 2609 A667800-F): Main coordinating center of the Hive Federation since 410. Center of the Glean Cluster, an unusually rich grouping of 16 Hiver-habitable worlds which are mutually accessible by jump-1 shipping.

Good War/Bad War: The terms "good war" and "bad war" are expressions used by mercenaries to differentiate between small-scale actions within the Imperium and full-scale wars between the Imperium and outside forces.

Small-scale actions are viewed as good because the Imperial rules of war are in effect, and a unit knows that it will not be subject to weapons of mass destruction as such. Good wars are usually short and not particularly bloody. A unit in a tight spot need merely surrender and activate its repatriation bonds to be removed from combatant status. Even anti-guerrilla actions are good, under this classification, because of the fact that although most guerrillas usually observe no restraint with captured government forces, captured mercenaries can usually be ransomed to serve as a source of income.

A war is bad when no such controls are in effect, and a mercenary unit will be subject to the full horrors of war. Mercenary units are understandably reluctant to accept bad war contracts, but they may be forced into them by circumstances.

Grand Prince(ss): Imperial title of the heir to the Iridium Throne. Under Imperial custom, the eldest child of an emperor is granted the title at the age of 12. An Imperial Edict (q.v.) is issued which actually confers the title on the heir's birthday, but the formal investiture ceremonies are normally delayed until the next Holiday (see p. 38) after the birthday. It is extremely rare, but not unknown, for an emperor to withhold the title for a few years or never appoint one. A childless emperor formally designates a successor by granting that person the title grand prince (again, a rare event). If a grand prince dies before ascending the throne, another is normally appointed as soon as possible. It is, of course, not required that an emperor be designated grand prince in order to take the throne. See *Ciencia Iphegenia*, p. 25.

Great Rift: Broad expanse of space with a very low density of stars lying spinward of the main region of the Third Imperium. The Great Rift is a pronounced impediment to interstellar travel, and it constrains jumps through Corridor sector to the Spinward Marches.

The Great Rift is one of many astrographic terrain features which have provided long-term security for the Third Imperium. By its very nature, the Great Rift has made outside incursions difficult, which has made the interior of the Imperium a secure population center.

Guaran (Ricenden/Guaran 0827 A565800-F): Homeworld of the Hivers. Guaran has no special political importance, although it attracts millions of tourists annually from all over the Federation. See *Hive, Hive Federation.*

Hive: Intelligent major race with a large federation trailing the Imperium. Individuals are called Hivers, average 4½ feet from ground to top of upraised head, and weigh about 75 lbs. Descended from omnivore gatherer/scavenger stock, they are the most alien of the major races from a Human standpoint. Hivers exhibit a modified six-fold radial symmetry; the body has a calcareous internal skeleton consisting of a series of rings supporting the limbs and a fused carapace protecting the brain and internal organs.

The head is a modification of one of the limbs, and contains six eyestalks and six manipulative tentacles, plus paired infrared sensor organs. The other five limbs are identical (except for slight modifications of the hand opposite the head) and are used as arms and legs indiscriminately. Each limb ends in a six-fingered radial hand. Fingers are very flexible and have muscular suction cups on the lower surface about halfway to the tips. Hiver arms and hands are generally weaker than a Human's, but are very tough and difficult to injure.

The mouth (digestive opening) is on the lower surface of the body. There is no sound-producing organ, but Hivers do have three ears placed around the neck near the head.

Hivers have only one sex. Reproductive cells are exchanged each time that Hivers meet, using the modified rear hand (the process has been termed by Humans "shaking hands"). The cells are kept in a reproductive pouch on the lower body surface where they conjugate and exchange genetic material. Once every 40 days or so, a cell will develop into a larva, which then drops from the parent's body.

Hive planets are mostly wilderness, and the larvae enter the wilds, where most are killed. After about a year, survivors return to civilization, where they are welcomed into any nest (the first they come to) and begin their education as citizens. Parental instinct in Hivers is very strong, and the entire nest adopts the young. (Note that this instinct applies only to the year-old returnees; Hivers have no concern for the younger larvae, and in fact they consider them minor pests.)

Hiver language is a combination of arm/tentacle waving and physical contact. The written language is ideographic and is used as a standard language among the races of the Hive Federation. Hivers talking among themselves use all three aspects of language (gesture, touch, and writing) at once, a process capable of great subtlety and sophistication, but unintelligible to the outsider.

Travellers' Aid Society

TAS is an interstellar organization dedicated to assisting its members as they travel throughout the Imperium and beyond. With offices at most major starports, TAS provides several services:

■ Member hostels at all Class V starports (fees depend on local conditions).

■ Free access to the *Traveller News Service* on all worlds with TAS offices, and free Travel Zone advisories (p. 70).

■ One paid middle passage per *month*, redeemable on any starship line, or for Cr1,575 in cash.

A one-time MCr1 fee purchases a membership, or sometimes the Imperium awards one for long service or acts of extreme heroism. Membership costs no character points, but bestows Comfortable Wealth. Characters of lesser Wealth must pay for the upgrade.

Customs

Continued on next page . . .

Minutes out of J-space we were hailed and ordered to stand to for customs inspection. You don't argue with the customs service, so we meekly allowed their cutter to dock, cursing not a little as a MarchLines subbie that came out of jump just after us sailed straight in without an inspection. MarchLines must have negotiated docking priviliges, the swine!

The inspection team came aboard: two techs, an officer-in-charge, and a pair of armored goons with rifles. Like we were going to start anything! Ever since those lunatics at Bevy tried to take the inspection team out they've backed up the cutters with an SDB. You can't do much with a battery of lasers aimed at your bridge.

The techs departed, each accompanied by a goon, to mess about with bits of my ship in the hope that they might find something interesting – like I could afford to buy anything worth smuggling! The officer asked for the ship's papers. Why do they call them that? It's just a set of data entries on the computer. Anyway, I handed over the datachip, and she went through the little ritual of inserting it in the reader and scrutinizing every line. Like she hadn't already interrogated the ship's computer from her cutter, read everything there was to know about us and cross-checked it with naval records.

I can see the point of the inspection. I could tell my computer to lie about the ship – falsify the papers if you like – but why read the same data twice? If it's on the so-called papers, it's in the computer!

Maybe they just do it to make us think we're getting our money's worth out of the customs service. Whatever.

She handed me the papers. "All in order."

Hivers are unique among major races in that they had a complex culture before becoming sentient. Originally, they lived in the tunnels and built-up mounds of a large (2,000-pound) burrowing animal (known as *snohl*, or burrowers). In exchange for shelter, they gave food. They farmed fungus and foraged outside for decaying plants and dead animals as a source of food for the fungus.

Snohl were allowed to graze in the farm tunnels. Hivers ate the fungus and whatever fresh food they could find outside. Intelligence arose as the outside environment changed, forcing the foraging parties to travel farther to discover new sources of food and fertilizer; foragers advanced from simple scavenging and gathering efforts to complex cooperative efforts of hunting and trapping live game.

Today, fungus remains the staple of the Hiver diet; fungus-growing is a highly developed art. Most buildings retain the beehive shape and large underground tunnel complexes of the original burrowers, but they are constructed by machines; the burrowers are now reduced to the secondary function of keeping the tunnels clean. Hiver attachment to them is essentially non-rational; they just feel more comfortable with *snohl* around.

Society. Hive society is highly individualistic. The term "Hive" results from an early Human misconception stemming from the appearance of the Hivers' building and tunnel complexes, which were seen as resembling a nest of social insects, and labeled a "hive." Nests contain from five to 500 individuals, who are usually centered around some common endeavor.

While 100 is an average size for a nest (and was the largest size in pre-civilized times), larger groups may come together for some civilized purpose such as large manufacturing companies or universities. Small nests are usually spaceship crews or isolated research parties. A young Hiver will spend his first 15 years in his home nest; thereafter, nest changes may take place as often as a modern Human might change jobs.

Because of the nature of their reproduction, Hivers never experienced the population pressures so important to Human history. The population of the homeworld is now only a few hundred million, only 10 times greater than it was in prehistoric times. Predators control the young; when the adult survival rate rises, thus increasing the numbers of young produced, the predator population increases proportionately and the balance is maintained. Space colonization arose not from pressure but from curiosity, with which Hivers are amply endowed.

The Hivers have colonized only those planets with climates most pleasant to themselves; if the planet has no predators that eat Hiver larvae, they are imported. Because of the high birth rate, a colony will rapidly reach its maximum population level of a few hundred million and then stabilize. Hivers like planets of diameter 6,500 miles or less, with thin or standard atmospheres and unvarying climates. Hiver enclaves for commercial or scientific purposes are found on worlds of more extreme characteristics.

Hive industry and business excel at communications technology and robot construction. Major exports include artificial and computer languages, translators, and sophisticated electronic hardware of all types. Hiver mathematical systems are much in demand for their power and elegance.

Hive Federation: Human term for the loose interstellar community dominated by the Hivers; Hive Confederation is also sometimes used. The Hivers have only one culture and one language; the Hiver genotype (with individual variations similar in degree to differences between individual Humans of the same race) is also constant.

The Federation government (if such a term is at all applicable) is mostly concerned with maintaining the uniformity of the Hiver culture and species. This is accomplished by frequent reproductive embassies from one planet to another. Members of many different nests will shake hands with everyone nearby in a sort of farewell party, and will then board a large embassy ship bound for a far-off world. Once there, they will meet with as many people as possible, shaking hands and exchanging news, art, gossip, scientific information, political views, and so on for about a year. They will then return home for another year-long round of parties, discussions, and handshaking.

Most disputes among communities are handled in these embassies; others, considered too urgent or transient to wait for an embassy, are settled by judges. There is a considerable body of Hiver common law and custom, and a judge is a person who has spent years in study of the law; judges' decisions are not necessarily binding and are open to compromise, but they carry a great weight of custom.

The discovery of alien races and their integration into society required a slightly more formal organization, which grew out of the coordinating body whose job it was to schedule embassies. Two additional bodies were established: the Federation Navy and a development agency.

The Hiver parental instinct was aroused by the discovery of numerous intelligent species less fortunate than themselves, and work began immediately to lift the "children" to civilization. An early experience with an aggressive race led to the establishment of a system of quarantined worlds, denied entry to (or knowledge of) interstellar society.

Covert operations are in progress on quarantine worlds to modify overly aggressive cultures into acceptable members of the Federation, and several quarantined planets have been opened since the beginning of the program. So far, no quarantined race is close to achieving interstellar travel on its own; public debate continues on what to do in such a case.

The navy is the main instrument of military force. Hivers came late to the concept of war and are more comfortable with high-tech, long-range violence; they dislike the personal approach of ground combat.

When ground forces are absolutely needed, other races of the Federation generally supply the troops. Federation armed forces are essentially a deterrent force and are seldom used as an instrument of policy.

Other races of the Federation are equal partners in society, although the structure of society is Hiver-generated, and those races able to adapt best to a Hiver way of life and customs have been most successful. All races participate in the embassies, although in a modified form.

Some associated species retain strong internal governments or police forces to regulate the aggressive tendencies of their members, but whatever solution is reached, all Federation member societies are non-aggressive.

Most worlds of the Federation have communities of several species; races inhabit the worlds they find most pleasant.

Customs

[Continued]

"Thank you, ensign," I said, trying to be nice in the hope of getting to the port a bit quicker. But no. Not a chance.

"Tell me, captain. Are you really shipping frozen prawns? Eighty tons of them?"

"Yes, ensign. Frozen prawns. Nothing but. You can have a free sample if you like."

"I don't think so. I have reason to believe you're carrying contraband. I'll have to order a full search of the ship. It'll take about three hours."

*"Three hours!" I burst out. "But I have a buyer waiting. The **March Eagle** is already in port. I'll lose the deal!"*

She smiled stonily, her right hand close to her sidearm just in case, "You could always try to bribe me. In which case the inspection will take all day."

"Did MarchLines pay you to hold me up?"

The smile went away as she snapped, "No. Just a routine inspection to keep cutthroats like you from shipping nerve gas or Gauss rifles to the peasants. Take me to your bridge and I'll call in the second inspection squad."

"Certainly, ensign." I was about to add something but bit it back. I had a feeling that the inspection would take twice as long if I said what I really thought.

Meanwhile MarchLines was already in port, selling their cargo. They'd nobbled me again. But I had an idea . . .

– Captain Rik Frain,
*Free Trader **St. Hilaire***

Other Holidays

We do not specify other holidays in the Imperial calendar; these are left up to the individual GM, who may or may not consider such details important. There will certainly be days of significance to individual worlds as well: veterans honored, battles lost and won, religious events, and so on.

Off to a Bad Start

We'd made a deal. The Human, Halsine, had outlined the job. I'd quoted our fee. He'd winced. We'd bargained. He handed me a datachip in its protective case, reached across the desk and shook my hand . . .

. . . and I heard someone breathe "Now!" outside the office door.

By the time the door slammed open, propelled by a heavy boot, I was out of my chair and diving for the far corner of the room. Before the two Human goons had cleared the doorway I'd landed hard and rolled up against the wall. My autopistol was already clear of its holster.

Halsine, moving fast for a pink, had time to reach into his desk drawer before they shot him. Both of them fired twice, throwing my new employer back in his chair. He slumped back, his unfired pistol falling from his hand.

They started to turn in my direction, but I wasn't waiting to touch noses. I fired from the floor, slamming a dozen rounds into the nearest one. His packmate tried to step to the side for a clear shot, but if he got one off, it went wide. I nailed him at least twice, in the neck and head. No question about that kill, either.

Or about Halsine. My employer had taken four heavy rounds in the chest. Humans are tough, but not that tough. The room stank of blood and propellant, and I had to get out of there. I closed his staring eyes – the Humans have that custom, too, did you know that? – and was out of the office and down the hall at a trot.

I had to find a phone and warn the others, and I didn't know who might be looking for us. There was more to this than Halsine had said, and I had the feeling that the datachip in my pocket was going to be a lot of trouble. But we'd made a deal.

Holiday: The first day of the year, 001. A day of secular celebration in commemoration of the end of one year, but primarily celebrating the start of a new one. On most worlds, the day is one of rest and recreation, but some cultures choose to celebrate it differently, and a few not at all. All but essential Imperial offices are closed on Holiday, and most worlds follow suit.

Holiday Year: The year zero in the history of the Third Imperium, established by Emperor Cleon I to commemorate the establishment of the Third Imperium. Technically an aspect of calendar reform, the use of the year zero provides a central date point for counting years back into the Long Night and forward into the future of the Imperium.

The actual advantages of a holiday year are slight: Centuries begin in the hundredth numbered year instead of the first, and the number of years between any two dates before and after the year zero can be determined by simple subtraction.

More important at the time, the holiday year was used as part of the public-relations campaigns impressing the authority of the Imperium upon local governments. The minor nuisance of changing to the new calendar was used to gauge the cooperation of those governments. See *Imperial Calendar*, p. 39.

Humaniti (former spelling Humanity): Collective name for Human races, including Solomani, Vilani, Zhodani, and others. See *Humans.*

Humans: Intelligent major race dominating the Imperium and several additional interstellar communities. Humans stand approximately 5'10" and weigh about 170 lbs. Descended from omnivore gatherers, Humans developed intelligence in response to shifting climatological factors.

The most unusual aspect of Humaniti is the fact that Humans are present on many different worlds and stand at various levels of development on those worlds. The Solomani Hypothesis (see p. 61) states that Humans evolved on Terra (Solomani Rim/Sol) from indigenous life, and were scattered to many different worlds by an unknown agency (now believed to be the Ancients) for reasons unknown. The result is that many different, parallel Human races exist and coexist throughout known space.

The three most widespread Human races are the Solomani (Humans from Terra), the Vilani (Humans from Vland), and the Zhodani (Humans from Zhodane). Most branches of Humaniti are interfertile, although some of the more extreme variants are not. For taxonomic purposes, all are included in the family Hominidae, and the vast majority are genus *Homo*. Solomani and Vilani are *H. sapiens sapiens*, Zhodani are *H. zhdotlas*.

See also *Ancients, Humaniti, Solomani Hypothesis, Solomani, Vilani, Zhodani*. See **GURPS Traveller Alien Races 1** for more on the Zhodani.

Ilelish, Domain of: A domain of the Third Imperium, consisting of the Ilelish, Zarushagar, Reaver's Deep, and Daibei sectors.

Imperial Calendar: Calendar established at the creation of the Third Imperium as a universal calendar reform. Dates count from the founding of the Imperium, the year "zero." Dates before zero are negative; dates after are positive. For example, Terra invented jump drive in -2431. The Imperium was founded in zero. Emperor Strephon will celebrate his Golden Jubilee in 1121.

Calendar Conversion Table

January	1-31	001-031	July	1-31	182-212
February	1-28	032-059	August	1-31	213-243
March	1-31	060-090	September	1-30	244-273
April	1-30	091-120	October	1-31	274-304
May	1-31	121-151	November	1-30	305-334
June	1-30	152-181	December	1-31	335-365

The year is divided into 365 standard days, which are grouped into 52 weeks of seven days each. The lengths of days and weeks is a legacy of Terran domination during the Second Imperium. Days are numbered consecutively, beginning with 1. The first day of the year is a holiday and is not part of any week. For example, the first day (Holiday) of the year 1120 is 001-1120. The last day of the year is 365-1120.

Imperial Edict 97: This executive order is the enabling act for the use of Imperial warrants. Unusually obscure for such a wide-ranging and powerful edict, it is nonetheless on file at all Imperial installations. The edict text runs to 34 pages, much of it pure legalese; when distilled down, it proves very direct. It requires all Imperial officials to assist the holder with all the power of their office. Only the emperor has the power to issue these warrants.

A similar edict (Imperial Edict 3,097) provides limited power to the archdukes of the Imperium to issue similar warrants, although they are limited in their duration and territory.

Imperial Edicts: Proclamations of the emperor, usually reserved for extremely important matters. Imperial Edicts are numbered in the order in which they are issued, and are commonly referred to by these numbers.

Imperial Identity Document: Also known as the Universal Identity Document, Universal ID, ID card, and a number of other names. The record of every citizen's identity, taken first when birth is registered, and supplemented and expanded as time passes. The record consists of a full genetic work-up, full body and head-and-shoulders holograms, retinal pattern, fingerprints, and other identifying information. The Imperial enabling legislation does not define the

Ine Givar

Every empire has its opposition, and the Ine Givar fill the bill for the Imperium. When we wrote up some of the first *TNS* dispatches, we needed someone to blame for an explosion and invented a band of terrorists. We continued to use them from time to time when we wanted "bad guys." The name was simply a couple of nice-sounding nonsense words.

The Ine Givar often find themselves in the role of scapegoat. Every two-bit criminal and half-baked crackpot revolutionary group prefers to blame their actions on the Ine Givar, and the Ine Givar goes along because it makes them seem larger than they really are. On more than a few worlds, the only Ine Givar presence is an underground propaganda cell taking credit for acts of violence committed by other groups.

Another terrorist group, Solomani in origin, is *Rule of Terra,* p. 58. Links between the two groups are a subject of much speculation. Also see *Ine Givar* library entry on p. 43.

At Standard Noon, 062-1120 . . .

They had bumped and jolted through the mountains for a whole day, until riding in the ATV felt like being inside a huge blender. Finally, they crested the last ridge, and there was the mining camp spread out below.

Sandra popped the hatch and breathed deep as she took in the scene: the prefabricated base sections, the vehicle shelters, and the humming of powered-up machinery.

And the bodies, scattered about the camp like a child's neglected toys.

■■■

It'd been years since he was here. The last time he'd seen Stanley Highport was as he climbed into a transport to go home with the rest of the battalion. They'd fought hard and well, and the war was won.

Sixteen years later the memories were blurred a little, but the faces hovered at the edge of memory. He saw few of them now, not since a terrorist bomb had earned him a medal and a medical discharge. Now there was a new life as medical officer aboard the Free Trader Harlequin. But he missed the army life, missed his old comrades. Missed the regiment. He turned back to the viewport with mixed feelings.

What would it be like, coming back to this place as a civilian?

■■■

The suit was bulky and just a shade too hot, the gloves clumsy on his hands. There was that worrying cold spot on his lower back where the environment control wasn't working properly. Danev put it all aside, tried not to look at the stars as they gyrated in his peripheral vision.

The last hit had screwed the maneuver drive but good. The ship was spinning in space without power, but that was the least of their troubles. In three hours they'd touch the upper atmosphere of Avastan and their problems would all be over.

Join the Scout Service and see the stars! Explore worlds! Meet Humans and aliens! Carry vital information! Serve the emperor! Travel and Adventure for All – never a dull moment! At least the last part was right.

Danev blanked out the stars and kept working.

form of the documentation, but does specify what data must be recorded for various sophont species, and how the data is to be verified at all tech levels within the Imperium. Additional information – such as criminal, medical, and educational records – may be recorded on the portable form of the document. Planetary governments at all tech levels are capable of issuing the most primitive form of the document, which consists of a plastic card incorporating a data chip with the minimum data recorded within, and with holographic images, thumbprint, and other features on the surface. Sophisticated versions of the ID are capable of carrying a virtual dossier in their data-storage systems, and are capable of projecting and displaying all of the data in a wide variety of formats.

Although in theory every citizen must have an Imperial ID, in practice they are needed only by those who engage in interplanetary or interstellar travel. Full ID checks are rather a nuisance, and their implementation is at the referee's discretion.

Imperial Research Station: The worlds of the Imperium manifest a wide range of technological levels. The Third Imperium has always allowed its member worlds a wide degree of latitude, and it meddles very little in local affairs. With communication limited to the same speed as transportation, a single off-world query can involve weeks, months, or even years before a reply is received. In addition, the cost of off-world transportation (in both time and money) tends to limit the interchange of information, the shipment of experimental prototypes, and other such activities that are basic to the dissemination of scientific knowledge.

Most worlds have found that simply purchasing advanced technology from a neighboring world is impractical. Not only is such high technology expensive, putting it to any cost-effective use requires that the technology be understood.

Consider: As useful as TL8 solid-state chip circuits are, they cannot be used on a large scale without the knowledge of electronics or the ability to provide supporting circuits (power circuits, circuit boards, and so on), which further implies a knowledge of photo processing, and even crystal culture. In the final analysis, attempting to jump to a higher tech level without passing through any of the intervening tech levels just doesn't work: One must pass through the lower stages of technological development on the way to higher tech levels.

Regardless of what the individual member worlds do, there are also certain large-scale interests in the Imperium which back research projects. Such research is generally privately backed (such as under contract by multiworld corporations), and it is sometimes performed in Imperial Research Stations.

The Imperium finances research into a variety of areas. Sometimes this is an attempt to duplicate technology observed or reported in neighboring cultures and not yet within the ability of the best known science in the Imperium. Other times, the research covers an area of interest expressed by some Imperial body (such as spinal-mount weapons research performed by the Imperial Navy).

Imperial-backed research may delve into many areas. Some examples include black holes (both large-scale and miniature versions), instantaneous transmitter development (so far proving impossible), antimatter containment, new weapon development (such as disintegrator beams), black globes (force-field technology left behind by the Ancients), deep planetary scanning, psychohistory, mass population behavior prediction, genetic transformation of living organisms, self-aware robots and starships, stasis and time travel, personal shields, memory transfer, and total rejuvenation.

Imperial research stations may be located on worlds which need a boost to the local economy or in remote systems far from the potential disturbance of Imperial politics. Many different stations may be located in several systems of the same region, and many different areas of knowledge may be under investigation at one time.

In general, however, each station is constructed for one purpose, and it continues delving into a single area of knowledge for its entire span of usefulness. Its size, personnel roster, power plant capacity, and even visibility profile are dependent on its area of investigation.

Private Research: On a scale as vast as the Imperium, it's often cheaper to duplicate research than search out and contract for technology elsewhere in the Imperium. However, trade between worlds tends to introduce new knowledge and technology to those who do not yet have it. If a certain off-world item proves useful, local companies may try to achieve the same technology with the goal of entering into local manufacture. Local manufacture has the advantage of taking into account local preferences, as well as providing local employment. It also avoids potential problems with licensing agreements and arrangements.

Imperial Rules of War: To mitigate most of the potentially disastrous aspects of armed conflict, the "rules of war" evolved as an accumulation of unwritten concepts, which were established on a case-by-case basis.

The rules of war have never been officially codified, both to prevent them being seen as an Imperial endorsement of war and to keep formal precedent from preventing Imperial intervention whenever the Imperium deemed it necessary.

The main aim of the rules is maintaining the economic and military well-being of the realm. They give the Imperium the right to intervene only when local military action threatens this well-being. The primary causes of instability, as viewed by Imperial analysts, have been long-term economic dislocation and excessive extra-planetary influence.

Long-term social or economic dislocation is suffered when a region loses its ability to carry on at its prewar level of economic activity.

Excessive extra-planetary influence is even more vague. Historically, the Imperium has tolerated the use of force as an outlet for built-up sociopolitical pressures. In such cases, a short war is deemed preferable to continuing tension, sabotage, political agitation, etc. Attempts by extra-planetary forces, such as off-world governments or large commercial interests, to seize control of a world's affairs are beyond the scope of the "safety valve" rationale.

"Assistance" is tolerated so long as it is deemed appropriate to the level of legitimate interest in the affairs of the world held by the extra-planetary organization. For example, the Imperium has often tolerated the provision by megacorporations of training cadres, arms, equipment, etc., on a limited scale, and even of providing fully equipped combat units to local governments. When it has appeared that the primary burden for the conduct of the war has been car-

A Concise History of Ziru Sirka, Part II

Prepared for Solomani readers by the Vilani Historical Documents Subcommittee, Kasiiga University Press, Ishimaga, Vland, 001-1116

Exploration and Exploitation

Between 4400 and 1400 B.C., the Vilani explored, exploited, and settled virtually every world they contacted. Initially, their emphasis was on exploration and contact, but over the centuries, Vilani settlement inexorably followed. Worlds closest to Vland were settled first, but the star catalogs were bulging with worlds ripe for colonization and exploitation. Barren worlds were exploited for immediate gain; their resources were strip-mined and shipped off to feed Vland's growing industries.

Inhabited worlds were subjected to exploitation as well, but on a more subtle basis. Exploration revealed a number of technologically primitive races on worlds within 60 parsecs. None had developed interstellar travel; few had advanced even beyond the Iron Age. All were ripe for domination by the Vilani. The Vilani imposed their culture, their law, and their interstellar economic community on all the worlds they encountered. The subject races made few objections; the rewards were far too great when compared to the sacrifices they were called upon to make. Vilani help (or interference) gradually brought the subject races to a high technology level. The Vilani culture had no concept of a "prime directive" banning interference with local cultures. Instead, Vilani culture and technology were handed out wholesale to bring the many non-Vilani races forward. Early Vilani conquests were not military; they were more subtle exercises in economic subjugation.

Continued on next page . . .

ried by an extra-planetary power, the Imperium has intervened, claiming the power is using the misfortune of a local dispute as a pretext for aggression.

Imperial intervention is also guaranteed if any group makes use of or possesses weapons of mass destruction such as biological, chemical, or nuclear weapons. Precisely what constitutes a weapon of mass destruction is not formally defined, and Imperial officers are given vast discretionary powers in enforcement of the restrictions.

Imperial Stationery: The Imperial family has reserved (both by custom and by law) a distinctive design for its personal stationery. Well-known throughout the Imperium through its use for routine messages and for Imperial appointments, the form is cream-colored, embossed with the Imperial sunburst in gold, and incorporates a watermark and other technological security features. Both physical and electronic versions of the stationery are used.

Because it is used for Imperial appointments (even when issued in blank for offices in the Marches and other outlying areas), all Imperial officials are familiar with the design and can readily tell physical forgeries from the real thing. Electronic versions are data-encrypted with a special code lock and require a special hardware key to be unlocked, thus making even electronic forgeries difficult.

Imperial Sunburst: The symbol of the Third Imperium established by Cleon (the first emperor) when the empire was proclaimed. Images show him standing before the original banner with a golden yellow sunburst against a black background, representing Capital's type G star against dark space.

In 247, the Eliyoh (a non-Human minor race) joined the Imperium. To that race the symbology was unimpressive. The Eliyoh vision centered in the far infrared, which resulted in distinction between the official colors of black and yellow being impossible. So the Empress Porfiria declared that the symbol would have no official color.

The original banner in the Imperial throne room is still black with a yellow sunburst. The Imperial Interstellar Scout Service uses a red sunburst, the Imperial Navy yellow, the Imperial Army black, and the Imperial Marines maroon.

Imperial Warrant: Instrument of power issued by Imperial dukes, archdukes, or the emperor. A warrant is a written or electronic document on Imperial stationery provided to trusted agents of the Imperium as a method of bypassing the bureaucracy. Typically, a warrant is provided to an individual who uses the power it provides to accomplish some mission of interest to the issuing official. Missions may include establishment of colonies in areas requiring development, the assumption of military command in the midst of a crisis, or the unilateral establishment of new noble lines to administer provinces which have suffered from war or economic collapse.

For example, Strephon sometimes exercises power through agents rather than directly through the bureaucracy of the Imperium. These instances are rare, although there is reason to believe that such agents are more numerous than it appears. The Imperial warrant would contain a statement similar to this example:

"Capital. The bearer of this warrant is acting for the good of the Imperium and the Emperor. Extend him every assistance. Strephon."

The most recent Imperial Warrant (at least the most recent known to the general public) was that issued to Duke Norris of Regina shortly before the outbreak of the Fifth Frontier War (q.v.), and used by him with great effectiveness during that conflict.

See also *Imperial Edict 97, Fifth Frontier War.*

Ine Givar: An anti-Imperial terrorist organization, primarily active in the domain of Deneb, but with branches throughout the Imperium. Little is known of the history and organization of these terrorists, but Imperial intelligence sources believe they are at least partly funded by the Zhodani (something which some cells of the Ine Givar deny, but which others acknowledge).

Also see *Ine Givar* sidebar, p. 39.

Interdiction: The Imperial practice of interdiction of worlds within the boundaries of the Imperium had long been a source of contention between liberal and conservative factions in the government. Interdictions must be approved by the emperor or one of the archdukes, but generally such approval is given in response to a request from an interested service, which is almost always the Scouts or the Navy, and is virtually automatic.

It is generally held that the Scouts recommend interdiction to shield a young or sensitive culture from the interference that trade and commerce will bring.

The Navy is held to be more vindictive in its recommendations, the accusation being that it uses interdiction to punish local governments or to hide its own mistakes.

Interdicted worlds are awarded "travel zone red" ratings by the Travellers' Aid Society (p. 35).

See also *Red Zone.*

Iolanthe (b. 1052): Imperial Empress Iolanthe Guuilbataashullibaa Alkhalikoi. Iolanthe, the daughter of the senior duke of Gushemege sector and member of a prominent Vilani noble family, married Strephon in 1079. Her primary avocation is the preservation of developing cultures within the Imperium. See also *Strephon, Ciencia Iphegenia.*

Iridium Throne: The symbol of the office of emperor of the Third Imperium.

The term originally referred to the physical throne, constructed of the metal iridium, but over time has acquired a larger meaning.

Isis: (b. 1088) Isis Arepo Ilethian, archduchess of Ilelish, daughter of Archduke Dulinor (q.v.) and Lady Jessica Ilethian. She was appointed archduchess 001-1117, succeeding her father, who died the previous year.

Archduchess Isis was born on the same day as Grand Princess Ciencia Iphegenia (see p. 25), and (being of families from the Imperial court) attended the same schools. Because of this, the two have become close friends.

The Coming of the Bureaux

This 3,000-year period of exploration and exploitation was perhaps the most vital in Vilani history. But an empire more than 60 parsecs across is difficult for any government to rule. By 1480 B.C., a starship took more than 60 weeks to cross Vilani territory from border to border. It was impossible for the careful, constant control endorsed by the Vilani to be exercised across such vast distances. Over the course of several decades, the Vilani homeworld government established three subordinate governments – the bureaux – which were each assigned a portion of the overall territory to govern, defend, and exploit. Makhidkarun controlled the territory in the direction of the galactic core. Naasirka received territories nearer to Vland. And Sharurshid, controlled by interstellar merchants, was assigned territories in the direction of the galactic rim.

Each bureau was a complete interstellar government operated for a profit, but responsible for the welfare of its citizens, control of its subjects, and defense of its territory. Each bureau had rights of taxation, defense, and legislation in its territory. A bureau's fleets protected its shipping and trade; its armies defended its installations and conquered new worlds if necessary. Mutual assistance agreements allowed the bureaux to call upon each other for help. But while each bureau was a self-sufficient government controlling vast numbers of worlds, all three were nominally responsible to a central ruling council on Vland, the Igsiirdi.

The Igsiirdi ruled Vland. It received tribute (or taxation) payments from the bureaux and used the funds to administer public works on Vland. It also allocated newly discovered territories to the bureaux. The three bureaux appointed the Igsiirdi's members, and in practice, it served as a forum within which the bureaux could communicate, interact, and eventually reach decisions governing them all.

Alternate FTL Drives

If desired, Game Masters may incorporate other FTL interstellar drives than jump drives (as described on p. 13 and in the *Jumpspace* entry on this page), provided that they are slower than one week per parsec (3.26 light years). While this is not the case in the formal background history, no major violence will be done to the background if any number of alternate means of interstellar travel are allowed to exist, provided that the jump drive remains the fastest.

GMs may even introduce FTL radio, should they wish, provided that it is also slower than the speed of physical travel (although this may have unforeseen repercussions).

Further Research Is Needed . . .

"Many will think my next statement to be intended in humor, but I assure you that I am completely serious: Those who are not confused by the details of jump theory have not studied it deeply enough. I envy those of you who feel you understand what happens when a ship enters jump – I felt the same myself, 60 years ago when I was an undergraduate. By the time this course is over, you will be as mystified – and as fascinated – as everyone else in the field."

– Professor Chiraa Khoor,
Lecturer in the Physics of Jumpspace,
University of Regina

Jump Dimming: The transitions to and from jumpspace are momentous occasions during an interstellar trip. Following an old Vilani superstition, the pilot of a ship customarily dims the ship's interior and exterior lights before going into jump. Historically, this custom derived from the need for most of the ship's power to be diverted into the computer and jump-drive systems, so that the jump drive could be guided into creating the jump field properly. Non-Vilani pilots do not follow this tradition, which has not been necessary for centuries.

Lights on a ship are typically dimmed for a period of about two minutes; the lights are brought back up to full strength as soon as the ship is in jumpspace.

Jumpspace: The basic concept of interstellar travel, that of an alternate space. Jump is defined as the movement of matter from one point in space (called normal space) to another point in normal space by traveling through an alternate space called *jumpspace*. The benefit of jump is that the time required is relatively invariant – about one week. If the distance traveled is greater than can be covered in one week in normal space, then a gain has been made. Jumpspace makes possible enormous gains. Jump drives are described by the distance they allow, from jump-1 (1 parsec per week-long jump) to jump-6 (6 parsecs in the same time).

Entering jump is, in theory, possible anywhere, but perturbations due to gravity make it safest to begin a jump at least 100 diameters out from a massive body such as a world or star. Ships are naturally precipitated out of jumpspace before they get too deep into a gravity field.

Normal jumps take 168 hours (plus or minus up to 10%) to complete, regardless of the distance traveled. That range is between 6 days, 7 hours, 12 minutes and 7 days, 16 hours, 48 minutes.

Sometimes a jump goes wrong. Catastrophic failures (called misjumps) can destroy the ship and its crew. Other failures can destroy a drive or send a ship in the wrong direction. Some misjumps reduce a jump-6 to a mere jump-1, or convert a jump-1 into jump-10, -20, or higher, and in a random direction.

Kedzudh, Commonality of: Loose interstellar government in the Vargr Extents. The Commonality dates from 1044, when several world governments joined together in an attempt to suppress piracy. The Commonality government has limited powers of taxation; government institutions include a small navy/police force and a university. Individual worlds conduct their own interior and exterior relations. See pp. T:AI76, 78-79.

Kirur (Ruupiin/Thirty 1315 B863A03-F): Homeworld and capital of the Two Thousand Worlds, the interstellar empire of the K'kree. The planet's oceans are extremely shallow and the world exhibits almost no volcanic activity, which is very unusual for a world of its size. Kirur has one large continent, which was conquered in prehistoric times by the current ruling clan. Kirur is one of the most politically stable planets known. See *GURPS Traveller Alien Races 2*.

K'kree: The K'kree (occasionally called Centaurs by Humans) are the most massive of the major races and are the only major race to be descended from herbivores. An adult K'kree stands about 5′ at the shoulder and between 6′ and 7′8″ tall when standing erect. Weight averages 1,000 lbs. They are bilaterally symmetrical, hexapedal, and homeothermic. They bear some resemblance to the centaurs of ancient Terran myth, a trait noted by the earliest Human explorers.

The arrangement of the manipulative organ (or hand) on the front limb is one of their most interesting features. Complex or cartilaginous tubes permit the fingers of the K'kree hand to telescope up out of the way when the hand is used as a weapon. Fully extended, the fingers are mutually opposable to each other and to the "thumb," which is in reality an extension of the ulna. The K'kree hand is very flexible, but somewhat weaker in grasping power than the Human hand.

Like mammals, the K'kree are covered with a short gray or black fur and with a dense black mane covering the head and neck and upper back of both sexes. Unlike mammals, the young are fed partly digested, regurgitated food instead of milk. Males average 15% to 20% larger than females.

Rightness

K'lat'rr cannot be closely translated, but gives the scent of far horizons beyond rolling and unbounded prairie, red-golden backek releasing its flowery-sweet pollen in waves before the gentle breeze, on which floats the dark, wet, and ozone-tingling smell of recent thunderstorms, mingled with the wet and comforting scents of family close by. Can such a scene fail to excite you, to set both hearts pounding in joy and . . . rightness?

Rightness . . . belonging . . . these perhaps best describe K'lat'rr, which signifies that everything is in its proper place, in its proper order, as it should be. An old Terran songweaver spoke of "God's in his heaven and all's right with the world." If by "God" he meant Ghik'keeriklk'ak T't'kahk Xeng Kirr Tkexirr, he scented the concept with perfection.

*– Noble Diplomat K'agzi,
of the K'kree mission to Capital,
in an interview transcribed 227-1110*

Y.AMERICA'98

Disgusting?

"I always wondered if some of the hatred many Imperial citizens feel for the K'kree isn't really revulsion and disgust at the manner in which they nurse their young. I looked it up, and the standard references all have some circumlocution, but basically they barf and their kids eat it.

"Now, really – is this any more disgusting than a lot of things you Terrans eat? Do any of you know what honey really is? Think about that for a while next time you're dumping on the poor K'kree!"

– Humorist Anton Wilson Peale III

K'kree are extremely conservative in all aspects of their culture. Ceremonial military units (such as bodyguards) are armed with equipment which K'kree military technology outdated centuries ago, and (aside from modifications made necessary by the invention of spaceflight) K'kree government has not changed significantly in centuries.

Because of their origins as plains-dwelling herd animals, the K'kree are claustrophobes; they cannot stand to be enclosed. K'kree cities are clumps of low, broad buildings; the interior is never more than one story in height, which allows the sky to be visible. Internal building divisions are achieved with curtains or tapestries, but these are very rare. Modern buildings incorporate walls and roofs of glass or other translucent materials. Internal ventilation creates artificial random "breezes" within the building to keep up the illusion of open space.

K'kree are extremely gregarious. They are never found alone, and will quickly sicken and die if removed from other K'kree for any length of time. Receiving a trade or diplomatic delegation from the K'kree means entertaining the entire family (one or more wives, servants, scribes, assistants, etc.) of the merchant or the ambassador. The K'kree word for "my" refers to a possession of an individual's herd, not to that of an individual. Privacy and individuality are exotic and little-understood concepts for the K'kree.

Society: K'kree society is divided into castes. The system is a remnant of ancient times which no longer fits K'kree culture perfectly, but the K'kree stick with it because it is traditional. There are hundreds of castes, but the distinctions are too faint for non-K'kree to understand. For simplicity, castes can be divided into three general groupings: noble, merchant, and servant. It is possible for a family to rise in caste, but this is a rare occurrence.

The lowest caste, the servants, has come to include farmers, factory workers, and unskilled laborers, as well as servants for all classes.

The next higher caste, the merchants, includes most skilled workers, scientists, engineers, technicians, scribes, and government administrators, as well as merchants and businessmen.

Nobles are the governmental officials (the Krurruna and others), the high military officers, diplomats, and heads of trade and manufacturing concerns. Nobles are usually garbed in much more ornate fashion than the lower castes.

Every male K'kree must serve a term in the military upon coming of age. Warriors are drawn from all castes; rank in the military is determined by the caste of origin (nobles enter the service as general-officer trainees, merchants as lower officers and non-commissioned officers, etc.). Upon completing the required term of service, a warrior returns to his original caste and position. Warriors are the only K'kree permitted to bear weapons, and they are further distinguished by their peculiar flared and horned helmets. They serve as soldiers, police, firefighters, and bodyguards for diplomatic and mercantile expeditions.

Female K'kree are casteless, and take on the caste of their father or husband. Females have no position in government or society other than the rearing of young.

Government: The basis of K'kree government is rooted in the traditional herd system. The basic unit of government is the herd, which consists of thousands of individuals of all sexes, castes, and ages led by *krurruna* (literally: bosses) under a single steppelord.

In recent times, most herds have been assigned specific geographic areas (several may be assigned to a city or a single herd may be assigned millions of hectares of farmland). A number of herds are governed by a single "lord of step-pelords" (usually the ruler of a planet); and the K'kree race as a whole is ruled by a "Steppelord of the 2,000 Worlds."

Calendar: The K'kree calendar is based on the period of Kirur (the K'kree homeworld) around Gzang, its star. The K'kree *pimlbigr* (year) is 439.56 standard days in length.

See also *Kirur, Two Thousand Worlds,* and *GURPS Traveller Alien Races 2.*

Kuzu (Dark Nebula/Kilane 0406 A876986-E): Homeworld of the Aslan race and capital of the Aslan Hierate. For more information, see *GURPS Traveller Alien Races 2.*

L

Lair (Provence/Grnouf 2402 A8859B9-F): "Homeworld" and capital of the Vargr Extents. Lair has never been accorded any particular status in the hearts and minds of the Vargr race, unlike worlds such as Terra, Vland, Zhodane, Kuzu, and Kirur. Lair was only recently united; several sections of the planet boasted independence until only a few years ago – which is unusual for the homeworld of a major interstellar race. For more information, see *GURPS Traveller Alien Races 1.*

Lancia: Cultural region in the Gushemege sector of the Third Imperium. The area was extensively ravaged during the Vilani Pacification Campaigns, and afterward resettled from the Vland sector under a special program sponsored by the Makhidkarun (p. 76).

Lanthanum: A rare earth element, the first of the inner transition metals. Vital to the construction of the inner coils of interstellar jump-drive units.

Lesser Rift: Broad expanse of space with a very low density of stars trailing the main region of the Third Imperium. This rift is a pronounced imped-iment to interstellar travel, for it constrains jumps through the Empty Quarter. The Lesser Rift is "lesser" only in comparison with the larger, more prominent Great Rift spinward of the Imperium.

The Lesser Rift, like the Great Rift, has provided long-term security for the Third Imperium by constraining access to the Imperium's borders.

Llellewyloly: Sophont race native to Junidy (Spinward Marches/Aramis 3202 B434ABD-9). Llellewyloly have five multijointed limbs which function as hands and feet interchangeably; main sensory organs are also located on the limbs. The spherical central body is covered with long, coarse hair. Many body features are adaptations to the extreme temperature variations of Junidy's day.

Llellewyloly have a complex society with many dimensions of social precedence; the same individual may be entitled to high status in one situation and low in another, and to make an error concerning propriety is a serious matter.

Loeskalth: Minor Human race from Gushemege sector; known only from ancient First Imperium records. During the early stages of the First Imperium the Loeskalth culture absorbed a great deal of science and technology indirectly from the Vilani and founded a small empire which embraced, at its height, most of their home subsector.

About 5,400 years ago, the Vilani consolidation destroyed the Loeskalth Empire and absorbed the civilization into the mainstream of Vilani culture. An aggressive and warlike race, the Loeskalth resisted but were ultimately overwhelmed. What is known of their culture survives only in Vilani records of the war, and in fables on several worlds in the region.

A Concise History of Ziru Sirka, Part III

Prepared for Solomani readers by the Vilani Historical Documents Subcommittee, Kasiiga University Press, Ishimaga, Vland, 001-1116

The Consolidation Wars

Although Vilani territory was 60 parsecs in diameter in 1480 B.C., Vilani influence was felt far beyond their established borders. Cultures on the fringes of the Vilani sphere received the benefits of Vilani technology without being subjected to Vilani government. Many such cultures acquired jump-drive technology and explored territories even farther beyond the limits of Vilani exploration. It was inevitable that clashes would occur between the Vilani and these independent cultures.

In 909 B.C., the Vilani invented jump-2 and could travel directly to worlds 2 parsecs distant. Moreover, because of circumstances of stellar placement, many jump-2 routes took significantly less than half the time to run than comparable jump-1 routes.

Vilani ships after 909 B.C. had at least twice their previous speed and a vastly enhanced strategic mobility. The Vilani kept the jump-2 drive a jealously guarded secret for millennia: The drive immediately gave the Vilani the weapon they needed to keep the rest of the universe under control. In 880 B.C., after several centuries of sputtering conflict, the Igsiirdi (expressing the will of the bureaus) launched the Consolidation Wars and committed all of Vland's forces to subjugating the many states on the fringes of the Vilani Empire.

Continued on next page . . .

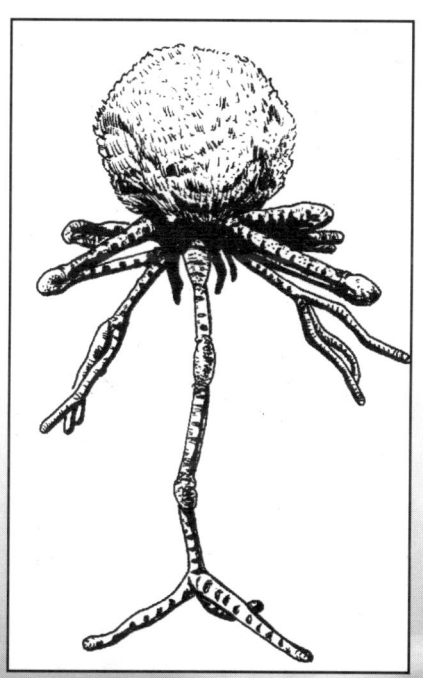

A Concise History of Ziru Sirka, Part III

[Continued]

When the wars ended in 476 A.D., the Vilani had almost tripled the size of their domain. Consolidation brought a marked change in the texture of Vilani society. Before, it had stressed peaceful expansion as neighboring worlds were assimilated in a trade community and absorbed into Vilani society. Now, armed might and superior technology were used to force any and every neighboring culture into the fold. Over the next 1,000 years, the Vilani conquered all of civilized space and absorbed enemies, allies, and neutrals alike. The Vilani jump-2 advantage virtually assured their ultimate victory in the Consolidation Wars. The Igsiirdi arranged coordination between the bureaux, shared the burden equitably, and prevented over-expansion. The Igsiirdi also allocated new territory to the bureaux once it was conquered, although the bureaux generally agreed before the fact how such territories would be distributed. The Igsiirdi managed the absorption of conquered states. Interstellar states continued to exist as subject states. They were absorbed into Vilani society as much as possible. Races that were unable to fit into Vilani society were severely restricted.

The Grand Empire of Stars

Vland colonized widely between 700 B.C. and 521 A.D., through several decades past the end of the Consolidation Wars. Vland had expanded until no uncolonized civilized states remained on its borders. Beyond those borders were only uncivilized worlds and empty systems.

In 476, the Igsiirdi declared the Ziru Sirka. The Vilani calendar dates from this point. The peace imposed by this Imperium lasted for nearly 1,200 years, but the cost to the Vilani and their subject races was immeasurable. The Ziru Sirka initially had no emperor. Within 10 years, the chairman of the Igsiirdi (elected for life by the council) was the *ishimkarun* – the shadow emperor – an anonymous leader who accepted or rejected the decisions of the council. He ruled through published proclamations, never appearing in public. Upon his death, the Igsiirdi elected a successor from its members.

With cultural maturity, the Ziru Sirka reached a pinnacle of interstellar diplomacy. Client states under Vilani protection or patronage numbered in the thousands. This stability led to raised world tech levels, living standards, and trade levels. At its height (1000 A.D.), the First Imperium contained over 15,000 worlds (via worlds absorbed from conquered states, settled regions which graduated from "territorial" to "sector government" status, and continued colonization of explored space).

Long Night (-1776 to 0): The period of almost universal chaos following the break-up of the Rule of Man (q.v.). The Long Night continued until the establishment of the Third Imperium by Cleon Zhunastu in the year 0. See also *Twilight, Third Imperium.*

Longbow: Acronym for "Long Baseline Observation Window," the name for a system created in the 800s for observation of the galactic core and the Zhodani axis of exploration toward the core. The largest known application of aperture synthesis ever constructed, Project Longbow was a deep Imperial secret throughout its existence, but has since been de-classified. Longbow was created to observe the Zhodani core expeditions, and, after many decades of data accumulation and calibration, was actually able to measure Zhodani shipping activity along the core axis. Because sensor signatures propagate at the speed of light, the observations were not in real time. Rather, the deeper into the core the sensor "looked," the older the signatures.

The Longbow collector plane was located in the Depot/Lishun (1219 Lishun) system as part of the sprawling Imperial Navy facility there, aiding in its concealment. The collector plane was a disk of billions of linked receiver elements 26 billion miles in diameter. This collector yielded a resolution at 1,500 parsecs of 33' in long-wavelength infrared, and of half a meter in visible light (meaning that objects larger than 1½' in the smallest dimension could be detected, and two such objects more than 1½' apart could be distinguished as two objects). According to the Imperial Navy public-relations office, the collector was dismantled when the project was shut down.

Persistent rumors of a second Longbow project continue to circulate.

M

Main: Any grouping of systems forming a chain of worlds all reachable by jump-1. This grouping provides a sort of "corridor" allowing jump-1 capable ships to travel to any world along the chain.

Many such groupings of worlds exist in the Imperium. Prominent examples include the Spinward Main in the Spinward Marches, the Vilani Main centered in the Vland sector, the Sylean Main in Core sector, and the Antares Main originating in the Antares sector.

Major Race: An arbitrary distinction based on the achievement of a specific intelligent race. A race which achieves interstellar travel (jump drive) through its own efforts is classed major; one which does not is classed minor.

To date, generally accepted major races include Humaniti (Zhodani, Solomani, and Vilani, but not other examples), Aslan, the Hive, K'kree, Vargr, Ancients, and Droyne.

The Suerrat (a Human race) are considered minor because their method of interstellar travel utilized generation ships. Similarly, the Geonee were originally thought to be a major race, but their development of the jump drive was based on recovered Ancient artifacts rather than on true racial efforts. Geonee dispute this and hold the (generally unshared) view that they are of major standing.

The Droyne have been demonstrated to be major, for they are now known to have developed jump drive as far back as -7000. At present, however, they do not build or use jump drives to any great degree (there are a few Droyne merchants), and most remain in their scattered systems of their own volition.

Mercenary: The remote centralized government of the Imperium is possessed of great industrial and technological might, but it is also unable, due to the sheer distances and travel times involved, to exert total control everywhere within its star-spanning realm.

Extensive home rule provisions allow planetary governments to choose their own forms of government, raise and maintain their own armed forces for local security, pass and enforce laws governing local conduct, and regulate (within limits) commerce. Defense has been a cooperative effort of local indigenous forces, which is stiffened by Imperial naval bases manned by extremely sophisticated forces. Conflicting local interests have often settled their differences by force of arms, with Imperial forces looking quietly the other way, unable or unwilling to intervene en masse. Imperial forces have been able to operate as a police force so as to not jeopardize their primary mission of defense of the realm. Only when local conflicts threaten either the security or the economy of an area have Imperial forces taken an active hand, and then with overwhelming speed and force.

In this environment, the soldier for hire has found active employment. The tolerance exhibited by the forces of the Imperium have made the hired military force a practical matter. Imperial policy has allowed the marketplace to provide military force to those who can afford it; one line of thought has been that a hired military can be more effectively controlled if it gets out of hand, as opposed to nationalistic or politically motivated military forces. See *Good War/Bad War* and ***GURPS Traveller Star Mercs***.

Minor Race: An intelligent race which has not achieved jump drive through its own efforts. For most races, this classification is appropriate. Many are contacted before they have reached a technological level capable of even considering jump drive, thus permanently prejudicing their potential.

Indeed, the shock of such classification, and the realization that this classification pervades interstellar society, is often sufficient to relegate a race to a permanent role as shopkeepers and accountants. Some slump, while others violently resist the classification. The fact that the categorization is informal and arbitrary, and tends to elevate those already in power, has made resistance difficult, if not impossible.

Monadium: Impenetrable bluish-gray metal alloy used as the basic construction material by the Ancients at the site on Antiquity (Corridor/Ian 0816). It has defeated all efforts to determine its exact composition; some experts believe it contains titanium. Even modern TL12 plasma and fusion weapons have been unable to penetrate it, and it cannot be worked, melted, or modified by any known process. Paint can be applied but adheres very poorly, and flakes off within a few weeks.

Moot: The Imperial government's only deliberative body. It has few powers and rarely exercises them. In theory, the Moot includes all Imperial nobles of baronial or higher status, but most nobles do not find it convenient to travel to Capital, and so many of those seated hold proxy votes. Large blocs of these votes can be wielded by a single influential noble.

Technically, the Moot is supreme in the Imperium, but its power is extremely limited. In practice, its deliberations are advisory to the emperor, and he is wise to heed them. The one power of the Moot is to dissolve the Imperium. When this power is invoked, it compels compromise among opposing factions.

When an emperor dies, abdicates, or otherwise becomes unfit for office, the Moot becomes important as the validating body for the new emperor. It has the power to examine the qualifications and credentials of the heir apparent and, in unusual situations, to reject him.

The Moot holds its sessions in the Moot Spire, which, at 5,741' high, is the tallest building on Capital. By tradition, the Spire is the only building allowed to tower above the Imperial Palace, which is 2½ miles away. Elevators with gravitic compensators can speed visitors from the bottom to the top in 18 seconds. At the top of the Spire is the High Moot, where select committees hold the most private deliberations.

A Concise History of Ziru Sirka, Part IV

Prepared for Solomani readers by the Vilani Historical Documents Subcommittee, Kasiiga University Press, Ishimaga, Vland, 001-1116

Stagnation

Vilani culture achieved stability at the cost of stagnation. Maintaining centralized control over this vast expanse created a cultural rigidity. The three bureaux became increasingly identical. The old Vilani culture which developed during the First Imperium adhered to a rigid caste structure. Hereditary positions became commonplace in all three bureaux. Each citizen had a specific and set place in the universe, and it was each citizen's duty to remain in that place. Society could not afford to let individuals do as they pleased.

Continued on next page . . .

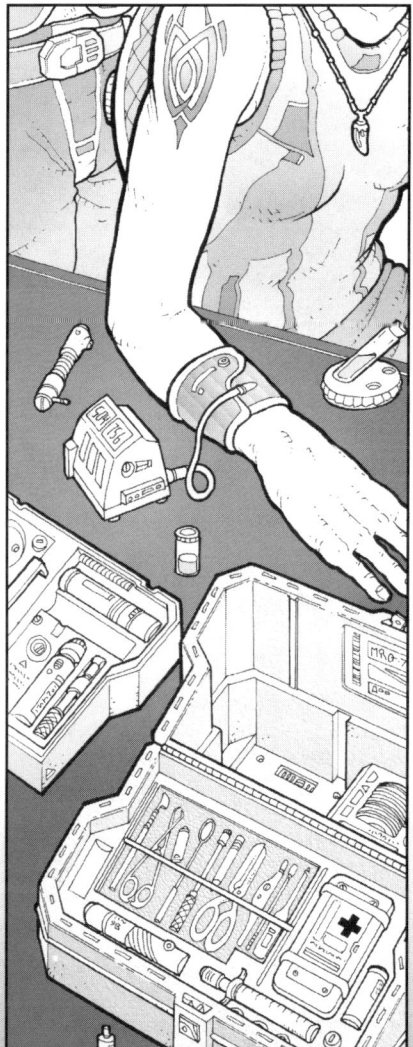

A Concise History of Ziru Sirka, Part IV

[Continued]

The Ziru Sirka began a long decline about 1500 A.D. The many subject races of the Imperium grew restive, impatient with the imposed culture of the Vilani. Imperial power was waning and stretched thin, and the Ziru Sirka could no longer afford to absorb new interstellar states. The Imperium had been safe as long as no exterior threat arose. But now, despite all efforts, technology had leaked across the borders to aid new interstellar states developing outside of Vilani control. Many threats pushed at many different places along the border. Some detached small portions of the Imperium; Imperial reactions crushed others.

The Crumbling Empire

About 1800 A.D., it was clear even to insiders that the rigid Vilani culture was, in reality, brittle. The young governments took larger and larger chunks of territory, often with the open acceptance of the local citizenry. The texture of Vilani culture was decaying. Officials in the fringe territories began to fabricate their reports rather than reveal the truth to their superiors. Appeals for help or support cost heavily in personal power, so officials simply reported success. Meanwhile, local governors took to hiring and equipping "barbarians" from outside the Imperium for personal power plays. Civil wars, mutinies, and insurrections became increasingly common.

The Imperium used diplomacy to play off enemies against one another where it could. But there was still substantial territorial shrinkage over the centuries, and the Imperium gradually lost territory along its coreward and trailing marches. A movement away from the established, civilized territories started as the Ziru Sirka began to fail.

About 2100 A.D., the wolf-like barbarian Vargr began pillaging the Imperium's civilized territories in the direction of the galactic core. Between then and 2800 A.D., Vargr fleets were a significant factor in the Imperial retreat out of coreward territories. Other border territories were in revolt, and even some interior territories were becoming unruly in their demands for self-government and less rigid controls from above.

It was against this background of a decaying empire that the first Imperial contact with Terra took place. In 2097 A.D., Terran explorers encountered the Vilani at Barnard's Star. The Terrans were understandably surprised to learn that someone else already owned the stars. The Imperium, on the other hand, dismissed the Terrans as simply another barbarian race of little consequence.

Naval Base: Port facility for the support, maintenance, repair, and refit of naval vessels. Planetary surface facilities are generally provided for vessels of 1,000 tons or less; orbital facilities handle larger ships.

A naval base has several distinct parts. The typical naval base is composed of an orbital berthing area, a surface berthing area, a maintenance section, and an administrative headquarters.

Berthing areas provide locations for ships to lay over, for a day or for months. All berthing areas include provisions for refueling from storage tanks or fuel lighters.

Maintenance sections at naval bases vary from base to base. Where such a section would be redundant to the local starport shipyard, it is small, and repairs or alterations are carried out under contract by the local facility. Where adequate facilities do not exist, the naval base itself may have a large maintenance section capable of extensive repairs and refits. Maintenance is performed on the ships on the world surface or in orbit as necessary.

The administrative headquarters handles the day-to-day operations of the base, as well as its paperwork (including the allocation of funds, distribution of personnel, and disbursement of maintenance and repair contracts).

The naval base is not a tactical unit. It has no battle forces of its own, and it does not exert control even over local system-defense boats (which are under a separate command). The naval base is responsible for supporting the fleet and keeping it in optimum condition for its combat missions.

Naval Depot: Depots serve as focuses for naval efforts: supplying a fleet's every need, providing construction and repair facilities, and producing and testing experimental ship prototypes. A depot generally occupies an entire system. Facilities, material, and personnel are extensive enough to repair and resupply a large fraction of the fleet at any time. A depot may be isolated from outside contact for years at a time without serious setbacks. As depots cover large parts of a system, there is no distinction between orbital and surface berthing.

In peacetime, the main function of a depot is the design and testing of ships. For this reason a large staff of naval architects and construction personnel is maintained at every depot.

In wartime, depots serve as repair and resupply centers for the fleet. In emergencies, the depot's construction yards are sometimes pressed into service for production of military ships.

Since a depot is obviously a very sensitive installation, security is tight. An extensive array of both entry and exit codes are employed to ensure no unauthorized vessels enter or leave the system. Contingents of marines and system-defense boats are stationed throughout the system, and they are constantly ready for action.

There is usually no more than one naval depot per sector. Depots are placed in systems where they will be close enough to the expected action to be useful, but far enough back to ensure that they will not be captured.

Nobility: The foundation of interstellar government within the Imperium. The Imperium depends on nobles ranging from knights to archdukes to carry the chain of authority and the mantle of responsibility from the Emperor to the people (see p. 9).

Nth Interstellar War: Any one of an indeterminate number of interstellar wars fought between the Terran Confederation and the First Imperium during the period -2408 and -2219.

The First Interstellar War (-2408 to -2400) marked the initial clash between Terra and Vland. The peace that concluded the hostilities was both uneasy and short. The second through seventh wars were marked by seesaw exchanges of territory, mostly confined to the Dingir and Sol subsectors. These initial wars were fought, on the Vilani side, with only the forces available to the Vilani provincial governor; the central government was preoccupied with other problems. This was fortunate for the Terrans, as Vilani power, even at this late date, was sufficient to crush the Terrans in short order had it been applied.

The Eighth Interstellar War broke the stalemate; the Terrans took Dingir and reached farther. Finally, the emperor took notice, and dispatched major fleet elements to the area, but the time for action had passed. Terran invention of the jump-3 drive made the Ninth Interstellar War a crushing victory for Terra and forced the Vilani to relinquish most of the Solomani Rim. Thereafter, the Terrans were almost constantly on the offensive.

In the centuries after the conclusion of the wars, no consensus could be reached in the academic community as to when the later conflicts began or ended; all were interrupted several times by armistices, cease-fires, or shaky periods of peace (indeed, a new war would often break out along the front lines before the existence of a peace treaty could be communicated to the respective capitals).

Periods of warfare are lumped together or split apart depending on the historian's individual point of view, and a single war to one historian can be identified as two or more wars by others. The situation is complicated by the fact that records for some of the years in question are sketchy. To clarify matters, an accommodation was arrived at which simply labels all interstellar wars after the Ninth with the indeterminate variable N. Proper usage calls for the war to be defined with the actual years being discussed. Many history texts use this system to refer to all the wars except the first.

The Nth Interstellar War (-2235 to -2219) ended the series when the Vilani Grand Imperium collapsed, as much from its own weight, age, and decadence as from Terran victories. The Terrans moved quickly to occupy the remaining Vilani territory.

See *First Imperium, First Interstellar War, Rule of Man.*

Nuclear Damper Technology

Nuclear dampers are force-field devices that focus on nuclear warheads or isotopes to prevent or disrupt nuclear reactions by making atomic nuclei more or less stable.

Statistics for nuclear damper modules for spacecraft are in the design rules. Dampers are also described on p. VE72 and p. UT80. In the *Traveller* universe, bulky models are available as early as TL11, rather than being limited to TL15+. If designing dampers using *Vehicles*, multiply weight, volume, and cost by 16 at TL11, by 8 at TL12, by 4 at TL13, or by 2 at TL14.

"Damper boxes" that prevent radioactive decay of unstable isotopes also exist. They weigh 80 pounds, take up 1.6 cubic feet, cost Cr40,000, and require 160 kW per cubic foot of cargo capacity that they possess at TL11. Halve all attributes at each higher TL.

The Regina System

Following Imperial custom, systems are most commonly identified by the name of the most important world in the system rather than the star. Almost without exception, this world contains the system starport (although the system may contain other, smaller ports and bases).

The Regina system, capital of the Spinward Marches, is a trinary star system – the primary Lusor and its dwarf companion Speck form the major system, while Darida orbits at about 5,000 AU distance. Among them, the three stars possess eight planets with 17 satellites.

Regina is only one of seven worlds in the trisystem that boast a breathable atmosphere, and only one of four habitable moons in orbit around the gas giant Assiniboia in the life zone of Lusor. With the best conditions of the group, it was settled first in 75 by an expansion wave of the Third Imperium. It soon became a trade center within the Spinward Marches, and was established capital of its subsector when it joined the Imperium in 250.

Regina supports the highest population. Its companion satellites of Brumaire and Harcourt have been extensively colonized as well.

The Darida system proved much less hospitable, and has been only minimally exploited. It does host a few small settlements devoted to prospecting and mining available ores, a few scientific and technical survey stations, and a small military base maintained by the Imperial Navy.

Continued on next page . . .

Octagon Society: Established in 342, the Octagon Society was the first major distressed-spacefarer assistance operation to appear in the Spinward Marches. The group thrived on public contributions and on some tax revenues for 150 years. It collapsed in the late 400s when scandals emerged over the quality of shelter construction and the disposition of certain funds.

Society shelters were generally of an octagonal shape. Large hostels were established on major worlds, while smaller weather shelters were placed on frontier or unsettled worlds. The characteristic octagon-shaped buildings are still visible on various worlds, although none are still in use as shelters for distressed spacefarers.

The Octagon Society was dissolved in 499, and its assets were sold at auction.

Oort Cloud: A spherical shell around most stars containing numerous small bodies of cometary material. A typical Oort cloud is about 0.5 to 1 light year from its primary and has an aggregate mass about that of Terra; density is thus extremely low. The main constituents of cometary bodies are ice and dust ("dirty snowballs"). Bodies in the Oort cloud are occasionally perturbed by collisions or by the influence of nearby stars into orbits which pass near the star; these form the visible comets. The Oort cloud around Terra was named after its discoverer, Terran astronomer Jan Oort, and the term was applied to other systems during the Second Imperium.

Outworld Coalition: Traditional name for the belligerent groups allied against the Imperium during the First and Second Frontier Wars. Commonly applied to any alliance of powers threatening the Spinward Marches and Imperial territories spinward of the Great Rift.

The original Outworld Coalition was formed in the early 500s at the instigation of the Zhodani Consulate. Vargr allegiances vacillated, but memories of the Imperial campaigns against certain Vargr states in the Corridor swayed some into membership. Zhodane, as the major partner, contributed military aid and assistance (such as technicians and advisors). While some Vargr governments contributed personnel and naval units, other Vargr remained neutral or sided with the Imperium.

The initial history of the coalition was one of continuing struggle for organization, as the Zhodani were constantly occupied in establishing Vargr governments, and then maintaining them in power. The intent was for the Vargr to raid the coreward edge of the Spinward Marches, especially Regina and Aramis subsectors, while the major thrust from Zhodane took Cronor and Jewell subsectors. The Vargr portions of the offensive failed dismally, which resulted in the collapse of the coalition.

The internal Imperial upheavals (the Civil War) which followed the First Frontier War (it was just called the Frontier War then) exposed a continuing weakness in the Imperium, and the Outworld Coalition reformed after a hiatus of five years. The reformed Coalition again attacked the Marches, this time taking portions of Jewell subsector. Although the Vargr again failed to take any territory permanently, their performance as a whole was considerably improved.

Traditionally, frontier wars in the Spinward Marches have involved coalitions of Zhodani and certain Vargr states. The Sword Worlds have also joined the coalition at times. See ***GURPS Traveller Behind the Claw***.

Regina Trinary Star System
Shown Cluster: Lusor Speck Binary

Trinary Companion
Darida – 5000 au

0.2 au Clement
0.4 au Austen

0.7 au Burgund
1.0 au Glybrius

1.6 au Assiniboia
Regina

Region of L-Spk Oort Cloud

LSW 5/5

P

Pacification Campaigns (76-120): A series of economic, diplomatic, and military operations directed at forcing membership in the Imperium upon those worlds which resisted the initial efforts to annex them.

Although the campaigns were predominantly economic and diplomatic in nature, the Imperium was not averse to using force when peaceful methods failed. Imperial battlefleets and ground forces rarely failed when brought to bear.

By 120, the pacification campaigns ended, and the initial phase of the Imperium's growth came to a close.

Four specific Pacification Campaigns were undertaken, each by an archduke of the Imperium. The Vilani Pacification Campaign was targeted at portions of Dagudashaag and Gushemege sectors. The Ilelish Pacification Campaign was aimed at the Darmine region. The Antarean Pacification Campaign hit much of Lishun sector. The Sylean Pacification Campaign operated in Delphi and Fornast sectors.

Peerage: The hierarchy of nobles within the Imperium.

Phoenix Project: Reported plot by Solomani guerrillas on Terra to destroy Imperial forces occupying Terra. Imperial intelligence reported penetration of the project command in 1045, with subsequent compromise of its basic plans and dismantling of its structure.

The Phoenix Project was supposedly born in the final years of the Solomani Rim War (990 to 1002) as Solomani leaders saw the possibility of their defeat and the loss of the homeworld to the invading Imperials. The project was said to have consisted of two distinct parts: pre-positioned caches of military goods to supply the coming uprising and a continuing program for the training of guerrillas.

The caches were concealed in many different places on Terra in areas calculated to preclude accidental discovery over the years. Each cache contained large quantities of munitions, weapons, vehicles, and medical supplies, all of varying technological levels so as to be of use regardless of the technical knowledge of the users. Each cache was hidden with its location entrusted to a single local family. These families were to form the core of the guerrilla forces when the rising was to take place.

A massive Imperial counter-guerrilla effort in 1040 to 1045 was directed at the discovery and destruction of the caches and the arrest of the families entrusted with their secrets.

Persistent rumors of two additional aspects of the project – Lambda (a codeword to trigger the uprising) and Omega (the reinforcement of the uprising by off-world Solomani) – have been dismissed as baseless by Imperial officials.

Many historians believe that the extent of the plot was greatly exaggerated by Imperial authorities, and hold that it was little more than an extreme example of wishful thinking on the part of the Solomani leadership. At any rate, the Phoenix Project no longer threatens the security of the Imperium, if indeed it ever did.

Postal Union: A group of political units associated to a greater or lesser degree for the purpose of communication among citizens, businesses, and governmental units.

The Regina System

[Continued]

Most planets orbiting Lusor (the primary star) and its dwarf companion Speck are named for persons and places associated with St. Regina. Worlds orbiting Darida are named in the Vilani language after famous Vilani authors.

The Phoenix Project

The notion of the Phoenix Project arose out of a need for a particular adventure to have what Marc Miller calls a "pull," an objective which the characters will seek out over the course of the adventure. In this case, the objective was to discover one or more caches of weapons and materiel accumulated to supply a planned rebellion against the Imperium by Solomani plotters. It represented something for the characters to hunt, in the process of which they could be drawn into the real adventure plot-line. There was never any intention of using the uprising itself as an adventure seed, but the possibility that such a centuries-old supply depot might still exist has proven compelling for many players.

Psionics

Psi powers have been a staple of science fiction since the inception of the genre, and *Traveller*'s designers felt that the subject merited attention. We decided that a too widespread use of psionics would require our Imperial society to be too different for the vast majority of gamers to enjoy, but at the same time we wanted to show what effects such powers could have on society (and we knew that if we included them in the game, every power player on Earth would have them). Our solution to these mutually contradictory goals was to create two societies, one in which psi is common (the Zhodani) and another in which it occurred, but was uncommon (the Imperium).

Making psionics a crime in the Imperium gave every character who wanted to have the advantages of psi powers a corresponding disadvantage: You are persecuted and hunted by most of the population. Unless, of course, you choose to hide your light under a bushel, which means that your powers have to be used with tact and discretion. Non-psionic individuals view any trace of psi talents with suspicion: You can read their minds. You can kill them with a thought. You can plant thoughts into their mind and make them do horrible things. Society is better off without you . . .

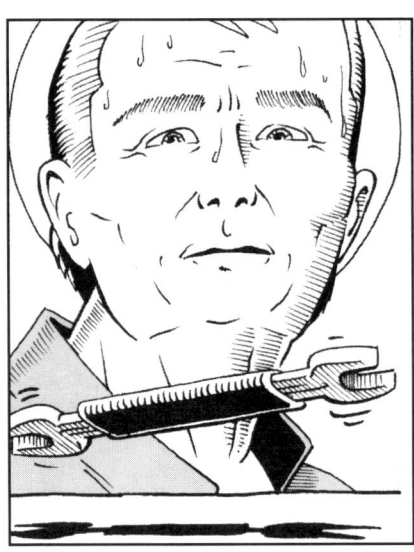

Of course, the game reality is more complicated than this. The widespread public distrust of psi powers forces the Imperial government to publicly call for their suppression, but the extreme usefulness of the talents mean that they also promote and employ them secretly. Publicly, all psionic training institutes are clandestine, illegal underground organizations. In reality the Imperial government operates a number of them (albeit hidden from public view).

Continued on next page . . .

Nearly all star systems are members of one postal union or another. Governments cooperate along their borders in order to allow the efficient flow of communications between them. Members of a postal union forward mail through their territories (subject, of course, to local security needs, acts of war, and so on) to the proper addresses. On the average, communication is at the speed of the fastest available transportation, which means about 3 or 4 parsecs per week in theory or short-term application, much less routinely.

Psionic Suppressions (800 to 826): Between 772 and 798, a series of financial, ethical, and moral scandals within the Psionic Institutes of the Imperium shifted public opinion against them. At the same time, it became clear that a good number of the Institutes were under the control of the Zhodani Consulate. In 800, the Imperium moved against the institutes by canceling their charters, jailing their leaders, and passing laws restricting the teaching or practice of psionics. Many institute figures went underground to espouse their cause in a type of guerrilla war.

The Psionic Suppressions had a profound influence on Imperial opinion. Over the course of 26 years, the suppressions equated psionics with the Zhodani and established in the average Imperial citizen a distaste for both that continues to the present day. The average citizen will admit to a general dislike of psionics, and if pressed, will usually state that psionics violate a person's right to mental privacy.

Psionics: The criminal use of mental powers for the manipulation of matter and energy and for communication. It has been demonstrated that minds (Human or non-Human, conscious or unconscious, intelligent or unintelligent) contain some capacity to operate without apparent use of physical facilities. For an individual to seek out such training is a criminal act.

Until circa -1000, psionics was little studied in most regions except on a disorganized level (parapsychology, the occult, spiritualism, and so on). It was known and practiced among the Zhodani and by some minor races, but it was by no means widespread.

During the Long Night, many races (Human and others) turned introspective. As a result, many finally began to engage in serious research in psionics, which revealed much about the empirical nature of the phenomenon, although the principles involved were, and remain, little understood.

Even though it assumed scientific validity, psionics remained a backwater science until about 650, when it underwent a tremendous burst of popularity. Psionics within the Imperium reached its peak in the latter half of the 700s. In the 790s, however, the crest of popular opinion broke with the revelation of scandals within the Psionics Institutes; the result was the Psionic Suppressions (800 to 826), which shifted public opinion away from support of psionics.

Psionics Institute: Any clandestine organization devoted to the illegal training of individuals in the use of psionics talents. Active Imperial campaigns to eradicate the Institutes have been pursued for more than 200 years.

Organizations of this nature have existed since before the advent of space travel, but they attained prominence only during the Long Night, when reproducible scientific discoveries made psionics a teachable, learnable science.

In the Imperial antebellum period, psionics institutes were rare, and they were formed only on a few scattered worlds which, for one reason or another, had an unusually high rate of psionic talents appearing, or which encouraged psionics for social, political, or commercial reasons. In the years after the Civil War, institutes were organized on most high-population worlds within the Imperium.

"Psionics Institute" is a generic name; each institution was independently organized and maintained. Institutes were generally supported by that portion of

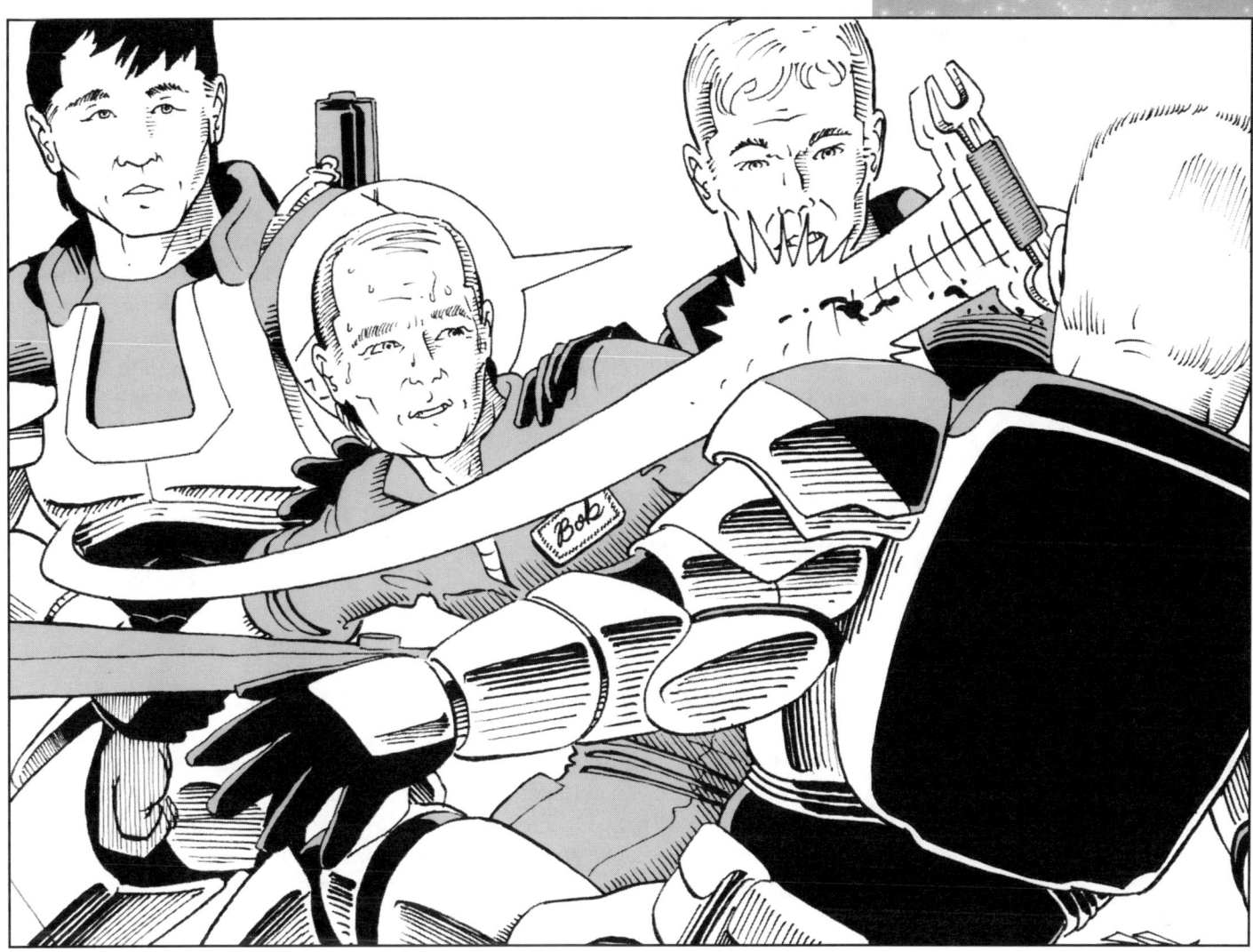

the population which had psionic talents; since that portion was small, they were viable only on high-population worlds (roughly 1 billion or more inhabitants).

During the Psionic Suppressions, the institutes' charters were revoked, and talented individuals were persecuted. In some cases, the individuals fled to assume new identities on other worlds; in others, whole families emigrated to the Zhodani Consulate or to other places beyond the frontiers of the Imperium.

Following the suppressions, there were theoretically no institutes remaining. In practice, however, illegal underground institutes are rumored to still remain on many worlds.

See *Psionic Suppressions*.

Psychohistory: The science of historical prediction and macrosocial manipulation. The main thesis of psychohistory is that the actions of trillions of individuals take on a fluidity and predictability which can be compared to that of molecules in a gas. The very size of the population being dealt with factors out individual peculiarities and allows the prediction of its behavior. With the ability to predict the reaction of a population to a particular stimulus comes the ability to manipulate that population, psychohistorians reason.

Psychohistory began as a combination of public relations/advertising techniques and behavioral science, and although its techniques have been put on a more rigorous footing, the basic principles are still not well understood. A number of minor experiments have confirmed the general validity of the science, but it was also shown to be too expensive to be of any practical utility. Research continues at a small number of Imperial universities.

Psionics

[Continued]

In the Zhodani, we present the opposite view: Psi powers are welcomed and supported by the populace at large. Zhodani citizens with psi powers realize that their talents are accompanied by a social responsibility. Telekinesis is used for delicate surgery rather than breaking and entering. Telepathy is used as a tool for the treatment of mental illness.

We introduced the Thought Police to keep Zhodani society from seeming too utopic. Thought Police read minds without permission, but only with the best of intentions. Feel like stealing? Willingly convey false information? Have lustful thoughts about your neighbor's spouse? The Thought Police will help you overcome these and other antisocial tendencies. You will no longer want things that are not yours. You will see no reason to lie. You will recognize lustful thoughts as common to us all, and feel no guilt over them (and certainly no urge to take improper action on them).

A Concise History of Ziru Sirka, Part V

Prepared for Solomani readers by the Vilani Historical Documents Subcommittee, Kasiiga University Press, Ishimaga, Vland, 001-1116

Arrival of the Terrans

Terrans, during this period of vast interstellar colonization, were pursuing their own history while confined to their homeworld. It was not until the 1960s that Terrans ventured into space, and not until 2000 A.D. that they were actually exploring space on a permanent basis. The Terran Confederation dates as a centralized world government to the signing of the Treaty of New York in 2022 A.D. (although it was not officially called that for another century). This treaty allowed the placement of the armed forces of the major nations of Terra under the centralized control of the United Nations (until then, a loose organization of nation-states, with no governmental authority).

In 2090 A.D., Terrans invented the jump drive. Initially, it was used only within the solar system, since the range of a jump-1 drive was insufficient to reach the nearest stars. Terrans remained restricted to their solar system for 43 years, and this long incubation period worked in their favor. They developed an extensive variety of jump-capable ships and had produced them for decades when they finally ventured to a neighboring star system.

Meeting the Vilani

An expedition placed intermediate refueling supplies and traveled to a nearby system, Barnard's Star, early in 2097 A.D. It encountered a Vilani mining outpost there. The tales its members heard of the Imperium's size staggered them. Joint international expeditions met with the Vilani and explored nearby systems. It came as a shock to the Terrans that most of the worlds beyond a few parsecs away were already claimed. More than a dozen Human races had already colonized the worlds around Earth. A quick effort was made to settle Barnard's Star even as Vilani prospectors were working on that world. Individual nations built starships and expanded their armed forces. Outposts were quickly reinforced and strengthened.

Interstellar War

The first interstellar war between the Imperium and the Terran Confederation began when a Vilani trade caravan ignored Terran traffic-control signals. Fortunately for the Terrans, the Vilani scarcely knew that a war was going on, as the UN exercised only tenuous control over the several national squadrons.

Continued on next page . . .

Rachele Society: Secret Vilani supremacist group founded on Pretoria/Pretoria by Zid Rachele in 992. Genocidal policies favored by the group culminated in the attempted takeover of the Pretorian government in 1010. An attempt at nuclear blackmail backfired when 26,000 people (including 1,900 Rachelean commandos) were killed by a nuclear explosion after the Society seized Imperial Scout facilities on Saki (Deneb/Pretoria). Zid Rachele disappeared in 1015 after escaping from the prison world Exile in Usani subsector (Deneb/Usani 1928).

In 1103, Zid Rachele and the Rachele Society surfaced again in Lishun in a brief power play at the Dynam Naval Depot (Lishun/Masionia 1219). Rachele and his followers attempted the theft of several mothballed naval warships, but were quickly defeated. Rachele's vessel was destroyed in the battle.

See *Rachelean Revolts*.

Rachelean Revolts (1010-1011): Major uprising on Pretoria (Deneb/Pretoria) fomented by the Rachele Society, which resulted in martial law under the Imperial Navy since that time. The Imperium as a rule does not interfere with local politics, but their intervention was forced when a Scout base on Saki (Deneb/Pretoria) was destroyed by nuclear weapons.

See *Rachele Society*.

Ramshackle Empire: Common term used during the Long Night to refer to the Rule of Man, also known as the Second Imperium. As the successor to the First Imperium, the Rule of Man took over the territories (and the problems) of its predecessor. Pro-Second Imperium histories contend that the Rule of Man delayed the inevitable collapse. Pro-First Imperium histories claim that the First Imperium was stagnant, but stable, and that the Ramshackle Empire actually precipitated the Long Night by looting subject worlds and promoting Terran superiority.

See *Rule of Man*.

Red Zone: The Travellers' Aid Society classification for a nation, world, or system which is dangerous to travelers. In general, the imposition of a red zone classification indicates the location is quarantined, interdicted by higher authority, or at war.

Quarantine indicates that a dangerous disease is present, and the danger of war is self-explanatory, but interdiction requires further discussion. Interstellar

governments often find it necessary to restrict access to worlds or systems for political or military reasons, and they do so by publishing interdictions.

Enforcement of interdiction varies with the reason for the restriction. Interdiction may be imposed on a world if it is a military base or other sensitive installation, a private reservation belonging to a powerful family desiring seclusion, a developing society which the government has elected to allow to evolve in isolation, or home of valuable resources being conserved for later development or exploitation.

Regina (Spinward Marches/Regina 0310 A788899-C): Capital of the Spinward Marches subsector. See sidebar, p. 52.

Repatriation Bond: A document guaranteeing passage of an individual to a specified location upon completion of contract work or upon suspension of contract work for any reason. Repatriation bonds are guarantees given as inducements to workers who might otherwise be wary of leaving their own worlds with no assurances that they could return. They are most commonly used by mercenary units.

Repatriation bonds are usually administered by a financial institution which holds the necessary funds in escrow.

Rule of Man (-2204 to -1776): A short-lived interstellar empire formed after the conquest of the Vilani Imperium by the Terrans. The conquered territories were under military rule from -2219 to -2204. Vilani military forces were incorporated into the Terran forces. Terran naval officers took over key posts in the Vilani bureaucracy (which was otherwise retained intact).

In -2204, the Terran Secretariat attempted to transfer control directly to Terra and to incorporate the conquered regions into the Terran Confederation. The commander in chief of the Terran Navy, Admiral Hiroshi Estigarribia, realized that the Confederation government could not possibly control the vast territories of the Vilani Imperium. He proclaimed himself Regent of the Vilani Imperium and Protector of Terra, so both states were now united in the Rule of Man. Nearly all the fleet sided with Estigarribia, both because it was composed largely of colonials (who were under-represented in the Terran Confederation government) and because of Estigarribia's careful preparation. The Confederation was dissolved without significant resistance.

The Terran fleet headquarters on Dingir became the capital of the Rule of Man. The bureaucratic center of the Imperium remained on Vland, although arrangements were undertaken to gradually transfer it elsewhere.

Upon Estigarribia's death, he was succeeded by his chief of staff, who crowned himself Emperor Hiroshi II. Estigarribia, even though he did not actually assume the crown, is therefore known to history as Emperor Hiroshi I.

Hiroshi II transferred all functions of government from both Vland and Dingir to a more centrally located world, renamed bilingually Hub/Ershur. This world was to remain the capital of the Rule of Man for the next 400 years.

During the Rule of Man, large numbers of Humans from Terra and its oldest colonies emigrated throughout the Imperium.

People of Terran ancestry or culture (many of them assimilated Vilani) assumed positions of power on most worlds and became industrialists and administrators.

A Concise History of Ziru Sirka, Part V

[Continued]

This war, considered a Terran victory, began the period of Terran ascendance and led to strengthening of the central Terran government. In 2123 A.D., representatives from the Terran colonies were admitted to the General Assembly.

The Terran government then changed its name to "The Terran Confederation."

The peace that concluded the first war was both uneasy and short. The second through seventh wars were marked by seesaw exchanges of territory, mostly confined to the Dingir and Sol subsectors. The Terrans applied every force they could bring to bear on their enemy, and believed that their successes in gradually expanding their territory were entirely of their own making. After winning the first three wars, they finally realized the Grand Imperium's immensity. They also realized that they could win in spite of that size.

Other problems than the Terrans preoccupied the Vilani central government. Vilani power, even at this late date, was sufficient to crush the Terrans had it been applied. But the Vilani fought these initial wars with only the forces available to the affected provincial governor. He was charged to win wars and maintain the empire's power on a limited budget. Appeals to the emperor were avoided because they cost heavily in personal power. The local governors often compromised, agreed to some territorial concessions, and then reported victory.

A Concise History of Ziru Sirka, Part VI

Prepared for Solomani readers by the Vilani Historical Documents Subcommittee, Kasiiga University Press, Ishimaga, Vland, 001-1116

A Major Victory

The Eighth Interstellar War finally broke open the frontier and ended in the first major Terran victory. After the capture of Dingir, Terran Grand Admiral Manuel Albadawi exploited Vilani confusion by reaching beyond Dingir to seize and fortify other worlds of the Imperium. The Treaty of Ensular (which ended the war) ceded all of the Imperium rimward of Vega to the Terrans. This series of interstellar wars ended when the Grand Imperium capitulated to a combination of Terran military successes and its own weaknesses. It collapsed when its leaders lost the support of the people and the will to resist.

Terran Occupation

The Terrans moved quickly to occupy the remaining Vilani territory. Many Vilani subject races, such as the Vegans, welcomed the Terrans. Terran naval officers were dispatched throughout the Grand Imperium. Between 2302 and 2317 A.D., more than 100,000 naval officers were sent to take control of the reins of government, direct local bureaucracies, and maintain peace and order. The Terran officers carried their technology with them. They occupied key posts in the Vilani bureaucracy, which otherwise retained intact. In some cases, Terran ensigns administered worlds, and mere commanders ruled whole subsectors. Vilani military forces were incorporated into the Terran forces.

The conquered territories were under military rule from 2302 to 2317 A.D. During this period, the Terran Navy learned to deal effectively with the Vilani and to be sympathetic to the Vilani people. That the Vilani openly accepted the Terrans made it easier to view them as friends deserving of respect and protection. The Terrans had to administer an immense empire that had already admitted it could not do the job itself. If the bureaucracy had collapsed (and trade ceased), hundreds of worlds would have died as supplies were cut off.

Continued on next page . . .

The problems of sheer size and scientific stagnation, which had brought about the fall of the Vilani Imperium, continued to plague the Rule of Man. The Vilani had coped with the problems of ruling a large empire by a rigid caste system with all citizens rooted permanently in their places, but this system could last only as long as there was no significant external threat. The Terrans did away with this system but were not able to replace it with a new social order. The destruction of the caste system swept away the foundations of society. Key industries fell apart as their workers became free to move elsewhere.

The -1776 date for the end of the Rule of Man is arbitrary; it notes the financial collapse of the central government, which occurred when the Treasury at Hub/Ershur refused to honor a monetary issue of the branch treasury at Antares. The resulting lack of confidence within monetary circles marked the end of large-scale interstellar trade and of effective governmental power within the Rule of Man. Although the Imperium did not completely fall apart for many years, the Rule of Man had effectively ceased to exist as a viable interstellar community, and the period known as Twilight had begun.

The Third Imperium refers to the Rule of Man as the Second Imperium, which emphasizes its own roots in the Solomani-dominated Second Imperium and the Vilani-dominated First Imperium. Anti-Solomani elements emphasize the failure of the Solomani-dominated Ramshackle Empire.

Rule of Terra: Solomani terrorist group active in selected regions of the Solomani/Imperial border. Violently anti-imperial even by the standards of most Solomani political groups, the Rule of Terra seeks to force the return of all "rightful Terran property" to Solomani hands through assassination and other acts of violence.

The organization, although interstellar in scope, apparently was not very strong in the beginning. Some of its claimed attacks have proven to be accidents, while others were the work of different dissident individuals or organizations.

The Rule of Terra's acts, although not its goals, have been disavowed by many other Solomani groups, including the Confederation government; in return, the Rule of Terra has attacked even Solomani populations, by stating that "all who do not contribute to the Manifest Destiny of the Race are not worthy to be part of the Race."

The group has claimed responsibility for many recent terrorist acts on the border, some of which Imperial authorities are sure were committed by others.

See also *Ine Givar.*

Scout Base: Port facility for the support, maintenance, and repair of scout vessels. The Imperial Interstellar Scout Service maintains a variety of scout bases scattered throughout the Imperium, with installations tending to be on less well-developed worlds with starports of type II or III. Scout bases tend to be surface installations equipped with basic facilities for fueling and for minor maintenance activities oriented toward ships of 1,000 tons or less.

Scout bases are positioned in systems more out of the way than are naval bases for a reason. The scout bases serve as a source of ships carrying dispatches from the well-traveled Xboat lanes to more remote worlds.

Scout bases also have other responsibilities, and most have an administrative responsibility in addition to the maintenance and refueling of scout ships. Within a subsector, one base will hold responsibility for cartography in the subsector, another will be responsible for technical developments, and still another for contact or liaison activities. The scout base is more extensive than an Xboat station, but less comprehensive than a way station.

See *Way Station, Xboat Station,* and **GURPS Traveller First In***.*

Second Frontier War (615 to 620): Fought between the Outworld Coalition and the Imperium during the period of the barracks emperors. Arbellatra (587 to 666) was named grand admiral of the Marches by Cleon V and led the combined local and Imperial forces to defeat the Coalition, and then proceeded to reestablish the central Imperial authority.

Second Imperium: The successor to the First Imperium, established by the Terran Confederation Navy to rule the territories conquered from the Vilani Empire by Terra.

See *Rule of Man.*

Sector: Mapping unit in astrography equal to 16 subsectors. Average density 500 to 650 worlds per sector. Sectors are named, and several synonyms are in common use, including march (or marches), region, reach (or reaches), quadrant, and matrix. The Spinward Marches, for example, is a sector.

As a rough means of comparing size, the sector counts of the large interstellar states and areas of settlement are: the Imperium 27, the Aslan Hierate 18, the Hive Federation 17, the Two Thousand Worlds 14, the Vargr Extents 14, the Zhodani Consulate 13, and the Solomani Confederation 11.

Shudusham Accords: A series of agreements and the laws arising from them concerning robotics, cybernetics, and artificial intelligence. The accords basically declare mechanical and artificial intelligence to be non-sentient, and not subject to the rights and protections accorded sophonts in the Imperium. See *Robots and Artificial Intelligence*, p. 18.

See *Shudusham Concords.*

Shudusham Concords: Agreement signed by 12 worlds of the Sylean Federation at Shudusham (Core/Capital) in -110 which dealt with weaponry carried by robots. The Concords have no legal force now, of course, but many worlds have adopted similar or identical standards using the Concords as a template, and most robots produced commercially in the Imperium are designed with these restrictions in mind.

See *Shudusham Accords.*

Signal GK: Abbreviation for *Gashimeku Kaalariin,* Vilani for "vessel in distress." The code signal GK originated on Vland as a distress signal in maritime and aviation activity, and it was one of the standard communications codes of the Vilani Imperium. When the Second Imperium succeeded it, signal GK was retained as a distress code co-equal with the Terran SOS and Mayday signals.

A Concise History of Ziru Sirka, Part VI
[Continued]

The Rule of Man

In 2317 A.D., the Terran Secretariat voted to transfer control of the conquered territories directly to Terra and to incorporate the Grand Imperium into the Terran Confederation. Such a move would have made every Terran a millionaire, but at an untold cost to the citizens of the Imperium.

Admiral Hiroshi Estigarribia, the commander-in-chief of the Terran Navy, realized that the Confederation government could not possibly control the vast territories of the Imperium. He proclaimed himself regent of the Vilani Imperium and protector of Terra, with both states now united in the Rule of Man.

The Confederation was dissolved without significant resistance. Terran fleet headquarters at Dingir became the capital of the Rule of Man. Upon Estigarribia's death, his chief of staff succeeded him and crowned himself Emperor Hiroshi II. Hiroshi II transferred all government functions from Dingir and Vland to a more centrally located world, renamed bilingually Hub/Ershur.

The Fall of Night

This world remained the capital of the Rule of Man for the next 400 years. Unfortunately, Terran rule was no more enlightened or progressive than that of the Vilani. From a tight, paternalistic economic empire, the pendulum swung to a disjointed military empire. Neither was really tenable over such a large domain. The drift toward disintegration was too strongly rooted in the fabric of the Ziru Sirka. All too soon the Long Night, the inevitable result of centuries of oppressive rule, descended over the stars which had been the Ziru Sirka.

LSW 5/98

Peacekeepers

"It's hard, what we're doing now. Harder than the war, that's for sure. Then it was 'assault that bunker' or 'hold this town.' If it was armed and didn't wear Imperial uniform, we shot it. We knew who the enemy was and what they'd do to us if we didn't do it first. But this peace-keeping business?

*"I'm not a peacekeeper. I'm a target. I have a card in my pocket that says I have to challenge three times before firing. They don't want us shooting civilians, you see. Laudable enough, unless those civilians are throwing rocks and firebombs. Unless they're hiding the sniper who's just shot the corporal. Unless it's **your** friend lying dying in the street. Unless it's **your** barracks they just firebombed.*

"Then the issue gets a little cloudy."

The Imperial Navigation Act of 103 requires all vessels, whether military or civilian, to respond to the GK, SOS, or Mayday signals, provided such response does not endanger the ship and crew of the responding vessel.

Six Races: Traditional term for the intelligent races which dominate this region of the galaxy. It appears independently in Human, Aslan, Vargr, and K'kree literature.

There is some disagreement as to the meaning of the term and the identity of the races involved. Most commentators agree that all of the six races must be major races; the candidates are Aslan, Droyne, Hive, K'kree, Solomani, Vargr, Vilani, and Zhodani. Various racially based hypotheses have emerged, but none has gained ascendancy. See p. 10.

Soegz: Admiral Soegz was a loyal supporter of Arbellatra in the final years of the Civil War, and he was elevated to archduke of Antares by her decree, which incidentally and simultaneously ordered the execution of the previous archduke for the treason of not supporting her.

Soegz, a Vargr and a subordinate admiral under Arbellatra, commanded a task force during the fleet actions of the Second Frontier War and late in the Civil War.

Sol, Domain of: A Domain of the Third Imperium, consisting of the Diaspora, Old Expanses, Solomani Rim, and Alpha Crucis sectors.

Solomani: Strictly, a member of that Human race which developed on Terra from the original Human stock (*Homo sapiens sapiens*). The term Solomani is often used to refer to members of the Solomani race (or, more palatably to some, to members of the Human race of Solomani descent) or to members of the Solomani political movement.

Its original meaning is obscure, but the word seems to have originally meant either "men of Sol" or "sole men."

After the Solomani developed jump drives in -2431, Solomani Humans scattered to the stars in several waves. Early colonization efforts first settled the worlds closest to Terra; the later conquest of the First Imperium and the establishment of the Rule of Man sent more Solomani Humans out primarily to occupy the formerly Vilani-controlled regions.

See *Humans*.

Solomani Autonomous Region: Area within the Imperium granted self-government through a charter from Empress Margaret I in 704. The charter granted control of the region of space within a radius of 50 parsecs of Terra (hence the name Solomani Sphere) to a Solomani governing body, which was given broad powers of authority.

For 200 years, the Imperium effectively ignored the region and concentrated instead on its coreward frontiers.

By 940, Solomani oppression of non-Human (and non-Solomani) worlds forced Empress Margaret II to revoke the region's charter. After years of diplomatic actions proved fruitless, it was decided to forcibly reintegrate the region into the Imperium. The Solomani resisted, and the Solomani Rim War (990 to 1002) began.

See *Terra*.

Solomani Confederation: In 871, the government of the Solomani Autonomous Region reorganized itself as the Solomani Confederation in an attempt to strengthen its claims to the heritage of the old Terran Confederation. Although tantamount to a declaration of independence, the reorganization was officially ignored by the government of the Imperium until the increasingly belligerent and extremist policies of the Solomani caused many border worlds under Solomani rule to petition the Imperium for redress.

The branches of the Solomani Confederation's government took the names of the government of the Terran Confederation, but the present institutions have little resemblance to those of the past. The chief governing body of the Solomani Confederation is the Secretariat. The Secretariat is presided over by the secretary general, who is elected from its membership. The secretary general is the chief administrative officer of the Solomani government, and while the office holds great power, it is fully accountable to the Secretariat.

Representatives to the Secretariat are appointed by the governments of the individual districts. The number of representatives each district may appoint is determined according to that district's contribution to the Solomani economy.

A district typically consists of a single world, but low population worlds or depressed areas are combined into multiworld districts. In the case of a district such as this, an election is held to determine the representative from that district. These, however, are not elections in the normal sense; the governments vote, rather than the populace. Each government of such a district is allocated votes (again, according to its economic importance), which are used to elect a representative for that district.

All government officeholders and officials must be members of the official party, the Solomani Movement. Although once waning in power and influence, the party is gaining in popularity as a result of successful Solomani incursions on the Imperium's rimward border. Still, the real power in the Confederation is held by the government and its factions.

Because of the greater degree of local autonomy that exists in the Solomani Confederation, interworld factionalism exists to a much greater degree than had been allowed in the Imperium. Coalitions of worlds exist outside the normal government channels, which sometimes give them equal political importance within a given region. For example, the Near Bootes cluster, in the Capella subsector, dominates large portions of the adjacent subsectors both economically and politically. Bootean mercantile interests have traditionally favored peaceful trade with the Imperium, and their influence has been held to be largely responsible for many peace negotiations between the Imperium and the Solomani Confederation.

Another example of this factionalism is the ongoing trade war (in Solomani Rim/Kukulcan) between Kukulcan and the coalition of Thetis and Laputa. The war has been causing severe damage to the economy of Kukulcan, but the Thetis coalition has thus far been able to muster enough power to prevent effective intervention by the Confederation.

Solomani Hypothesis: When the Solomani invented jump drive in -2431, they also discovered that more than a dozen Human races had already colonized the worlds surrounding Earth. At the time, there was no satisfactory explanation for the more than 40 genetically identical Human races.

The Solomani Hypothesis, first proposed by Magis Sergei haut-Devroe (64 to 141), theorized that all of the many widely scattered Human races of the galaxy originated on Terra. He thought that they were transported to their current homeworlds by an alien race (which haut-Devroe called the Ancients) for purposes which even today remain unclear. The approximate date of the scattering has been established as between -400,000 and -300,000.

Quid Nomine?

Over the years, science-fiction writers have used a variety of terms to refer to the inhabitants of planet Earth. "Earthling" is one of the earliest, and now seldom used because of that. "Terran" seems to be the odds-on favorite for the last few decades – so why isn't it used in *Traveller*? And why Solomani?

Firstly, we felt that the term Terran was becoming overused, and we wanted to use something different. "Humans" didn't seem quite right, but "Humanity" did find its way into the game, albeit with the alternate spelling of "Humaniti" (of which more below).

"Solomani" suggested itself from the phrase "Sol men" or "men of Sol" after the name applied to our own star (the Latin word for "sun"). The "i" ending of "Solomani" (and of "Zhodani," "Humaniti," and so on) came from rather a roundabout route. One of Loren Wiseman's early games was *Eagles,* dealing with the interactions of the Roman army along the Rhine frontier with various German tribes. Because of the Latin forms plurals, the vast majority of Germanic tribal names were Latinized and recorded as ending with either a single or double "i" – for example Suebii, Hermandurii, Langobardii, and so on. Marc Miller liked the sound of these names, and applied the same principle to the names of the various Human races in *Traveller*.

The Terra System

In the early years of space exploration, colonies were established throughout the Terran system. Every satellite was explored at least superficially, and expeditions even ventured into the depths of Jupiter's atmosphere. Although all colonies except Luna were abandoned during the Long Night, they have since been re-established.

Sol (G2V)

AU	World/Satellite	Notes
0.4	**Mercury**	
0.7	**Venus**	
1	**Terra**	Class V Starport
	Luna	Research lab, colony
1.5	**Mars**	Military base, colony
	Phobos	
	Deimos	
2.8	**Planetoid Belt**	Mining colony
5.2	**Jupiter**	(Only major satellites listed)
	Ring System	
	Io	
	Europa	
	Ganymede	Military base
	Callisto	
9.5	**Saturn**	(Only major satellites listed)
	Ring System	
	Janus	
	Mimas	
	Enceladus	Research lab
	Tethys	
	Dione	
	Rhea	
	Titan	
	Hyperion	
	Iapetus	
	Phoebe	
19.2	**Uranus**	(Only major satellites listed)
	Ring System	
	Miranda	
	Ariel	
	Umbriel	
	Titania	
	Oberon	
30.1	**Neptune**	(Only major satellites listed)
	Ring System	
	Triton	
	Nereid	
39.5	**Pluto**	Research lab
	Charon	

Worlds in the Terra system are named for various deities of old Terran religions, taken from the Greco-Roman pantheon.

When Terra was incorporated into the Imperium in 588, a small historical mission verified much of haut-Devroe's work. The hypothesis was already generally accepted by the majority of the Human population in the Imperium.

More than 40 known Human races have been located (and several more of them failed to adapt to their new worlds and are now extinct). Only three of these Human races have reached widespread prominence; they are the Vilani, the Zhodani, and the Solomani.

Most other Human races accept the hypothesis but lend it no special importance. The hypothesis is used by the Solomani Movement as a basis for its claims of Solomani racial superiority.

See *Humans.*

Solomani Movement: An organization devoted to the doctrine that Humans of Solomani descent are superior to all others and most fit to rule the galaxy.

Solomani Rim War (990 to 1002): War between the Third Imperium and the Solomani Confederation during which a large portion of the Solomani Rim sector was returned to Imperial control.

Hoping to profit from Imperial preoccupation with the Third Frontier War and the disorganization which followed upon the abdication of Styryx in 989, the Solomani reasserted their control over the complete Solomani Sphere, including those portions reabsorbed into the Imperium (see *Solomani Autonomous Region*). The Imperium declared war in 990.

The initial phase of the war went very well for the Solomani. Although the Imperium maintained sizable fleets along the border, they were inferior in strength to the massed naval elements of the Solomani Confederation. In most areas, the Solomani regained the border worlds lost to the Imperium in the last half century and even occupied a number of worlds that had never been part of the Solomani Sphere.

Solomani fortunes were checked in 993 when a large invasion force attempted to regain the worlds in the Old Expanses sector. It encountered near-fanatical resistance and was repulsed with heavy losses.

The period from 993 to 998 was one of stalemate. The Solomani abandoned their plans for further expansion in order to rebuild their forces. Their policy of inflexibly defending every border world was a constant drain on their resources, and the Solomani were not able to regain the initiative. By 998, the Imperial Navy had achieved strategic dominance as the greater industrial base of the Imperium made its power felt.

The last phase of the war, 998 to 1002, consisted of a near continual advance by Imperial forces into the heart of the Solomani Sphere. The basic Imperial strategy was to attack along two parallel axes of advance, with lesser task forces spreading out to create a huge pocket of Solomani territory to be reduced at leisure.

Although the Solomani occasionally achieved a tactical success against a task force (such as in the Battle of Kagukhasaggan in early 1002), they were unable to halt the main advances. With the liberation of the Vegan district in 1001, the Imperium gained the secure base envisioned in the reign of Styryx. The loss of the Vegan district prompted the Solomani to embark on a desperate gamble. Recalling the time when the outnumbered Terran Confederation was able to defeat the Vilani Imperium, the Solomani consolidated their remaining naval forces into a single fleet and struck at the Imperial fleet that was advancing out of the Vegan district.

At the Battle of Dingir, in early 1002, the Solomani Grand Fleet was scattered and substantially destroyed. The remnants of the Solomani fleet fell back deeper into the Sphere, and the Imperial forces firmly established themselves in Terra's own subsector.

The Imperial high command decided that Terra would have to be invaded in order to end forever all claims of Solomani superiority, and thus the use of Terra as a rallying standard elsewhere in the Sphere. In order to invade Terra, a sizable fraction of the Imperial forces in the Solomani Sphere were assembled into an assault force, which effectively ended the pursuit of the defeated Solomani fleet. The invasion began in the second quarter of 1002, and the hard-fought campaign lasted until nearly the end of the year.

In the end, the Imperium conquered the planet, but the battle for Terra had consumed so much of the Imperial military resources that the Imperial high command felt they lacked sufficient strength to resume their advance into the rest of the Solomani Sphere. Accordingly, they negotiated a temporary armistice with the Solomani military commanders, who were glad to gain a respite to regroup their remaining forces. The war ended on this basis as both the Imperial and Solomani civilian governments, who were concerned with the strain placed on their economies by the protracted war, informally agreed to extend the armistice indefinitely.

Scholars have debated the wisdom of invading Terra; some claim that the battle was a marginal if not a Pyrrhic victory for the Imperium. The general consensus has been that the war as a whole was a victory for the Imperium. A substantial amount of the Solomani Sphere was reabsorbed by the Imperium, and a vigorous Vegan Autonomous District was set up to oversee Imperial interests along the new border.

Solomani Security: Also known as SolSec, this organization is the secret police force maintained in service to the Solomani Confederation for the purpose of maintaining state secrets, conducting espionage, and implementing political policies of the government.

Solomani Security maintains both a network of contacts which provide information from outside the Confederation and a network of informants which provide information within the Confederation. Solomani Security agents themselves are highly trained individuals capable of conducting espionage and sabotage.

Solomani Sphere: The territory governed by the Solomani as the Solomani Autonomous Region.

See *Solomani Autonomous Region.*

Sophont: A generalized term for an intelligent life form.

Sophontology: Also called *xenology.* The study of intelligent life. Subsidiary branches of this science include *cultural sophontology,* the comparative study of sophont societies; *physical sophontology,* the study of the genetic and physiological makeup of intelligent life; and *developmental sophontology,* the study of the various means by which life forms evolve intelligence.

Solomani Names

The philosophy of names for characters in science-fiction games varies depending on the "style" of the players. Names like Lance Starhawk will be perfectly acceptable to some groups, and not to others.

Traveller was written with the assumption that characters of Solomani descent would represent the full range of the languages and cultures of Earth. When choosing names to use in adventures, articles, and the *Traveller News Service* – at **www.sjgames.com/gurps/traveller/news.html** – the authors tried to mix names from a variety of cultures: Stashu Nagoya, for example, is a combination of olish and Japanese names.

Those looking for a source of personal (usually, but not always the first) names can consult the myriad "baby name" books in the local library (they often explain the meaning of the name and give details of the ethnic and cultural backgrounds). There are a variety of books which explain the origin and background of family names. A search of the Internet will reveal a number of sites dealing with names.

Non-European ethnic and cultural backgrounds are especially encouraged, as it is the contention of *Traveller*'s original designers that all of Earth's peoples participated in the settlement of space. This may result in the use of triple names from some cultures (Vasili Pavlovich Zhukov, Marcus Tullius Cicero) or names where the family name is the first name (Kim Sung).

Starports: Extrality

The major portion of a starport is surrounded by a barrier demarking the limit of Imperial extraterritoriality (often shortened to *extrality*). The region inside this is under direct Imperial authority and the local planetary laws do not apply. Goods may be purchased here without duty, and taxes are limited to a small Imperial income tax and such customs duties as the Imperium levies. Violators of local laws, especially political "criminals," may find asylum and sanctuary from restrictive local regimes, but if the fugitive is sought for an offense that is also a violation of Imperial law (murder, most felonies, and so on), Imperial officials will hold and extradite the fugitive.

Depending on the nature of the planetary government, the extrality limit may be marked by a simple wire fence or more complex barriers resembling the Berlin Wall of old Terra. This usually is done to prevent citizens of the planet from leaving without authorization and to enforce local customs laws.

Although, strictly speaking, the law level of the starport permits any weapon to be carried openly, the Imperial laws against property damage, murder, and extortion are rigidly enforced by Imperial authorities, backed up by Imperial military forces as necessary. The owners of most businesses frown on open displays of weaponry and will usually refuse to serve walking arsenals . . . and are usually fairly well-equipped themselves.

Each facility has its own unique features, and the number of variants is almost equal to the number of downports (that portion of the starport located on the surface of the planet – orbital facilities, or highports, are all extraterritorial). Almost every downport has an associated urbanization surrounding the downport (in many cases completely). Residential areas are often allowed inside the extrality barrier for employees of the port and its associated businesses (which are as numerous as those associated with a terrestrial airport or seaport of the present). It shouldn't take much imagination to come up with adventures hinging on extrality.

An escaped criminal, for example, might seek asylum inside the extrality barrier. Since it is in the best interest of the downport to maintain cordial relations with local governments, if the crime was particularly heinous (in local terms), there might be a tendency on the part of the starport officials to overlook exculpatory evidence. The accused might seek help in eluding starport officials until he can gather evidence to clear his name. Adjust the details to fit an individual campaign.

See pp. T:FT66-67 for more information.

Spinward Marches: The Imperium's farthest frontier sector, containing 437 star systems divided along a coreward/rimward line by the Imperial border. The region is dominated by two major powers: the Imperial Spinward Marches sector and the frontier provinces of the Zhodani Consulate. In the independent territory between the two powers lie four small territories: the Federation of Arden, the Sword Worlds Confederation, the Border Worlds (a splinter state cut from the Sword Worlds during the Fifth Frontier War), and the Darrian Confederation. Each follows its own diplomatic line designed to maintain independence from both the Zhodani and the Imperium.

The Spinward Marches has been settled since the 400s and is still a frontier sector. High-tech worlds are scattered among empty, fallow worlds; there is potential for exploration, exploitation, and development for centuries to come.

GURPS Traveller Behind the Claw describes the Marches in detail.

Starport: An establishment for the landing, servicing, refueling, and control of starships. Starports range in quality from I (the worst, little more than a spot of cleared ground) to V (the best and most extensive).

Starports generally have two facilities, surface and orbital. The surface facility includes cargo-handling installations, a landing field, control towers, and other necessary areas. Surface starport components are frequently called Down (as in Credo Down Starport on Regina). Orbital facilities are present (usually in stationary orbit above the surface component) to enable handling of unstreamlined ships and to allow construction of heavy craft in orbit. The orbital component is often called Orbital (as in Credo Orbital Starport).

Type I and II starports have no extensive orbital facilities, but they usually have navigational satellites or similar equipment. Non-streamlined ships at these starports must be serviced by shuttles. Starports, being the primary point at which starships interact with a system, are usually the location for shipyards and additional bases, such as scout bases, naval bases, or other military installations.

Strephon (b. 1049): Strephon Aella Alkhalikoi, 43rd emperor of the Imperium; eldest son of Emperor Paulo III (981-1071); born 1049; coronation 1071. His Golden Jubilee (50th anniversary of his coronation) is to be celebrated in 1121. He married Iolanthe Guuilbataashullibaa (p. 43) in 1079. They have one issue, the Grand Princess Ciencia Iphegenia (p. 25).

Subsector: Mapping unit in astrography. Average density: 30 to 40 worlds per subsector.

Subsectors are noted within a sector by their position using the first 16 letters of the alphabet (A-P). In addition, they are named and may be called by a variety of synonyms for subsector, including province, cluster, or district. Imperial convention is to assign numbers to districts (for example, District 268) which are under Imperial protection because they are pending integration into the Imperium.

Superheavy Elements: Although elements heavier than uranium are increasingly unstable and radioactive (with half-lives measured in fractions of a second), quantum theory predicts an "island of stability," consisting of the elements with atomic numbers 114 to 122, which have half-lives measured in the millions of years. These superheavy elements, also called eka-metals or island metals, are generated in small amounts in supernova explosions. Only a few grams have ever been discovered in nature, which is just enough for scientists to determine that superheavies would be immensely valuable to industry if a source could be found.

Survey, First (published 420): The first comprehensive astrographic and demographic survey of the Imperium, which was performed by the Imperial Interstellar Scout Service. More than 100 years in the making, its publication in 420 made available the Imperium's records on its component worlds for public use.

Survey, Second (published 1065): The second comprehensive survey of the Imperium, which was performed by the Scout Service, and which updated the long obsolete and incomplete data in the First Survey. The Second Survey was 70 years in compilation, went to greater lengths than its predecessor, and included more world data as well as more complete astrographic data. In addition, the expansion of the Imperium since 420 had added many new worlds that had to be included.

Sword Worlds Confederation: A loose confederation of worlds in the Spinward Marches, spinward of Imperial space and coreward of the Darrians. The first settlement in the region was on Gram in -399.

By circa -200 the settlement of the area was largely complete, and the first interstellar government in the region, the Sacnoth Dominate, was formed in -186. Consisting of the 20 worlds settled up to that point, the Dominate lasted until -102, when it was fractured by rebellion into several smaller states.

During the ensuing centuries, various Sword World governments rose and fell; they sometimes coalesced all the worlds under a single world's domination and sometimes splintered into several small states. Contact with Imperial traders in 73 brought increased trade and had a stabilizing influence on the region, but this stability was short-lived.

The First Frontier War brought a desire for cooperation among the various squabbling worlds, and the end of the war saw the formation of the first unified confederation in centuries, which was centered on Sacnoth and which was referred to as the Second Dominate. As a result of the Outworld Coalition's victory, the Sword Worlds annexed Terant 340, Torment, Trifuge, and Cunnonic, which are all in the Darrian subsector.

The Second Dominate held power until 698, when it was overthrown by a coalition headed by Gram. The Gram Coalition ruled until 788, when a short war with the Darrian Confederation resulted in the loss of the four worlds gained during the First Frontier War.

Public outrage at the mishandling of the war caused the subsequent fall of the Gram government. The replacement for the Gram Coalition was the Trilateral Alliance, a decentralized organization headed by Narsil, Sacnoth, and Durendal. The Alliance broke up in 848 due in large part to the inherent weakness of its organization, and an interregnum of essentially independent worlds lasted until Gram reasserted its influence (helped substantially by Zhodani money and advisors, rumor has it) in 852. This government has remained in control to the present.

The government allows almost complete local autonomy. Individual worlds maintain separate military forces, pass their own laws, and completely regulate their own internal affairs. The Confederation government regulates interworld trade, handles diplomatic relations with outside powers, and adjudicates interworld disputes.

In peacetime, the Confederation government maintains a pool of high-ranking military officers (selected from the military forces of all worlds) who are trained in large-unit command and staff operations.

Blood Bonds

Soldiers get captured in any war, and elaborate procedures have been created over the years to deal with them. Often, one side trades prisoners with the other, usually on a 1-for-1 basis. In a mercenary war of the sort that takes place in *Traveller*, the losing side is not usually able to conduct negotiations or provide funds. We speculated that part of the cost of hiring a mercenary unit would involve pre-paying their passage home after their services were no longer required, and the concept of a repatriation bond was born.

Repatriation bonds were partly inspired by the use of "documents" called *blood chits*, which evolved as a way of getting pilots home more or less intact. One prominent use was in China in 1940 by the American Volunteer Group (the "Flying Tigers"). Each pilot had a silk square sewn onto the back of his jacket with an American flag printed on it, and an inscription in Chinese, English, and several other languages announcing that anyone who helped the pilot get to American lines would receive a reward, usually paid on the spot in gold.

See *GURPS Traveller Star Mercs* for more information on repatriation bonds.

Square Pegs?

Cleon II: Also known as Cleon the Weak; only Issue of Cleon I. Born 21, proclaimed emperor 53, abdicated 54.

In fact, history testifies that "weak" may be an unfair description of Cleon II. Apparently unsuited to devious palace politics, but still recognizing the need to consolidate the power of the fledgling Imperium, Cleon abdicated in favor of his brilliant chancellor, Artemsus Lentuli.

Vitally concerned with the welfare of his former realm, Cleon spent the remainder of his active, colorful, and (from all accounts) happy life on the frontier as a self-appointed (and extremely effective) one-man fire brigade. His personal magnetism, combined with the romance of his abdication, made him an extremely effective advocate. The most famous example was in 56, when he single-handedly averted the potential rebellion on Thutmose by mediating a marathon 39-hour negotiation session between all three political parties on that world.

Cleon III: Born 201, proclaimed emperor 244, assassinated 245. In the dynastic crisis caused by the death of Martin II without direct issue, Cleon Zhunastu, a great-great-great-grandson of Cleon II, appeared to be the most legitimate claimant to the throne. Since Cleon III was soon nicknamed "Cleon the Mad," it appears that while Cleon's claim to the throne was sound, he was not. His behavior in office soon convinced surviving members of the government that he was a homicidal maniac, and a decision to dispose of him was made and implemented in short order.

*– Chadwick, Miller, et al.,
"Emperors of the Third Imperium"*

During time of war, all military forces are confederalized and placed under a single unified command. For ground forces, divisions will be commanded by generals from the individual worlds, corps and higher organizations by Confederation officers. The component forces of a division will be from the same world whenever possible. For naval forces, individual ships are under the command of local officers, squadrons or higher organizations under Confederation officers.

See *GURPS Traveller Behind the Claw* for more information.

Sylea: Capital of the Sylean Federation. Renamed Capital by Cleon I.

Sylea, Domain of: A domain of the Third Imperium, consisting of the Core, Fornast, Massilia, and Delphi sectors.

Sylean Federation (-650 to 0): Large interstellar federation which served as the basis for the Third Imperium.

Established on Sylea in -650, the Federation grew slowly, absorbing several surrounding worlds and increasing trade and interaction between worlds.

By -30, the real power in the Federation was an industrial consortium headed by Cleon Zhunastu. Cleon, a Solomani noble of great vision, used his family industrial base and the support of other families (obtained by the persuasiveness of his personality) to obtain behind-the-scenes control of the Federation government and to begin an active campaign to increase the number of worlds under its control.

After 30 years of economic and diplomatic maneuvering (and occasional military action), Cleon had increased the size of the Federation and extended its control to the edge of what is now Core sector. Cleon envisioned a territory larger than a single sector, however, and concluded that the tightly controlled, highly centralized nature of the government of the Sylean Federation was not suitable for a large, star-spanning empire.

Cleon decided the Federation had served its purpose, and he began plans for a more suitable form of interstellar government, which would allow greater local autonomy but maintain cohesion over large distances. In addition, to restore the past glories of the Rule of Man (and therefore lay claim to all former territories of the First and Second imperiums), Cleon proposed to revive the Imperium.

This was made possible by the fact that in the closing years of the period known as Twilight, one of the last claimants to the throne of the Rule of Man had made Sylea his capital. Cleon traced the legitimacy of the Sylean Federation backward through this emperor to the Rule of Man and (since the Rule of Man claimed to be the lawful successor to the Vilani Imperium) to the First Imperium as well.

In the 651st year of the Sylean Federation, the Grand Senate of the Federation "persuaded" Cleon to accept the Imperial crown. That year he was crowned First Emperor of the Third Imperium, and he proclaimed the 651st year of the Sylean Federation to be the Year Zero of the Third Imperium.

System: A star and its family of planets and satellites. The term "system" denotes a major world and its associated star, plus any other planets, satellites, asteroids, and other bodies.

System-Defense Boat: A non-starship specifically intended for defensive operations inside a star system. It was developed on the principle that a non-starship (because of the increased armament made possible by its lack of jump drives) can normally defeat a starship of equal tonnage. SDBs are typically stationed at the vital points of a system (the gas giants, the asteroid belt, the major world, and so on), and they attack invading vessels according to one or more predetermined plans.

System-defense boats range in size from 100 to 5,000 tons and are constructed at all tech levels from 8 to 12. There are hundreds of different types, which depend upon the specific mission for which they are designed.

Terra (Solomani Rim/Sol 1827 A867A69-F): Also known to its inhabitants as Earth, Terra is the origin world of the genetic stock from which all races of Humaniti are descended, former capital of the Terran Confederation, former capital of the Old Earth Union, and former capital of the Solomani Autonomous Region. The word Terran (used in the past to refer to an inhabitant of this world or to a citizen of the Terran Confederation) is derived from the name of this world. See sidebar, p. 62, for a discussion of the Terra system.

Terran Confederation (-2398 to -2204): Interstellar government consisting of Terra and its colony worlds. The Terran Confederation has its roots in the formation of the United Nations Space Coordination Agency (UNSCA) circa -2500. In addition to handling mundane responsibilities that helped avoid conflict, UNSCA soon became a clearinghouse for space operations.

One of UNSCA's natural directions was research. In 2087 A.D., UNSCA researchers in the system's asteroid belt who were looking for better drives to transport ores invented jump drive. The first jump drives were used only in the solar system – they were too weak to be used for interstellar travel. In 2096 A.D., for various reasons, the first interstellar jump expedition traveled to Barnard's Star rather than Alpha Centauri.

Upon their return in 2097 A.D., the expedition members were hurried into a hushed meeting with UNSCA. The expedition had encountered intelligent life – Human life! The expedition members had encountered a Vilani prospecting outpost, an outpost on the very fringe of a vast, advanced empire controlled by alien Humans. It came as quite a shock to the Terrans that many of the worlds only a few parsecs away were already claimed. Politicians echoed the popular sentiment that it was unfair for people from several hundred light-years away to claim worlds near Terra. Individual nations began expanding their armed forces and building starships.

Is the Truth Really Out There?

A question that is as hotly discussed among *Traveller* fans as speculations about angels and pinheads among medieval philosophers is this: To what extent did the Vilani have contact with Terrans prior to the official first contact in 2097? How could the Vilani have missed such an important world? Are all the 20th-century reports of ET contact really grounded in Vilani surveillance of Terra? If the Vilani knew about the Terrans, how could they have come as such a surprise in the various frontier wars?

Some *Traveller* fans hold that the Vilani did not know of the Terrans, but that a lesser Vilani subject race (perhaps the Vegans) did. Were the bodies allegedly recovered at Roswell, New Mexico, in 1947 Vegan merchants killed in some kind of accident? Was the Tunguska event in Siberia in 1908 a Vegan spacecraft crash? Did the Vegans or some other spacefaring group give the secret of jump drive to the Terrans in the late 20th or early 21st century?

Traveller canon has always avoided the question, but the present author has one fervently held opinion: Terran invention of jump-drive was through their own efforts – it was not given, taken, or acquired in any way other than through independent research.

LSW 5/98

A Great Golden Crown

"The Imperium is our contribution to the endless history of civilization that came before us and that will continue on after us. It is what we leave to the future, and is in some finite way better than what the past left to us. No great civilization is ever dead. They all remain as the foundations upon which future societies are built. The Terran Confederation, the Vilani Bureaux, Cleon's Sylean vision, the United States of America, the Roman Empire, the Gimmini city states. All are still with us.

"The Third Imperium is a great golden crown, the greatest achievement of Human history, and each of us are tiny gems set within it. But this crown is not meant to be worn by any emperor. It is a treasure that belongs to every Imperial citizen, and each of these must be free to fashion his or her own addition to this treasure, to attach him or herself to this priceless offering that we leave to the future."

– Emperor Strephon Aella Alkhalikoi, from a speech to the Imperial Moot, 1110, on the occasion of his order to lift martial law on Terra

The Lifeblood of Empire

"The only measure of this Imperium's value is its economic strength and vitality. We may aggregate all manner of high purposes and beliefs to this civilization, but we must not forget that it exists only to allow its citizens to effectively interact on an economic basis.

"All interactions between intelligent beings are economic because economics is the satisfaction of natural biological needs by social means. We create societies by trading; we do not create societies and then decide to trade to have something to do with our time. Politics, statecraft, religion, and our own glorious Imperium; these are all methods to create an environment within which beings can go about their most basic business of trading the necessities for healthy, meaningful lives."

– Duchess Margaret Tukera, address to the 500th Oracle, 103-1116

Over the course of the next three decades, UNSCA and the United Nations transformed itself into a true world government, which administered the defense of Terra against the Vilani Empire. Terran colonies formed on other worlds were granted membership in the United Nations. In -2400, the UN officially changed its name to the United Worlds. Two years later, the name was changed again to the Terran Confederation. Modern historians, for simplicity, use this term exclusively.

The Terran Confederation fought a series of interstellar wars with the Vilani Imperium over the period -2408 to -2219. These wars ultimately resulted in the fall of the Vilani Grand Imperium. The Confederation was dissolved in -2204 upon the proclamation of the Rule of Man to replace the Vilani Imperium.

See also *Rule of Man, Nth Interstellar War,* and *Solomani.*

LSW 5/98

Third Frontier War (979 to 986): The long period of uneasy peace between the Imperium and the Zhodani Consulate erupted into war in 979 with simultaneous blows by the Zhodani in the Querion and Jewell subsectors. Imperial reaction was deficient, and the hostilities continued for nearly six years with little to show for it. The armistice finally signed in 986 gave each side little, and it brought about the abdication of Emperor Styryx in 989.

Third Imperium (0 to present): Also called The Imperium. Founded in 0 by Cleon Zhunastu from the Sylean Federation in what is now Core sector. The Imperium grew swiftly during the pacification campaigns, and more slowly thereafter until stability was reached in the 600s, by which time the Imperium had absorbed much of the territory of the First and Second imperiums.

Government Structure: The Imperium can be best thought of as a form of feudal confederation. Member worlds of the Imperium agree to pay taxes and obey a few fundamental laws which the Imperium promulgates, known as the High Laws. In return, the Imperium agrees to patrol the space between the worlds, to protect interstellar trade, to encourage travel and commerce, and to arbitrate diplomatic relations between worlds. Beyond this, individual worlds are left to their own devices so long as they acknowledge the power of the Imperium to rule the space between the stars.

Imperial power is present on member worlds in the form of consulates, bureaucratic offices, and bases. Sometimes, larger enclaves of Imperial power are placed where they can enhance the emperor's strength.

The Imperium's territory is divided into sectors, which are in turn divided into subsectors and systems. Groups of sectors called domains have been created above the sector level.

During the Pacification Campaigns, Emperor Artemsus divided space into six regions, labeled them domains, and appointed an archduke over each of them. To each archduke, he assigned the continuing pacification of the domain's many systems and their integration into the Imperium. The domains were: Sylea (Core, Fornast, Massilia, Delphi), Vland (Corridor, Vland, Gushemege, Dagudashag), Gateway (Ley, Glimmerdrift Reaches, Gateway, Crucis Margin), Ilelish (Ilelish, Zarushagar, Reaver's Deep, Daibei), Antares (Lishun, Antares, Mendan, Amdukan), and Sol (Diaspora, Old Expanses, Solomani Rim, Alpha Crucis). Most of the domains were never totally absorbed into the Imperium.

In 589, during the First Frontier War, a seventh domain was established: Deneb (Spinward Marches, Deneb, Trojan Reach, Reft). The intent was to appoint an archduke to be responsible for their supervision. However, the Civil War broke out before an archduke was appointed, and it was not until over 500 years later that Emperor Strephon would be persuaded to appoint Norris Aella Alledon as archduke of the domain of Deneb.

Following the Civil War, the emperors expressed concern about individuals with powers equaling their own, so they moved to lessen the power of the archdukes in the Imperial government. As a result, the domains came to have little practical significance. Each archduke did retain the power to create knights and baronets.

In the years after the Fourth Frontier War, and after the problems it presented from lags in communication, Emperor Strephon felt a strengthened archduke position could enable the Imperium to more quickly respond in defending the realm. Against the protests and opposition of some prominent members of the Moot, Strephon reestablished the domain as a level in the bureaucracy of the Imperial Navy, and returned to the domain the ability to collect taxes. Still later, Strephon gave the archdukes the ability to legislate and enforce the desires of the emperor on the local level.

See *Sylean Federation*.

Thoengling Empire: Large, centralized state in the Vargr Extents. The Thoengling Empire is one of the most stable of the Vargr states and has existed in its current form since 792. The emperor, who has great governmental authority, is chosen for life by vote of an elected assembly; by law, no member of his family may succeed him. Sons and daughters of the higher nobility are brought up at the Imperial court, where every effort is made to inculcate personal loyalty to the emperor.

The Thoengling Empire has become a major trading partner of the Imperium and generally supports Imperial interests in the Vargr Extents.

Trade Routes: Routes which jump-capable starships travel between major worlds and which connect vital suppliers with essential markets, important government worlds with high-population worlds, and strategic resources with exploiting industry. Trade routes are a natural outgrowth of economic and market pressures. When a market is no longer profitable, the trade routes bypass it.

The trade routes are typically the territory of the Imperium's largest trading companies. They maintain fleets of commercial transports and merchants who serve these trade worlds, and they reap large profits in doing so.

But the trade routes directly serve fewer than a tenth of the worlds of the Imperium. The other 90% of the Imperium's worlds are served by feeder lines, tramp freighters, and free traders. These smaller companies and unscheduled ships carry passengers and cargo between worlds off the main trade routes.

Trade Routes

One of the problems with space is that it is essentially empty. Isaac Asimov once wrote that if star systems were atoms (he mentioned that our system would be a fluorine atom), the universe was an excellent example of a hard vacuum. What this means is that there is almost nothing resembling terrain for interstellar maps, and no one direction is superior to any other direction. An essentially random distribution of stars results in clumps and patterns, however, and this helps a little.

The concept of the jump drive creates limitations to free travel, however. Most ships in *Traveller* cannot travel more than 1 or 2 parsecs at a time, and this means that "roads" in space will follow the paths of these short-hop jump routes. An analogy can be made to rivers. Rivers are naturally occurring transportation routes, and cities located on them had greater access to trade than those not so fortunate. Worlds located on the "trade routes" formed by the strings of 1-parsec jumps will tend to be more prosperous than those not so favored.

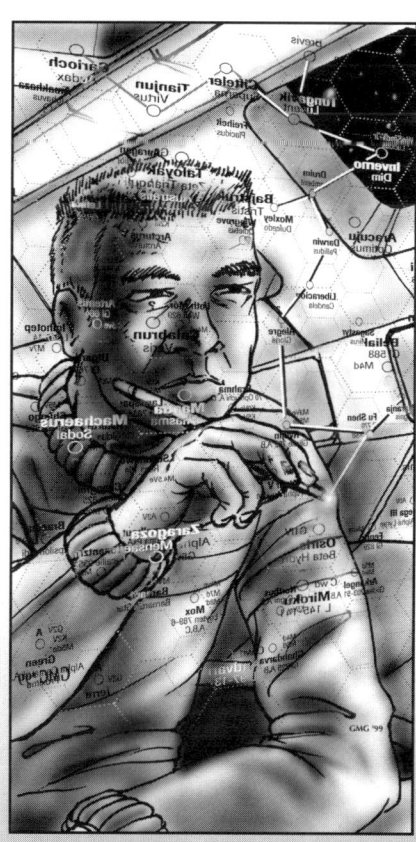

K'kree Religion

"The K'kree are unlike the vast majority of sophonts in that their religious beliefs are monolithic throughout their culture, and essentially unchanged since the earliest K'kree civilization. They have been almost totally unaffected by exposure to outside influences, or the advancements of science and technology. K'kree religion is not so much a way of worship as it is a way of thought and belief. While K'kree religious writings abound in myths and legends, and there is a definite belief in divinity and in divine purpose, the K'kree never seem to have evolved the notion that their deities could be swayed by prayer, offerings, promises, or good behavior. As suits a harsh and militant people, the divine play is distant, inscrutable, and unrelenting.

"The K'kree religion is a fatalistic one – they believe that events have been long since preordained, and are quite unchangeable by any mortal agency. This fatalism, however, is tempered by an absolute faith in their own glorious destiny. Thus, fatalism does not hamper them; instead it makes them almost fanatical. If a K'kree soldier has been fated to die, he will die – no amount of running from destiny will stop him from being killed, or from doing what he is fated to do. Thus, he is more inclined to put his every effort into the battle.

"As befits their natures, the religion of the K'kree is perhaps the most supremely polytheistic religion practiced by any race anywhere. The K'kree believe that each and every living K'kree is the worldly counterpart of a divine being. The religion holds that there is an ideal universe, somewhere in time and space, in which all K'kree who ever were (or will ever be) live. It is a single, immense prairie, on which all can live in complete peace and harmony, under a divine steppelord who rules over all equally.

Continued on next page . . .

Travel Zone: Standard form of classification for worlds in terms of relative danger. As a service to spacefarers, the Travellers' Aid Society (see p. 35) publishes travel-zone classifications which indicate the degree of danger a world presents to visitors. Standard classifications are green (no danger), amber (caution advised), and red (severe danger).

See *Amber Zone*, *Red Zone*.

Trojan Points: In a gravitational system composed of a small body orbiting a much larger one (such as a planet and star, or a moon and planet), there are two stable points lying in the small body's orbit 60 degrees ahead and behind it, and equidistant from the small and large bodies. These are called Trojan points (also LaGrangian points, which are abbreviated as L4 and L5).

The Trojan points of a gas giant near an asteroid belt commonly collect a cluster of asteroids. The name comes from the first such cluster discovered by Terrans at Jupiter in the Sol system; the asteroids were named after mythical heroes of the Trojan War.

Twilight (-1776 to -1526): The failure of the Rule of Man triggered the collapse of most interstellar civilization. While interstellar travel and commerce continued, it was at a greatly reduced rate, and the many worlds of the Imperium turned in on themselves. The period of collapse is termed Twilight, and it lasted for 250 years.

Modern historians consider Twilight to have begun in -1776 when the treasury on Hub/Ershur refused to acknowledge a monetary issue of the branch treasury at Antares, which triggered a financial collapse and the destruction of large-scale trade within the Imperium. The end of Twilight is commonly accepted as the year -1526, when the last governmental body claiming to be the Rule of Man ceased to exist. This ushered in the Long Night (see p. 48).

Twilight's Peak: Legendary or apocryphal story of lost starfarers on an unknown world who discovered fantastic structures and devices while surviving a terrifying winter. Phrased as an epic poem of execrable quality, the story is most notable only in that it may be based on fact: A task force was lost in the time period specified, and it has not been recovered or accounted for.

Two Thousand Worlds: Most common name in the Imperium for the region of space ruled by the K'kree. "Two thousand worlds" is a literal translation of the K'kree *T't'tkahk Xeng Kirr*. The same words can also be rendered idiomatically as "universe." In times past, the words meant "night sky," for roughly 2,000 stars can be seen from one hemisphere of *Kirur*, the K'kree homeworld. The name should not be taken to mean that there are exactly 2,000 worlds in the K'kree empire.

The K'kree government is highly conservative. The current dynasty ruling the Two Thousand Worlds has been in power since prehistoric times, and the form of the government has remained unchanged except for a few minor modifications made necessary by the problems inherent in governing an interstellar empire.

K'kree expansion into space progressed very slowly after the invention of the jump drive in -4142. The conservative nature of society and the technical limitations placed upon spaceflight by that society (K'kree spaceships must be very large, for example) combined to inhibit early exploration and colonization.

The discovery of other sophonts caused a xenophobic reaction in K'kree society. The realization that intelligent carnivores might exist somewhere in space sparked the K'kree obsession to convert the universe to herbivorism. This obsession stimulated the growth of the Two Thousand Worlds to its present size and still dominates K'kree culture. Local cultures are tolerated and other aspects of K'kree society are not heavily enforced, but all races within the Two Thousand Worlds are herbivorous.

K'kree contact with the Hive Federation was soon followed by the Hiver-K'kree war of -2029 to -2013. The military technology of the K'kree proved superior in the first stages of the war. The war ended due to nonmilitary considerations, however, when the Hive Federation demonstrated a plan to radically alter the K'kree social order through the use of psychohistorical techniques and threatened to implement it. The K'kree withdrew to the antebellum borders, and the border between the two states has remained stable to this day.

The K'kree Empire eventually stopped in its expansion. Increasing problems of administration over interstellar distances and contact with other starfaring races (such as Hivers and Humaniti) have stabilized the Two Thousand Worlds at its present size.

See *K'kree* and ***GURPS Traveller Alien Races 2***.

K'kree Religion
[Continued]

"Each mortal K'kree is a living embodiment of his respective divine counterpart, born into the world for the dual purpose of carrying forward the divine plan for this shadow world, and of testing the individual's worth.

"These divine K'kree become mortal once, live out a lifetime in this universe (which is but an instant in their own), and then return when their part is done. The way in which they stood up to the trials of this universe determines their standing in the other.

Vargr: Intelligent major race derived from Ancient genetic manipulations of Terran carnivore/chaser stock, which apparently dates from approximately the same time that Humaniti was scattered to the stars.

Inhabiting a region rimward of the Imperium, the Vargr were a puzzle to xenologists. The biochemistry and genetic makeup are almost identical with a number of terrestrial animals, but they differ radically from most of the flora and fauna indigenous to Lair, which is the purported Vargr home world.

Research during the early years of the Third Imperium concluded them to be the result of genetic manipulation of transplanted Terran animals of the family *Canidae*, almost certainly of genus *Canis*. The obvious conclusion – supported by the archeological evidence – is that the race known as the Ancients was responsible for this.

The typical Vargr is about 5'2" and 130 lbs. They are upright, bipedal carnivores, with rear limbs digitigrade and hands very similar in size and appearance to those of a Human, although there are significant internal differences. They have approximately the same physical parameters as Humans, and are able to use the same equipment without modification or additional instruction.

*"Details of these concepts are hard to translate to the Human mind. There seems to be little concept of a 'good' life or an 'evil' life, or of rewards or punishments handed out for conduct. Ethics and morals are not so much the object of judgment as the ability of the individual to play his part without complaint, doing what needs to be done. In many respects, these religious concepts can be acquainted with certain philosophical teachings of Terra's ancient Greek and Roman cultures, particularly certain of Plato's doctrines (see especially **The Republic**, Book VII) and some aspects of Stoic philosophy.*

"That the K'kree believe themselves to be reflections of divine beings in temporary mortal form is an interesting concept. It is the basis for their extremely rigid dislike of other races, for the K'kree religion makes no provision for non-K'kree in their paradise world. Thus, all non-K'kree they meet, no matter how intelligent, are of the shadow world (our universe) alone, and hence inherently inferior.

Continued on next page . . .

K'kree Religion
[Continued]

"Yet the K'kree know themselves to be mortal in this life; their divine essence is no more and no less immortal than the Human concept of the soul.

"The shape of the divine plan for this 'shadow world' in which the K'kree live out their mortal lives is also an interesting one. The closest approximation to the K'kree belief possible in Human terms (and the approximation is by no means exact) is that the K'kree come into this world to shape it into a new paradise, into which some other people will eventually emerge and, in turn, descend into another 'shadow world' to shape its progress toward paradise. It is an infinitely repeating cycle of creation through a multitude of universes. Just who is to inherit this universe is hard to say; some K'kree writings seem to indicate that it is another race of K'kree, but a few translations could be interpreted to mean that it is some K'kree client race that will ultimately emerge as the 'divinities' who will descend into the next shadow world from ours. This would seem to be at the core of the K'kree efforts to shape certain subject races into a pattern conforming with their own ways. All other shadow races are, of course, nothing but obstacles in this life to be overcome.

"K'kree religious belief, at least among the leaders, was badly strained by the results of the Hiver-K'kree War. The K'kree backed down from the conflict, but the details of the true nature of the conflict were never made public. A certain weakening of the faith in the upper classes of K'kree society seems to have taken place, but their conservative nature made the idea of religious innovation unthinkable.

Continued on next page . . .

On the average their reactions are slightly faster than those of the typical Human, but individuals vary widely. The Vargr senses of smell and sight are superior to those of Humans.

Government: There is no central Vargr government; indeed, there is no governmental type that can be said to be "typically Vargr." Every conceivable form of governmental organization can be found somewhere in the Vargr Extents. The only cohesive force in the Extents is a fierce racial pride which causes a slight tendency toward racial cooperation.

The higher the level of the Vargr government, the more unstable it becomes because of the difficulty of obtaining consent of all Vargr involved.

Vargr in the Imperium: While only a few planets populated completely by Vargr exist within the Imperium, there are millions of Vargr citizens of loyal subject planets. Additionally, Vargr adventurers, criminals, mercenaries, and traders can be found throughout the coreward reaches of the Imperium.

Society: The key elements shaping Vargr societies are a very strong centrifugal force resulting from an emphasis on consensus and informal lines of authority, and an equally strong centripetal force resulting from a deeply ingrained family/clan/tribe/national loyalty.

Centralized authority is extremely limited at the upper levels of Vargr society, and action is based on broad coalitional concerns, with a constant splitting and rejoining of dissident factions. Traditionally, this has made it very difficult for more centralized and organized societies such as the Imperium to deal on a meaningful basis with what passes for Vargr states.

The Vargr have little respect for formal authority, and what respect they might have decreases as that authority becomes more remote. Vargr tend to respect informal authority figures more, and they obey superiors who are better known to them.

The Vargr have an intense racial pride, and they are easily insulted. They are prone to enter into fights without regard to possible consequences. Vargr social organization is difficult to characterize in Terran terms, but it can be most closely compared to the Dakota Sioux of North America in the 1800s, if the analogy is not pressed too far.

Even among the most stable Vargr governments, a highly charismatic leader can attract followers for almost anything. The neighbors of the Vargr are constantly the subject of impromptu raids and scattered piracy by bands of Vargr (totally without government sanction, of course) who have been talked into a raid, a battle, or a war by a charismatic leader.

See *GURPS Traveller Alien Races 1* for more information.

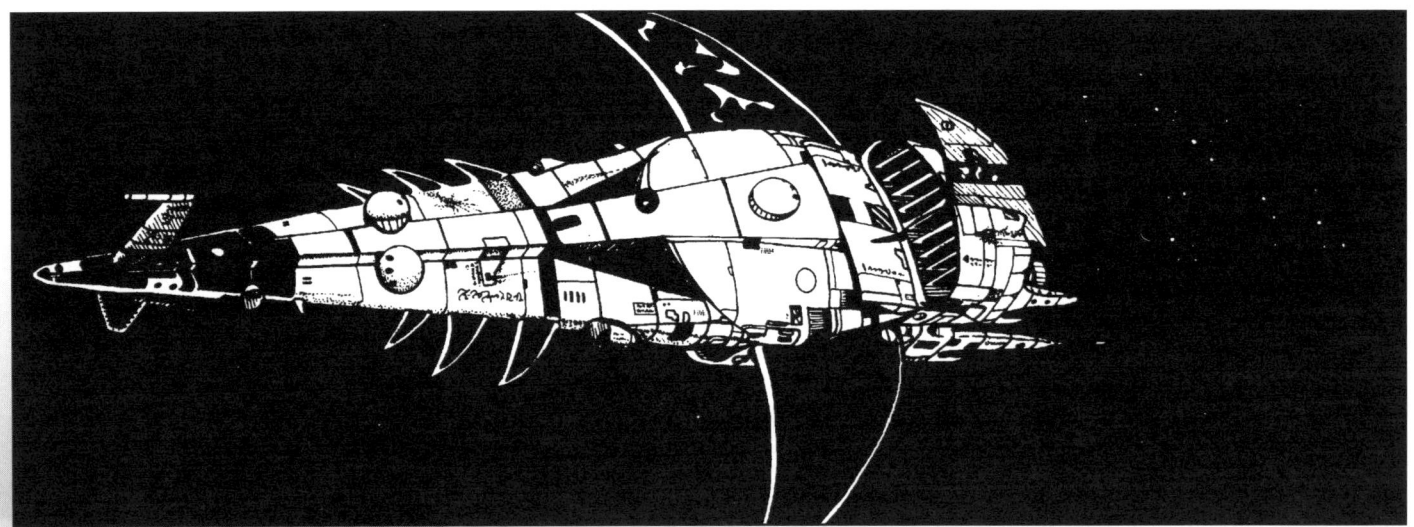

Vargr Campaigns (220 to 348): The series of wars, encounters, conflicts, and disputes between the Imperium and the various Vargr states in Vland, Corridor, and Deneb sectors along the coreward edge of the Imperium.

As the Imperium expanded, it initially recruited worlds which were former members of the Second and First Imperiums. As its borders reached still farther, the Imperial expansion met already established Vargr states of varying sizes. The Imperium struggled for over a century to secure its territory against the Vargr; the inevitable series of conflicts which resulted are collectively called the Vargr Campaigns.

Vargr Extents: The territory dominated by Vargr governments. The term Vargr Extents refers to those sectors with major Vargr populations. Extents are situated roughly coreward of the Imperium and especially coreward of the Spinward Marches, Deneb, Corridor, and Vland sectors. See *GURPS Traveller Behind the Claw* and *Alien Races 1*.

Vegan: An intelligent race originating on Muan Gwi (Solomani Rim/Vega 1717 A456A86-F) and inhabiting the Vegan Autonomous District; they are named by Humans after the bright star near their home-world.

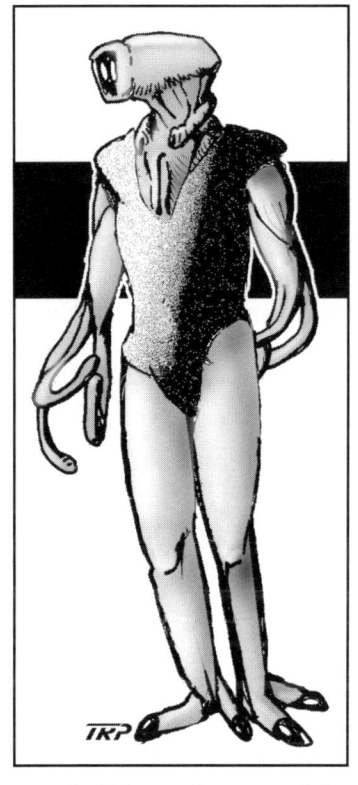

General: Vegans are upright, bipedal, and bilaterally symmetrical, and they average 7′2″ in height. They are bisexual, homeothermic oxygen breathers with an average life span of more than 200 years. Because of their low-gravity origin, they are physically quite weak and are unable to live on high-gravity worlds.

The head serves both as braincase and as sensory appendage. Auditory organs are located in the collar-like structure around the neck. Despite external appearances to the contrary, Vegans have two eyes located inside the hood-like fleshy structure which dominates the head.

The paired eyes are covered by a transparent eyelid-like structure, which acts as a polarized light filter. This structure protects the eyes from glare, like built-in sunglasses, and also serves to keep windblown dust out of the eyes. This filter can be retracted when not needed. The eyes themselves are large and pick up radiation well into the infrared portion of the spectrum, an adaptation to Muan Gwi's small red sun. Since the skull is fixed solidly in place, a Vegan cannot turn its head, but the fleshy hood containing the eyes can turn through a large arc.

The mouth is a vertical slit in the upper thoracic region with paired breathing/vocal slits on either side of it. Two mandibles are located inside the upper chest, and they grind food between their opposing sets of teeth.

Where the forearm and hand would be on a Human, Vegans have three tentacles, which serve them as manipulative organs. Their legs end in broad, splayed feet, which prevent them from sinking into the soft sand.

The urogenital opening is a vertical slit located ventrally in the lower abdomen. There are no external differences between sexes.

Vegans have a number of adaptations to the arid dry region of Muan Gwi where they developed. Their tall, thin bodies are designed for maximum radiation of heat. The torso is covered with a thick integument. Its convoluted surface is richly supplied with blood vessels.

Epithets

Most sentient creatures assign nicknames for other races – derogatory epithets, mere vulgarisms, or attempts at humor. The examples below are translated into Anglic for clarity.

Imperial Nicknames for Zhodani: "Joes," "Zhos," "Joe Danny," "Sike" (or "Psike," referring to the fact that many Zhodani are trained psionics).

Zhodani Nicknames for Imperials: "Buzz," "dead-head," "blockhead" (a reference to the repression of psi powers within the Imperium).

Human Nicknames for Vargr: These aim at their perceived speech patterns, and include "Snarl," "Gral," and "barker." The ultimate insult, however, is "doggie."

Vargr Nicknames for Humans: The Vargr tend to refer to the color of human skin ("pinkie," "brown-hide"), to the human's relative lack of hair ("baldy") or to the peculiar odor of humans ("stinker").

Sword Worlders: The immensely proud Sword Worlders expect to be addressed as "Sir" or "Madame." A powerful insult, when it can be gotten away with, is to omit the use of any honorific, especially with officials. Similarly, an easy way to ingratiate oneself with a Sword Worlder is to adopt an attitude of deference; even an extreme or satiric pose ("Most Esteemed, Most Highly Evolved Sir . . .") will be mistaken by some Sword Worlders for sincerity. But many Sword Worlders have caught on to the trick over the years . . . and they have retained a dueling culture.

Other Times, Other Places

The vast background history of the *Traveller* universe provides many eras for adventuring, but this book is limited to just one – the year 1120. Some GMs, however, will undoubtedly find that this setting places too many restrictions on the types of campaigns they wish to run, but will still want to use the *Traveller* background as inspiration. Several options are open.

The Beginning: Many GMs are attracted to campaigns set in the first few decades of the Third Imperium, under the reigns of the two Cleons and Artemsus. This is a time of rebuilding, expansion, exploration, and recontact after a period of chaos and barbarism, with many opportunities for the aspiring empire-builder.

This is the time period covered by *Traveller, 4th Edition* in the 20+ published books produced by Imperium Games. It will require very little effort on the part of the GM to convert this material to *GURPS*, since the adventures and campaign materials are usable independently of the rules system.

Interstellar Wars: Another popular period is the time of the first contact between the Terrans and the decadent Vilani Empire, around the 24th century. The "explosion" of the Terrans onto the interstellar stage provides an excellent backdrop for adventure. However, no material on this period has been published as yet, which means that GMs will have to create their own.

By increasing or decreasing the supply of blood to the integument, heat radiation from the torso can be regulated to optimum effect (more during the day, less at night). This arrangement obviates the necessity for sweating and its consequent water loss. All orifices of the body can be sealed to prevent unnecessary moisture loss.

History: The Vegans received the jump drive about -6000 from Vilani-influenced traders, and they colonized several nearby worlds before being absorbed by the First Imperium in -4404. They were severely restricted under Vilani rule, as were all races who resisted being integrated into the rigid Vilani culture. Because of this, they welcomed Terran victory in the Interstellar Wars and the advent of the Rule of Man.

The Vegan Polity prospered under the Rule of Man and survived the Long Night largely intact. With the advent of the Third Imperium, the Vegan area was broken into individual planetary states in accord with Imperial policy; non-Humans were treated as full citizens, but – in order to cement Imperial authority – no multiworld governmental units were allowed.

Under the Solomani, the Vegans were again restricted. Human colonies were founded on many Vegan worlds to maintain Solomani influence there, and Solomani governors were installed on all Vegan worlds. After the Solomani Rim War, the present Vegan Autonomous District was formed as a counterweight to the Solomani.

Society: Vegan society is divided into hundreds of different *tuhuir,* which might be roughly translated as culture, philosophy, or tao. Each *tuhuir* has its own customs and traditions and its own interpretation of the proper way to live. The civil service which governs the Vegan District is a *tuhuir* which oversees and mediates among all the other *tuhuir.* Although rare, heretical and rebellious *tuhuir* do exist.

Archeology shows that the *tuhuir* were once separate societies and each was associated with a particular geographic location, like countries on ancient Earth. Now, however, they are mixed together in complex patterns.

Tuhuir are not hereditary; when a Vegan nears sexual maturity, he enters a period of search which may last for many years. Eventually, the individual chooses a *tuhuir;* once made, the choice is for life. In practice, about 50% of all Vegans enter the *tuhuir* of their parents (the exact percentage varies with each *tuhuir);* about 0.5% find that they enjoy the search as a way of life and never join a *tuhuir.*

Vegan Autonomous District: After the hard-fought victory over the Solomani at Terra in 1002, the Imperium found that it could not completely conquer and absorb the rest of the Solomani Sphere. The Imperial high command decided to create the Vegan Autonomous District to act as a counterweight to the remnants of the Solomani Confederation. The Vegans have complete internal control over their district, but free passage is guaranteed for Imperial citizens and goods.

Although many factors have contributed to the present peace and stability along the Solomani Rim, it cannot be denied that the creation of the Vegan Autonomous District has achieved its original purpose.

The worlds of the Vegan Autonomous District are under a single, centralized government. State power is contained in a civil service and is chosen and promoted by competitive examinations.

Vilani: Human major race (*H. sapiens*) which developed on Vland from Human stock placed there by the Ancients.

History: The world of Vland, while possessed of a hospitable environment, boasted an alien ecology based on its own independently evolved biology, a biology that produced proteins, sugars, and amino acids that were difficult for Humans to digest and metabolize. The Humans could not use most local plant and animal life for food without considerable modification.

One of the oldest occupations in Vilani society is that of *shugilii* (which translates roughly as "miller"). The *shugilii* was a person who could transform raw food into edible food through special aging and chemical treatment. The *shugilii* task was more akin to shaman or witch doctor than cook. Since much food on Vland was inedible without some treatment, *shugilii* were powerful members of society.

The alienness of Vland was reciprocal. Humans were unsuitable as food for predators. Parasites and bacteria could not infect the Human system. Even most viruses were unable to invade and take over Human cells. Consequently, the primitive Human society found little need for medically oriented shamans. Vilani medical and biological science was very slow to develop because of this.

Vilani legends are full of accounts of the wars of the gods, terrible destruction, and occasional intervention in Human affairs by the gods. Legends exist of early explorers who found lands with great living stone-metal gods possessed of immense magical powers and immortality. Modern archeologists now believe these "gods" were actually great robot warriors and juggernauts used by the Ancients in their final war. Apparently, the last of these machines finally ran down circa -20,000.

Society: Early Vilani society was dominated by three groups: the *shugiliis*, the aristocrats, and the merchants. Aristocrats were the natural leaders of society, the *shugiliis* were the all-important food processors, and the merchants controlled trade.

With the flowering of Vilani society (circa -11,000) and its attendant industrial revolution, each of these three forces gained power rather than lost it; each participated in the creation of the industrialized wealth of Vland.

A Matter of Taste

While awaiting dinner, I was served a Vilani beer, which is something every gourmet should experience once. It was very dark, but not completely opaque. Light passed through it in a very diffused manner. The head was small, but persistent, and the aroma was heavy, yeasty, and faintly reminiscent of newly baked rye bread on Terra, with subtle hints of spices and seasonings that I cannot describe.

My first sip convinced me that I had been given water drained from aging sweatsocks. I thought for a moment it was a joke until I noticed my hosts swigging theirs with gusto.

– Kinmon Denisovitch, "An Innocent on Vland"

Vilani Conservatism

Q: How many Vilani does it take to change a lightbulb?

A: Six. One from the ladder carriers' guild of the maintenance bureau to bring the ladder in and set it up, one from the ladder holders' guild of the same bureau to steady the ladder once it is set up, one from the clerks' guild of the government bureau to make sure the proper forms are filled out for changing light bulbs and to pay the proper fee to the energy bureau, one from the lightbulb-changers' guild of the energy bureau to change the bulb, one from the wick-trimmers' guild because it is traditional, and one from the supervisors' guild because his presence is required by law whenever five or more workers are engaged in the same task.

When the Vilani first encountered the Terrans (now called Solomani), one of the chief surprises for the Vilani was the rapid pace of Terran technological change. Research was undertaken for its own sake, discoveries made as a result of that research, inventions devised based on those discoveries, and society changed by those inventions – all in a mere heartbeat as far as the Vilani were concerned. Why are the Vilani so slow compared to the Terrans, when both races originated from the same stock?

The most common theory holds that their distrust of innovation and technology stems from a dimly held prehistoric memory of conditions on Vland. Many scientists believe that a substantial number of Ancient war robots roamed Vland, fighting each other on behalf of a dead race for many centuries after the last of the Ancients had been destroyed. Until the power sources of these machines were exhausted, the Vilani led a shadowy existence in the hills, mountains, and jungles where the machines could not travel, developing civilization only after the last of the machines went silent. Technology is inherently chaotic, reasoned the early Vilani, and must be carefully controlled or it will destroy itself and everything else with it.

On a primitive world where interesting gadgetry lay everywhere (and could easily destroy the one who played with it, and all his family, too), and where even experimenting with a new food item was gambling your life, it's possible that the desire for innovation was literally bred out of the Vilani!

In -9235 the Vilani made their ultimate breakthrough – one that would assure their ascendance for the next 6,000 years. A research team working on the fringes of the Vland system created the first working prototype jump drive and demonstrated its effects.

The Vilani found intelligent life forms on other worlds within 60 parsecs of Vland. None of the races had progressed enough to have begun interstellar travel. The Vilani found it easy to dominate these less technically advanced races. The Vilani were able to impose their culture and law; however, the Vilani conquered through economic subjection rather than by military means.

As their sphere of influence was expanding, the Vilani found it difficult to maintain control across such great distances with jump-1 as their maximum rate of travel and communication. At the same time, each of the three power classes of Vilani society found itself threatened by the forces around it. Three bureaux were established, each independent of the other two, and each assigned a territory among the stars for which it was responsible. Each of the three bureaux was effectively identical, but they initially espoused different philosophies, based on their origins. The bureaux maintained their own governments within their territories.

Sharurshid, originating within the merchant class, emphasized interstellar trade. Makhidkarun, originating with the aristocracy, emphasized interstellar government. Naasirka, originating with the *shugiliis*, floundered after it found that it could not control food supplies on most of the worlds it dealt with, but it ultimately became a broad-line organization which emphasized energy, transport, and luxury goods.

In -5430, the Vilani finally invented the jump-2 drive. No other race had jump-2, and the Vilani maintained their monopoly by jealously guarding its secrets from all subject races. Beginning in -5400, a series of wars to subjugate the resisting fringe cultures was waged. This period of consolidation wars lasted until -4045.

Grand Empire of Stars: In -4045, the ruling Vilani council, the Igsiirdi, declared the Grand Empire of the Stars, or in the Vilani tongue, the *Ziru Sirka*. The Vilani calendar starts from this date.

At first, the empire had no emperor. Within 10 years, the chairman of the Igsiirdi (elected for life by the council) was the *Ishimkarun* – the "Shadow Emperor." He ruled through published proclamations, but never appeared in public. In -3610, the Shadow Emperor became the Emperor of the Stars, who was the absolute monarch of the empire. Successors were elected from the Igsiirdi upon the death of the old emperor.

For nearly 1,200 years the Grand Empire of the Stars kept the peace among its star-spanning population. However, the empire insisted on cultural rigidity. Exploration was stopped by -4000. Scientific research was controlled and then stopped altogether by -3800.

The beginning of the end of Vilani domination was signaled by the contact with the Terrans in -2422. By -2408 the Terrans and the Vilani were at war; by -2219 the Terrans had surpassed the Vilani technologically and were marching through the cities of Vland as conquerors, and the Grand Empire of the Stars was at an end.

Currently, Vilani is a cultural rather than a racial or national labeling, and it is applied to those within the Imperium who retain some of the old ways. Dialects of the old High Vilani language survive in certain places, along with a few fragments of Vilani culture, such as musical forms and other fine arts.

Certain of the old Vilani noble families have maintained more of the old culture, particularly the families who control the Vilani megacorporations. Some Imperial officials wonder how much of the old Vilani agenda they retain as well.

Vilani Calendar: The Vilani calendar is based on the period of Vland (the Vilani homeworld) around Urakkalan, its star. The Vilani *gurkala* (year) is 478.72 standard days in length.

See also *Vland, First Imperium,* and the *Concise History of the Ziru Sirka* sidebars on pp. 33, 42, 47, 49, 56, and 58.

Vland (Vland/Vland 1717 A967A9A-F): Homeworld of the Vilani, former capital of the Vilani Imperium, current capital of the Vland sector. Vland remains a major trade and cultural center for the Imperial core/spinward regions.

Vland, Domain of: A domain of the Third Imperium, consisting of the Corridor, Vland, Gushemege, and Dagudashag sectors.

W

War: Major violent conflict between nations, megacorporations, or races. See *Good War/Bad War, Imperial Rules of War.*

Way Station: Link in the express boat network. The way station is a large (for the Scout Service) base devoted to the overhaul and refit of express boats at points in their journeys. During a normal tour of duty, an express boat will jump from system to system, and occasionally change pilots, but steadily work its way farther and farther down the line. At each stop (Xboat station), the Xboat is routinely checked, refuelled, reprovisioned, and sometimes recrewed. Ultimately, however, it must undergo maintenance and possible repair after the rigors of its mission. The way station performs this function.

Way stations have repair and maintenance equipment, as well as trained staffs of service personnel. They are the equivalent of naval bases, although they are capable of servicing only smaller tonnage ships (10,000 tons and less).

See **GURPS Traveller First In**.

Vilani Names

Names for those of Vilani ancestry will of course be in Vilani. Space does not permit a full discussion of Vilani naming practices – simply pick a personal name and a family name from the list below.

Vilani Personal Names

The most common male personal names are: Adkhar, Eneri, Enli, Ganidiirsi (short form Gani), Shannash, Mazun, and Khugi, although they are not the only ones by any means.

The most common female personal names are: Gamaagin (short form Gam), Nashu, Sharikkamur (short form Sharik), Shana, Iikush, Mususup; again, these are not the only ones.

Vilani Family Names

Vilani family names are like their Solomani counterparts, in that most of them have their origins in occupations long past.

Aadkashli	Kigiisii
Aakmir	Kiigashshiim
Aardashpiur	Kiirumim
Aershugginkh	Lagkhuundaa
Akis	Lanashraa
Ama	Laragii
Anshii	Linkirgir
Aru	Linuuksa
Ashi	Lishenii
Ashran	Maarera
Bamasmur	Maariishe
Biisana	Maasaaru
Dargiimkam	Madkashgerg
Dashkhur	Makrus
Digeruu	Menkiin
Direma	Miigakl
Dshurkemshirp	Mimrak
Durashnish	Mirakru
Durirrii	Mirgakre
Ekiir	Murnas
Enleshkaadshar	Mushiiru
Gaakshirum	Namiirna
Gaarirra	Nirkra
Gaarrasa	Numar
Ganaare	Nurashu
Ganaran	Riisha
Garshansem	Rishar
Gashkhimkl	Sagaruu
Gemana	Sargkham
Giinshiirnir	Shaarshiim
Giirdudshamsher	Shaim
Gimmini	Sharama
Iiken	Shasharshi
Ilgud	Shashiig
Imgbukkhlum	Shemi
Inshard	Shgapgunshusgis
Irkirkhaamn	Shimannii
Kakaakam	Shirika
Kakarku	Shirrushi
Kamsash	Shmeshkdumshir
Karise	Shumim
Kdgergadm	Shumma
Kerana	Shuramshi
Khaasira	Siikuna
Khamkharlamdd	Uamdar
Khemiris	Uddenkhadsg
Khiikanu	Umrunkkir
Khiishimshu	Zisduurkhaar

Low Passage

This is the fiscal and social equivalent of traveling steerage on a 19th century passenger liner. Low passengers spend the entire trip in suspended animation, and thus have no life-support requirements other than a trickle of power to run the low berth (see p. 108). Low passage normally costs Cr175 per jump, regardless of the number of parsecs traveled.

On larger passenger vessels, a ship's medical officer puts people into low berths and revives them at the end of the voyage. On smaller vessels, where stewards (with or without medical training) see to low passengers, there is a chance of death upon revival.

The Low Lottery: This last has led to a form of gambling on some vessels called the "Low Lottery," where crewmembers place small wagers on how many low passenger will not survive the trip. The winner receives all the wagers; if there is no winner, the prize rolls over to the next trip. By custom, the person actually "freezing and thawing" the low passengers is forbidden from betting, for obvious reasons. It is considered bad taste to mention the low lottery to the passengers themselves, but seasoned travelers will know of the custom, and sometimes place bets of their own.

Middle Passage

Middle passage is a step up from low passage, and is substantially more expensive (Cr1,750 per jump, again regardless of the number of parsecs traveled). On large passenger liners, middle- and high-passenger staterooms are segregated on different decks, each with separate lounge areas, galleys, and so on. Smaller vessels often mix the two types of passengers on the same level.

Aside from the bridge, the cargo deck, and engineering, passengers are normally allowed the run of the ship during the week in jump, although smaller vessels encourage them to remain in their staterooms or in the passenger lounge. Food service is provided as part of the passage, and is served in the lounge.

High Passage

High passage is more expensive than middle passage, and is virtually identical except for a higher standard of service and food. On large liners, high passengers have their own decks, lounges, and food service. Some ships give high passengers larger, more luxurious staterooms. On smaller ships, the main difference is in the quality of food and the behavior of the stewards. High passage normally costs Cr3,500 per jump, regardless of parsecs traveled.

Xboat: See *Express Boats* and *GURPS Traveller First In*.

Xboat Station: Facility for handling Xboats at a star system. At each system served by the Xboat network, an express boat station is maintained to handle the message traffic and to manage incoming and outgoing Xboats.

Usually located near the edge of a star system, the station picks up messages beamed to it by incoming Xboats and relays the data to the local world for delivery. Messages destined for worlds farther down the line are transmitted to a waiting Xboat which then jumps for the next world in the network.

The Xboat station contains receiving and retransmission equipment; refueling and support facilities for the local staff and waiting crew are also provided. The Xboat station maintains a local office on the system's major world for the acceptance of Xboat messages, as well as to handle delivery of the messages to addresses on the world.

Year Zero: The base year of the Imperial calendar and the founding year of the Third Imperium. By selecting a base year numbered 0 (instead of the generally selected year 1), the Imperial dating system became a standard number line extending forward and backward in time.

Years before the founding of the Imperium become simple negative numbers, and the differences between dates before and after the founding of the Imperium can be determined by simple subtraction.

Z

Zhdant (Zhdant 2719 A6547C8-F): Capital of the Zhodani Consulate and homeworld of the Zhodani people. Unlike the capitals of other empires, Zhdant is largely divided into the estates of the members of the ruling Zhodani council, which makes the world's population unusually low. Zhdant is often spelled "Zhodane" in Anglic texts.

Also see *GURPS Traveller Alien Races 1*.

Zhodani: Human major race (*H. zhdotlas*) inhabiting the Zhodani Consulate, a region far spinward of the Imperium.

The Zhodani are a branch of Humaniti similar in most respects to other Human races. In general, they tend to be taller than Solomani or Vilani and lithe of build. Their most important difference is the acceptance and use of psionics.

Society: Zhodani society is divided into three classes: nobles, intendants, and proles. Nobles are the enfranchised ruling class, and they receive psionic training from childhood. Intendants are managers and administrators of society, and they also receive early psionic training. Proles constitute the masses; they are forbidden the use of psionics and do not receive training.

Within this rigid class system exist two opportunities for promotion to a higher class. All prole children are tested for psionic potential, and those showing high scores are taken from their families and adopted into the intendant class. Intendants are rewarded for great diligence, service to the state, or victory in the psionic games through the granting of noble titles.

The presence of psionics in the hands of those in power means that many aspects of society work at high efficiency. Psychology, behavioral science, com-

munications science, and education are more refined and exact than in other societies. Educational methods are finely tuned and capable of teaching concepts rapidly and accurately. Mental deviance or criminal tendencies can be detected early and corrected with facility.

Zhodani society is generally a happy one. Individuals are members of a functioning whole, and each makes a contribution to its success. The relative lack of upward mobility for the proles is offset by the possibility for their children to move upward if they have the proper potential. The burden of responsibility imposed on the intendants is lightened by the ever-present possibility of reward through elevation to the noble classes. The nobles themselves temper their burden of authority with comfort derived from their station in life.

Morality: The Zhodani have a general distaste for other Human races which do not practice psionics. Effective indoctrination and the ever-present possibility that one's mind is being read have removed dishonesty and deviance as common features of society. The *Tavrchedl'* (Thought Police) are a special branch of the government who are charged with maintaining right thought in the population.

Imperial citizens have a strong distaste for the Zhodani. Because the Zhodani practice psionics, an Imperial cannot be sure that a Zhodani is not invading his mental privacy at any time. Imperials feel exposed and uncomfortable when they are knowingly in the presence of Zhodani.

Because of their psionic abilities, the Zhodani have the most effective authoritarian rule in history. Imperial citizens, who are used to a great degree of local autonomy, fear Zhodani conquest because of the loss of freedom they believe it would entail.

Government: The Zhodani consulate is a participatory democracy in which only nobles are allowed to vote. Executive and judicial functions are the responsibility of a series of councils of varying sizes. Each council elects one of its number as executive officer and a number of its members as delegates to the next higher council.

A city, for example, will elect several of its council members to be representatives to the world council. The process continues upward through several layers of councils to the overall Grand Council of the Zhodani. Nominally, each member of a council serves for one olympiad (three Zhodani years), but in practice, each councilor serves until his replacement arrives and replaces him officially, or until word of his reelection to another term is received. Oftentimes, the district from which a councilor is elected will have only his relatives as voters, and his reelection is virtually assured.

Standard practice (when possible) calls for Zhodani councils to submit important questions to a plebiscite of those affected. The principle can be suspended where immediate action is required, but the official ordering the action stands responsible to the voters and must justify his actions as soon as possible.

Supreme executive power is vested in three consuls; one is elected each year for a term of one olympiad by and from the members of the Grand Council. No consul may be elected twice in succession, and retired consuls become life members of the Grand Council.

Zhodani-Imperial Relations

The history of Zhodani-Imperial relations has been a stormy one. Five major wars and many small conflicts have broken out in the 1,020 years since the two cultures made contact, and the political situation has always been tense.

The primary bone of contention has been the Spinward Marches, or, more properly, Imperial expansionism into that region. The Consulate stabilized itself at its present size around -1000. The Zhodani believe that their polity has reached its optimum size, and feel no current need for further territory When the Imperium entered the Spinward Marches, the Zhodani did not respond immediately, as a few settlers posed no significant threat. As the years passed, however, and the expansionist intent of the Imperium became clear, the Zhodani (and their Vargr allies) responded with what is now seen as a preemptive war to throw the Imperial timetable off-balance (the First Frontier War of 589-604). The Imperium won the war, but instead of taking advantage of his victory at the front, Imperial Admiral Olav hault-Plankwell took his fleet to Capital, assassinated Empress Jaqueline, and seized the throne. The resulting chaos and civil war effectively stalled Imperial expansion Spinward.

There is no evidence that hault-Plankwell intended to cause a civil war, or that he was intentionally furthering Zhodani political aims, but the results were certainly in Zhodani favor. The fact that the Zhodani did not take advantage of the civil war to expand into the Spinward is clear evidence that they had no territorial ambitions in the region.

Zhodani aims in the Second Frontier War (615-620) are more of a mystery. The Zhodani and Vargr attacked, the Imperial Navy under Admiral Arbellatra responded, and the Imperium was once again triumphant. Did the Zhodani see in Arbellatra a future empire builder, one whose aspirations needed to be deflected? There is no evidence Arbellatra intended to set up her own empire in the Spinward and expand into the Zhodani Consulate, but like Admiral hault-Plankwell a generation earlier, she moved to Capital and took over, first as regent, then as empress. What were Zhodani intentions? We do not know, but the result was a lengthy period of peace (albeit an uneasy one).

The peace was broken in 979 when the Zhodani/Vargr coalition (by then known as the Outworld Coalition) attacked once again. The war continued for six years, and ended in an armistice, but the allegations of Imperial incompetence brought about the abdication of Styryx in 989.

Continued on next page . . .

The Fourth Frontier War (1082-1084) was also inconclusive, though the Imperium claims to have won on the basis of its victory at the Battle of Two Suns. The Fifth (and last) Frontier War, (1107-1110), again brought no territorial changes.

Viewed from an expansionist perspective, the continual Zhodani aggressions have been singularly unsuccessful. However, it would seem that the Zhodani have succeeded admirably well in keeping the Imperium away from their borders. Is this what was intended all along?

Imperiallines

Imperiallines is a tramp-freighter operator with trade stations located at many type III starports throughout the Spinward Marches. The company maintains a low profile as the operator of a fleet of jump-2 Frontier Transports carrying cargo from outlying systems to the major trade route worlds.

The company operates elsewhere in the Imperium (under a variety of names), always using the *TI*-class Frontier Transport – and a smaller fleet of secret *TJ*-class transports. Ships of the *TJ* class are designed to be externally identical, but capable of jump-6 instead of only jump-2. *TJ*s can carry cargo, passengers, and electronic messages.

History: The Zhodani date their empire from the traditional date of the first organized use of psionics on Zhodane, -6731 Imperial, the year of the first olympiad. They achieved jump drive about 1,300 years later, in -5415 Imperial.

The expansion of the Zhodani was gradual and uneventful. Although some states on the fringe resisted absorption into the Consulate, most were annexed peacefully. The Zhodani first came into conflict with the Third Imperium in the 500s, which started the First Frontier War in a dispute over present and future limits to settlement in the Spinward Marches area. Frontier wars over the next 600 years have failed to resolve the basic differences between the two empires.

Zhodani Calendar: The Zhodani calendar is based on the period of Zhdant (the Zhodani homeworld) around Pliebr, its star. The Zhodani *chten* (year) is 275.19 standard days in length. Zhodani dating uses three *chten* called the *thequzdij* (olympiad). A Zhodani date is written as olympiad.year. For example, 3173.1 is the first year of the 3,173rd olympiad.

See also *Zhdant* and **GURPS Traveller Alien Races 1**.

For Game Masters Only

The following sections are intended for the eyes of Game Masters only, as they contain information not generally known to the populace of the Imperium in general, or (in some cases) known only to GMs.

THE MYSTERY OF THE ANCIENTS

Who or what were the Ancients? The Ancient "race" started with one individual specimen, a Droyne who found he had remarkable mental and psionic powers. This individual, who calls himself "Grandfather," is still alive today, hiding out in his own private "pocket universe."

Grandfather was an incredible specimen of an otherwise fairly ordinary intelligent race. His psionic powers enabled him to regenerate any damage, including that leading to normal aging, which rendered him virtually immortal. His mental prowess, on the other hand, fueled a burning curiosity for anything and everything that he could learn.

He started researching, but realized that he needed competent assistants. He tried to fulfill this need in three different ways. The first method was that of procreation: Grandfather sired 20 children, each of whom had 20 children of their own, all nearly as intelligent as Grandfather. With 420 offspring, Grandfather decided he had enough and stopped.

His second method was to experiment with other species of life. In his attempt to find good help, he carried Humans from Terra to many other worlds in this part of the galaxy. He and his descendants also experimented with Terran canine stock, and genetically created intelligence in the race now known as the Vargr.

Last, Grandfather created a number of different models of super-intelligent robots to assist him in his research. Only this last method proved successful, with living beings proving to be unreliable.

Grandfather assigned research projects to each of his children and grandchildren, and progress was rapid, with many new discoveries made by the teams of scientists on their various worlds. Grandfather, basking in the light of this success, decided to take a vacation, and traveled about Droyne space seeing all that there was to see.

When he finished with this vacation, he decided to explore the remaining frontiers of existence. He called all of his children to come and help him, but they had started on their own projects and were too busy to show up.

Grandfather started his work anyway, but he soon found that his children's experiments interfered with his own. His decision to have children long ago was an error, he realized, and now he must rectify it. He began a campaign to eliminate all of his offspring.

The children found out about his campaign and resisted. The war of Grandfather against his children was a long and complicated one. Initially, his opponents did not understand that he meant to totally eliminate them; later, they adopted his tactics of total destruction.

The war went on for 2,000 years. Staggering weapons were used, including planet-busters, nova triggers, bombardment with asteroids, and such ordinary weapons as tailored plagues, poison gas, and nuclear devices.

The war ended when Grandfather had destroyed all of his children (he kept careful count). The galaxy was somewhat the worse for wear; it had many new asteroid belts and quite a few ravaged worlds.

Grandfather determined that he would, in the future, limit himself to more easily controlled assistants. He improved on the robots he had built before, and constructed a corps of robots and androids to help him in his experiments. Then he pinched off a pocket universe around his base world and retreated there to pursue his studies unhindered by the concerns of the larger universe.

Who in the Imperium today knows these facts? No one knows them all, but there are a few scattered sophontologists who have come to the conclusion that the Droyne are the modern-day descendants of the Ancients, and they are somehow not as intelligent as the earlier race. The fact that the "Ancients" still exist (in the form of Grandfather) is not known by anyone except Game Masters.

See *Andory, Chirpers, Church of the Chosen Ones, Droyne, Solomani Hypothesis, Vargr, Major Races (Solomani/Vilani/Zhodani, Vargr, Hiver, K'kree, Aslan,* and *Droyne*).

LONGBOW II

The Library Data entry is correct, although incomplete. A more ambitious project, Longbow II, based on the lessons learned from the first Longbow, was begun under Strephon's direction in 1103. This project will use the entire width of the Imperium as its long baseline. With its sensor termini located in the Spinward Marches and Antares Sectors, in resolution but not sensitivity, Longbow II replicates a passive sensor dish with a diameter of 160 parsecs (about 18 trillion miles), sensitive in all electronic bands, from gamma and X-rays down through visible light and infrared all the way to long-wavelength radio. Longbow II will be able to achieve a theoretical resolution of 0.0196 inches at a range of 8,000 parsecs, the distance to the galactic core.

Unlike the original Longbow with its disk-shaped receiver providing two-dimensional resolution (width and length), Longbow II's long baseline will lie only in the width dimension, along the galactic plane. This means that this spectacular theoretical resolution will be only in width, not height. Longbow II data will be collected at all of the listening points along the "bowline" and carried by jump-6 Imperiallines (see p. 80) couriers to its "focal point" at Depot/Lishun, where the data will be synchronized (by such methods as pulsar emissions within in the common field of view of all the sensors), compiled, filtered, and enhanced by lengthy and demanding computer runs.

The calibration of such a complicated system is a massive undertaking. It will probably be decades before meaningful observations of the galactic core can be extracted from the raw data. The existence of Longbow II is not openly acknowledged, and it will be described only as a top secret communications project if it must be discussed at all. The Longbow data and all analysis of it has one of the highest security classifications in the Imperium.

Secrets

From the beginning, *Traveller* was a game of secrets. One of the rewards for adventuring was not an increasing pile of gold coins, but knowledge of the universe. One of the first secrets, revealed slowly, over the course of several adventures, was the flow of events leading to the Fifth Frontier War (see p. 32), which took place as the game timeline slowly advanced. Another secret was the true nature of the Ancients, the who and why behind Humaniti's distribution among the stars. We have another one building in *GURPS Traveller*, but you'll have to wait to find out what it is going to be . . .

There is a problem with secrets in RPGs, however. If you tell anybody, it is not a secret anymore, but it is rather hard to tell just GMs (who really need to know such things) without also telling their players (who need to puzzle secrets out over the passage of time). No matter how well the GM strives to keep players in the dark, they all find out eventually.

So what's the solution? Create your own secrets. It's your campaign, and if every one of your players owns the books and knows that Grandfather still lives in his own little pocket universe, you make that fact the red herring, the false lead, and come up with something else equally exciting, but at the same time something that resides in your head alone.

CHAPTER THREE

Characters

Careers

In the original *Traveller*, a character's pre-game career greatly shaped him. *Classic Traveller* offered six careers (Navy, Marines, Army, Scouts, Merchants, and Other). This grew to 18 types in *Megatraveller* and 40 in *Traveller the New Era*. Careers limited the skills a character could acquire, and helped generate a background story. Certain careers gave benefits upon leaving them.

The career templates in this chapter are optional, but usage is strongly recommended to maintain the flavor of *Traveller*.

Tech Levels

The Imperium's base TL is 10. In *GURPS*, people from worlds with lower TL should take Primitive (p. B26). Those with higher-TL backgrounds should take High Technology (p. CI26).

Classic *Traveller* did not distinguish between TL backgrounds once characters began adventuring. First edition *GURPS Traveller* "fudged" similarly, mentioning Primitive but not High Technology. Therefore, GMs would be justified in adjusting High Technology's cost – but this second edition will assume a full 20 points for TL11 characters and 50 points for TL12.

These high costs help explain why TL10 equipment is the standard. TL12 goods may be relatively common and cheap; TL12 technicians and operators are neither. See *Technical Difficulties*, p. 108.

The advanced wealth rules (p. 83) can help offset High Technology's cost.

Characters in *GURPS Traveller* will emerge from two backgrounds. Some will be created directly for *GURPS Traveller*, using *GURPS Basic Set* and the notes in this chapter. Others will be converted from pre-existing campaigns in a previous version of *Traveller*. The latter process is discussed in *Character Conversions*, pp. 124-129.

CREATING A CHARACTER

The GM should have access to the *GURPS Basic Set* and (optimally) to *Compendium I*. The discussion below is for Solomani (p. 75) and Vilani (p. 60) Humans, and applies to both unless otherwise noted.

The Vargr and Zhodani are dealt with briefly in sidebars in this chapter, and in more detail in the *Alien Races 1* sourcebook. The sidebar information should be sufficient for GMs to explore the two races as NPC characters.

GURPS Traveller is designed for 150-point starting characters. This allows a "standard" 100-point character with a TL12 background, a standard TL10 PC with a nice ship, an elite background such as Imperial Marine commando with a few points to spare, or plenty of room for unique concepts.

Basic Attributes

The Solomani and Vilani both possess the normal Human attributes defined by *GURPS*. The normal limitations apply to characters from these races – no more than 100 points in attributes, no more than 40 points of disadvantages, and no more than 5 quirks at -1 point each.

Minor Human races may have small (or even radical) differences in their racial template at the GM's discretion.

Physical Appearance

Physical appearance follows the standard guidelines on p. B15. Solomani run the full panoply of appearances as on 20th-century Earth. Vilani racial appearance (hair, eyes, skin color, etc.) has the same extremes as Solomani – their differences are primarily cultural and social. For all physical purposes, Vilani and Solomani are the same (Vilani tend to be a few pounds heavier for a given height).

Careers

Careers are presented as templates, beginning on p. 86. *GURPS Traveller* pre-game careers don't generate service histories or carry the risk of death as in classic *Traveller* character generation. Players should create their own service history. Those who miss the other feature may roll 1 die. On a 1 or 2, crumple up your character sheet and start over.

Wealth

Average starting wealth is Cr15,000.

For more advanced economics, adjust average starting wealth for the character's TL, per p. T:FT48. TL0 is Cr150, TL1 Cr250, TL2 Cr350, TL3 Cr500, TL4 Cr1,000, TL5 Cr1,500, TL6 Cr2,500, TL7 Cr3,750, TL8 Cr6,000, TL9 Cr10,000, TL10 Cr15,000, TL11 Cr25,000, and TL12 Cr50,000. The GM could rule this a one-time penalty/bonus for Primitive and High Technology respectively, or actually charge for starting-wealth adjustments per p. T:FT100.

For more starting-wealth options, including an ownership stake in a starship, see *GURPS Traveller Far Trader*. Controlling interest – though not ownership – in a starship is discussed in *Ship Patron*, pp. 84-85.

Status

Status roughly equates with the Social Standing characteristic of *Traveller*.

STATUS AND COST OF LIVING

Level	Status	Monthly Cost of Living
8	Emperor/Empress	nil
7	Archduke/Archduchess	Cr50,000+
6	Duke/Duchess	Cr30,000
5	Marquis/Marchioness	Cr15,000
4	Count/Countess, High Official	Cr8,000
3	Baron/Baroness, Middle Official	Cr4,000
2	Knight/Dame, Low Official	Cr2,000
1	Doctor, Industrialist, etc.	Cr1,000
0	Average Individual	Cr500
-1	Poor, Non-Citizens, etc.	Cr200
-2	Beggar, Known Outlaw, etc.	Cr100

Players purchasing high Status can assume it includes the noble title indicated on the table, should they so choose at character creation.

Reputation

Reputations tend to be campaign-specific, and need be crafted in consultation with the Game Master.

Vargr

The wolflike Vargr (see p. 71) are found throughout known space. Vargr make good player characters. Enthusiastic, curious, egotistical, and quick, they are natural scouts or pilots.

Vargr average 4″ shorter than a Human of the same ST, and weigh proportionately less. Their hearing is in a higher range than that of Humans.

Attributes

ST -1 [-10]; DX +1 [10]. Vargr are significantly smaller than men, but have faster reflexes on the average.

Advantages

Acute Taste/Smell +3 [6]; Acute Vision +1 [2]; Alertness +1 [5]; Claws [15]; Enhanced Move 1 (doubles Move, with the limitation that running fatigue starts applying after 5 seconds, -30%) [7]; Fur [4]; and Teeth (1d+1 bite in close combat) [5].

Disadvantages

Cannot Kick [-5]. Their digitigrade posture probibits Vargr from kicking in close combat (except stamping on prone foes). This disadvantage was set at -5 points, offsetting the cost of their Teeth.

Chummy [-5]. The Vargr retain a certain "pack mentality," and are happiest in groups . . . not necessarily just groups of Vargr, but any group they have come to consider trustworthy

Curious [-5]. Even more than Humans, a Vargr will go out of his way to investigate new things. This is one reason their race is so widespread.

Easy to Read [-10]. Vargr society is far more open than that of Humans; disguising their feelings is quite alien to them. Emotional signs (posture, facial expression, ruffled fur) are obvious even to Humans . . . especially since Vargr are descended from earthly canines, and humans have been reading their dogs' body language (and vice versa) for millennia.

Proud [-1]. Vargr are always concerned with their own status within their individual group, and with their group's status in society. They are also quick to take offense at racial slights.

Reduced Fatigue -1 [-3].

Reduced Hit Points -1 [-5].

Reputation -2 (Flaky, easily swayed, potentially even disloyal) [-10].

Special Effects

Reaction bonuses and penalties for Charisma are doubled with Vargr. Success or failure at important tasks will affect a Vargr's self-esteem much more than they would a Human's, and Vargr self-esteem is contagious, especially to other Vargr! This can justify a Vargr buying added levels of Charisma (or giving them up) during play.

See *GURPS Traveller Alien Races 1* for more information.

Zhodani

Zhodani (see p. 78) are thought of by most Imperials as tall, swarthy, frightening mind-readers, by many as the enemy (and may have Social Stigma or a Secret because of it).

Zhodani are standard Humans, and are built as Human characters with only a few changes. The most important is height. Calculate a Zho's height normally for his ST; then figure weight from that height; then go back and add 7″ (!!) to height. They are lithe and slender, but not skinny.

Zhodani tend toward darker skin, eye, and hair colors, with less variation than the Solomani, but all skin and hair colors are known. They have 28 teeth instead of 32.

In the Zhodani Consulate, Status 2 is a prerequisite for psionics (if you don't have it before your talent is discovered, you get it immediately), but you may buy psionic skills without any Unusual Background. (Campaigns in the Imperium follow the rules as given under *Psionics*, even for Zhodani characters.)

Almost all Zhodani will have Honesty and Truthfulness, unless renegades or officials dealing routinely with non-Zhodani.

See *GURPS Traveller Alien Races 1* for more information.

New Advantage: Ship Patron

Your former service (or some patron appropriate to your past) gave you the use of a ship. You don't own it (the patron does), and you must pay for all expenses, but it's yours to do as you please. The patron *must* make sense with respect to your background. Usually this means a former employer.

Cost depends on the ship and terms of control. A basic ship – jump-1 with fuel for 1 jump, either streamlined or with a ship's vehicle, with up to 1 G acceleration – costs 10 points. To this, add:

■ If the ship can carry jump fuel sufficient for more than 1 parsec (regardless of how many jumps it takes):

Fuel Cap. in Parsecs	Cost
2	+5
3	+10
4	+13
5	+15
6	+16
7	+17

■ In addition, add +3 points for each jump-drive level after jump-1.
■ Add +1 for each +0.5 Gs acceleration after 1 G, rounding down. Figure this with total loaded mass (see p. 158) assuming 5 tons per cargo space. (Sample ships list this as their Accel.)

Continued on next page . . .

ADVANTAGES, DISADVANTAGES, AND QUIRKS

The universe is a vast, often unusual place. Most advantages, disadvantages, and quirks have their place somewhere in the Imperium. Those that don't:

Literacy is assumed for citizens of *Traveller*'s empires; therefore it costs no points. Barbarian sorts and others may take Illiteracy as a disadvantage.

Magic only manifests in the superior technology left behind by the Ancients, so Magic Aptitude, Magic Resistance, and most mystical advantages and disadvantages have no place in Traveller.

Military Rank applies to those currently serving in a military. Those with Imperial military experience should take the appropriate Courtesy Rank (p. CI23), though the GM may rule it isn't mandatory. ("I never mention that I used to be *Captain* Blugh, because I don't want people to recall the *De'stre A'toll* incident.")

Bionics are very rare, and subject to considerable social stigma in the Imperium, especially if unconcealed. Medical replacements that do not enhance function are tolerated, especially if cosmetically concealed.

Skills

Some GMs may wish to restrict certain skills (and advantages such as Jack-of-All-Trades, p. 125) to certain careers. This is in keeping with the original game.

Psionics

Psionics face a Social Stigma through most of the Imperium (see *Psionics* and related subjects on p. 54). A 10-point Unusual Background is required to buy psionic powers and skills. In general, enhancements are not allowed without GM approval; limitations are common. The specific powers and skills available – and their further restrictions – are detailed below.

Psionics Institute: Upgrading to a 15-point Unusual Background will also give the psi access to a Psionics Institute. Other psionics must hunt for one . . . and the GM may rule they must pay the extra 5 points if they establish a stable, long-term patronage once one's found.

Psionic Training: Characters who have not undergone training at a Psionics Institute may only purchase latent powers: All skills can be bought at Power 1 only, and are unreliable (per the sidebar on p. B176). A teacher must be had to buy off a power's unreliability and to learn any new skill. Generally, instruction can only be found at a Psionics Institute, though the GM may allow for lone masters willing to take on a new student.

Telepathy: The skills of Mind Shield, Life Detection (see p. T:AI137), Emotion Sense, Telereceive, Telesend, Mental Blow, and Mental Stab may be acquired.

ESP: Clairvoyance, Clairaudience, and Seekersense skills may be acquired.

Psychokinesis: The skills of Levitation and Telekinesis may be acquired.

Teleportation: The skills of Autoteleport and Exoteleport may be acquired with restrictions. The -50% limitation that objects retain orientation and speed is mandatory. The "carry nothing and arrive nude" -50% limitation is an option. Exoteleport must include the -40% limitation, "only to carry along more weight

- If both the ship and one of its vehicles can land on planet surfaces: +2.
- Four low berths: +1.
- Additional low berths: +1 point for each 20, round down.
- Fuel processors: +2.
- One armed turret: +5.
- Each additional armed turret: +2.
- Cargo capacity: +1 for every 3 spaces, round down. Count empty turrets here (3 spaces per turret, or +1 apiece).
- Staterooms, if ship suitable for commercial passenger service: +1 per 2 staterooms after the first 3.

Terms of control vary. The one universal constraint is that the ship can't be legally sold; a small duty usually is attached as well for 0 points. A more serious Duty (on 9 or less) is worth -5 points. A mercantile patron will share in any profits, giving -1 point for every 5% taken. See p. T:FT p. 102 for more ideas.

Some patrons will pay for crew salaries, maintenance, or upkeep, or some combination thereof. The GM should add to Ship Patron cost depending on the value of this support, generally between +2 (free fuel) to +25 (all expenses on a large ship).

For full or partial ownership of a starship, see Ship Owner, p. T:FT 101.

Scout Ship   24/28 points
Imperial Interstellar Scout Service veterans (p. 99) with at least 12 years' service may receive a 100-ton *Sulieman*-class scout/courier as a mustering-out benefit. Just like the user, the ship is subject to recall to active service at the discretion of the IISS; the user must therefore inform the IISS of their location each time they enter a starport. This reduces ship cost by -5 points. The ship is not fitted suitably for commercial passenger service. The ships are issued unarmed (24 points), but weaponry may be installed (+4 points).

Free Trader   36+ points
A company may hand over an older ship to a former employee with at least 12 years' experience. (Note that most *current* employees have little say in their ship's operations, so rarely pay for it with Ship Patron.) This *Beowulf*-class free trader's cost is reduced -5 by its mix of patron profit-taking and upkeep. Add +1 to cost if an air/raft is carried; +4 to arm one turret; +5 to arm both.

Yacht   33+ points
Those with Status 3+ may be given a 200-ton *Vanderbilt*-class yacht as a personal interstellar transport. The staterooms are not set up for commercial service. Add +4 to arm one turret, +5 to arm both. If the patron pays all (routine!) expenses, +10.

---

with Autoteleport." GMs may wish to implement the ruling that failure at Exoteleport still deposits the psi at the destination, but without clothing or equipment. Teleportation over any significant distance on a planetary surface carries other risks (as noted by Larry Niven in his SF collection *All the Myriad Ways*). Teleportation on a world's surface is limited to 300 miles or less. Teleportation from 30 to 300 miles carries with it great risk of disorientation: -6 to Body Sense rolls. For distances of from 3 to 30 miles roll at -4, under 3 miles -2, and under 300 yards roll vs. Body Sense skill normally.

Teleportation at ranges greater than 300 miles is not allowed because of the problems of conservation of momentum. The potential injury is huge; a teleport traveling from sea level at Earth's equator to sea level at one of the poles would arrive with a total velocity over 1,000 mph different from that of the ground at his destination. Changes in altitude (and any other changes in gravitational potential) will result in potential energy changes, manifesting themselves in changes in body temperature. Teleports who lose altitude will increase body temperature; teleports who gain altitude will lose body temperature. Teleports may not make altitude changes of more than 400 yards in one jump, and cumulative jumps of more than 600 yards up or down per hour may not be undertaken without death or serious brain damage.

Healing: The "self-only" limitation is mandatory. All skills except Sense Aura are available.

CHARACTER TEMPLATES

A character template is a list of attributes, advantages, disadvantages, and skills that a player can use in order to quickly build a specific type of character without neglecting important abilities or getting bogged down in the rules. The point costs of these abilities are listed, and the sum is given as the "template cost." The player pays this cost, specifies the options he wants, writes those abilities down on his character sheet, and spends his remaining points to customize his character (see below).

Templates are never required – they simply purchase many abilities at once, have no in-play effects, and offer no "package discount." **GURPS Traveller** GMs may require them, because they can emulate the semi-limited character generation that provided part of classic **Traveller**'s flavor. If not required, templates can be treated as nothing more than recommendations, exactly like those listed in the *Character Types* sections of other **GURPS** books.

Skills

In the templates in this section, *primary skills* are skills that are absolutely required, *secondary skills* are helpful skills that it's hard to imagine the character not having, and *background skills* are skills chosen for descriptive reasons rather than utility. Skills are listed in the following format:

Skill Name *(Difficulty)* Relative Level **[Point Cost]**-Actual Level

Customizing Templates

Once the template has been purchased, the player must customize it by spending any remaining character points. The template does not influence how these points are spent. If the template has fewer disadvantages than the campaign permits, more may be taken, giving extra points to spend.

Quirks are rarely listed on templates, and are always optional; they should be selected by the player.

Altering Templates

Templates are *guidelines,* not rules. When customizing a template, the player is free to alter any or all of the items that came with it. Subtracting items from a professional template may result in a character who will be regarded as incompetent by his peers, however.

Character Templates vs. Racial Templates

Character templates are *not* the same thing as racial templates, such as the Vargr template on p. 83. Racial templates use attribute modifiers instead of attribute levels, may include advantages unavailable on a less-than-racial basis, and include disadvantages that don't count against the campaign disadvantage limit.

When using character templates with other races, simply add or subtract any racial attribute modifiers from the template's attribute levels.

Letters of Marque

Letters of Marque and Reprisal (to give them their full name) are documents by which a government authorizes private persons to fit out armed vessels and seize civilian shipping belonging to that government's enemy. Such vessels are known as privateers. They are legally distinguishable from pirates in that they operate under color of authority, and operate only against a specified foe. The value of a letter of marque is twofold. It usually entitles you to use (non-secret) military bases, though not without paying for what you receive. And it keeps you from being executed out of hand if you're caught by the foe . . . if, that is, he recognizes your letter as authority to make war on him!

Historically, a government issues letters of marque when it needs a fleet of commerce raiders and doesn't have the time or money to create it. A privateer is even better than a mercenary, because the privateer doesn't have to be paid; he just keeps what he takes from your foes! The problem with privateers is that they often get out of hand, embarrassing the nation that "authorized" them. (On the other hand, a privateer may be scrupulous about following the laws and courtesies of war, just to build up a good reputation against the day he needs mercy from his foes.)

A true letter of marque, if issued in a form likely to be respected by its foes, can be considered a form of Patronage: a single powerful patron, whose assistance is sometimes available, worth 10 points. The Imperium has not issued a true letter of marque for many, many generations. However, some surrounding governments still do. And, outside Imperial borders, some megacorps issue letters of marque against their rivals!

The Imperium does, very occasionally, hire private warships to suppress pirates or smugglers, in times and places where its own forces are stretched thin. This would represent Legal Enforcement Powers (p. B21) worth 15 points.

The Extremely Hazardous Duty (p. CI78) to go a-privateering could be the condition under which a Ship Patron offers you a vessel! This will *reduce* the cost of a ship by 20 points.

ATHLETE   90 POINTS

A former professional athlete, in whatever sport the player chooses. For whatever reason, he has retired – perhaps he suffered an injury, ran afoul of professional gamblers, or grew bored with his former occupation.

Attributes: ST 12 [20], DX 12 [20], IQ 10 [0], HT 12 [20].

Advantages: A total of 20 points in Ambidexterity [10]; Double-Jointed [5]; Extra Fatigue [3/level]; Fit or Very Fit [5 or 15]; High Pain Threshold [10]; Rapid Healing [5]; Reputation (Famous athlete) [varies]; Toughness (DR 1) [10]; Wealth [10 or 20]; and +1 ST, DX, or HT [10].

Disadvantages: A total of -20 points chosen from Bad Back [-15]; Code of Honor (Sportsmanship) [-5]; Compulsive Gambling [-5 to -15]; Enemy (Gamblers, 6 or less) [-10]; Greed [-15]; Jealousy [-10]; Overconfidence or Glory Hound [-10 or -15]; Selfish [-5]; and Sense of Duty (Anyone on his "team") [-5].

Primary Skills: Tournament Law (sport) (M/E) IQ+2 [4]-12, plus any one of Bicycling or Swimming, both (P/E) DX+4 [16]-16; Boxing, Fencing Sport, Sports (any), or Wrestling, all (P/A) DX+3 [16]-15; Judo Sport, Karate Sport, Skating, or Skiing, all (P/H) DX+2 [16]-14; and Lifting (P/H; ST) ST+2 [16]-14 or Running (P/H; HT) HT+2 [16]-14.

Secondary Skills: A total of 6 points in any of the above and any of Jumping (P/E); Climbing or Dancing, both (P/A); Hiking (P/A; HT); and Acrobatics or Throwing, both (P/H).

Background Skills: A total of 4 points in any of Acting, Gambling, Intimidation, or Leadership, all (M/A); Sex Appeal (M/A; HT); and Carousing (P/A; HT).

Customization Notes: A "star" athlete should consider spending most of his remaining points to boost an Athletic skill, ST, or DX up to a very high level. He should also use at least some of his designated advantage points to buy a Reputation. Note that it's rare for athletes to be cross-trained in many disciplines.

ATTORNEY   60 POINTS

A lawyer. Perhaps not the most appealing character from a roleplaying standpoint, but one which can have certain advantages in some kinds of campaigns.

Attributes: ST 10 [0], DX 10 [0], IQ 13 [30], HT 10 [0].

Advantages: Comfortable Wealth [10] and 10 points chosen from among Charisma [5/level]; Sanctity [5]; Single-Minded [5]; Status 1 [5]; Voice [10]; and more Wealth [10].

Disadvantages: A total of -20 points in Bully [-10]; Code of Honor (Professional ethics) [-5]; Compulsive Lying [-15]; Greed [-15]; Honesty [-10]; Odious Personal Habits ("Pedantic," "Shameless," etc.) [-5 to -15]; Overweight [-5]; Reputation (Lawyer) [-5]; Secret (Dishonest) [-10]; Sense of Duty (Clients) [-5]; and Workaholic [-5].

Primary Skills: Law (M/H) IQ+3 [10]-16; Research (M/A) IQ+2 [6]-15; and one of Bard (M/A) IQ+2 [6]-15, Diplomacy (M/H) IQ+1 [6]-14, or Fast-Talk (M/A) IQ+2 [6]-15.

Secondary Skills: Administration (M/A) IQ-1 [1]-12 and Writing (M/A) IQ-1 [1]-12.

Background Skills: A total of 6 points in Criminology, Interrogation, Intimidation, or Politics, all (M/A); Accounting, Detect Lies, or Psychology, all (M/H); and improved levels with any of the other skills on this template.

Customization Notes: Pick a specialty and choose your skills to reflect this. E.g., a corporate lawyer is likely to have Accounting and extra points in Administration, while a district attorney is more likely to have a very high level in Politics. A successful attorney of any kind will spend some of his remaining points on Reputation and additional Wealth.

BARBARIAN   50 POINTS

This template represents a standard fixture of science fiction: a character from a primitive world, forced to cope with things beyond his ken. He's not stupid; he's just unacquainted with life in a technological society.

Attributes: ST 11 [10], DX 12 [20], IQ 10 [0], HT 11 [10].

Advantages: A total of 10 points chosen from Alertness [5/level]; Animal Empathy [5]; Fit [5]; Immunity to Disease [10]; Night Vision [10]; Pitiable [5]; Plant Empathy [5]; Rapid Healing [5]; and Resistant to Poison [5].

Disadvantages: Primitive (-4 TLs) [-20]; plus another -15 points in Confused [-10]; Curious [-5 to -15]; Gullibility [-10]; Innumerate [-5]; Non-Iconographic [-10]; Semi-Literacy [-5] or Illiteracy [-10]; Social Stigma (Barbarian) [-15]; Space Sickness [-10]; Technophobia [-15]; Uneducated [-5]; and more levels of Primitive [-5/level].

Primary Skills: Survival (any) (M/A) IQ+2 [6]-12; 10 points in low-tech Combat/Weapon skills (Bow, Brawling, Broadsword, etc.) and one of Hiking (P/A; HT) HT+1 [4]-12, Riding (P/A) DX+1 [4]-13, or Running (P/H; HT) HT [4]-11.

Secondary Skills: Camouflage (M/E) IQ+1 [2]-11; Cooking (M/E) IQ+1 [2]-11; Stealth (P/A) DX [2]-12; Swimming (P/E) DX [1]-12; and Tracking (M/A) IQ+1 [4]-11.

Background Skills: A total of 4 points in Animal Guise (M/A), Animal Handling (M/H), Climbing (P/A), Fishing (M/E), and Mimicry (any) (P/H; HT).

Customization Notes: If enough skills are taken, it will probably be more efficient to raise DX or IQ by one or more levels. This is in keeping with the archetype: SF barbarians always seem to catch on fast!

BELTER   75 POINTS

Belters are rude, crude, rough-and-tumble space prospectors who hunt among the tumbling rocks of the asteroid belt, looking for the strike that will make them rich and let them retire. Some tire of the quest and take up other pursuits.

Attributes: ST 11 [10], DX 12 [20], IQ 12 [20], HT 10 [0].

Advantages: A total of 20 points in 3D Spatial Sense [10]; Alcohol Tolerance [5]; Alertness [5/level]; Fit [5]; G-Experience [10]; Improved G-Tolerance [5 or 10]; Intuition [15]; Light Hangover or No Hangover [2 or 5]; and Luck [15].

Disadvantages: A total of -20 points in Alcoholism [-15]; Compulsive Carousing [-5]; Compulsive Gambling [-5 to -15]; Greed [-15]; Lecherousness [-15]; Loner [-5]; Obsession (Finding the big strike) [-5]; Odious Personal Habits ("Doesn't wash," "Foul mouth," etc.) [-5 to -15]; and Social Disease [-5].

Primary Skills: Area Knowledge (Belt) (M/E) IQ+2 [4]-14; Engineer (Mining) (M/H) IQ [4]-12; Free Fall (P/A) DX [2]-12; Geology (M/H) IQ [4]-12; Navigation (M/H) IQ [4]-12; and Prospecting (M/A) IQ [2]-12.

Secondary Skills: Astrogation (M/A) IQ-1 [1]-11; Piloting (Starship) (P/A) DX-1 [1]-11; and Vacc Suit (M/A) IQ-1 [1]-11.

Background Skills: A total of 2 points in Cartography, Gambling, Merchant, or Planetology (Rock/Ice), all (M/A); and Brawling (P/E) and Carousing (P/A; HT).

Customization Notes: Long-time belters should spend some additional points on higher levels in Free Fall and Vacc Suit. A successful belter might actually have some Wealth! Since belters spend a lot of time in space and live in cramped quarters, neither Claustrophobia nor Space Sickness is appropriate.

BOUNTY HUNTER   65 POINTS

A bounty hunter makes his living finding people who don't want to be found: bail jumpers, escaped criminals, merchants who "skip out" on scheduled starship payments, and fugitives of all kinds. The hunter takes custody of the fugitive and escorts him to the nearest legal authority.

Attributes: ST 11 [10], DX 12 [20], IQ 12 [20], HT 10 [0].

Advantages: Legal Enforcement Powers (Bounty-hunter's license) [5], plus 15 points chosen from Acute Senses (any) [2/level]; Alertness [5/level]; Combat Reflexes [15]; Contact (Police; skill-15, 9 or less, usually reliable) [4]; Intuition [15]; Reputation [varies]; and Single-Minded [5].

Disadvantages: A total of -20 points chosen from Bully [-10]; Callous [-6]; Delusion ("I'm a cop!") [-5 to -15]; Enemy (Rival or escaped criminal, 6 or less) [-2] or (9 or less) [-5]; Greed [-15]; Honesty [-10]; Intolerance (Crooks) [-5]; No Sense of Humor [-10]; Reputation [varies]; and Stubbornness [-5].

Primary Skills: Area Knowledge (any) (M/E) IQ [1]-12; two of Interrogation, Research, or Streetwise, all (M/A) IQ [2]-12; one of Beam Weapons (any) or Guns (any), both (P/E) DX+2 [1]-14*; and a total of 3 points in Blackjack (P/E), Brawling (P/E), Judo (P/H), and Wrestling (P/A).

* Includes +2 for IQ.

Secondary Skills: Stealth (P/A) DX-1 [1]-11; one of Detect Lies (M/H) IQ-2 [1]-10 or Intimidation (M/A) IQ-1 [1]-11; and one of Shadowing or Tracking, both (M/A) IQ-1 [1]-11.

Background Skills: A total of 3 points in Criminology, Fast-Talk, Gambling, or Holdout, all (M/A); as well as Fast-Draw (any) (P/E) and Carousing (P/A; HT).

Customization Notes: A bounty hunter can be an honest "free-lance cop" or a low-life who is no better than those he hunts; consider spending some points on skills from the Law Enforcer (p. 94) or Rogue (p. 98) template, respectively. Successful bounty hunters may also want to spend a few points on Wealth.

BUREAUCRAT   50 POINTS

Paper-pushers sometimes leave their jobs to take up the traveling lifestyle. There are many reasons for this, most of them involving boredom and the lack of a sense of purpose. Bureaucrats are invaluable in certain situations; i.e., anything involving paperwork.

Attributes: ST 10 [0], DX 10 [0], IQ 13 [30], HT 10 [0].

Advantages: A total of 20 points in Administrative Rank [5/level]; Common Sense [10]; Imperturbable or Unfazeable [10 or 15]; Security Clearance 1-2 [2/level]; Single-Minded [5]; and Wealth [10 or 20].

Disadvantages: A total of -20 points chosen from Bad Sight (Correctable) [-10]; Cowardice [-10]; Hidebound [-5]; Honesty [-10]; Incurious or Obdurate [-5 or -10]; No Sense of Humor [-10]; Odious Personal Habits ("Boring," "Officious," etc.) [-5 to -15]; Overweight or Skinny [-5]; Stubbornness [-5]; Unattractive (Geeky) [-5]; Unfit [-5]; and Workaholic [-5].

Primary Skills: Administration (M/A) IQ+2 [6]-15.

Secondary Skills: Computer Operation (M/E) IQ [1]-13; Research (M/A) IQ+1 [4]-14; Speed-Reading (M/A) IQ-1 [1]-12; and Writing (M/A) IQ-1 [1]-12.

Background Skills: A total of 7 points in Savoir-Faire (Servant) (M/E); Politics (M/A); Accounting, Law, or Diplomacy, all (M/H); and Typing (P/E).

Customization Notes: Choose your background skills to reflect your former job; e.g., a civil servant might have Politics and Savoir-Faire (Servant), an accountant should have Accounting, and a low-level secretary would have Savoir-Faire (Servant) and Typing.

COMPUTER TECHNICIAN   60 POINTS

Another character with a variety of reasons for traveling, ranging from ennui to pursuing enemies. Computer technicians have many skills of immediate value, but most are light on combat skills and reflexes, and need backup in tense situations.

Attributes: ST 10 [0], DX 10 [0], IQ 14 [45], HT 10 [0].

Advantages: A total of 15 points chosen from Claim to Hospitality (Contacts on the net) [1 to 10]; Less Sleep [3/level]; Lightning Calculator [5]; Mathematical Ability [10]; Security Clearance 1-2 [2/level]; Versatile [5]; and Zeroed [10].

Disadvantages: A total of -20 points in Addiction (Stimulants) [-5]; Bad Sight (Correctable) [-10]; Clueless [-10]; Curious [-5 to -15]; Delusions ("Computers are people," "The net is real life," etc.) [-5 to -15]; Klutz [-5]; Low Empathy [-15]; Oblivious [-3]; Overweight or Skinny [-5]; Shyness [-5 to -15]; Unattractive (Geeky) [-5]; and Unfit [-5].

Primary Skills: Area Knowledge (Net) (M/E) IQ [1]-14; Computer Operation (M/E) IQ+1 [2]-15; Computer Programming (M/H) IQ [4]-14; and Electronics Operation (Computers) (M/A) IQ [2]-14.

Secondary Skills: Computer Hacking (M/VH) IQ-1 [4]-13; Electronics (Computers) (M/H) IQ-1 [2]-13; Mathematics (M/H) IQ-2 [1]-12; and Research (M/A) IQ-1 [1]-13.

Background Skills: A total of 3 points in Administration or Hobby (Computer Games), both (M/A); and Artificial Intelligence or Cryptanalysis, both (M/H). Note that hobby skills are taken at half price; see p. B54.

Customization Notes: This template is intentionally on the cinematic side to make it interesting. This can be taken even further (if the GM permits) by adding Neural Cyberdeck Interface [20 to 30] and Cyberdeck Operation (M/VH).

CORSAIR   75 POINTS

There is a certain romance in vicarious law-breaking, hence the rather romantic term "corsair." Call them what you will, these people are *pirates* (although those who operate under a Letter of Marque, p. 86, are more correctly called "privateers").

Note: Piracy is hotly debated among *Traveller* fans. Decisions over the long-term viability of piracy in a given campaign rest with the GM and players.

Attributes: ST 11 [10], DX 12 [20], IQ 12 [20], HT 11 [10].

Advantages: A total of 20 points in 3D Spatial Sense [10]; Alcohol Tolerance [5]; Ally Group (2-5 75-point pirates, 9 or less) [10]; Charisma [5/level]; Combat Reflexes [15]; Contact (Military; skill-18, 9 or less, somewhat reliable) [3]; Daredevil [15]; Fearlessness [2/level]; G-Experience [10]; Light Hangover or No Hangover [2 or 5]; Luck [15]; and Zeroed [10].

Disadvantages: Enemy (Imperium, 6 or less) [-20]; and -15 points chosen from Alcoholism [-15]; Bad Temper [-10]; Callous [-6]; Code of Honor (Pirate's) [-5]; Compulsive Carousing [-5]; Compulsive Gambling [-5 to -15]; Greed [-15]; Laziness [-10]; Reputation [varies]; Selfish [-5]; and Trademark [-1 to -15].

Primary Skills: Either Beam Weapons (any) or Guns (any), both (P/E) DX+3 [2]-15*; and Intimidation (M/A) IQ+2 [6]-14.

Secondary Skills: Free Fall (P/A) DX [2]-12 and Vacc Suit (M/A) IQ [2]-12, plus any two of these 6 options:

1. Astrogation (M/A) IQ [2]-12 and Piloting (Starship) (P/A) DX+1 [4]-13.

2. Armoury (Spaceship weaponry) (M/A) IQ [2]-12 and Gunner (any ship-mounted) (P/A) DX+3 [4]-15*.

3. Engineer (Vehicles) (M/H) IQ [4]-12 and Mechanic (any) (M/A) IQ [2]-12.

4. Electronics Operation (Comm) (M/A) IQ [2]-12 and Traffic Analysis (M/H) IQ [4]-12.

5. Electronics Operation (Sensors) (M/A) IQ [2]-12 and SIGINT Collection/Jamming (M/H) IQ [4]-12.

6. Leadership (M/A) IQ [2]-12 and Tactics (M/H) IQ [4]-12.

* Includes +2 for IQ.

Background Skills: A total of 6 points in Area Knowledge (System) (M/E); Electronics Operation (Security Systems), Gambling, Heraldry (Ship's markings), or Streetwise, all (M/A); Brawling or Knife, both (P/E); Shortsword (P/A); and Carousing (P/A; HT).

Customization Notes: Choose secondary skills to reflect your specialties: (1) pilot, (2) gunner, (3) engineer, (4) comm, (5) sensors/ECM, and (6) captain. Two choices are required because most pirate crews are small and experience heavy attrition.

DIPLOMAT   80 POINTS

The problem with being an ex-diplomat is that no one you run into is *quite* willing to believe you're retired. Are you the former under-assistant trade attaché to Regina, or are you really a spy? Nevertheless, diplomats have a wide variety of useful skills.

Attributes: ST 10 [0], DX 10 [0], IQ 13 [30], HT 10 [0].

Advantages: A total of 30 points in Administrative Rank [5/level]; Alternate Identity [15]; Legal Immunity [5 to 20] (20 points is Diplomatic Immunity); Patron (Agency, 6 or less) [15]; Security Clearance [2/level]; Status 1-4 [5/level]; and Wealth [10 or 20]; plus 10 more points in Acute Hearing [2/level]; Charisma [5/level]; Fashion Sense [5]; Language Talent [2/level]; Sanctity [5]; and Voice [10].

Disadvantages: A total of -20 points chosen from Duties [-2 to -15]; Enemy (Rivals, enemy agents, etc.; 6 or less) [-10]; Fanaticism (National or political cause) [-15]; Overconfidence or Glory Hound [-10 or -15]; Secret (Spy) [-5 to -20]; and Sense of Duty (Nation, planet, or system) [-10].

Primary Skills: Administration (M/A) IQ [2]-13; Bard (M/A) IQ [2]-13; Diplomacy (M/H) IQ+2 [8]-15; Savoir-Faire (M/E) IQ [1]-13; and a M/A language at IQ [2].

Secondary Skills: Politics (M/A) IQ-1 [1]-12; Research (M/A) IQ-1 [1]-12; and Writing (M/A) IQ-1 [1]-12; one of Acting or Fast-Talk, both (M/A) IQ-1 [1]-12; one of Detect Lies or Psychology, both (M/H) IQ-1 [2]-12; one of Economics, History, Intelligence Analysis, or Law, all (M/H) IQ-1 [2]-12.

Background Skills: A total of 7 points in Chess (M/E); Disguise, Holdout, Lip Reading, or Photography, all (M/A); Beam Weapons (any) or Guns (any), both (P/E); Fencing (P/A); and Carousing (P/A; HT).

Customization Notes: Choose an agency, planet, political cause, etc., and build your character around it . . . or the goal of destroying it! Pick options that suit an archetype: Diplomatic Immunity, Law, and Chess for a top-hat-wearing traditionalist; Alternate Identity, Intelligence Analysis, and Guns for a spy, etc.

ENGINEER   60 POINTS

In the days of steam-powered surface ships, the engineering crews were known as "black gangs" because the coal dust and smoke turned their uniforms black. Engineers still have a tendency to get dirty, even though they deal with liquid hydrogen instead of coal.

Attributes: ST 10 [0], DX 10 [0], IQ 13 [30], HT 10 [0].

Advantages: A total of 15 points in Double-Jointed [5]; G-Experience [10]; Lightning Calculator [5]; Manual Dexterity [3/level]; Mathematical Ability [10]; Temperature Tolerance 1-2 [1 or 2]; and Versatile [5].

Disadvantages: A total of -15 points chosen from Curious [-5 to -15]; Delusion ("The engines have feelings!") [-5]; Duty (As crewman) [-2 to -15]; Loner [-5]; Odious Personal Habit ("Dirty") [-5]; Sense of Duty (Ship) [-5]; Stubbornness [-5]; and Workaholic [-5].

Primary Skills: Engineer (Vehicles) (M/H) IQ [4]-13; Mechanic (J-Drive) (M/A) IQ+1 [4]-14; Mechanic (M-Drive) (M/A) IQ+1 [4]-14; and Mechanic (Power Reactor) (M/A) IQ+1 [4]-14.

Secondary Skills: Computer Operation (M/E) IQ-1 [½]-12; Free Fall (P/A) DX+2 [8]-12; Mathematics (M/H) IQ-1 [2]-12; Scrounging (M/E) IQ-1 [½]-12; and Vacc Suit (M/A) IQ-1 [1]-12.

Background Skills: Any two of Armoury (Spaceship armor), Armoury (Spaceship weaponry), Electronics Operation (any), Mechanic (other), or Shipbuilding (Starship), all (M/A) IQ-1 [1]-12; or Electronics (any), Engineer (other) or Photonics (any), all (M/H) IQ-2 [1]-11.

Customization Notes: Consider spending a few points on additional technical skills such as Mechanic (Robotics) or Engineer (Electrical). In a larger-than-life game, the GM may also permit Gadgeteer [25]. High Technology is essential for servicing TL11 or TL12 equipment. Finally, an engineer should never have Technophobia unless he acquired it after beginning his career!

ENTERTAINER   80 POINTS

The entertainer-turned-traveler can be useful to a group with more than gunfights on their agenda. Depending on specific talents and local tastes, entertainers are often more able to earn pocket change than many other spacefarers.

Attributes: ST 10 [0], DX 12 [20], IQ 12 [20], HT 11 [10].

Advantages: A total of 20 points chosen from Appearance [5 or 15]; Charisma [5/level]; Empathy [15]; Fashion Sense [5]; Luck [15]; Manual Dexterity [3/level]; Musical Ability [1/level]; Rapier Wit* [5]; Reputation [varies]; Versatile [5]; Voice [10], and Wealth [10 or 20].

  *With GM's permission!

Disadvantages: A total of -20 points chosen from Chummy or Gregarious [-5 or -10]; Compulsive Carousing [-5]; Jealousy [-10]; Lecherousness [-15]; Overconfidence or Glory Hound [-10 or -15]; Poverty [-10 or -15]; and Trademark [-1 to -15].

Primary Skills: Any two of Acting, Bard, or Performance, all (M/A) IQ+3 [8]-15; Musical Instrument (any) (M/H) IQ+2 [8]-14; Singing (P/E; HT) HT+3 [8]-14 or Dancing (P/A) DX+2 [8]-14.

Secondary Skills: Any two of Musical Notation (M/E) IQ+2 [4]-14; Poetry or Snake Charming, both (M/A) IQ+1 [4]-13; Musical Composition or Ventriloquism, both (M/H) IQ [4]-12; Juggling (P/E) DX+2 [4]-14; Fire Eating or Stage Combat, both (P/A) DX+1 [4]-13; Acrobatics or Sleight of Hand, both (P/H) DX [4]-12; or a total of 8 points in any of the primary skills.

Background Skills: A total of 6 points in Make-Up or Savoir-Faire, both (M/E); Scene Design, Video Production, or Writing, all (M/A); Sex Appeal (M/A; HT); Fireworks (M/H); and Carousing (P/A; HT).

Customization Notes: Choose a profession and pick your skills accordingly; e.g., a traveling vaudeville performer might take Acrobatics-12 [4]; Dancing-14 [8]; Juggling-14 [4]; Make-Up-13 [2]; Scene Design-13 [4]; and Singing-14 [8]; while a classy opera star is more likely to have Performance-15 [8]; Savoir-Faire-15 [6]; and Singing-15 [16].

Entertainers who know Leadership (M/A) at 12+ can also learn Choreography (M/A) (requires Dancing at 12+), Conducting (M/A) (requires two Musical Instrument skills at 12+), Directing (M/H) (requires Performance at 12+), or Fight Choreography (M/A) (requires Stage Combat at 12+).

FARMER   25 POINTS

Another classic sci-fi character: the bucolic youth infected with wanderlust who leaves his backwater world and becomes caught up in the excitement of interstellar adventure. He can bring either youthful enthusiasm or comic relief, depending on the situation.

Attributes: ST 11 [10], DX 10 [0], IQ 10 [0], HT 11 [10].

Advantages: A total of 15 points chosen from Animal Empathy [5]; Common Sense [10]; Extra Fatigue 1-3 [3/level]; Fit [5]; Less Sleep [3/level]; Luck [15]; Sanctity [5]; Serendipity [15]; and Strong Will [4/level].

Disadvantages: A total of -25 points chosen from Bowlegged [-1]; Charitable [-15]; Clueless [-10]; Curious [-5 to -15]; Easy to Read [-10]; Gluttony [-5]; Gullibility [-10]; Hidebound [-5]; Honesty [-10]; Impulsiveness [-10]; Low Self-Image [-10]; Overconfidence [-10]; Poverty [-10]; Shyness [-5 to -15]; Truthfulness [-5]; and Youth [-2/level].

Primary Skills: Agronomy (M/A) IQ+2 [6]-12; Driving (any) (P/A) DX+1 [4]-11.

Secondary Skills: Any two of Carpentry or Gardening, both (M/E) IQ+1 [2]-11; Blacksmith, Mechanic (Gasoline Engine), or Weather Sense, all (M/A) IQ [2]-10; Animal Handling (M/H) IQ-1 [2]-9; or Riding (any) (P/A) DX [2]-10.

Background Skills: Any one of Fishing (M/E) IQ [1]-10; Distilling or Merchant, both (M/A) IQ-1 [1]-9; Swimming (P/E) DX [1]-10; Guns (Rifle or Shotgun) (P/E) DX+1 [1]-11*; or Bolas or Lasso, both (P/A) DX-1 [1]-9.

  *Includes +1 for IQ.

Customization Notes: Of course, the farmer who becomes an adventurer is liable to be exceptional! Given the low price of this template, a farmer could have much higher attributes and more of everything. If you choose Youth, though, remember that points in skills cannot exceed (2 × age).

HUNTER/GUIDE 90 POINTS

Any group that plans to spend much time in a wilderness area should include a skilled hunting guide. Even if the guide isn't familiar with the specific territory, there are certain general skills that carry over.

Attributes: ST 11 [10], DX 11 [10], IQ 13 [30], HT 11 [10].

Advantages: A total of 20 points chosen from Absolute Direction [5]; Acute Senses (any) [2/level]; Alertness [5/level]; Combat Reflexes [15]; Composed or Imperturbable [5 or 10]; Danger Sense [15]; Fit [5]; Night Vision [10]; Peripheral Vision [15]; and Temperature Tolerance 1-2 [1 or 2].

Disadvantages: A total of -15 points in Claustrophobia [-15]; Demophobia [-15]; Guilt Complex [-5]; Loner [-5]; Overconfidence [-10]; and Sense of Duty (Those he's guiding) [-5].

Primary Skills: Area Knowledge (any) (M/E) IQ+1 [2]-14; First Aid (M/E) IQ [1]-13; Orienteering (M/A) IQ [2]-13; Survival (any) (M/A) IQ [2]-13; and one of Beam Weapons (any) or Guns (any), both (P/E) DX+2 [1]-13*.

* Includes +2 for IQ.

Secondary Skills: Leadership (M/A) IQ-1 [1]-12; Naturalist (M/H) IQ-1 [2]-12; Tracking (M/A) IQ-1 [1]-12; and any two of Driving (any), Powerboat, or Riding (any), all (P/A) DX+1 [4]-12, or Hiking (P/A; HT) HT+1 [4]-12.

Background Skills: A total of 5 points in Camouflage or Savoir-Faire (Servant), both (M/E); Animal Handling (M/H); Knife or Swimming, both (P/E); Climbing or Stealth, both (P/A); Skiing (P/H); and higher level with Beam Weapons or Guns.

Customization Notes: Consider higher DX or other Area Knowledge and Survival skills. The hunter can be everything from a boy scout leader (Climbing, Hiking, and Swimming) to the Great White version (Guns, Riding (Elephant), and Stealth).

JOURNALIST/REPORTER 50 POINTS

Travel is grist for the writer's mill, and the average group of travelers will provide more than enough subject matter! Of course, the journalist may be a news-maker himself, the driving force behind the group.

Attributes: ST 10 [0], DX 10 [0], IQ 13 [30], HT 10 [0].

Advantages: A total of 20 points chosen from Alertness [5/level]; Charisma [5/level]; Contacts (Any kind; skill-18, 9 or less, somewhat reliable) [3/contact]; Imperturbable [10]; Intuition [15]; Patron (Publisher or network, provides "press pass," 9 or less) [15]; Reputation [varies]; Serendipity [15]; Single-Minded [5]; and Strong Will [4/level].

Disadvantages: A total of -20 points chosen from Curious [-5 to -15]; Delusion ("I'm immortal when I'm carrying a note pad, camera, microphone, etc.") [-5 to -10]; Impulsiveness [-10]; Jealousy [-10]; Obsession (Get the story) [-5]; Odious Personal Habits ("Aggressive," "Rude," etc.) [-5 to -10]; Reputation [varies]; Stubbornness [-5]; Vow ("Always publish the truth") [-5]; and Workaholic [-5].

Primary Skills: Research (M/A) IQ+1 [4]-14; Writing (M/A) IQ+1 [4]-14; and native language skill at IQ+2 [2]-15.

Secondary Skills: Speed-Reading (M/A) IQ-1 [1]-12; and any two of Savoir-Faire (M/E) IQ+1 [2]-14; Bard or Fast-Talk, both (M/A) IQ [2]-13; Detect Lies (M/H) IQ-1 [2]-12; and 2 more points in Writing.

Background Skills: Any one of Conspiracy Theory (M/VH) IQ-3 [1]-10; Literature (M/H) IQ-2 [1]-11; or Shadowing (M/A) IQ-1 [1]-12; plus a total of 4 points in Computer Operation (M/E); Electronics Operation (Comm), Photography or Video Production, all (M/A); and Typing (P/E).

Customization Notes: Decide what kind of journalist you are and choose skills appropriately: Paparazzi will want Shadowing and Photography, a tabloid writer will have Conspiracy Theory, and a learned author might focus on Literature. A successful journalist should consider adding Wealth.

Law Enforcer 90 points

Cops and ex-cops have many reasons for traveling: an unsolved case from years past, vengeance over justice denied, or perhaps even a need to escape from enemies acquired in the line of duty.

Attributes: ST 10 [0], DX 12 [20], IQ 12 [20], HT 10 [0].

Advantages: A total of 30 points chosen from Alertness [5/level]; Combat Reflexes [15]; Contacts (Street; skill-18, 9 or less, somewhat reliable) [3/contact]; Fearlessness [2/level]; Fit [5]; Higher Purpose (Oppose all criminals of one type, etc.) [5]; Intuition [15]; Legal Enforcement Powers* [5 to 15]; and +1 to ST, DX, IQ, or HT [10].

Disadvantages: A total of -25 points chosen from Bully [-10]; Cannot Harm Innocents [-10]; Curious [-5 to -15]; Duty* (To force) [-5 to -15]; Enemy (Gangsters, 6 or less) [-15]; Guilt Complex [-5]; Honesty [-10]; Intolerance (Criminals) [-5]; Odious Personal Habit ("Authoritarian") [-5]; Overconfidence [-10]; Secret (Crooked) [-10]; Sense of Duty [-5 to -15]; and Workaholic [-5].

* Police officers must have at least 5 points of Legal Enforcement Powers and a -5-point Duty; ex-cops will have neither.

Primary Skills: Area Knowledge (Beat) (M/E) IQ+2 [4]-14 and Law Enforcement (M/A) IQ+2 [6]-14; one of Beam Weapons (any) or Guns (any), both (P/E) DX+2 [1]-14†; a total of 7 points in Brawling, Fast-Draw (Pistol), or Shield (Riot Shield), all (P/E), or Judo, Short Staff, or Tonfa, all (P/H).

†Includes +2 for IQ.

Secondary Skills: Administration (M/A) IQ [2]-12; Computer Operation (M/E) IQ [1]-12; Criminology (M/A) IQ [2]-12; First Aid (M/E) IQ [1]-12; Holdout (M/A) IQ-1 [1]-11; Research (M/A) IQ-1 [1]-11; Shadowing (M/A) IQ-1 [1]-11; and Stealth (P/A) DX [2]-12; any three of Interrogation, Intimidation, Leadership, or Streetwise, all (M/A) IQ [2]-12, or Detect Lies, Diplomacy, or Psychology, all (M/H) IQ-1 [2]-11; any two of Motorcycle (P/E) DX+1 [2]-13, Driving

(any) or Riding (any), both (P/A) DX [2]-12, or Running (P/H; HT) HT-1 [2]-9.

Background Skills: A total of 6 points in Armoury (any) or Electronics Operation (any), both (M/A), or Animal Handling, Explosive Ordnance Disposal, Forensics, Law, or Tactics, all (M/H).

Customization Notes: Choose skills to suit your service specialty. A K9 officer will want Animal Handling, a bomb-disposal expert will want Explosive Ordnance Disposal, etc. Many policemen train outside the force; thus, extra Beam Weapons, Guns, and unarmed combat skills are likely.

Manager 55 points

Like *Attorney* (p. 87) and *Bureaucrat* (p. 89), this may seem an odd choice. Why would a normal businessman choose a life of excitement and danger over one filled with mind-numbing boredom and tedious attention to minor details?

Attributes: ST 10 [0], DX 10 [0], IQ 13 [30], HT 10 [0].

Advantages: A total of 20 points in Administrative Rank [5/level]; Common Sense [10]; Intuition [15]; Single-Minded [5]; Status 1-2 [5/level]; Strong Will [4/level]; and Wealth [10 or 20].

Disadvantages: A total of -20 points in Age [-3/year]; Bully [-10]; Compulsive Spending [-5 to -15]; Extravagance [-10]; Greed [-15]; Hidebound [-5]; Incurious or Obdurate [-5 or -10]; Migraine [-5 to -20]; Miserliness [-10]; Overweight [-5]; Secret (Dishonest) [-10]; Stubbornness [-5]; and Workaholic [-5].

Primary Skills: Administration (M/A) IQ+1 [4]-14; Leadership (M/A) IQ+1 [4]-14; and any two of Bard, Fast-Talk, Intimidation, or Teaching, all (M/A) IQ+1 [4]-14, or Detect Lies or Diplomacy, both (M/H) IQ [4]-13.

Secondary Skills: Accounting (M/H) IQ-1 [2]-12; Computer Operation (M/E) IQ [1]-13; Economics (M/H) IQ-1 [2]-12; Merchant (M/A) IQ-1 [1]-12; and Writing (M/A) IQ-1 [1]-12.

Background Skills: A total of 2 points in Carousing (P/A; HT), Savoir-Faire (M/E), and Sports (Golf) (P/A).

Customization Notes: Select skills that reflect your management style. A tough, self-made, owner-operator type might have Fast-Talk, Intimidation, and Carousing, while a graduate from a posh business school is more likely to have Bard, Diplomacy, and Savoir-Faire. Any manager can justify lots of Wealth in the form of bonuses or stock options.

MARTIAL ARTIST   90 POINTS

Depending on the campaign, there may be use for someone whose previous career was learning how to kill people with his bare hands or a large wooden club.

This template may be combined with *Athlete* (p. 87) or *Entertainer* (p. 92).

Attributes: ST 11 [10], DX 13 [30], IQ 10 [0], HT 11 [10].

Advantages: A total of 20 points chosen from Combat Reflexes [15]; Daredevil [15]; Enhanced Block* [6]; Enhanced Dodge* [15]; Enhanced Parry* [6 or 10]; Fit or Very Fit [5 or 15]; High Pain Threshold [10]; Iron Hand* [10 or 15]; Strong Will [4/level]; Style Familiarity [1 to 15]; Toughness (DR 1) [10]; +1 or +2 to ST or HT [10 or 20]; and +1 to DX [15].

Disadvantages: A total of -20 points chosen from Bad Temper [-10]; Bully [-10]; Code of Honor [-5 to -15]; Obsession (Become a master) [-5]; Overconfidence [-10]; Pacifism (Cannot harm innocents) [-10] or (Cannot kill or Self-defense only) [-15]; Post-Combat Shakes [5]; and Vow (Never use weapons) [-15].

Primary Skills: A total of 24 points in the skills and maneuvers of a martial-arts style from *GURPS Martial Arts*; see Spacer Kung Fu (p. MA115) for a style especially useful to travelers. Alternatively, take any three of Brawling DX+3 [8]-16; Boxing, Sumo Wrestling, or Wrestling, all DX+2 [8]-15; or Judo, Karate, Short Staff, Staff, or Tonfa, all DX+1 [8]-14.

Secondary Skills: Acrobatics (P/H) DX [4]-13; Jumping (P/E) DX [1]-13; and one of Intimidation, Leadership, or Teaching, all (M/A) IQ+2 [6]-12.

Background Skills: A total of 5 points in First Aid, Savoir-Faire (Dojo), or Tournament Law, all (M/E); Armoury (Hand Weapons) or Holdout, both (M/A); Body Language, Style Analysis, or Tactics, all (M/H); Meditation* or Physiology, both (M/VH); Garrote or Knife, both (P/E); and Stealth (P/A).

* With GM's permission!

Customization Notes: The biggest decision to make when customizing a martial artist is choosing the style he uses. As a result, this template really only comes into its own with the addition of *Martial Arts*.

GMG '99

MECHANIC/TECHNICIAN 60 POINTS

Although less respected (and less well-paid) than engineers (p. 91), mechanics and techs fill a vital role in any group.

Attributes: ST 10 [0], DX 10 [0], IQ 13 [30], HT 10 [0].

Advantages: A total of 15 points in Common Sense [10]; Intuition [15]; Less Sleep [3/level]; Lightning Calculator [5]; Manual Dexterity [3/level]; Single-Minded [5]; and Versatile [5].

Disadvantages: A total of -15 points chosen from Bad Sight (Correctable) [-10]; Clueless [-10]; Curious [-5 to -15]; Duty (As crewman) [-2 to -15]; Overweight or Skinny [-5]; Shyness [-5 to -15]; Stubbornness [-5]; and Workaholic [-5].

Primary Skills: Scrounging (M/E) IQ+2 [4]-15; and any two specialties of Armoury (see list, p. B53), Mechanic (p. B54), or Electronics Operation (p. B58), each (M/A) IQ+2 [6]-15.

Background Skills: Computer Operation (M/E) IQ [1]-13; and three additional specialties of Armoury, Mechanic, or Electronics Operation, each (M/A) IQ [2]-13.

Secondary Skills: A total of 7 points in Armoury (any), Electronics Operation (any), Lockpicking, Mechanic (any), Vacc Suit, or Video Production, all (M/A); Mathematics or Metallurgy, both (M/H); and Driving (any), Free Fall, or Piloting (any), all (P/A).

Customization Notes: Choose skills that reflect your area of expertise. A Marine armourer will have Armoury (Beam weapons), Electronics Operation (Weapons), and a few points in Free Fall and Vacc Suit; a robot repairman is more likely to have high skill levels in Electronics Operation (Computers) and Mechanic (Robotics). Like engineers (p. 91), the GM may permit techs and mechanics to take Gadgeteer [25] and should usually forbid Technophobia!

MEDICAL DOCTOR   90 POINTS

Passenger vessels all have medical requirements, and no group of any size can afford to be far from a trained physician.

Attributes: ST 10 [0], DX 10 [0], IQ 14 [45], HT 10 [0].

Advantages: Comfortable Wealth [10]; and a total of 20 points in Composed [5]; Disease-Resistant or Immunity to Disease [5 or 10]; Higher Purpose (Heal the sick) [5]; Less Sleep [3/level]; Manual Dexterity [3/level]; Sanctity [5]; Sensitive or Empathy [5 or 15]; Single-Minded [5]; Status 1-2 [5 or 10]; and more Wealth [10 or 20].

Disadvantages: A total of -20 points in Addiction (Stimulants) [-5]; Charitable [-15]; Code of Honor (Hippocratic oath) [-15]; Greed [-15]; Guilt Complex [-5]; Honesty [-10]; Nightmares [-5]; Pacifism (Cannot harm innocents) [-10] or either (Cannot Kill or Self-Defense Only) [-15]; Selfless [-10]; Sense of Duty [-5 to -20]; and Workaholic [-5].

Primary Skills: Diagnosis (M/H) IQ+1 [6]-15; Electronics Operation (Medical) (M/A) IQ+1 [4]-15; and Physician (M/H) IQ+1 [6]-15.

Secondary Skills: Any two of Hypnotism, Pharmacy, or Psychology, all (M/H) IQ [4]-14; or Genetics, Physiology, or Surgery, all (M/VH) IQ-1 [4]-13.

Background Skills: Administration (M/A) IQ-2 [½]-12; Computer Operation (M/E) IQ-1 [½]-13; and Diplomacy (M/H) IQ-2 [1]-12; plus another 9 points in Leadership, Research, Tattooing, or Teaching, all (M/A); Poisons or Veterinary, both (M/H); or any primary or secondary skill.

Customization Notes: Use secondary skill choices and the flexible background skill points to reflect your specialty. An army field medic might pick Leadership-13 [1], Psychology-14 [4], and Surgery-15 [12]. A "doctor" at a seedy starport clinic would probably get more mileage out of Hypnotism-14 [4], Pharmacy-15 [6], Poisons-15 [6], and Tattooing-13 [1].

MEDICAL TECHNICIAN   45 POINTS

As noted under *Medical Doctor* (above), characters with medical skills are almost mandatory in a group of adventurers. Smaller passenger vessels tend to have medical techs rather than full-fledged doctors.

Attributes: ST 10 [0], DX 10 [0], IQ 13 [30], HT 10 [0].

Advantages: A total of 20 points chosen from Combat Reflexes [15]; Disease-Resistant or Immunity to Disease [5 or 10]; Less Sleep [3/level]; Sensitive or Empathy [5 or 15]; Single-Minded [5]; and Versatile [5].

Disadvantages: A total of -20 points in Addiction (Stimulants) [-5]; Charitable [-15]; Chummy [-5]; Delusion ("I'm a doctor!") [-5]; Guilt Complex [-5]; Honesty [-10]; Overconfidence [-10]; Pacifism (Cannot harm innocents) [-10] or (Cannot kill or Self-defense only) [-15]; Selfless [-10]; Sense of Duty [-5 to -15]; and Workaholic [-5].

Primary Skills: Diagnosis (M/H) IQ+1 [6]-14; Electronics Operation (Medical) (M/A) IQ+1 [4]-14; and First Aid (M/E) IQ+1 [2]-14.

Secondary Skills: Pharmacy (M/H) IQ-1 [2]-12.

Background Skills: Computer Operation (M/E) IQ-1 [½]-12 and Scrounging (M/E) IQ-1 [½]-12.

Customization Notes: On very small ships, "medical technician" is probably a part-time job. If so, this template could be combined with Mechanic/Technician (p. 95) or (for pirate crews) Corsair (p. 90), with the GM's assistance.

MERCHANT   75 POINTS

Many campaigns will focus on the crew of the futuristic equivalent of a tramp steamer, moving from place to place and eking out a living on the edge of the frontier. A keen eye for a bargain, and a sharp sense of profit and loss (and, in some places, a quick draw!) are vital job skills.

Attributes: ST 10 [0], DX 10 [0], IQ 13 [30], HT 10 [0].

Advantages: A total of 30 points in Ally Group (2-5 75-point crewmen, 9 or less) [10]; Charisma [5/level]; Claim to Hospitality (Trade guilds, etc.) [1 to 10]; Contacts (Business; skill-18, 9 or less, somewhat reliable) [3/contact]; Cultural Adaptability [25]; Empathy [15]; Intuition [15]; Language Talent [2/level]; Lightning Calculator [5]; Luck [15]; Strong Will [4/level]; and Wealth [10 to 30].

Disadvantages: A total of -20 points in Code of Honor (Merchant's) [-5]; Compulsive Gambling [-5]; Compulsive Generosity [-5]; Compulsive Spending [-5]; Enemy (Bounty hunter, 6 or less) [-5]; Extravagance [-10]; Greed [-15]; Jealousy [-10]; Miserliness [-10]; Overweight or Fat [-5 to -20]; Selfish [-5]; Stubbornness [-5]; and Workaholic [-5].

Primary Skills: Merchant (M/A) IQ+2 [6]-15.

Secondary Skills: Accounting (M/H) IQ [4]-13; Administration (M/A) IQ [2]-13; Computer Operation (M/E) IQ [1]-13; Economics (M/H) IQ [4]-13; Fast-Talk (M/A) IQ [2]-13; Freight Handling (M/A) IQ [2]-13; and Leadership (M/A) IQ [2]-13.

Background Skills: A total of 12 points in Area Knowledge (any) or Gesture, both (M/E); Astrogation, Gambling, Holdout, Language (any), or Streetwise, all (M/A); Detect Lies, Forgery, or Law, all (M/H); Appreciate Beauty (M/VH); Beam Weapons (any), Brawling, Fast-Draw (Pistol), or Guns (any), all (P/E); Piloting (Starship) (P/A); Carousing (P/A; HT); or any primary or secondary skill.

Customization Notes: Background skills should reflect your market, goods, and the size of your operation. A "lone wolf" selling stolen military technology out of the back of a scout ship will want Astrogation-13 [2], Piloting-12 [8], and Streetwise-13 [2]; the master of a corporate trading vessel is likely to use those points to get Administration-16 [8] and Economics-16 [10].

....

PROFESSOR   70 POINTS

This template represents an academician who spends more of his time teaching than in research (compare *Scientist,* p. 98).

Attributes: ST 10 [0], DX 10 [0], IQ 14 [45], HT 10 [0].

Advantages: A total of 20 points in Claim to Hospitality (Universities) [1 to 10]; Language Talent [2/level]; Lightning Calculator [5]; Mathematical Ability [10]; Reputation (Famous academician) [varies]; Status 1-2 [5 or 10]; Strong Will [4/level]; Tenure [5]; Versatile [5]; Voice [10]; and Wealth [10 or 20].

Disadvantages: A total of -20 points chosen from Absent-Mindedness [-15]; Age [-3/year]; Bad Sight (Correctable) [-10]; Clueless [-10]; Duty (Teaching; non-hazardous, 12 or less) [-5] or (15 or less) [-10]; Hard of Hearing [-10]; Indecisive [-10]; Intolerance (Uneducated people) [-5]; Oblivious [-3]; and Sense of Duty (Anyone who needs tutelage) [-10].

Primary Skills: Teaching (M/A) IQ+1 [4]-15; plus either **two** of Anthropology, Archaeology, Artificial Intelligence, Astronomy, Botany, Chemistry, Computer Programming, Cryptology, Ecology, Economics, Geology, History, Law, Literature, Mathematics, Paleontology, Philosophy, Physician, Physics, Psychology, Theology, or Xenology, all (M/H) IQ+2 [8]-16, or **one** of Genetics, Linguistics, or Physiology, all (M/VH) IQ+2 [16]-16.

Secondary Skills: Computer Operation (M/E) IQ-1 [½]-13; Research (M/A) IQ-1 [1]-13; Speed-Reading (M/A) IQ-1 [1]-13; and Writing (M/A) IQ-1 [1]-13.

Background Skills: Bard (M/A) IQ-2 [½]-12; Language (any) (M/A) IQ-2 [½]-12; and Savoir-Faire (M/E) IQ-1 [½]-13.

Customization Notes: If choosing two fields, make sure the combination is logical; e.g., Archaeology and Paleontology, Botany and Ecology, Philosophy and Theology. Professors often have skill in advanced fields like Biochemistry (M/VH) (requires Chemistry at 12+), Hyperspace Physics (M/VH) (requires Mathematics, Nuclear Physics, and Physics at 15+), Nuclear Physics (M/VH) (requires Mathematics and Physics at 15+), and Paraphysics (M/VH) (requires Physics and Biochemistry at 12+).

ROGUE 85 POINTS

"Rogue" is a more romantic term than "criminal." Literature is filled with lovable, roguish criminal/heroes, from Robin Hood to Simon Templar, touching base with Jesse James and Butch Cassidy along the way, and culminating in a merchant/smuggler-turned-rebel named Han Solo.

Attributes: ST 10 [0], DX 13 [30], IQ 13 [30], HT 10 [0].

Advantages: A total of 30 points chosen from Alertness [5/level]; Charisma [5/level]; Contacts (Street; skill-18, 9 or less, somewhat reliable) [3/contact]; Danger Sense [15]; Daredevil [15]; Double-Jointed [5]; Luck [15]; Manual Dexterity [3/level]; Night Vision [10]; Sanctity [5]; Versatile [5]; and Wealth [10 to 30].

Disadvantages: A total of -30 points chosen from Callous [-6]; Code of Honor (Rogue's) [-5]; Compulsive Gambling [-5 to -15]; Compulsive Lying [-15]; Enemy (Law-enforcement agency, 6 or less) [-15]; Greed [-15]; Kleptomania [-15]; Laziness [-10]; Light Sleeper [-5]; Loner [-5]; Overconfidence [-10]; Paranoia [-10]; Reputation (Crook) [varies]; Secret (Almost anything!) [-5 to -20]; Selfish or Self-Centered [-5 or -10]; Social Stigma (Outlaw) [-15]; Status -1 [-5]; Trademark [-1 to -15]; and Trickster [-15].

Primary Skills: Area Knowledge (any) (M/E) IQ [1]-13; Stealth (P/A) DX [2]-13; and Streetwise (M/A) IQ [2]-13.

Secondary Skills: Computer Operation (M/E) IQ [1]-13 and Running (P/H; HT) HT-2 [1]-8; and three skills off each of these two lists (or just spend a net 12 points on them):

I. Panhandling (M/E) IQ+1 [2]-14; Acting, Courtesan, Fast-Talk, Fortune Telling, Gambling, Intimidation, or Merchant, all (M/A) IQ [2]-13; or Sex Appeal (M/A; HT) HT [2]-10.

II. Electronics Operation (Security Systems), Holdout, Lockpicking, Shadowing, and Traps, all (M/A) IQ [2]-13; Brawling (P/E) DX+1 [2]-14; Beam Weapons (any) or Guns (any), both DX+3 [2]-16*; Climbing or Filch, both (P/A) DX [2]-13; or Escape, Pickpocket, or Sleight of Hand, all (P/H) DX-1 [2]-12.

* Includes +2 for IQ.

Background Skills: A total of 6 points in Gesture (M/E); Disguise or Survival (Urban), both (M/A); Forgery or Poisons, both (M/H); Computer Hacking (M/VH); Fast-Draw (any) or Knife, both (P/E); Carousing (P/A; HT); or Mimicry (Human Speech) (P/H; HT).

Customization Notes: This template is *adaptable*. Decide on what kinds of crimes you'd like to commit, then pick skills (and disadvantages!) to match. A mob knee-breaker might take Brawling, Fast-Talk, Gambling, Guns, Holdout, and Intimidation; a sweet-talking street girl might lean toward Acting, Courtesan, Holdout, Pickpocket, Sex Appeal, and Sleight of Hand.

SCIENTIST 70 POINTS

The term "scientist" is applied to those academicians who spend more time in research than teaching (compare *Professor*, p. 97).

Attributes: ST 10 [0], DX 10 [0], IQ 14 [45], HT 10 [0].

Advantages: A total of 20 points in Ally (76-100 point grad student, 9 or less) [5]; Claim to Hospitality (Universities) [1 to 10]; Imperturbable [10]; Intuition [15]; Language Talent [2/level]; Lightning Calculator [5]; Mathematical Ability [10]; Reputation (Famous academician) [varies]; Single-Minded [5]; Status 1-2 [5 or 10]; Strong Will [4/level]; Tenure [5]; Versatile [5]; and Wealth [10 or 20].

Disadvantages: Curious [-5]; and -20 points chosen from a higher level of Curious [-5 or -10]; Absent-Mindedness [-15]; Age [-3/year]; Bad Sight (Correctable) [-10]; Clueless [-10]; Delusion (Crazy theory) [-5]; Dependent (26-50 point grad student, 9 or less) [-3]; Hard of Hearing [-10]; Intolerance (Uneducated people) [-5]; Oblivious [-3]; Obsession (Proving his theory) [-5 to -15]; Stubbornness [-5]; and Workaholic [-5].

Primary Skills: Either **two** of Anthropology, Archaeology, Artificial Intelligence, Astronomy, Botany, Chemistry, Computer Programming, Cryptology, Ecology, Economics, Geology, History, Law, Literature, Mathematics, Paleontology, Philosophy, Physician, Physics, Psychology, Theology, and Xenology, all (M/H) IQ+4 [12]-18; or **one** of Genetics, Linguistics, or Physiology, all (M/VH) IQ+4 [24]-18.

Secondary Skills: Research (M/A) IQ [2]-14; Writing (M/A) IQ [2]-14; and either Computer Operation (M/E) IQ [1]-14 or Electronics Operation (any) (M/A) IQ-1 [1]-13.

Background Skills: Any two of Language (any) (M/A) IQ-2 [½]-12; Leadership (M/A) IQ-2 [½]-12; Savoir-Faire (M/E) IQ-1 [½]-13; and Teaching (M/A) IQ-2 [½]-12.

Customization Notes: All notes given for Professor (p. 97) also apply here.

SCOUT   90 POINTS

Veterans of the Imperial Interstellar Scout Service share a problem with ex-spies and ex-diplomats: Nobody really believes they're no longer working for their "former" employer. And, of course, sometimes they are.

Attributes: ST 11 [10], DX 11 [10], IQ 13 [30], HT 11 [10].

Advantages: A total of 20 points in 3D Spatial Sense [10]; Acceleration Tolerance [10]; Alertness [5/level]; Claim to Hospitality (Former scouts) [10]; Collected or Imperturbable [5 or 10]; Combat Reflexes [15]; Common Sense [10]; Danger Sense [15]; Daredevil [15]; Fit [5]; G-Experience [10]; Improved G-Tolerance [10]; Intuition [15]; Luck [15]; Strong Will [4/level]; and Versatile [5].

Disadvantages: Duty (Reactivation, 9 or less) [-5]; and -20 points in Code of Honor (Scout's) [-5]; Curious [-5 to -15]; Impulsiveness [-10]; Loner or Reclusive [-5 or -10]; Overconfidence or Glory Hound [-10 or -15]; Shyness [-5 to -15]; Stubbornness [-5]; Workaholic [-5]; and Xenophilia [-5 or -15].

Primary Skills: Astrogation (M/A) IQ [2]-13; Cartography (M/A) IQ [2]-13; Electronics Operation (Sensors) (M/A) IQ [2]-13; and Piloting (Starship) (P/A) DX+2 [8]-13.

Secondary Skills: Area Knowledge (Galaxy) (M/H) IQ-1 [2]-12; Computer Operation (M/E) IQ-1 [½]-12; Electronics Operation (Comm) (M/A) IQ-1 [1]-12; Engineer (Vehicles) (M/H) IQ-1 [2]-12; Free Fall (P/A) DX+1 [4]-12; Mechanic (J-Drive) (M/A) IQ-1 [1]-12; Mechanic (M-Drive) (M/A) IQ-1 [1]-12; Photography (M/A) IQ-1 [1]-12; and Vacc Suit (M/A) IQ-1 [1]-12.

Background Skills: Astronomy (M/H) IQ-2 [1]-11; First Aid (M/E) IQ-1 [½]-12; Intelligence Analysis (M/H) IQ-2 [1]-11; Navigation (M/H) IQ-2 [1]-11; Planetology (any) (M/A) IQ-2 [½]-11; and Survival (any) (M/A) IQ-2 [½]-11; plus 3 points in Area Knowledge (any) (M/E), Beam Weapons (any) (P/E), Gunner (any ship-mounted) (P/A), Guns (any) (P/E), and Tactics (Space) (M/H).

Customization Notes: A scout can justify having been almost anywhere. Use extra Area Knowledge, Planetology, and Survival skills to reflect the systems, planet types, and terrain types (respectively) that your scout has encountered. The Scout Service isn't intended for combat, but some Scouts are "cowboys" and may have decent levels in Gunner and Tactics (also see *GURPS Traveller First In* for combat-oriented branches of the IISS). Remember that scouts often work alone: It pays to be versatile rather than specialized.

UNDERCOVER AGENT   90 POINTS

For obvious reasons, a retired spy often needs to keep moving. The talents, contacts, and enemies acquired during an active career as an agent can make life exciting for anyone who comes into contact with him!

Attributes: ST 10 [0], DX 13 [30], IQ 13 [30], HT 10 [0].

Advantages: A total of 25 points in Alertness [5/level]; Alternate Identity [15]; Appearance [5 or 15]; Charisma [5/level]; Collected or Imperturbable [5 or 10]; Combat Reflexes [15]; Contacts (Any; skill-18, 9 or less, somewhat reliable) [3/contact]; Danger Sense [15]; Intuition [15]; Language Talent [2/level]; Luck [15]; Sanctity [5]; Strong Will [4/level]; Versatile [5]; Voice [10]; and Zeroed [10].

Disadvantages: A total of -25 points in Curious [-5 to -15]; Delusion ("Enemy agents are after me!") [-5 to -15]; Duty (Agency, 9 or less) [-5]; Enemy (Enemy agents, 6 or less) [-15]; Insomniac [-10 or -15]; Light Sleeper [-5]; Loner [-5]; Mistaken Identity [-5]; Nightmares [-5]; Overconfidence [-10]; Paranoia [-10]; Secret [-5 to -20]; and Sense of Duty (Nation) [-10].

Primary Skills: Area Knowledge (any) (M/E) IQ [1]-13; Language (any) (M/A) IQ [2]-13; and two skills from each of these three lists (or just spend a net 12 points on them):

I. Savoir-Faire (M/E) IQ+1 [2]-14; Acting, Fast-Talk, or Interrogation, all (M/A) IQ [2]-13; Sex Appeal (M/A; HT) HT [2]-10; Detect Lies (M/H) IQ-1 [2]-12; or Carousing (P/A; HT) HT [2]-10.

II. Demolition, Electronics Operation (Security systems), Lockpicking, or Traps, all (M/A) IQ [2]-13; Climbing or Stealth, both (P/A) DX [2]-13; or Escape (P/H) DX-1 [2]-12.

III. Electronics Operation (Comm), Electronics Operation (Sensors), Lip Reading, Photography, or Shadowing, all (M/A) IQ [2]-13; or Body Language or Traffic Analysis, both (M/H) IQ-1 [2]-12.

Secondary Skills: Computer Operation (M/E) IQ-1 [½]-12; Disguise (M/A) IQ-1 [1]-12; Holdout (M/A) IQ-1 [1]-12; Intelligence Analysis (M/H) IQ-1 [2]-12; Research (M/A) IQ-1 [1]-12; Speed-Reading (M/A) IQ-1 [1]-12; and one of Beam Weapons (any) or Guns (any), both (P/E) DX+1 [½]-14*.

* Includes +2 for IQ.

Background Skills: One of Driving (any) or Piloting (any), both (P/A) DX-1 [1]-12; and 7 points in Cartography or Heraldry (any), both (M/A); Cryptanalysis, Cryptography, Forensics, Forgery, Poisons, or SIGINT Collection/Jamming, all (M/H); or Computer Hacking (M/VH).

Customization Notes: Primary skills reflect the kind of agent you are. A "social engineer" might have Body Language, Fast-Talk, Lip Reading, Lockpicking, Savoir-Faire, and Stealth. An assassin might have Demolition, Electronics Operation (Sensors), Shadowing, and Traps, and skip List I to add points to combat skills. The best agents have a good mix of skills, though.

WEALTHY TRAVELER (REMITTANCE MAN)   85 POINTS

This template represents someone, usually a non-heir, who is paid by his family to stay away from home. The reasons are many and varied, and are left up to the imaginations of the player and GM. There are certain limitations (the need to check in with a bank from time to time, for one), but the character is largely free to do what he wants (except go within a parsec of home or gain too much notoriety).

Attributes: ST 10 [0], DX 10 [0], IQ 10 [0], HT 10 [0].

Advantages: Either Filthy Rich [50] or Patron (Wealthy family, provides cash, 12 or less) [50]; plus 25 points in Alcohol Tolerance [5]; Ally Group (2-5 75-point bodyguards, 12 or less) [20]; Appearance [5 to 25]; Claim to Hospitality (Other rich people) [5 to 10]; Fashion Sense [5]; Heir [5]; Light Hangover or No Hangover [2 or 5]; Luck [15]; Reputation (Celebrity) [varies]; Status 1-5* [5/level]; and +1 or +2 to any attribute [10 or 20].

 * Filthy Rich provides +1 Status; see p. B18.

Disadvantages: A total of -30 points in Addiction [varies]; Alcoholism [-15]; Chummy [-5]; Compulsive Carousing [-5]; Compulsive Gambling [-5 to -15]; Compulsive Spending [-5 to -15]; Delusion ("Everyone thinks I'm great!") [-5]; Extravagance [-10]; Greed [-15]; Impulsiveness [-10]; Incompetence (Administration) [-1]; Intolerance (Poor people, lower classes, etc.) [-5]; Laziness [-10]; Lecherousness [-15]; Overconfidence [-10]; Selfish or Self-Centered [-5 or -10]; and Short Attention Span [-10].

Primary Skills: Savoir-Faire (M/E) IQ+4 [8]-14.

Secondary & Background Skills: Any two of Chess or Games (any), both (M/E) IQ+8 [16]-18; Falconry or Gambling, both (M/A) IQ+7 [16]-17; Sex Appeal (M/A; HT) HT+7 [16]-17; Appreciate Beauty (M/VH) IQ+2 [16]-12; Dancing, Driving (any), Fencing, Piloting (any), Riding (any), or Sports (any), all (P/A) DX+3 [16]-13; or Carousing (P/A; HT) HT+3 [16]-13.

Customization Notes: A character like this is mainly useful for his money, but his skills can be chosen to give him an edge in adventuring situations. Be sure that they reflect your character's background. The scion of a powerful military family might know Chess and Fencing, while the daughter of a rock star is more likely to have Carousing and Sex Appeal.

ARMY (ENLISTED)   90 POINTS

Soldiers are trained to follow orders and kill people for a living, which is occasionally useful in their subsequent careers. This template represents a former soldier in a land army, whether local (planetary), Imperial, or extra-Imperial.

Attributes: ST 11 [10], DX 13 [30], IQ 11 [10], HT 11[10].

Advantages: A total of 20 points in Combat Reflexes [15]; Courtesy Rank 0-2 [1/level]; Fearlessness [2/level]; Fit or Very Fit [5 or 15]; Hard to Kill 1-2 [5 or 10]; High Pain Threshold [10]; Reputation (Decorated) [varies]; and Toughness (DR 1) [10].

Disadvantages: A total of -20 points in Bloodlust [-10]; Callous [-6]; Chummy [-5]; Code of Honor (Soldier's) [-5]; Duty (Reactivation, 6 or less) [-2] or (9 or less) [-5]; Fanaticism (Patriotism) [-15]; Flashbacks [-5 to -20]; Intolerance (Enemy race or culture) [-5]; Nightmares [-5]; Overconfidence [-10]; Post-Combat Shakes [-5]; and Sense of Duty (Comrades in arms) [-5].

Primary Skills: Either Beam Weapons (any) or Guns (any), both (P/E) DX+2 [2]-15*; plus Gunner (any) (P/A) DX+1 [2]-14*; NBC Warfare (M/A) IQ+1 [4]-12; and Savoir-Faire (Military) (M/E) IQ+1 [2]-12.

Secondary Skills: Armoury (Small Arms) (M/A) IQ [2]-11; Camouflage (M/E) IQ [1]-11; Electronics Operation (Comm) (M/A) IQ-1 [1]-10; First Aid (M/E) IQ [1]-11; Hiking (P/A; HT) HT-1 [1]-10; Orienteering (M/A) IQ-1 [1]-10; Stealth (P/A) DX-1 [1]-12; Survival (any) (M/A) IQ-1 [1]-10; and Tactics (M/H) IQ-1 [2]-10; plus a total of 3 points in Brawling (P/E), Judo (P/H), Knife (P/E), Spear (P/A), and Throwing (P/H).

Background Skills: A total of 6 points in Scrounging (M/E); Administration, Demolition, Forward Observer, Leadership, Mechanic (any), or No-Landing Extraction, all (M/A); Engineer (Combat), Explosive Ordnance Disposal, SIGINT Collection/Jamming, or Traffic Analysis, all (M/H); Beam Weapons (other), Guns (other), or Parachuting, all (P/E); and Battlesuit, Driving (any), or Gunner (any), all (P/A).

Customization Notes: Choose Courtesy Rank that reflects your former service grade: A private is Rank 0 [0], a sergeant is Rank 1 [1], and a senior sergeant (or specialist) is Rank 2 [2]. This becomes Military Rank [5/level] if reactivated!

Choose background skills appropriate to unit and MOS; e.g., *Airborne*, No-Landing Extraction-12 [4], Parachuting-14 [2]; *Artillery*, Forward Observer-12 [4], Gunner (Cannon)-14* [2]; *Engineer Corps*, Demolition-11 [2], Engineer (Combat)-11 [4]; *Mechanized Infantry*, Driving (Tracked)-13 [2], Mechanic (Gasoline Engine)-12 [4]; *Supply*, Administration-12 [4], Scrounging-12 [2]; etc.

 * Includes +1 for IQ.

ARMY (OFFICER)   90 POINTS

A former officer in one of the forces described under *Army (Enlisted)*, p. 100.

Attributes: ST 11 [10], DX 12 [20], IQ 13 [30], HT 11 [10].

Advantages: A total of 20 points in Charisma [5/level]; Combat Reflexes [15]; Courtesy Rank 3+ [1/level]; Reputation

(Decorated) [varies]; Status 1 [5]; Strong Will [4/level]; and Voice [10].

Disadvantages: A total of -20 points in Callous [-6]; Code of Honor (Officer's) [-5]; Duty (Reactivation, 6 or less) [-2] or (9 or less) [-5]; Fanaticism (Patriotism) [-15]; Honesty [-10]; Intolerance (Enemy race or culture) [-5]; Jealousy [-10]; Odious Personal Habit ("By the book") [-5]; Overconfidence [-10]; Sense of Duty (His command) [-10]; Stubbornness [-5]; and Workaholic [-5].

Primary Skills: Administration (M/A) IQ [2]-13; Leadership (M/A) IQ [2]-13; and Tactics (M/H) IQ [4]-13; plus 2 more points in one of those three skills; and Savoir-Faire (Military) (M/E) IQ [1]-13.

Secondary Skills: Either Beam Weapons (any) or Guns (any) (P/E), both DX+2 [1]-14*; plus Electronics Operation (Comm) (M/A) IQ-1 [1]-12; Gunner (any) (P/A) DX+1 [1]-13*; NBC Warfare (M/A) IQ-1 [1]-12; and Orienteering (M/A) IQ-1 [1]-12.

   * Includes +2 for IQ.

Background Skills: A net 4 points in Forward Observer, Heraldry (Military Insignia), Interrogation, or Survival (any), all (M/A); Cryptography, Engineer (Combat), Intelligence Analysis, Psychology, or Strategy, all (M/H); Parachuting (P/E); and Battlesuit, Driving (any), or Stealth, all (P/A).

Customization Notes: Courtesy Rank should reflect your former service grade: A lieutenant is Rank 3 [3]; a captain or major is Rank 4 [4]; a lieutenant colonel is Rank 5 [5]; a colonel is Rank 6 [6]; a brigadier is Rank 7 [7]; and a full general is Rank 8 [8]. This becomes Military Rank [5/level] if reactivated!

Choose background skills appropriate to unit and MOS (military occupational speciality); e.g., *Armor,* Driving (Tracked)-13 [4]; *CIC,* Strategy-13 [4]; *Intelligence,* Intelligence Analysis-12 [2]; Interrogation-13 [2]; *Psych Warfare,* Psychology-13 [4]; etc.

ARMY AVIATION (ENLISTED)   90 POINTS

Army aviation flies aircraft (helicopters, vertols, grav vehicles, and light jets) in support of land operations by the army. Since all Imperial aviation assets are assigned to the Imperial Navy, this template represents a veteran of a local (planetary) or extra-Imperial force.

Attributes: ST 10 [0], DX 12 [20], IQ 12 [20], HT 11 [10].

Advantages: A total of 25 points in Absolute Direction or 3D Spatial Sense [5 or 10]; Acceleration Tolerance [10]; Acute Vision [2/level]; Combat Reflexes [15]; Courtesy Rank 1-2 [1/level]; Danger Sense [15]; and Reputation (Decorated) [varies].

Disadvantages: A total of -20 points in Bad Temper [-10]; Callous [-6]; Code of Honor (Soldier's) [-5]; Duty (Reactivation, 6 or less) [-2] or (9 or less) [-5]; Fanaticism (Patriotism) [-15]; Intolerance (Enemy race or culture) [-5]; Overconfidence or Glory Hound [-10 or -15]; and Sense of Duty (Comrades in arms) [-5].

Primary Skills: Gunner (any) (P/A) DX+2 [2]-14*; Gunner (any other) (P/A) DX+2 [2]-14*; and Piloting (any military aircraft) (P/A) DX+2 [8]-14.
   * Includes +2 for IQ.

Secondary Skills: Aviation (M/A) IQ [2]-12; Electronics Operation (Comm) (M/A) IQ [2]-12; Electronics Operation (Sensors) (M/A) IQ [2]-12; Navigation (M/H) IQ [4]-12; NBC Warfare (M/A) IQ [2]-12; Parachuting (P/E) DX [1]-12; Savoir-Faire (Military) (M/E) IQ [1]-12; and Tactics (M/H) IQ [4]-12.

Background Skills: A net 5 points in Forward Observer, Leadership, Mechanic (any), No-Landing Extraction, Photography, Survival (any), or Vacc Suit, all (M/A); Free Fall, Gunner (any), or Piloting (any), all (P/A); and personal Combat/Weapon skills.

Customization Notes: Choose Courtesy Rank that reflects your former service grade; aviators are always at least sergeants (Rank 1 [1]), if not senior sergeants (Rank 2 [2]). This becomes Military Rank [5/level] if reactivated!

Choose your basic Gunner and Piloting skills to reflect your unit type; e.g., *Air Cav,* Gunner (Machine Gun) and (Rocket Launcher), Piloting (Helicopter); *CAS,* Gunner (Bombs) and (Machine Gun), Piloting (Heavy Airplane), etc. Choose background skills to reflect special training in things like extraction, reconnaissance, or SERE.

Note that aviators should never have Acceleration Weakness, Acrophobia, Confused, or Motion Sickness!

ARMY AVIATION (OFFICER)   90 POINTS

A former officer in one of the forces described under *Army Aviation (Enlisted),* above.

Attributes: ST 10 [0], DX 12 [20], IQ 13 [30], HT 11 [10].

Advantages: A total of 25 points in Absolute Direction or 3D Spatial Sense [5 or 10]; Acceleration Tolerance [10]; Acute Vision [2/level]; Charisma [5/level]; Combat Reflexes [15]; Courtesy Rank 3+ [1/level]; Danger Sense [15]; Reputation (Decorated) [varies]; and Status 1 [5].

Disadvantages: A total of -25 points in Callous [-6]; Code of Honor (Officer's) [-5]; Duty (Reactivation, 6 or less) [-2] or (9 or less) [-5]; Fanaticism (Patriotism) [-15]; Honesty [-10]; Intolerance (Enemy race or culture) [-5]; Jealousy [-10]; Overconfidence or Glory Hound [-10 or -15]; and Sense of Duty (His command) [-10].

Primary Skills: Gunner (any) (P/A) DX+2 [2]-14*; Gunner (any other) (P/A) DX+2 [2]-14*; Leadership (M/A) IQ-1 [1]-12; Piloting (any military aircraft) (P/A) DX+2 [8]-14; Savoir-Faire (Military) (M/E) IQ [1]-13; and Tactics (M/H) IQ [4]-13.

* Includes +2 for IQ.

Secondary Skills: Administration (M/A) IQ-1 [1]-12; Aviation (M/A) IQ-1 [1]-12; Electronics Operation (Comm) (M/A) IQ-1 [1]-12; Electronics Operation (Sensors) (M/A) IQ-1 [1]-12; Navigation (M/H) IQ-1 [2]-12; NBC Warfare (M/A) IQ-1 [1]-12; and Parachuting (P/E) DX [1]-12.

Background Skills: A total of 4 points in Forward Observer, No-Landing Extraction, Photography, Survival (any), or Vacc Suit, all (M/A); Intelligence Analysis or Strategy, both (M/H); Free Fall, Gunner (any), or Piloting (any), all (P/A); and personal Combat/Weapon skills.

Customization Notes: Choose Courtesy Rank that reflects your former service grade; if they fly, aviation officers are usually lieutenants (Rank 3 [3]), captains (Rank 4 [4]), or colonels (Rank 5 [5] or 6 [6]). This becomes Military Rank [5/level] if reactivated! See Army Aviation (Enlisted) (p. 101) for other recommendations.

MARINE (ENLISTED)   90 POINTS

Inside the Imperium, this represents a veteran of the Imperial Marines. Powers outside the Imperium sometimes have marine forces, while planetary forces within the Imperium have army units that serve the same function, but without the title. The Imperial Marines, after all, are unique.

Attributes: ST 11 [10], DX 12 [20], IQ 12 [20], HT 11 [10].

Advantages: G-Experience [10]; and 20 points chosen from 3D Spatial Sense [10]; Acceleration Tolerance [10]; Breath-Holding 1-2 [2 or 4]; Combat Reflexes [15]; Courtesy Rank 0-2 [1/level]; Fearlessness [2/level]; Fit or Very Fit [5 or 15]; Hard to Kill 1-2 [5 or 10]; High Pain Threshold [10]; Improved G-Tolerance [10]; Reputation (Decorated) [varies]; and Toughness (DR 1) [10].

Disadvantages: A total of -25 points in Bloodlust [-10]; Callous [-6]; Chummy or Gregarious [-5 or -10]; Code of Honor (Soldier's) [-5]; Duty (Reactivation, 6 or less) [-2] or (9 or less) [-5]; Fanaticism (Patriotism) [-15]; Intolerance (Enemy race or culture) [-5]; Overconfidence or Glory Hound [-10 or -15]; and Sense of Duty (Comrades in arms) [-5].

Primary Skills: Either Beam Weapons (any) or Guns (any), both (P/E) DX+3 [2]-15*; plus Free Fall (P/A) DX [2]-12; Gunner (any) (P/A) DX+2 [2]-14*; Savoir-Faire (Military) (M/E) IQ [1]-12; and Vacc Suit (M/A) IQ [2]-12.

* Includes +2 for IQ.

Secondary Skills: Armoury (Small Arms) (M/A) IQ-1 [1]-11; Computer Operation (M/E) IQ-1 [½]-11; Electronics Operation (Comm) (M/A) IQ-2 [½]-10; First Aid (M/E) IQ-1 [½]-11; Stealth (P/A) DX [2]-12; Tactics (M/H) IQ-1 [2]-11; one of Battlesuit or Exoskeleton, both (P/A) DX-1 [1]-11; one of Gesture (M/E) IQ-1 [½]-11 or Lip Reading (M/A) IQ-2 [½]-10; and a total of 3 points in Brawling or Knife, both (P/E); Shortsword (P/A); or Judo or Throwing, both (P/H).

Background Skills: A total of 5 points in Scrounging (M/E); Administration, Demolition, Leadership, or Mechanic (any), all (M/A); Engineer (Combat), Explosive Ordnance Disposal, SIGINT Collection/Jamming, or Traffic Analysis, all (M/H); Breath Control (M/VH); Beam Weapons (other) or Guns (other), both (P/E); Gunner (other) or Piloting (any), both (P/A); or any primary or secondary skill.

Customization Notes: Courtesy Rank should reflect your former service grade: A private is Rank 0 [0]; a sergeant is Rank 1 [1], and a senior sergeant (or specialist) is Rank 2 [2]. This becomes Military Rank [5/level] if reactivated. Choose background skills appropriate to unit and MOS; see Army (Enlisted) (p. 100) for examples. No marine should have Space Sickness!

MARINE (OFFICER)   90 POINTS

A former officer in the Imperial Marines.

Attributes: ST 11 [10], DX 12 [20], IQ 13 [30], HT 11 [10].

Advantages: A total of 25 points in 3D Spatial Sense [10]; Acceleration Tolerance [10]; Charisma [5/level]; Combat Reflexes [15]; Courtesy Rank 3+ [1/level]; G-Experience [10]; Improved G-Tolerance [10]; Reputa-tion (Decorated) [varies]; Status 1 [5]; Strong Will [4/level]; and Voice [10].

Disadvantages: A total of -25 points in Callous [-6]; Chummy [-5]; Code of Honor (Officer's) [-5]; Duty (Reactivation, 6 or less) [-2] or (9 or less) [-5]; Fanaticism (Patriotism) [-15]; Honesty [-10]; Intolerance (Enemy race or culture) [-5]; Jealousy [-10]; Odious Personal Habit ("By the book") [-5]; Overconfidence or Glory Hound [-10 or -15]; Sense of Duty (His command) [-10]; Stubbornness [-5]; and Workaholic [-5].

Primary Skills: Administration (M/A) IQ [2]-13; Free Fall (P/A) DX [2]-12; Leadership (M/A) IQ [2]-13; Savoir-Faire (Military) (M/E) IQ-1 [½]-12; Tactics (M/H) IQ [4]-13; and Vacc Suit (M/A) IQ-1 [1]-12.

Secondary Skills: Either Beam Weapons (any) or Guns (any) (P/E), both DX+2 [1]-14*; plus Computer Operation (M/E) IQ-1 [½]-12; Electronics Operation (Comm) (M/A) IQ-1 [1]-12; Gunner (any) (P/A) DX+1 [1]-13*; and one of Battlesuit or Exoskeleton, both (P/A) DX-1 [1]-11.
  * Includes +2 for IQ.

Background Skills: A total of 4 points in Astrogation, Electronics Operation (other), or Interrogation, all (M/A); Engineer (Combat), Intelligence Analysis, Psychology, or Strategy, all (M/H); and Piloting (any) (P/A).

Customization Notes: Courtesy Rank should reflect your former service grade; see Army (Officer) (p. 101) for ranks. This becomes Military Rank [5/level] if reactivated. As with other military careers, choose background skills appropriate to unit and MOS. Marine officers shouldn't have Space Sickness, but some paper-pushers have never been space-side . . .

MARINE COMMANDO (ENLISTED)   130 POINTS

A veteran of an Imperial marine commando unit. The genuine article is fairly rare.

Attributes: ST 11 [10], DX 13 [30], IQ 13 [30], HT 11[10].

Advantages: Combat Reflexes [15]; Fit [5]; G-Experience [10]; and 10 points chosen from 3D Spatial Sense [10]; Acceleration Tolerance [10]; Breath-Holding 1-2 [2 or 4]; Courtesy Rank 0-2 [1/level]; Daredevil [15]; Fearlessness [2/level]; Hard to Kill 1-2 [5 or 10]; High Pain Threshold [10]; Improved G-Tolerance [10]; Reputation (Decorated) [varies]; Toughness (DR 1) [10]; and Very Fit [10] (adds to cost of Fit).

Disadvantages: Fanaticism (Patriotism) [-15]; plus -15 points in Bloodlust [-10]; Callous [-6]; Chummy or Gregarious [-5 or -10]; Code of Honor (Soldier's) [-5]; Duty (Reactivation, 6 or less) [-2] or (9 or less) [-5]; Intolerance (Enemy race or culture) [-5]; Overconfidence or Glory Hound [-10 or -15]; and Sense of Duty (Comrades in arms) [-5].

Primary Skills: Two Beam Weapons or Guns skills, each (P/E) DX+3 [2]-16*; plus Free Fall (P/A) DX+1 [4]-14; Gunner (any) (P/A) DX+2 [2]-15*; Savoir-Faire (Military) (M/E) IQ [1]-13; Tactics (M/H) IQ [4]-13; and Vacc Suit (M/A) IQ [2]-13.

Secondary Skills: Another Beam Weapons or Guns skill, (P/E) DX+2 [1]-15*; plus Armoury (Small arms) (M/A) IQ-1 [1]-12; Battlesuit (P/A) DX-1 [1]-12; Brawling (P/E) DX [1]-13; Computer Operation (M/E) IQ-1 [½]-12; Demolition (M/A) IQ-1 [1]-12; Electronics Operation (Comm) (M/A) IQ-1 [1]-12; Engineer (Combat) (M/H) IQ-1 [2]-12; Explosive Ordnance Disposal (M/H) IQ-1 [2]-12; First Aid (M/E) IQ-1 [½]-12; Gesture (M/E) IQ-1 [½]-12; Judo (P/H) DX-1 [2]-12; Knife (P/E) DX-1 [½]-12; Piloting (Spaceship) (P/A) DX-1 [1]-12; Scrounging (M/E) IQ-1 [½]-12; Shortsword (P/A) DX-1 [1]-12; Stealth (P/A) DX [2]-13; and Traps (M/A) IQ-1 [1]-12.
  * Includes +2 for IQ.

Background Skills: Administration (M/A) IQ-2 [½]-11; Leadership (M/A) IQ-2 [½]-11; Mechanic (any space-related) (M/A) IQ-2 [½]-11; SIGINT Collection/Jamming (M/H) IQ-2 [1]-11; and Traffic Analysis (M/H) IQ-2 [1]-11.

Customization Notes: Courtesy Rank reflects your former service grade; see Marine (Enlisted) (p. 102). This becomes Military Rank [5/level] if reactivated. There is no choice in background skills here. Elite units have standardized training; the only choices are "qualify" or "wash out." Commandos should have no physical disadvantages (a retired soldier could, if he was wounded in action).

MARINE COMMANDO (OFFICER)   145 POINTS

A former officer in one of the Imperial Marines' commando units . . . even rarer than his enlisted counterpart!

Attributes: ST 11 [10], DX 13 [30], IQ 13 [30], HT 11 [10].

Advantages: Combat Reflexes [15]; Fit [5]; G-Experience [10]; and 15 points chosen from 3D Spatial Sense [10]; Acceleration Tolerance [10]; Breath-Holding 1-2 [2 or 4]; Charisma [5/level]; Courtesy Rank 3-5 [1/level]; Fearlessness [2/level]; Hard to Kill 1-2 [5 or 10]; High Pain Threshold [10]; Improved G-Tolerance [10]; Reputation (Decorated) [varies]; Status 1 [5]; Strong Will [4/level]; Toughness (DR 1) [10]; Very Fit [10] (adds to cost of Fit); and Voice [10].

Disadvantages: Fanaticism (Patriotism) [-15]; plus -15 points in Bloodlust [-10]; Callous [-6]; Chummy [-5]; Code of Honor (Officer's) [-5]; Duty (Reactivation, 6 or less) [-2] or (9 or less) [-5]; Honesty [-10]; Intolerance (Enemy race or culture) [-5]; Overconfidence or Glory Hound [-10 or -15]; Sense of Duty (His command) [-10]; Stubbornness [-5]; and Workaholic [-5].

Primary Skills: Two Beam Weapons or Guns skills, each (P/E) DX+3 [2]-16*; plus Electronics Operation (Comm) (M/A) IQ [2]-13; Free Fall (P/A) DX+1 [4]-14; Gunner (any) (P/A) DX+2 [2]-15*; Leadership (M/A) IQ+1 [4]-14; Savoir-Faire (Military) (M/E) IQ [1]-13; Tactics (M/H) IQ+1 [6]-14; and Vacc Suit (M/A) IQ [2]-13.

Secondary Skills: Another Beam Weapons or Guns skill, (P/E) DX+2 [1]-15*; plus Administration (M/A) IQ-1 [1]-12; Armoury (Small arms) (M/A) IQ-1 [1]-12; Battlesuit (P/A) DX-1 [1]-12; Brawling (P/E) DX [1]-13; Computer Operation (M/E) IQ-1 [½]-12; Demolition (M/A) IQ-1 [1]-12; Engineer (Combat) (M/H) IQ-1 [2]-12; Explosive Ordnance Disposal (M/H) IQ-1 [2]-12; First Aid (M/E) IQ-1 [½]-12; Gesture (M/E) IQ-1 [½]-12; Interrogation (M/A) IQ-1 [1]-12; Intelligence Analysis (M/H) IQ-1 [2]-12; Judo (P/H) DX-1 [2]-12; Knife (P/E) DX-1 [½]-12; Piloting (Spaceship) (P/A) DX-1 [1]-12; Scrounging (M/E) IQ-1 [½]-12; Shortsword (P/A) DX-1 [1]-12; Stealth (P/A) DX [2]-13; and Traps (M/A) IQ-1 [1]-12.
   * Includes +2 for IQ.

Background Skills: Mechanic (any space-related) (M/A) IQ-2 [½]-11; SIGINT Collection/Jamming (M/H) IQ-2 [1]-11; and Traffic Analysis (M/H) IQ-2 [1]-11.

Customization Notes: Commando officers lead from the front, and are just as tough as their men. Since commando units are company- or battalion-sized, these "fighting officers" are limited to Military Rank 5; therefore, commando officers are often passed over for promotion, and may even have to accept a demotion to join the unit. Courtesy Rank should reflect this, and is limited to lieutenant (Rank 3 [3]), captain (Rank 4 [4]), or colonel (Rank 5 [5]). This becomes Military Rank [5/level] if reactivated.

   See *Marine Commando (Enlisted)* (p.103) for other notes.

NAVY (ENLISTED)   90 POINTS

This template can represent a former member of the Imperial Navy or a local planetary navy, either inside or outside the Imperium. Local navies within the Imperium tend to be mislabeled customs and anti-piracy patrols.

Attributes: ST 10 [0], DX 12 [20], IQ 12 [20], HT 11 [10].

Advantages: G-Experience [10]; and a total of 20 points in 3D Spatial Sense [10]; Acceleration Tolerance [10]; Combat Reflexes [15]; Courtesy Rank 0-2 [1/level]; Fit [5]; Improved G-Tolerance [10]; and Reputation (Decorated) [varies].

Disadvantages: A total of -20 points chosen from Chummy or Gregarious [-5 or -10]; Code of Honor (Soldier's) [-5]; Duty (Reactivation, 6 or less) [-2] or (9 or less) [-5]; Fanaticism (Patriotism) [-15]; Intolerance (Enemy race or culture, Pirates, etc.) [-5]; Overconfidence or Glory Hound [-10 or -15]; and Sense of Duty (Comrades in arms) [-5].

Primary Skills: Free Fall (P/A) DX+1 [4]-13; Savoir-Faire (Military) (M/E) IQ+1 [2]-13; Vacc Suit (M/A) IQ+1 [4]-13; and one of these 6 options:

1. Area Knowledge (System or sector) (M/E) IQ+1 [2]-13; Astrogation (M/A) IQ+1 [4]-13; and Piloting (Spaceship) (P/A) DX+2 [8]-14.
2. Armoury (any) (M/A) IQ+2 [6]-14 and Gunner (any ship-mounted) (P/A) DX+4 [8]-16*.
3. Cartography (M/A) IQ+1 [4]-13; Electronics Operation (Sensors) (M/A) IQ+1 [4]-13; and SIGINT Collection/Jamming (M/H) IQ+1 [6]-13.
4. Electronics Operation (Comm) (M/A) IQ+2 [6]-14 and Traffic Analysis (M/H) IQ+2 [8]-14.
5. Engineer (Vehicles) (M/H) IQ [4]-12; Shipbuilding (Starship) (M/A) IQ [2]-12; and two of Mechanic (J-Drive), (M-Drive), or (Power Reactor), each (M/A) IQ+1 [4]-13.
6. Leadership (M/A) IQ+2 [6]-14 and Tactics (Space) (M/H) IQ+2 [8]-14.

Secondary Skills: Computer Operation (M/E) IQ [1]-12; Shortsword (P/A) DX [2]-12; and either Beam Weapons (any) or Guns (any), both (P/E) DX+2 [1]-14*.
   * Includes +2 for IQ.

Background Skills: A total of 2 points in any of Scrounging (M/E); Administration or Heraldry (Ship's Markings), both (M/A); Brawling (P/E); or Carousing (P/A; HT).

Customization Notes: Courtesy Rank should reflect your former service grade: An ordinary space hand is Rank 0 [0], a chief is Rank 1 [1], and a master chief (or specialist) is Rank 2 [2]. This becomes Military Rank [5/level] if reactivated! Also choose primary skills that reflect your duty: (1) helmsman or pilot, (2) gunner or gunner's mate, (3) sensor operator, (4) radioman, (5) engineer, and (6) chief or master chief (which require Courtesy Rank 1 or 2, respectively).

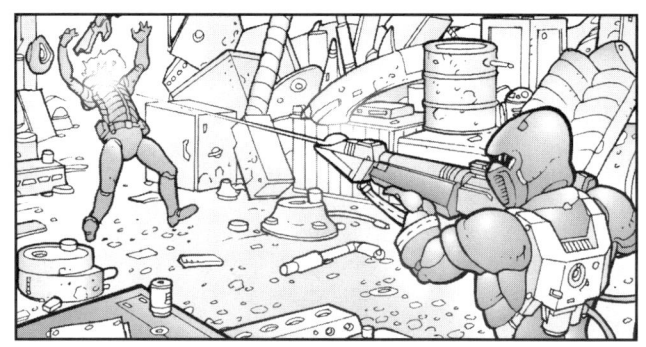

NAVY (OFFICER)   90 POINTS

A former officer in one of the forces described under *Navy (Enlisted)*, p. 104.

Attributes: ST 10 [0], DX 12 [20], IQ 13 [30], HT 11 [10].

Advantages: A total of 20 points in 3D Spatial Sense [10]; Acceleration Tolerance [10]; Charisma [5/level]; Combat Reflexes [15]; Courtesy Rank 3+ [1/level]; G-Experience [10]; Improved G-Tolerance [10]; Reputation (Decorated) [varies]; Status 1 [5]; Strong Will [4/level]; and Voice [10].

Disadvantages: A total of -20 points in Chummy [-5]; Code of Honor (Officer's) [-5]; Duty (Reactivation, 6 or less) [-2] or (9 or less) [-5]; Fanaticism (Patriotism) [-15]; Honesty [-10]; Intolerance (Enemy race or culture, Pirates, etc.) [-5]; Jealousy [-10]; Odious Personal Habit ("By the book") [-5]; Overconfidence or Glory Hound [-10 or -15]; Sense of Duty (His command) [-10]; Stubbornness [-5]; and Workaholic [-5].

Primary Skills: Leadership (M/A) IQ+1 [4]-14; Savoir-Faire (Military) (M/E) IQ [1]-13; Tactics (Space) (M/H) IQ+1 [6]-14; and one of these options:

1. Armoury (any) (M/A) IQ+2 [6]-15 and Gunner (any ship-mounted) (P/A) DX+3 [4]-15*.

2. Astrogation (M/A) IQ [2]-13 and Piloting (Starship) (P/A) DX+2 [8]-14.

3. Cartography (M/A) IQ [2]-13; Electronics Operation (Comm) (M/A) IQ [2]-13; Electronics Operation (Sensors) (M/A) IQ [2]-13; SIGINT Collection/Jamming (M/H) IQ-1 [2]-12; and Traffic Analysis (M/H) IQ-1 [2]-12.

4. Engineer (Vehicles) (M/H) IQ+1 [6]-14; Shipbuilding (Starship) (M/A) IQ-1 [1]-12; and all three of Mechanic (J-Drive), (M-Drive), and (Power Reactor), each (M/A) IQ-1 [1]-12.

Secondary Skills: Administration (M/A) IQ-1 [1]-12; Computer Operation (M/E) IQ-1 [½]-12; Free Fall (P/A) DX [2]-12; Vacc Suit (M/A) IQ-1 [1]-12; and either Beam Weapons (any) or Guns (any), both (P/E) DX+1 [½]-13*.

  * Includes +2 for IQ.

Background Skills: A total of 4 points in Heraldry (Ship's Markings) or Planetology (any), both (M/A); or Astronomy, Intelligence Analysis, or Strategy (Space), all (M/H).

Customization Notes: Courtesy Rank should reflect former service grade: ensign or junior lieutenant (Rank 3 [3]), lieutenant or lieutenant commander (Rank 4 [4]), commander (Rank 5 [5]), captain (Rank 6 [6]), commodore or rear admiral (Rank 7 [7]), or admiral (Rank 8 [8]). This becomes Military Rank [5/level] if reactivated! Primary skills represent practical experience on board ship: (1) weapons, (2) command, (3) systems, and (4) engineering. The GM may wish to allow those 10 points to be spent in other areas (e.g., on Administration for a logistics man). The Navy also plays a prominent role in Imperial military espionage, with an intelligence network to rival any dedicated agency's. Some former officers will combine naval and spy skills depending on how long they spent in each role.

NAVY AVIATION (OFFICER)   90 POINTS

A former naval officer (see *Navy (Officer)*, left), but trained to handle small craft (aerospace shuttles, fighters, etc.) as opposed to starships. Local navies within the Imperium rarely have "aviation assets" like this except for customs and anti-piracy duties.

Attributes: ST 10 [0], DX 12 [20], IQ 13 [30], HT 11 [10].

Advantages: One of 3D Spatial Sense [10] or Acceleration Tolerance [10]; plus 15 points Acute Vision [2/level]; Charisma [5/level]; Combat Reflexes [15]; Courtesy Rank 3+ [1/level]; Danger Sense [15]; Daredevil [15]; G-Experience [10]; Improved G-Tolerance [10]; Reputation (Decorated) [varies]; Status 1 [5]; and Strong Will [4/level].

Disadvantages: A total of -25 points in Callous [-6]; Code of Honor (Officer's) [-5]; Duty (Reactivation, 6 or less) [-2] or (9 or less) [-5]; Fanaticism (Patriotism) [-15]; Impulsiveness [-10]; Intolerance (Enemy race or culture, Pirates, etc.) [-5]; Jealousy [-10]; Overconfidence or Glory Hound [-10 or -15]; Sense of Duty (His command) [-10]; Stubbornness [-5]; and Workaholic [-5].

Primary Skills: Gunner (any) (P/A) DX+2 [2]-14*; Gunner (any other) (P/A) DX+2 [2]-14*; Leadership (M/A) IQ-1 [1]-12; Piloting (Starship) (P/A) DX+2 [8]-14; Savoir-Faire (Military) (M/E) IQ [1]-13; and Tactics (Space) (M/H) IQ [4]-13.

Secondary Skills: Administration (M/A) IQ-1 [1]-12; Astrogation (M/A) IQ-1 [1]-12; Aviation (M/A) IQ-1 [1]-12; Computer Operation (M/E) IQ-1 [½]-12; Electronics Operation (Comm) (M/A) IQ-1 [1]-12; Electronics Operation (Sensors) (M/A) IQ-1 [1]-12; Free Fall (P/A) DX [2]-12; and Vacc Suit (M/A) IQ-1 [1]-12.

Background Skills: Navigation (M/H) IQ-2 [1]-11; Parachuting (P/E) DX-1 [½]-11; and a total of 2 points in Photography or Survival (any) (M/A); Beam Weapons (any) or Guns (any), both (P/E); or Carousing (P/A; HT).
  * Includes +2 for IQ.

Customization Notes: Courtesy Rank should reflect your former service grade. Navy aviation officers either use the naval ranks listed for Navy (Officer) (above) or the following: flight lieutenant (Rank 3 [3]), squadron leader (Rank 4 [4]), wing commander (Rank 5 [5]), and group captain (Rank 6 [6]). The higher ranks don't get to fly (at least not as often as they would like, and never in combat). This becomes Military Rank [5/level] if reactivated.

JOB TABLE

Job (requirements), Monthly Income	Success Roll	Critical Failure
Poor Jobs		
Bouncer at Low Dive (ST 10+), Cr400	ST	LJ, 4d/8d
Starport Panhandler* (Panhandling), Cr300	PR	1d/4d
Street Entertainer* (any one of Bard, Dancing, Musical Instrument, or Singing 10+), Cr50 × Skill	PR	-1i
Struggling Jobs		
Actor/Actress* (Acting 10+), Cr50 × Skill	PR	-1i/LJ, 1d
Bouncer at Better-Quality Dive (ST10+, Intimidation), Cr650	Best PR	LJ, 4d/8d
General Laborer (ST 10+), Cr550	PR	LJ/5d
Journalist* (Research 12+, Bard, or Photography 12+), Cr70 × Best PR *plus* Cr500 × Reputation	Best PR	-2i/LJ, 2d
Mechanic/Technician (any Mechanic skill at 12+), Cr120 × skill	PR	-1i/-1i, LJ, 2d
Roadie (ST 10+), Cr650	PR	-1i/LJ
Sales Clerk (Merchant 10+), Cr600	PR + Reaction	LJ
Security Guard (any combat skill at 10+, ST 10+), Cr600	PR	-1i, LJ/LJ, 4d
Translator (two additional languages at 12+), Cr100 × skill	Best PR-2	-2i/-3i, LJ
Average Jobs		
Bodyguard (ST 11+, one combat skill at 12+), Cr90 × IQ	ST	-1i, LJ/-1i, LJ, 4d
Lab Assistant/Tech Worker (Computer Operation 10+, Research 11+, any Science skill 10+), Cr100 × worst PR-6	Worst PR	-2i/LJ, 2d
Local Law Enforcement: Patrol (Law Enforcement, Streetwise, and Criminology 12+), Cr75 × best PR	Worst PR	-3i, 2d/LJ, 4d
Low-level Spy (Fast-Talk, Research, and Stealth), Cr100 × Worst PR	Worst PR	4d, LJ/Jailed
Mercenary Trooper (any two combat skills 10+), Cr100 × Best PR	Best PR-2	-2i, 4d/8d, LJ
Private Detective (Law Enforcement, Research, and Streetwise 12+), Cr75 × best PR	Worst PR	-3i, 2d/LJ, 4d
Prospector/Belter* (Prospecting 10+), Cr100 × Skill	Prospecting	-3i, 1d/LJ, 3d
Starship Crew (Status 0+, appropriate shipboard skill 10+), Cr80 × best appropriate skill *plus* Cr200 × (Rank or Status)	Specific job's PR	LJ, 2d/LJ, 8d
Studio Musician (any Musical Instrument 10+), Cr100 × PR	PR	LJ
Comfortable Jobs		
Back-up Musician (any Musical Instrument 12+), Cr100 × PR	PR	LJ
Black Marketeer* (Streetwise 12+, Merchant 10+), Cr300 × Worst PR	Streetwise	-3i/-5i, arrested
Doctor (Physician 13+, Status 0+), Cr350 × PR	PR	-3i/-10i, lose license
Engineer (any Engineer skill at 12+), Cr200 × PR	PR	-2i/-4i, LJ
Lawyer (Law 12+, Status 1+), Cr300 × PR	PR	-2i/-2i, LJ, 2d
Local Law Enforcement: Detective (Status 0+, Law Enforcement, Streetwise, and Criminology 12+), Cr75 × best PR *plus* Cr10 × (Status)	Worst PR	-3i, 2d/LJ, 4d
Mid-Level Spy (Diplomacy, Intelligence Analysis, and Research), Cr375	Worst PR	-6i/LJ
Mercenary Officer (Rank 1+, any one combat skill, Leadership, and Tactics 10+) Cr100 × Skill *plus* Cr10 × (Rank or Status)	Best PR-2	-2i, 4d/8d, LJ
Scientist (Computer Operation 12+, Research 13+, any Science skill 14+), Cr300 × best Science skill	Worst PR	-2i/LJ, 2d
Starship Officer (Rank 1+, Leadership 10+, appropriate shipboard skill 10+), Cr100 × best appropriate skill *plus* Cr200 × (Rank or Status)	Specific job's PR	LJ, 2d/LJ, 8d
Wealthy Jobs		
Major Corporate Stockholder (Very Wealthy+), Cr50,000	10	-2i/-5i, -1 level of Wealth, 2d
Remittance Man/Woman* (Status 2+), Cr12,000 × Status	IQ + Status	LJ**
Rock Star* (Status 2+, Performance 12+), Cr1,500 × Status	PR	LJ†

Key to Table

PR: Prerequisite; LJ: Lose Job; "d": dice of damage suffered (the GM may opt to play this out); "i": months of income lost.

* Freelance jobs.   ** Family loses fortune and the supply of funds is cut off.

† Musical tastes change or band breaks up over artistic differences.

CHAPTER FOUR

Equipment and Supplies

Most of the existing equipment created for **GURPS** can be used in **GURPS Traveller**. Game Masters interested in the full range of equipment available should acquire **Ultra-Tech**, **Ultra-Tech 2**, and perhaps even **High-Tech** for TL4-7 adventuring. The Safetech parameters on pp. UTT9-10 should be consulted as the GM determines what's available and at what cost. In addition, the following setting parameters apply:

GRAVITIC TECHNOLOGY

Artificial gravity appears at TL8 in the **Traveller** universe, two TLs early. Contragravity appears four TLs early – thus, TL12 CG units are available at TL8, while TL13 CG units arrive at TL9. Grav belts are available, but "grav guns" and gravity-beam weapons are *not* used in the **Traveller** setting. Artificial-gravity units include automatic compensation for transient high-G accelerations (separate "grav compensators" aren't needed) to 3 Gs at TL8-9 or 6 Gs at TL10-12.

ENERGY STORAGE TECHNOLOGY

Non-rechargeable power cells are not in standard use. All power cells should be built as rechargeable (having half normal durations/energy storage/shots).

MEDICAL TECHNOLOGY

Braintaping and regeneration rays are unavailable. Low berths (aka cryotubes) are often installed on starships for use by low passengers (those who make the trip in suspended animation), and are often used in lifeboats to extend their capacity and range (see sidebar, p. 108).

BEAM WEAPON TECHNOLOGY

Beam weapons undergo several changes between "standard" **GURPS** and **GURPS Traveller**. See also the setting-specific design notes on p. 111.

Lasers fire pulses of coherent light. At TL10+, X-ray lasers become available. Lasers use backpack power packs; this is a *heavily* ingrained custom dating to the earliest, power-hungry models and their clunky power cells.

Plasma guns fire bolts of high-energy plasma, and are identical to the plasma blaster weapons described on p. UTT58, except that the cost is × 15, not × 1.5, for beams under 6,400 MJ output. *Fusion guns* are more powerful, higher TL plasma blasters. (They aren't **Ultra-Tech**'s fusion guns.)

Particle beams are commonly used as spacecraft weaponry, but are not available for use as personal weapons. If designing spacecraft p-beams using **GURPS Vehicles**, limit designs to neutral particle beams of 100,000 kJ or higher output.

Note: GURPS Traveller expresses prices in Imperial credits, abbreviated Cr (Cr500, Cr1, etc.). Large amounts are in megacredits (MCr1.23, MCr34.2, etc.) of 1 million credits each. Other **GURPS** books use the alternate symbol for credit, which is $.

Tech Levels

Traveller was the first science-fiction roleplaying game to make widespread use of tech levels, a device later used by **GURPS,** albeit with modifications. **GURPS Traveller** uses the **GURPS** tech levels, but since there is considerable possibility for confusion, a table for conversion is provided below. All references to Tech Levels or TLs will be to the **GURPS** system. Any reference to **Traveller** tech levels will be clearly labeled as such.

Traveller Tech Level	GURPS Tech Level
0	1-3
1	4
2	5
3	5
4	5
5	6
6	6
7	7
8	8
9	9
10	9
11	9
12	10
13	10
14	11
15	12
16	13

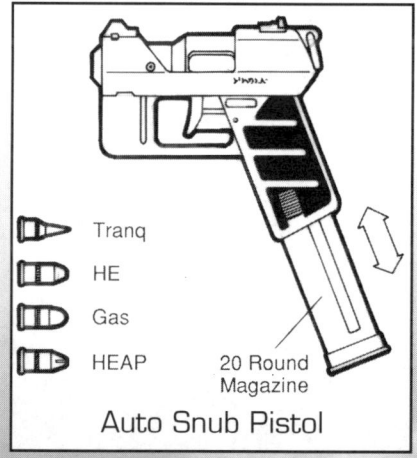

Tranq

HE

Gas

HEAP

20 Round Magazine

Auto Snub Pistol

Technical Difficulties

In *Traveller*, all Imperial military forces use top-of-the-line gear. In *GURPS*, the average marine, with his TL10 background, would be at -10 to use or repair most of his TL12 equipment!

Several solutions exist. The GM can rule that – even though the TL12 units get all the press – the Imperium actually fields units at TLs 10, 11, and 12. (This would make logistics sense, too, vastly multiplying potential "vendor" worlds.) The downsides are introducing multiple TLs of Imperial gear and bending *Traveller* canon.

A second option assumes all equipment is TL12, except items that require a Mental skill to use or might need field repair. In those cases, the trooper receives gear of his own TL. This creates even more multi-TL inventory muddle, but tweaks the setting a little bit less.

A third option is to ignore the situation, which would justify slashing the cost of High Technology (see p. 82).

Low Berths

Also called cryo-tubes (or freezers, a vulgarism starship crews never use . . . when passengers can hear). "Low passengers" (see p. 78) spend a star trip in suspended animation. Many lifeboats carry low berths to reduce life-support needs.

Entering: Entering a low berth takes five minutes, 10 without assistance.

Revival: Those outside a low berth can revive an occupant at any time. The berth can trigger revival after a set duration, or a linked computer can when certain preprogrammed conditions are met. Revival takes 15 minutes. Success is automatic if overseen by a person with Physician 10+ or Electronics Operation (Medical) 10+. Otherwise, roll against HT; the occupant dies on a critical failure. One person may only monitor four revivals at once.

Nerve guns are rare; increase their TL by 2 (i.e., they appear at TL12). They cost 10 times listed price. *Stunners* are rare; increase their TL by 3 (i.e., they appear at TL12). They also cost 10 times list.

Disintegrators were used by the Ancients, but their secrets were lost. Any that enter into the game will be one-of-a-kind artifacts, therefore highly valuable and very likely to be confiscated by the Imperial government if discovered.

Several *GURPS* beam-weapon types are not used in the *Traveller* setting: anti-particle beams ("pulsars"), blasters and electron-beam weapons (as personal weapons), displacers ("tachyon shotguns"), electrolasers, electron pistols/rifles, flamers, gamma-ray lasers ("grasers"), kinetic stunners ("forcebeams"), microwave disruptors ("masers"), paralysis guns, screamers, and space/time disruptors. Fusion guns as described in *Ultra-Tech* do not exist; use plasma blasters instead.

MESON TECHNOLOGY

Meson guns are designed as neutral-particle beams (p. VE123) except they first appear at TL10 and have a minimum output of 1 billion kJ, divided by 10 at each successive TL. They function like neutral-particle beams, except they ignore target armor PD and DR. Anyone not directly hit will suffer secondary explosive and radiation damage (which does *not* ignore DR and PD) as per antiparticle beams.

Meson communicators are identical in statistics and function to neutrino communicators (see *Ultra-Tech* and *Vehicles*) except weight, volume, and cost are multiplied by 10.

ELECTRONICS TECHNOLOGY

Bioscanner, chemscanner, and *multiscanner* devices do not exist. The radscanner *does* exist. *Ultrascanners* do not exist. *Neutrino communicators and receivers* are not available (but see *Meson Communicators*). *Intruder suits* and *intruder chameleon* armor, vehicle, and robot surfaces are unavailable.

FORCE FIELD TECHNOLOGY

All deflectors and force screens, and all related force-field technology (force shields, force swords, life-support belts, etc.) are unavailable. Exceptions include nuclear dampers (see p. 51), meson screens (see p. 154), and the ultra-rare "black globe" and "white globe" force fields derived from Ancient artifacts. Gravity ripple communications are not available.

NEURAL INTERFACE, IMPLANTS, AND CYBERNETICS

These are rare in *Traveller*. With the exception of simple prosthetics, which replace but do not augment missing body parts, bionics are not commercially available in the Imperium. This stems from Imperial distrust for technology that smacks of robotics or mind control ("Zhodani influences!").

On many planets, possession of obvious or known cybernetics is a Social Stigma. Nevertheless, most advanced societies, including the Imperium, have the technology to produce cybernetics and implants, and may do so on a limited basis (outfitting covert operatives, for example).

If introducing neural interface technology and cybernetics, GMs should use the TLs from *GURPS Ultra-Tech*, *Space*, and *Ultra-Tech 2* rather than from *GURPS Cyberpunk*, and reduce the bonus given by neural interfaces to +1 rather than +4.

ULTRA-TECH MELEE WEAPONS

Ultra-Tech melee weapons (vibroblade, monowire, sonic blade, neurolash, force sword, etc.) are rare or non-existent (GM's option) in the *Traveller* setting.

PSIONIC SHIELDS

The technology to block Psi powers exists in the *Traveller* setting, and has been incorporated into vehicles, buildings, and personal helmets. The helmets are described on p. 116.

DRUGS

Most medicinal and many non-medicinal drugs found in *GURPS* are available. Some non-standard drugs include:

Slow (TL10) slows down perceived time for the user, at a rate of 2-to-1. Treat as Altered Time Rate +1 (see p. CI49). A dose takes effect in one minute if taken as a pill, immediately if injected, and lasts 10 minutes. The user suffers 1d damage afterward. Cr2,000 in pill or injectable form.

Fast (TL10) is a powerful improvement of Suspend. A dose lasts 60 days (!), during which the subject requires only a single day's life support. At the end of its use, the user suffers 1d of damage. Fast is primarily used in survival situations, and tablets or injectors are often carried in lifeboat survival kits. Few people take the drug in the presence of those they do not completely trust. One dose costs Cr1,500 in either form. An antidote is available for Cr100.

Combat drug is an improved TL10 Adder (see p. UT97) providing +2 to ST, DX, and HT. Duration and onset are as for Slow drug. Unlike TL8 Adders, no HT roll is required, but

users do suffer -2 to ST, DX, and HT for 20 minutes afterward. Cost is Cr200 in pill form or Cr400 as an injectable.

Anagathics (TL12) are the only version of Anti-agathics (p. UT99) available in *GURPS Traveller*. Anagathics retard the aging process (by about 50-to-1), but cannot reverse it. Each monthly dose slows aging for that month; missing a dose requires making up any skipped aging rolls at one per week till the regimen is re-established or the rolls get caught up. Anagathics are rare and expensive. A monthly dose costs Cr30,000; finding it requires a 5-point Contact (he has 1d-2 doses every month) or a Streetwise roll (roll at -6 once every three months per TL12 world; success finds 1d doses).

ILLEGAL DRUGS

Given the size and diversity of the Imperium, just about anything can qualify as an illegal substance somewhere. Different races will be affected differently by some substances, and what is harmless to Humans will no doubt be deadly to some, hallucinogenic to others, and medicinal to a few. It is up to the individual GM to determine what is and is not an illegal drug for a given world, or portion of a world. The substances which the Imperium bans on an empire-wide basis are still fairly numerous, but the most important are the various types of psi drugs (see pp. T:AI140-141).

WEAPONS

The following sections detail the variety of personal weaponry commonly encountered in the Imperium. These models have informally become the "standards" – they can be purchased or repaired throughout most of Imperial space. For every "standard" model of weapon, at least 100 variants can be encountered on single worlds or in local regions.

Many weapons don't become "standardized" until one (possibly more) TLs past their introduction. For instance, ACRs can be developed at TL8, but the standard designs incorporated TL9 improvements by the time they filtered throughout the Imperium. Most TL8 militaries with a desire for ACRs simply import the TL9 Imperial standards rather than develop their own TL8 version.

PERSONAL SLUG THROWERS

Most Imperial slug-throwers are familiar, but not identical to 20th-century fare. Over thousands of years the standard calibers and design parameters have changed. Slight changes in weapon statistics result.

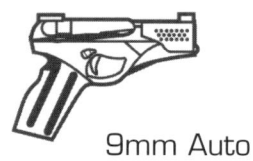
9mm Auto

9mm Mag

Body Pistol

Revolvers commonly fire 5mm, 7mm, or 9mm ammo.

Magnum revolvers fire a more powerful 9mm cartridge than the standard 9mm revolver. Ammo is not interchangeable. Many Imperial nobles carry ceremonial Magnums, in the same way that those of previous ages carried ceremonial swords as part of their formal costume.

Body pistols are small, non-metallic automatic pistols specially constructed to evade detection by all but the most advanced scanning equipment. Covert and criminal uses for the weapon abound, and it is a favorite of spies, smugglers, and others of their ilk.

Auto pistols are usually 7mm or 9mm.

Gauss pistols and *Gauss rifles* fire 4mm darts (sometimes called needles) accelerated by electromagnetic coils in the barrel rather than expanding gasses. They are almost completely silent except for the sharp crack of a supersonic round. (Some weapons can be adjusted to fire rounds at subsonic velocities; this option adds Cr500 to weapon cost and is required for firing tranq rounds. Subsonic rounds do ½ damage but make no more noise than a mosquito.) Standard upgrades to the Gauss rifle include gyrostabilization, laser sights, HUD sights, and a RAM-grenade hardpoint; the listed weapon includes these.

Gauss Rifle

Carbines and *rifles* are normally 7mm (carbines) or 7mm, 9mm, or 13mm (rifles). Their ammo does not interchange with corresponding pistol ammo. The 13mm rifle would have non-military utility on very few worlds.

Assault rifles usually are 5.5mm or 7.5mm. Models seen on Imperial worlds tend to slightly underperform their ancient Terran ancestors, a testimony to how long the Solomani have excelled at weapons-crafting.

Advanced combat rifles fire a variety of caseless ammunition in 7mm or 9mm. The standard models feature gyrostabilization, laser sights, HUD sights, and a RAM-grenade hardpoint.

Snub pistols and *accelerator rifles* fire small rockets, making them recoil-free and well-suited for zero-gravity work. The snub pistol also features very short range, ideal

for starship interiors. Both meet the varying demands of shipboard and hullside combat by firing a wide mix of ammo. These weapons could be *much* lighter, but manufacturers find that purchasers want some minimal "heft" to their small arms.

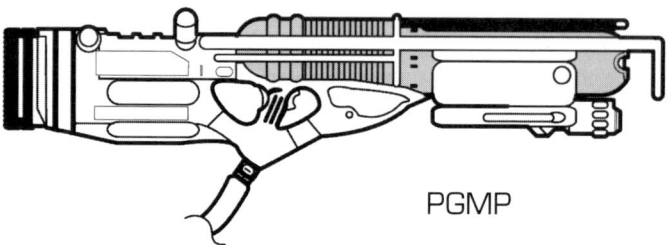
PGMP

SMGs and *shotguns* resemble their Terran ancestors, with small changes in performance over the centuries.

Light assault guns offer a relatively low-tech counter to armored infantry and some utility against unarmored threats.

ENERGY WEAPONS

Lasers, plasma guns, and fusion guns all include integral laser and HUD sights (Holographic HUD at TL9+). All have backpack powerpacks with rechargeable power cells; the weight and cost under *AWt* is the backpack. Add both together for total values. The backpack power supply usually attaches to the weapon via a cord; battle dress designed for firing the PGMP-10A or FMMP-11 may incorporate the power cord into the armor.

The PGMP-10A and FGMP-11 are designed to plug into battle-dress electronics to use its HUD; they cannot be fired without a suit.

The PGMP-11 and FGMP-12 use contragravity units in weapons and backpacks that reduce weight to 1% of actual weight; the FGMP-12 can even be used one-handed with the CG unit activated. When turned on, the CG unit drains 1 shot per 5.55 hours (PGMP) or 13.88 hours (FGMP) from the backpack.

HAND GRENADES

These are described on pp. UT67-68.

RAM GRENADES

Somewhat misnamed, RAM (*r*ocket-*a*ssisted *m*unition) grenades are rockets fired from hardpoints incorporated in the flash suppressors of ACRs or muzzles of Gauss rifles, much like TL7 rifle grenades. They come in anti-personnel and anti-armor versions.

The RAM grenade can only be launched from a rifle hardpoint; this provides minimal "standoff" distance and allows the grenade's firer to use any laser or HUD sights attached to his rifle. Though hardpoint-launched, they may be loaded in combat (takes 6 turns). The rifle cannot function normally while grenade-armed.

AMMUNITION NOTES

Most *GURPS Traveller* guns fire conventional ball rounds, but some have multiple ammunition types, listed on the tables on pp. 114-115. These are:

APS is armor-piercing saboted ammunition. DR protects at half value against it, as shown by the (2) after the round's damage, but damage after DR is also halved.

Beehive are flechette rounds described on p. VE189.

CHEM is a chemical-filled round. A common chemical filler is sleep gas, at Cr5 per dose, but other gasses can be substituted per p. UT70.

Gauss guns fire high-density dart ammunition. Armor DR is halved, but damage is *not* halved after penetrating DR.

HE is a high-explosive round that does damage using the explosion rules in *GURPS Basic Set* (p. B121). Fragmentation damage is shown in square brackets.

HEAT is a high-explosive shaped-charge round. The (10) after damage means target armor protects at $\frac{1}{10}$ DR against a direct hit. If fired against soft targets the round may not detonate: Roll 3d vs. armor DR+3 (or half armor DR if non-rigid); if it fails, the impact alone does only $\frac{1}{6}$ damage and armor protects at full DR.

Tranq rounds are available for all slug-throwers, including Gauss weapons, at TL8+. The slug is a drugged needle imbedded in a special gel. The round normally does no damage, though it will do 1 impaling hit to paper, eyes, and similarly fragile targets. It will penetrate any armor with DR 2 or less vs. impaling, delivering one dose of a drug, usually a Sleep agent. Tranq rounds cost three times as much as normal ammo, plus the cost of one dose of the drug. They have $\frac{1}{3}$ the range of normal rounds. See *Needlers* on p. UT50 for more general information and pp. UT70-71 for popular chemical agents.

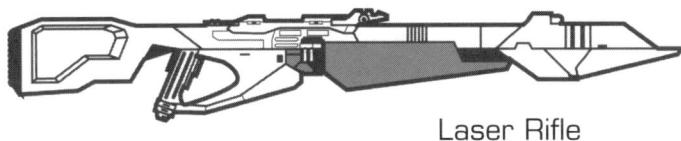

Laser Rifle

DESIGN YOUR OWN!

GURPS Traveller weapons were built using the *Vehicles* design rules to approximate the range, armor penetration, and weight of weapons from classic *Traveller*, *Striker*, and *MegaTraveller*.

GMs may wish to design more weaponry for *Traveller*. As previously mentioned, the weapons in this chapter are simply the most common in the Imperium. Variant models are plentiful. See *GURPS Vehicles*, *Ultra-Tech*, and *Ultra-Tech 2* for a vast variety of options.

GURPS Traveller Special Rules

When designing new weapons, keep in mind that many types aren't seen in the *GURPS Traveller* setting, some weapons cost more, and some have special restrictions, see pp. 107-108. The following special design rules also apply:

Gyrostabilization (TL8): This feature is similar to weapon stabilization for large weapons (see p. VE45), but is available for handheld weapons at TL8. It reduces the penalties for firing while moving (p. B117) by 1.

Weight is $0.05 \times$ empty weight (with stock, etc.) at TL8, negligible at TL9+. Cost is Cr200 × empty weight. Halve cost at TL9 and quarter it at TL10+.

High Energy Recoil: In *GURPS Traveller*, plasma blasters and fusion guns have a recoil penalty of (square root of KJ output) × M / (Empty weight + 5); M is 0.75 if tripod mount, 1.5 if shoulder stock or stock and bipod, 2.25 if pistol grip. This affects minimum ST.

Gravfield generators (TL8): These can be built into weapons and backpacks to reduce effective weight. Build it as a contragrav-lift unit supporting 90-100% of the weapon's weight (including the unit).

When calculating recoil, use actual empty weight including the weight of the unit; when calculating minimum ST, use the CG-reduced weight.

Full weight applies in all applications when the CG unit is turned off or has no power.

Standard Accessories

These accessories follow the "standard" *GURPS* rules. They are noted because they are the options most commonly found on Imperial small arms. ACRs, Gauss rifles, and all energy weapons already incorporate some accessories.

HUD Sights (TL8): These include a cable that plugs into a HUD or Holographic HUD helmet or goggles (see p. 116). The HUD displays a targeting reticle showing exactly where the gun is pointing. This reduces SS by 2 (with HUD) or 5 (with HoloHUD). If a laser sight is used as well, exact range-to-target data will be displayed as well, and snapshooting is even easier: Add half (round up) weapon Acc to unaimed shots. Cr500, negligible weight, powered by display unit.

Laser Sight (TL7): The sight's low-powered beam places a dot where the weapon is pointing. This adds 2 to Acc with aimed shots and reduces Snap Shot penalty to -1 at up to 50 yards or -2 at 51-100 yards. It can also be tuned to infrared. Cr200, weight negligible, 100 shots to a B cell.

RAM Grenade Hardpoint (TL6): This is usually incorporated into the flash suppressor or muzzle brake of a TL8+ firearm. A savvy TL6-7 world could easily design their weapons to fire imported TL8+ RAM grenades, though. There's no reason, other than tradition, that one could not be put on a beam weapon. Cost and weight negligible. Any weapon with a hardpoint may not exceed LC 1.

TL6-7 rifles may incorporate similar rifle-grenade launchers. See *GURPS High-Tech*, p. 78.

PERSONAL EQUIPMENT

Here's a brief list of ultra-tech equipment characters may find useful – see pp. B212-213 for lower-TL gear. Add 50% to any device's operating time on power cells for each TL after it first appeared. Operating durations have already been halved to account for using rechargable power cells.

Halve price and weight one TL after a device first appears; quarter them two TLs later. This doesn't apply to toolkits, air tanks, weapons, or armor.

Survival Gear

Air Mask (TL7): A face mask and air hose. Used on worlds with unbreathable but otherwise harmless atmospheres. If the atmosphere lacks enough oxygen (or has too much) air tanks are also required, while if it has enough oxygen but is contaminated or tainted, a filter (but no tanks) is required. Cr100, 2 lbs.; for another Cr50 has a mini-tank with 10 minutes of air.

Air Tank (TL7): Stores two hour's worth of air; usable with vacc suits, air masks, sealed armor, etc. Multiple tanks can be worn; each is Cr100, 10 lbs. An advanced rebreather (TL8, Cr200, 1 lb.) added to breathing gear multiplies tank duration by 10.

Filter (TL7): Used with air mask or any respirator, allows contaminated air to be breathed without resort to air tanks. The filter media require periodic replacement. Cr200, 1 lb. for CBR-rated filter usable against chemical agents, bioweapons, or radiation fallout; Cr100 for filter only rated for things like pollution, volcano fumes, or pollen. Replacement filter media (every 48 hours): Cr40 for CBR-rated, Cr10 otherwise, ¼ lbs. Note that to protect against contact agents like nerve gas or bioweapons, a sealed suit will also be necessary.

Pressure Tent (TL8): An airtight tent strong enough to be inflated to one atmosphere in a vacuum. Opening it completely evacuates the air; entering or leaving through the one-man lock takes a minute. Cr500 and 15 lbs. for a one-man tent; Cr1,500 and 30 lbs. for a two-man tent; Cr5,000 and 150 lbs. for an eight-man tent.

Respirator (TL9): Makes very thin and thin oxygen atmospheres safely breathable. Lasts two weeks on a B cell. Includes protective goggles and short-range communicator. Cr300, 3 lbs.

Reducing Respirator (TL9): As above except makes dense or very dense oxygen atmospheres safely breathable. Works for two weeks on a B cell and a chemical recharge (Cr50). Cr500, 5 lbs.

Rescue Ball (TL8): Also called an "enviro-bubble" or a survival bubble, this is a paperback-book sized package that inflates into an air-tight bubble with self-sealing flap. It can be erected in four seconds and holds 15 minutes of air – more if the wearer carries an air tank. It floats and is flexible enough to move in (Move 1). Merchant ships may issue these to passengers instead of vacc suits, since they're well-suited to use by untrained individuals. Cr800, 5 lbs.

Personal Reentry Kit (TL8): A foamed atmospheric ablative heat shield, chemical thruster and parachute allows an individual in a sealed suit (such as a vacc suit or battle dress) to reenter atmosphere on successive Free Fall (to reenter without burning up) and then Parachuting (to land safely) rolls. Cr15,000, 30 lbs.

Sensors

Atmosphere Tester (TL8): A simplified chemsniffer that tests the atmosphere it's in and displays the composition 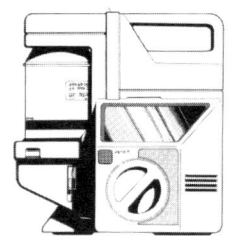 using a digital readout. Also, a light glows red if the atmosphere is unbreathable by Humans, green if breathable. Works for six months on a B cell. Cr400, 1 lb.

Biosniffer (TL10): An advanced chemsniffer that can recognize and categorize evidence of biological organisms. For example, it could determine what type of life-forms had previously occupied an area by picking up characteristic molecules produced by their exhalations, skin flakes, etc., and comparing

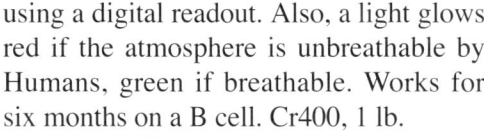

them to a database included in the device's computer. It has a range of up to 5 yards. An Electronics Operation (Sensors) roll is required to pick up something, with a -1 penalty per half hour that the trail is cold. Cr2,000, 2 lbs., three months on a B cell.

Chemsniffer (TL8): Analyzes chemical traces in the atmosphere. Range is 5 yards – can be used to determine atmospheric composition or find contaminants, drugs, explosives, etc. on a successful Electronics Operation (Security Systems) roll. Cr700, 2 lbs., works three months on a B cell.

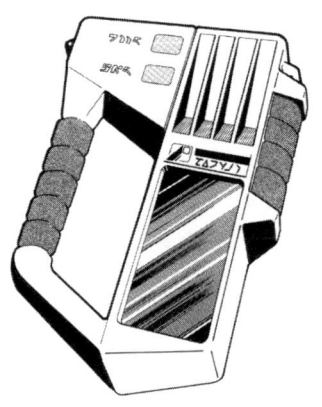

Densitometer (TL11): This gadget uses gravitic-imaging technology to map the interiors of objects. Effective range is 500 yards. A successful Electronics Operation (Sensors) roll is required to make a clear scan, which takes 1 second per 27 cubic feet (18.5 seconds per displacement ton). Failure means the scan must be repeated. When an object has been scanned, it stores the data as a 3-D plan in standard computer media (0.037 gigs per cubic foot/1.85 gigs per displacement ton) that can be accessed via computer for a "cutaway" view of the object. One C cell provides power for five minutes of scanning. Cr15,000, 10 lbs.

Goggles, Anti-Glare (TL8): Darken automatically to protect vs. ultrabright light. Cr150, 0.5 lbs. These or other goggles can add to a suit helmet for the same weight and price.

Goggles, Infrared (TL8): Gives wearer infrared vision (as per Infravision advantage, p. B237). Cr600, 0.5 lbs., three months on an A cell.

Goggles, Light-Intensifier (TL7): These halve all darkness penalties (round in user's favor) except in complete darkness. A laser hit will burn them out. Cr200, 1 lb. At TL-8+, Cr300 buys LI contact lenses with effectively no weight. They work one week on an AA cell.

Goggles, Multiview (TL8): Combines antiglare, infrared, and light-amplification goggles into one system. Works for six weeks on an A cell. Cr1,200, 1.5 lbs. At TL9+, a "sunglasses" version is available at Cr600 and negligible weight, three months on an A cell.

Neural Activity Sensor (TL12): A backpack display and processing unit with one or more handset antennas. It detects the electrical activity of a life form's nervous system at up to 300 yards. The display detects and classifies life-forms as IQ 1, IQ 2 (insect-equivalent level), IQ 3 (reptile-equivalent level), IQ 4-6 (mammal-equivalent level), or IQ 7+ (near-sapient/sapient). Insect-equivalent level lifeforms are generally shown as washes of color on the display representing density of lifeforms, while higher forms may be represented by individual "blips." Electronics Operation (Sensors) allows manipulation of various tools to call up graphs showing exact number of lifeforms and filter out or classify known types according to database information. It's blocked by psi shielding or solid objects. The handset is not attached to the backpack and can be operated out to 100 yards distance, further extending range. The backpack runs on a C cell, handsets on a B cell, for a week. Backpack: Cr15,000, 20 lbs. Handsets: Cr20,000, 0.5 lbs.

Sensor Visor (TL10): As multiview goggles (or helmet visor) but adds image enhancement with 100× magnification; +3 to Vision rolls. Works for two weeks on two B cells. Cr1,500, 2 lbs.

Televiewers (TL8): High-tech electro-optical binoculars with up to 50× magnification and built-in laser rangefinder (+2 to Forward Observer skill, range 5,000 yards). Infrared and light intensification (as per goggles) can be built in for an extra Cr300 each. Works for six weeks on a B cell. Cr950, 2 lbs.

Communication and Information

Communicator, Short-Range (TL8): Tiny two-way radio, often built into helmets. Base range 10 miles, ×10 at TL9 or ×50 at TL10+, increasable up to 100% on a successful Electronics Operation (Communication) roll at -1 per 10% extra range. Lasts six months with an A cell. Cr50, weight negligible. Disguiseable in wristwatch, earring, etc. for +10% cost.

Communicator, Medium-Range (TL8): A palm-sized radio; as above, but base range 100 miles. Lasts six months with a B cell. Video display available at double cost. Cr200, 1 lb.

Communicator, Long-Range (TL8): A book-sized or backpack unit. As above but base range 1,000 miles. A B cell powers it for six weeks of steady use. Cr600, 10 lbs. Add Cr100 for video display at TL8.

Com Scrambler (TL8): Attached to a communicator, scrambles messages so that only another scrambler tuned to the same combination can translate it. Cr500, ¼ lb.

Computer, Personal (TL7): A pocket-sized hand computer, also capable of interfacing with larger systems. Complexity equals TL-6. Cr1,000, 2 lbs., six months on a B cell.

Digital Camera (TL8): Takes full-color still or motion pictures, recording them on a computer disk. Runs for two weeks on a B cell. Cr500, 2 lbs.

TRAVELLER

PISTOLS – USE GUNS/TL (PISTOL) SKILL

Weapon	Malf	Type	Dam	SS	Acc	½D	Max	Wt	AWt	RoF	Shots	ST	Rcl	Costs	LC	Hld	TL
Revolver, 5mm	Crit.	Cr.	1d	9	2	75	1,100	0.7	0.03	3~	6	8	-1	60/0.01	3	+1	6
Revolver, 7mm	Crit.	Cr.	1d+2	10	3	130	1,500	1.4	0.08	3~	6	8	-1	65/0.04	3	0	6
Revolver, 9mm	Crit.	Cr.	2d	10	4	150	1,600	2.3	0.16	3~	6	8	-1	75/0.08	3	-1	6
Magnum Revolver, 9mm	Crit.	Cr.	3d-1	10	4	185	1,800	3	0.2	3~	6	10	-2	390/0.33	3	-2	7
Body Pistol, 5mm	Crit.	Cr.	1+2	9	1	90	1,200	1	0.04	3~	6	8	-1	300/0.06	3	+2	7
Auto Pistol, 7mm	Crit.	Cr.	2d-1	10	2	150	1,600	2.3	0.13	3~	7	9	-1	75/0.05	3	0	6
Auto Pistol, 9mm	Crit.	Cr.	2d+2	10	3	150	1,900	2.6	0.57	3~	15	9	-1	400/0.82	3	-1	7
Gauss Pistol, 4mm	Ver.	Cr.	6d (2)	9	6	500	3,200	1.6	0.03	8	15/A	8	-1	1,300/10.6	2	0	10

RIFLES AND CARBINES – USE GUNS/TL (RIFLE OR LIGHT AUTO) SKILL

Weapon	Malf	Type	Dam	SS	Acc	½D	Max	Wt	AWt	RoF	Shots	ST	Rcl	Costs	LC	Hld	TL
Carbine, 7mm	Crit.	Cr.	5d+1	12	8	400	3,000	9.4	0.6	3~	10	10	-1	140/0.21	4	-5	6
Rifle, 7mm	Crit.	Cr.	6d+1	14	10	700	4,000	10	1.2	3~	20	10	-1	830/1.7	4	-6	7
Rifle, 9mm	Crit.	Cr.	7d-1	14	9	600	3,400	11	1.3	3~	10	11	-2	910/1.8	4	-6	7
Rifle, 13mm	Crit.	Cr.	14d-1	20	11	1,200	5,400	33.1	4.6	1	10	16B	-3	2,140/6.6	1	No	8
Assault Rifle, 5.5mm	Crit.	Cr.	5d	12	8	400	3,000	7.7	0.9	12	30	9	-1	590/1.3	1	-5	7
Assault Rifle, 7.5mm	Crit.	Cr.	7d-1	14	10	800	4,100	11.6	1.5	11	20	11	-2	950/2.1	1	-6	7
ACR, 7mm	Ver.	var.	var.	12	10	Var.	Var.	7.2		10	20	10	-2	1,540	1	-5	9
with Solid		Cr.	6d+1			740	4,000		0.6					0.9			
with APS		Cr.	8d (2)			1,100	6,000		0.4					4.3			
ACR, 9mm	Ver.	var.	var.	12	9	var.	var.	8.6		10	20	11	-2	1,640	1	-6	9
with Solid		Cr.	7d-1			560	3,400		1.3					1.8			
with APS		Cr.	8d+2 (2)			840	5,100		0.9					9.1			
with HEAT		Exp.	3d-1 (10)			560	3,400		0.9					5.5			
Gauss Rifle, 4mm	Ver.	Cr.	8d+1 (2)	12	11	900	4,500	5.9	0.1	20	40/B	9	-1	2,620/32	0	-4	10

ZERO-G WEAPONS – USE GUNS/TL (GYROC) SKILL

Weapon	Malf	Type	Dam	SS	Acc	½D	Max	Wt	AWt	RoF	Shots	ST	Rcl	Costs	LC	Hld	TL
Snub Revolver, 10mm	Crit.	var.	var.	9	1	50	50	0.6	0.12	3~	6	–	0	275	2	+1	8
Auto Snub Pistol, 10mm	Crit.	var.	var.	9	0	50	50	1	0.56	3~	20	–	0	275	2	0	8
with Ball	Crit.	Cr.	1d+1											0.2 per round	2		
with HEAT (TL9)	Crit.	Exp.	6d (10)											0.5 per round	0		9
with CHEM	Crit.	Spcl.	Spcl.*											0.3 plus one dose of chem agent per round	2		
Accelerator Rifle, 10mm	Crit.	var.	var.	11	9	500	500	6	2.1	10	15	–	0	450	1	-3	9
with AP	Crit.	Cr.	5d (2)											20	1		
with HEAT	Crit.	Exp.	6d (10)											20	0		
with CHEM	Crit.	Spcl.	Spcl.*											17 plus 15 doses of chem agent per clip	2		

* Creates 2-yard-wide cloud of one dose of chemical agent, usually sleep gas – see pp. UT70-71

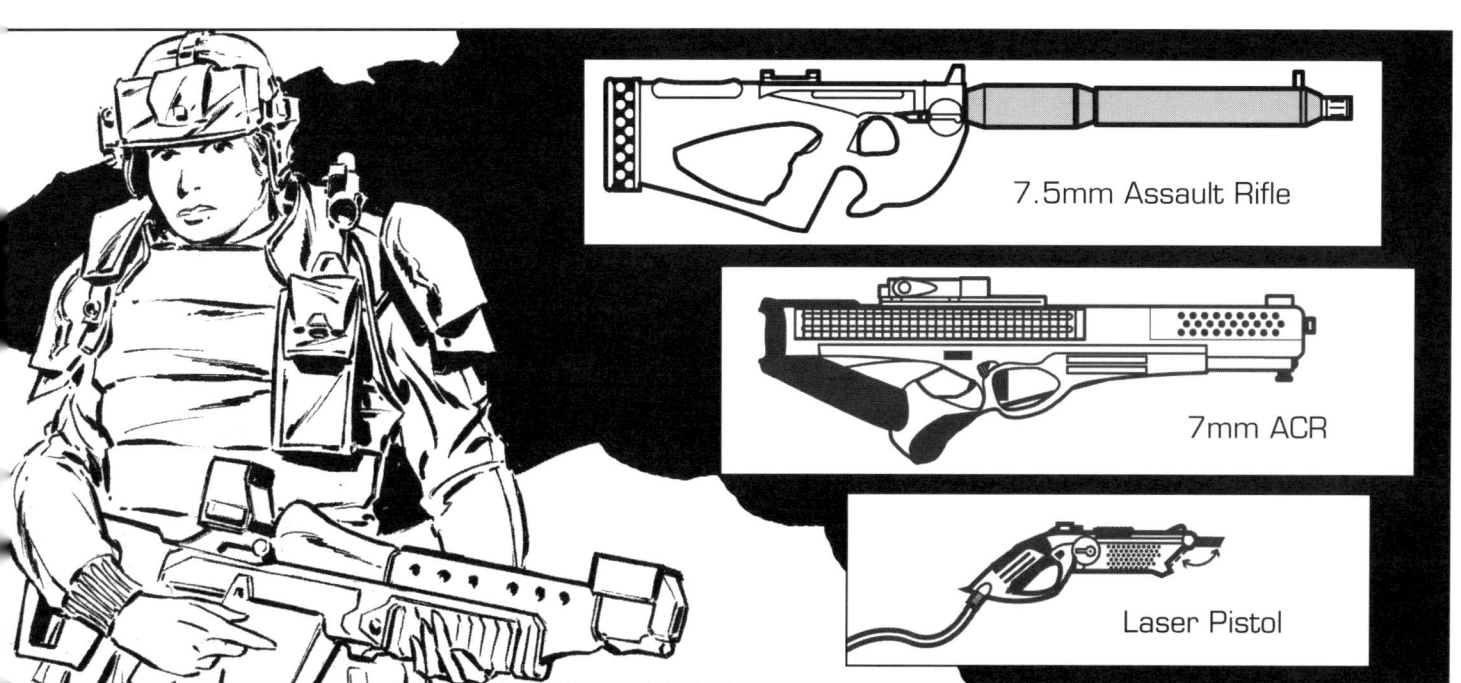

7.5mm Assault Rifle

7mm ACR

Laser Pistol

WEAPON TABLES

SUBMACHINEGUNS – USE GUNS/TL (LIGHT AUTO) SKILL

Weapon	Malf	Type	Dam	SS	Acc	½D	Max	Wt	AWt	RoF	Shots	ST	Rcl	Costs	LC	Hld	TL
SMG, 9mm	Crit.	Cr.	3d-1	12	6	190	1,800	7.1	1.2	10*	32	9	-1	540/1.8	2	-4	7

SHOTGUNS – USE GUNS/TL (SHOTGUN) SKILL

Weapon	Malf	Type	Dam	SS	Acc	½D	Max	Wt	AWt	RoF	Shots	ST	Rcl	Costs	LC	Hld	TL
Shotgun	Crit.	Cr.	4d	12	5	30	165	8.8	0.2	3~	5	10	-2	136/0.23	4	-5	6
Auto-Shotgun	Crit.	Cr.	4d	12	7	30	245	9.8	0.6	10*	10	10	-2	710/1.8	1	-6	8

ENERGY WEAPONS – USE BEAM WEAPONS/TL (LASER or FUSION) SKILL

Weapon	Malf	Type	Dam	SS	Acc	½D	Max	Wt	AWt	RoF	Shots	ST	Rcl	Costs	LC	Hld	TL
Laser Pistol-9	Ver.	Imp.	2d	10	10	580	1,200	2.8	3	4*	50/5C	7	0	1,300/500	2	-1**	9
Laser Carbine-8	Ver.	Imp.	2d+2	12	18	2,700	5,400	9	6	8*	50/D	7	0	1,900/500	1	-6**	8
Laser Carbine-10	Ver.	Imp.	2d+2 (2)	12	19	4,000	8,000	6	6	8*	50/D	7	0	1,475/500	0	-4**	10
Laser Rifle-9	Ver.	Imp.	4d	12	19	3,300	6,600	10	12	8*	100/2D	8	0	2,100/1,000	0	-6**	9
Laser Rifle-10	Ver.	Imp.	4d (2)	12	20	4,900	9,200	9	12	8*	100/2D	8	0	1,875/1,000	0	-6**	10
Laser Pistol-10	Ver.	Imp.	2d (2)	10	11	870	1,700	1.9	3	4*	50/5C	7	0	1,095/500	0	0**	10
PGMP-10	Ver.	Exp.	6d×8†	12	14	460	920	7.2	6	1	46/D	12	-3	16,675/500	0	No	10
PGMP-10A	Ver.	Exp.	6d×15†	17	15	740	1,500	19	120	1	450/5E	19	-3	36,175/2,500	0	No	10
PGMP-11	Ver.	Exp.	6d×15†	17	15	740	1,500	20	156	1	750/6E	9	-3	72,675/3,500	0	No	11
FGMP-11	Ver.	Exp.	6d×25†	17	16	1,100	3,300	17	192	1	500/8E	22	-4	63,175/3,000	0	No	11
FGMP-12	Ver.	Exp.	8d×20†	15	12	1,100	3,300	22	48	1	80/2E	10	-4	65,475/1,500	0	No	12

Can be fired at either RoF 3~ (semi-auto with three rolls to hit) or RoF 4 or 8 (full-auto using laser-autofire rules).

** Holdout figure is for laser weapon only. Power packs are separate items. A laser pistol power pack is -3 to Holdout; all others are -5.

† PGMP and FGMPs fire bolts of high-velocity star-hot plasma (treat as crushing; no damage multiplier). The splattering plasma also does ¼ damage to everyone else within 2 yards of the target.

SUPPORT WEAPONS – USE GUNS/TL (RIFLE) SKILL

Weapon	Malf	Type	Dam	SS	Acc	½D	Max	Wt	AWt	RoF	Shots	ST	Rcl	Cost	LC	Hld	TL
LAG, 20mm	Crit.	var.	var.	17	9	var.	var.	19.2		2~	5	15	-3	1,350	0	No	8
with APDS		Cr.	12d+2 (2)			630	4,300		1.2					12.8			
with HE		Cr.	1d+2 [2d]			420	2,900		1.2					5.1			
with Beehive		Imp.	1d			420	2,900		1.2					10.2			

RAM GRENADES – USE GUNS/TL (RAM GRENADE) SKILL

Weapon	Malf	Type	Dam	SS	Acc	½D	Max	Wt	HoF	Shots	ST	Rcl	Cost	LC	Hld	TL
4cm RAM-8 HEAT	Crit.	Exp.	5d×5 (10)	20	11	290	485	0.88	1/6	1	–	0	20	0	-3	8
4cm RAM-8 HE	Crit.	Exp.	6d×2 [4d]	20	11	290	485	0.88	1/6	1	–	0	18	0	-3	8
4cm RAM-9 HEAT	Crit.	Exp.	6d×6 (10)	20	11	370	850	1.1	1/6	1	–	0	17	0	-3	9
4cm RAM-9 HE	Crit.	Exp.	6d×3 [4d]	20	11	370	850	1.1	1/6	1	–	0	14	0	-3	9

Holdout figure is for the grenade alone. Attaching the grenade to a weapon lowers the weapon's Holdout by -2.

Note: Wt is loaded weight of weapon. AWt is weight of one clip or full load of ammo. Costs are weapon/(ammo clip or full load). See p. UT124 for explanation of other statistics.

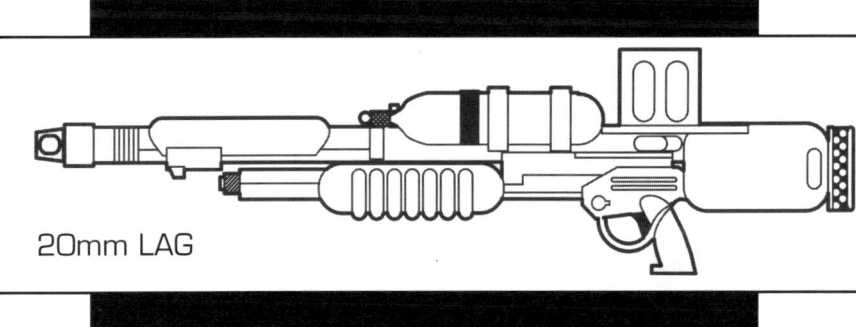

20mm LAG

Miscellaneous Devices

Automedic (TL9): Coffin-like computer-controlled medical bed that automatically treats patients. Has skill 14 in First Aid, and 13 in Diagnosis, Physician, and Surgery (+1 to skill per TL over 9). Cr50,000 at all TLs; weight 600 lbs. at TL9, 500 lbs. at TL10, 400 lbs. at TL11+. Drugpack (refill every 25 uses): Cr5,000, 50 lbs.

Electronic Lockpick (TL8): Gives +3 to Lockpicking or Electronics Operation (Security Systems) to break electronic locks, -2 per TL vs. higher-TL locks. Cr1,500, 3 lbs., three months on an A cell.

Disguise Kit (TL5): Suitcase-sized kit with makeup, wigs, etc. Gives +2 to Disguise skill. Cr300, 10 lbs.

Inertial Compass (TL8): Small device that indicates direction and distance traveled from any preset point on a planet accurate to within 1 yard per 1,000 miles. Must be calibrated for the planet (takes 1 hour and a Navigation or Electronics Operation (Sensors) roll). Works on an A cell for six months. Cr250, 1 lb.

Head-Up Display (HUD) (TL8): Mounted in a helmet or goggles, this displays information readouts from devices plugged into it, organizing and projecting them onto the wearer's goggles or visor at a handy eye-level. Any equipment that uses a visual display screen can be connected to a HUD by a short cable or communicator link – vehicle instrumentation, computers, sensor displays, etc. This adds +1 to skills where quick reaction is important (such as Driving, Piloting, and Free Fall); see HUD Sights on p. 112 for weapon bonuses. Note: Spaceship crew are assumed to be using HUDs, so there is no bonus for using them. A HUD runs off an A cell for six months or uses the same power as other helmet/suit systems. Cr500, ½ lb. At TL9 this becomes Holographic HUD with the same weight, cost, and power usage.

Medical Pouch: A doctor's bag with standard bandages, sedatives, injectors, skin patches, stimulants, and so on, plus a full set of physician's and surgeon's tools for the TL. Cost and weight don't drop at higher TLs – the contents just improve. It's the minimum requirement to use Surgery, Diagnosis, or Physician without penalty, and adds +2 to First Aid skill. A TL8+ physician performs as TL7 without this much gear. Cr700, 15 lbs.

Psi Shield (TL8): Protects wearer vs. telepathy as if it were a Mind Shield used by a telepath with a skill of 3 and a Power of 6 (plus 2 per additional TL). The shield circuits warn the operator when a telepath fails to penetrate the shields, but provide no warning if he succeeds. Works for two weeks on a B cell. Cr5,000, 1 lb. Psi shields can also be added to other headgear.

Tools (TL5+)

Tool Kit, Basic: Available for Engineering, Mechanic, Armoury, and Electronics skills. Anyone attempting repairs without an appropriate kit is at -5 to skill (using the wrong kit will reduce that to -3). An attempt to repair equipment of higher TL than the kit is -2 per TL difference. Mechanic or Engineer kits: Cr800, 300 lbs. Armoury or Electronics kits: Cr1,200, 100 lbs. No price or weight drop as TL increases.

Tool Kit, Portable: As above, but fits into a case or backpack. Major repairs are at -2 to skill; minor repairs at no penalty. Mechanic or Engineer kits: Cr600, 20 lbs. Armory or Electronics kits: Cr900, 10 lbs.

Tool Kit, Mini: A small belt-sized version of the above kit types. Routine repairs can be made at -2 to skill, major repairs at -4. Cr400, 2 lbs.

Cyberware and Bioware

Existing prejudices regarding bionics (see *Cybertechnology*, pp. 16-17) influence price and availability. Medical bionics that simply *replace* missing functions are at normal price, though the ⅕-price obviously bionic versions are hard to find. Non-obvious bionics that *enhance* in some fashion are very hard to find, and average twice the price listed in the **Ultra-Tech** books. Bionics that enhance *and* are obvious in use (heel spikes, cyberhair, etc.) are extremely hard to find and usually five times list price or more.

Apply the same guidelines to **GURPS Bio-Tech**'s offerings. A good place to look for both sorts of hard-to-find modifications is a military or intelligence employer.

Robots

Relatively dumb non-combat robots are purchased normally. Robots incorporating weapons or neural nets are very hard to find for sale. Sentient robots are extremely rare, and almost never for sale.

ARMOR AND PROTECTIVE GEAR

Most soldiers wear body armor; wise adventurers do, too. The following entries comprise the armor commonly found in the Imperium. The GM may choose whether to introduce armor from other *GURPS* sourcebooks.

Jack, mesh, ablat, reflec, and flak jackets can usually be worn as (or underneath) normal clothing without exciting undue comment. Vacc suits, cloth armor, and CES are tolerated around startowns if no helmet is worn, but outside of lawless worlds and war zones, wearing combat armor or battle dress is illegal.

As with firearms, some of these Imperial-standard pieces of equipment are a tech level later than their introduction.

Jack (TL1): The Imperial nickname for light leather armor. See p. B210 for leather, chainmail, plate armor, etc.

Cloth (TL7): A jacket and pants tailored from ballistic cloth (like Kevlar or Monocrys). It gives PD 2, DR 16 (PD 1, DR 2 vs. impaling attacks) over torso and limbs. Ballistic cloth works by distributing impact force across a wider area, so kinetic energy may cause bruising even when an attack fails to penetrate: Each "6" rolled on cutting or crushing damage dice inflicts *one* additional hit. Cr1,100, 14 lbs. At TL8+, Cr1,500, 12 lbs.

Flak Jacket (TL7): As cloth, but in vest form – it only protects the torso (locations 9-10 and 17-18). Cr425, 6 lbs. At TL8+, Cr600, 5 lbs.

Ablat (TL8): A cheap, bulky vest tailored from material that ablates (vaporizes) when hit by beam fire, carrying away its energy. Ablat is too bulky to wear under clothing, but can pass for winter clothing. It protects the torso only. Against lasers and plasma/fusion guns it has PD 4, DR 12, but every 4 hits stopped on a location drops its DR by 1, and for every 3 DR lost 1 PD is also lost. Against other attacks, it has PD 1, DR 2 (even if beam protection ablated away). A vest is Cr100, 15 lbs.; full suits that also cover the limbs are available (Cr300, 40 lbs.) but rarely worn due to their weight. Double DR at TL9, with 1 PD lost for every 6 DR ablated.

Mesh (TL7): Synthetic leather jacket reinforced with fine alloy mesh. Very light, mainly effective against blades and shell fragments rather than gun fire. It protects the torso and arms with PD 2, DR 4 (halved vs. impaling). Cr150, 1.5 lbs.

Light Infantry Helmet (TL8): An open-faced helmet, often worn with ablat, cloth, or mesh armor. It protects the brain (locations 3-4) with PD 4, DR 15 (+5 per DR over TL8). Cr30, 1.5 lbs.

Combat Infantry Helmet (TL8): A full helmet equipped with CBR filters, airtight with visor down. PD 4, DR 18 except visor, which is PD 2, DR 10. Add +10 DR at each higher TL. Cr240, 8 lbs.

Vacc Suit (TL8): A vacuum suit protects the wearer from vacuum, hazardous atmospheres, and low-level radiation. Getting in or out takes a minute (five seconds to put on the gloves, another five to put on the helmet, if already wearing the suit without either). Times are halved on a successful Vacc Suit roll. The suit holds enough air for five minutes till air tanks are attached. See p. UT25 for additional details. A PD 2, DR 3 model is Cr1,500, 20 lbs. An armored PD 4, DR 30 model is Cr4,000, 80 lbs.

Reflec (TL9): This armor (developed a TL later than listed in **Ultra-Tech**) is tailored from reflective material designed to deflect laser fire. It can be worn over other armor or clothing. It gives PD 6, DR 2 vs. lasers, PD 3, DR 0 vs. other energy weapons, and no protection otherwise. Full suit: Cr300, 2 lbs. Jacket (torso and arms): Cr150, 1 lb.

Combat Environment Suit (TL9): A neck-to-toe flexible form-fitting body suit of advanced closed-weave synthetic materials. Usually worn open at the neck and wrists, the suit can be sealed by donning gauntlets and a transparent hood and respirator or sealed combat helmet (it still is *not* vacuum-resistant). Its tight molecular mesh protects fully vs. impaling attacks (unlike cloth armor) but heat build-up is a problem. The suit uses a solid-state cooling system woven into the garment, but this gives it a pronounced infrared signature (+2 to spot with infrared sensors). A backpack coolant unit using a chemical chill can nullifies this problem, but after two hours the can is

exhausted (spares are Cr20, 1 lb.). CES gives PD 2, DR 24 protecting all locations except the head and hands. As with cloth armor, non-penetrating hits do 1 hit on every damage-die roll of "6." CES is Cr4,000, 12 lbs., or 14 lbs. if coolant system worn. *Note*: Treat this as a TL9 improvement of monocrys (p. UT74), with twice the cost and 75% of the weight. In addition to the heat problem, it can't be concealed by or disguised as ordinary clothing.

Combat Armor (TL9): An armored vacc suit (simply add air tanks) made of articulated plastic, advanced alloys, and carbon composites. It has PD 6, DR 38 on torso; PD 4, DR 28 on limbs; and PD 4, DR 20 on hands and feet. The helmet protects the head with PD 4, DR 26; visor protects face at PD 2, DR 18. Add DR 8 per TL over TL9. Cr2,250, 38.5 lbs.

IR Chameleon (TL9): This infrared-cloaking system blends the wearer's heat signature into the background (-3 to IR spotting and targeting; -10 to IR-homing projectiles). It can be added to combat armor or CES suits. A suit must be sealed for IR chameleon to work. Cr1,500, 5 lbs., works 12 hours on a pair of A cells.

Battle Dress (TL10): Imperials call powered combat armor "battle dress." (The "battledress uniform" on p. UTT73 is simply called "fatigues.") This armor enhances the wearer's strength as well as provides superior protection. Battle dress has PD 5, DR 150 on the body and head from the front or sides, PD 4, DR 100 from other angles, and PD 4, DR 75 on the limbs. Its laminate armor halves the armor divisor of shaped-charge explosive (HEAT-type) rounds; i.e., a RAM-8 round would do 5d×5 (5) rather than 5d×5 (10). Battle dress gives the wearer ST 25 and moves at Speed 5.5, Move 5.

Battle dress is air-tight and self-sealing. Its NBC filter removes nuclear, biological, or chemical contamination allowing unlimited operations in tainted or polluted atmospheres. It has a six-hour air supply (backpack tanks can extend this). Other features: IR chameleon; radar/laser detector; helmet HUD; medium-range scrambled communicator; global positioning system; passive imaging sensors giving choice of telescopic magnification, light-amplified night vision, or IR thermal imaging (2-mile range).

Battle dress runs off a rechargeable E cell for 88 hours, 53 minutes. A suit costs Cr58,050, stands 7' tall, and weighs 275 lbs. (empty). The weight does not count as encumbrance.

Improved Battle Dress (TL11): As above, but better armored. It has PD 5, DR 240 on the body and head from front or sides, PD 4, DR 160 from other angles, and PD 4, DR 120 on limbs. The armor incorporates a superconductor layer that doubles DR vs. beam weapons such as lasers and PGMP/FGMPs. Other systems are as TL10 battle dress except sensors have a 4-mile range and the suit's E cell powers it for 111 hours, 6 minutes. Improved battle dress costs Cr63,050. It weighs 261 lbs. (empty).

CHAPTER FIVE

Travel, Trade, and Commerce

HOW TO GET THERE

Reactionless thrusters are used to fly between worlds and jump drives between stars; any other technology is *very* rare.

Non-starships (anything under 100 tons or with no jump drive) require Piloting (Spaceship) skill. Starships are flown with Piloting (Starship).

Piloting (Spaceship) equates to Piloting (High-performance spacecraft) on p. V144. To emulate classic *Traveller*, have Piloting (Spaceship) default to Piloting (Starship)-2. GMs might also allow Piloting (Contragravity) to default to Piloting (Spaceship)-4.

INTERPLANETARY TRAVEL

Interplanetary travel requires success rolls vs. two skills: Piloting (Starship or Spaceship) and Astrogation. One crew member may fill both roles, but at -4 on any vehicle 200 tons or larger.

Ships *can* jump wholly within a star system – see *Micro-Jumps*, p. 121.

TRAVEL TIMES

This chart assumes constant acceleration to the halfway point, then constant deceleration to the destination (you could accelerate the whole distance, but this will make it harder to stop upon arrival).

Distance	1 G	2 G	3 G	4 G	5 G	6 G
0.2 AU	31 hrs	22 hrs	18 hrs	15 hrs	14 hrs	13 hrs
0.5 AU	2 days	34 hrs	28 hrs	24 hrs	22 hrs	20 hrs
1 AU	2.8 days	2 days	40 hrs	34 hrs	31 hrs	28 hrs
2 AU	4.1 days	2.8 days	2.3 days	2 days	43 hrs	40 hrs
5 AU	6.3 days	4.5 days	3.7 days	3.2 days	2.9 days	2.6 days
10 AU	9 days	6.3 days	5.2 days	4.5 days	4 days	3.7 days
50 AU	2.9 wks	2 wks	11.7 days	10 days	9 days	8.3 days
100 AU	4 wks	2.9 wks	2.4 wks	2 wks	12.8 days	11.7 days

Abbreviations: *wks:* weeks, *hrs:* hours.

Planetfalls

Streamlined spaceships (see pp. 150-151) can safely land on and leave planet surfaces, and skim gas-giant atmospheres. Unstreamlined ships avoid all three; their avionics aren't designed for the intricacies of atmosphere nor their hulls for landing.

Reaching Earth orbit requires an orbital velocity of 17,800 mph. For another planet, multiply 17,800 by the square root of (its mass in Earth masses divided by its diameter in Earth diameters). If mass is unknown, simply divide the planet's diameter by Earth's diameter (8,000 miles), then multiply by 17,800. Escape velocity is 1.414 times orbital velocity.

Divide orbital (or escape) velocity by (21.8 × ship's Accel) to find out how many seconds it takes a *streamlined* ship to reach (or escape) orbit from the surface. If a planet has no atmosphere, subtract local gravity from the ship's Accel first. Unstreamlined ships always subtract local gravity from Accel.

Arrivals take as much time as departures, plus 30 seconds of carefully setting down. In either case, vacuum worlds or an unstreamlined hull requires Accel to exceed local gravity.

For gas-giant skimming, figure an average escape velocity of 75,000 mph and local gravity of 1.25 G. Divide entry and exit times by 10; the ship's not even getting close to the surface.

For aerobraking streamlined ships without power, see p. VE164.

Skill Rolls

Safe planetfalls are routine, but not automatic. Make a Piloting roll for each arrival and departure. Skimming a gas giant is +0, landing in atmosphere +3, and landing in vacuum +4. Departures are +2. Weather and other circumstances can subtract -1 to -10. Pilots of skill 15+ can reroll mishaps per p. B69.

Unstreamlined ships can attempt any of these manuevers, at an additional -5. (Except in emergencies, this is *illegal* under Imperial law.) Even the best landing will likely cause some minor hull damage.

Gas Giants

Given their importance, gas giants were noted in *Traveller*'s star-system statistics. Unfortunately, *GURPS* stats don't normally mention whether a system has gas giants. *GURPS Traveller First In* provides a system for generating gas giants. For a quick reference in an unknown system, roll 2d. On a 9 or less, a gas giant is present.

Misdirected Jump Table

Roll	Deviation	Distance
2	0°	1d/2
3	30° starboard	1d
4	30° port	1d
5	30° starboard	2d
6	30° port	2d
7	60° starboard	3d
8	180°	3d
9	60° port	4d
10	60° port	4d
11	30° starboard	5d
12	60° starboard	5d

Roll 2d twice (once for each column).

This table allows the referee to place the ship at a random spot on a subsector (or sector) map. The deviation is away from the intended direction of the jump. The distance is the number of dice the GM rolls to determine how many hexes in the new direction the ship misjumps, starting at the departure hex. Note that it is possible for a ship to deviate 30 parsecs from its starting point during a misjump, the only time more than 6 parsecs per jump may be traveled.

INTERSTELLAR TRAVEL

Only one form of faster-than-light drive is available, the jump drive. Slower-than-light interstellar travel isn't unknown, but uncommon.

JUMP

Jump drives allow a ship to travel faster than the speed of light by entering jumpspace. Ships in jumpspace are completely out of communication with the normal universe, and with other ships in jumpspace. A ship's jump drives determine how far it can jump. The drives are rated in terms of their jump number, which can range from 1 to 6. (The number equals their maximum range in parsecs.) A ship can make a jump equal to or less than its jump number, but fuel requirements round up to the next even parsec (see below). All jumps take about a week (168 hours +/- 10%). Time spent in jump has no relation to the distance traveled; a 6-parsec jump and a 3-AU micro-jump both take about a week.

Each jump requires a quantity of liquid hydrogen. A portion is converted to energy in the ship's reactor to open the "hole" into jumpspace and to maintain the "bubble" around the ship once it enters, a portion is used as jump-drive coolant, and a portion is vented into jumpspace as part of the process of creating the jump "bubble" which separates and insulates the ship from jumpspace. For convenience though technically inaccurate, all of this is referred to as "fuel." Jump fuel is consumed at the rate of 10% of the ship's *displacement* tonnage per parsec jumped. In-system microjumps count as 1 parsec for consumption of fuel.

Ships may attach cargo pods, other ships, and such, then use their jump drives for the volume of the entire "assembly" as long as a ship's jump drives and fuel are sufficient for the increased volume. For instance, a normally jump-2 ship could carry another ship of its own volume through a jump-1.

Jump Types: When starships exit jump, they retain the velocity and direction they had on entering jumpspace. This leads to two basic types of jump:

Standing Jump: A standing jump attempts to give the emerging ship an orbital vector at the destination system. (Note that this will almost certainly require a non-orbital vector at the departure sytem.) Usually this is the safest type of jump, since it minimizes the possibility of colliding with a random asteroid or such. (Accidents still happen, which is why most starships have some armor.)

Running Jump: A running jump attempts to position the ship such that it need merely decelerate to approach the destination world. If poorly calculated, the ship will be off course and can waste considerable time maneuvering to the world.

The 100-Diameter Limit: Jump uses a straight line (called a jump line) in calculating courses. If that straight line intersects a 100-diameter sphere around an object larger than the ship, the ship is "precipitated out" of jump space. It is an astrogator's job to plot a course which avoids these pitfalls. Notice that this prevents a ship from emerging from jump within another object.

Jump Masking: A star's 100-diameter limit often blocks ("masks") the direct jump line from origin to destination world. Roll 8 or less on 3d for *both* origin and destination; success means that the jump point is unmasked. Masked jumps add about two days (44 hours) to normal travel time.

Micro-Jumps: It is possible to jump within a star system. The jump takes the standard time. A jump may be more efficient than using maneuver drives to travel from one world to another.

See p. T:FT59 for more detail on travel times.

MISHAPS

A successful jump requires three separate success rolls: Piloting (Starship), Astrogation, and Mechanic (J-Drive). A simple failure means the operation was unsuccessful, but may be attempted again (at a -1 penalty per subsequent attempt). A critical failure (or a simple failure, if the crew is rushed or fatigued) on any roll means that a potential mishap exists; roll again, with any success indicating that the mishap has been avoided, but the failure still counts. A second critical failure results in *disaster*. Mishaps can take several forms:

Attempting a jump using unrefined fuel is -2 to all rolls. Attempting a jump from within 100 diameters of another object is -4, within 50 diameters -8, within 10 diameters -12.

No Jump: A Piloting mishap results in no jump (the jump drive fails to operate – the Game Master may provide suitable sound effects if desired).

Misexit: An Astrogation mishap causes a misexit from jumpspace. Roll 1d. On a 1, the ship has exited near a solitary world, comet, or odd chunk of rock in deep space between major systems; on 2-3, the ship exits near a world or gas giant in the destination star system; on 4-6, the ship exits at a random point at the destination star's 100-diameter limit.

Misjump: A misjump occurs when the drive fails during the initial jump process (Mechanic mishap), or when a jump is failed because of penalties for being too close to another object. A misjump can take the form of no jump, a failed jump (the ship enters jumpspace, but emerges after about a week in the same place it started), or a misdirected jump, where the ship emerges from jumpspace in an unintended location, usually far in distance and location from the intended exit point (this result is different from a misexit). A failed jump and a misdirected jump are indistinguishable before the ship exits jumpspace. For the latter, consult the *Misdirected Jump Table* on p. 120.

Disaster: The ship experiences a high level of damage (or is completely destroyed, at the Game Master's option).

DETECTION OF JUMP

Jumps emit short bursts of energy. A previously undetected ship entering jump likely will reveal itself at the moment of jump, just as it disappears from sensor screens. Treat as +60 minus jumping ship's TL to radscanner readings, per p. 173, but don't also count the jumping ship's active transponder, radio, or active sensors unless they give a better bonus. A jump also give PESAs +25 minus twice TL. On a good sensors roll, the burst reveals the approximate size of the ship, and the time it left the system, if the scan is made in the same space-combat round as the jump. The direction of the jump (but not its distance) can be determined as well.

A ship *leaving* jump also emits a pulse of energy, which can reveal the approximate size of the ship and the time it entered the system. Halve the bonuses above for radscanners and PESAs for scans made in the same space-combat round.

A ship in jump cannot be detected in any fashion.

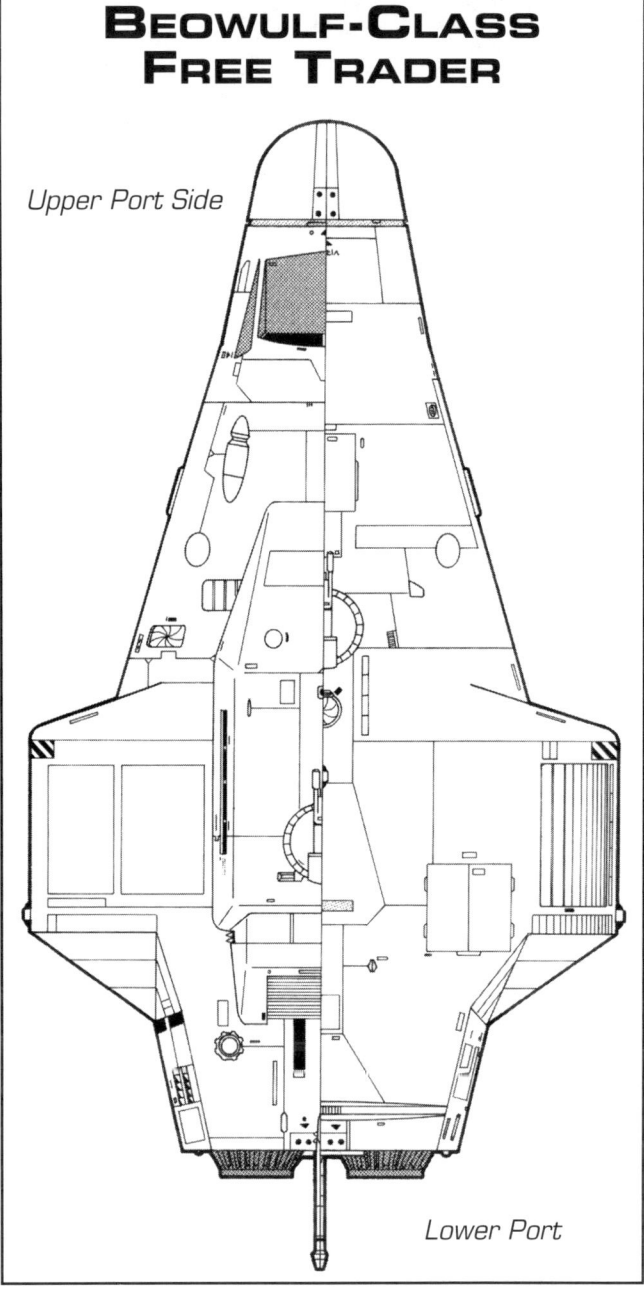

BEOWULF-CLASS FREE TRADER

Upper Port Side

Lower Port

Refined and Unrefined Fuel

Starports sell refined fuel (pure liquid hydrogen) for Cr350 per fuel module. Unrefined fuel has impurities and costs Cr50. Class I and II starports sometimes only have unrefined fuel available, whereas Class Vs rarely offer to sell it. Out-of-the-way locales may also offer only unrefined fuel, and the price can fluctuate with supply.

Any ship with fuel processors can create refined fuel from various compounds containing hydrogen, such as water, methane, or unrefined fuel.

Streamlined starships can skim unrefined fuel from a gas giant's atmosphere. Water from a planet's oceans can be converted with a fuel processor; some worlds prohibit this.

Merchant Ship Revenues

Item	Gross Income
High Passage (each)	Cr3,500
Middle Passage (each)	1,750
Low Passage (each)	175
Freight (per ton)	650
Mail (if fitted)	10,000
Speculative Cargo	(see text)

TRADE AND COMMERCE

Carrying cargo and passengers between worlds is the foundation of interstellar commerce. More detailed rules for such commerce are given in *GURPS Traveller: Far Trader*. GMs may override any of the following die rolls at their discretion (to declare no high passengers will be found in the outback of an underdeveloped colony world, for example).

Locate Passengers and Cargo: Passengers (see p. 78) and cargo may normally be found only at starports (they may be found elsewhere at the GM's discretion). Any character with Merchant skill may make one attempt to find each type of passenger and one attempt to find each type of cargo (mail, freight, and speculative cargo) once per day.

Locating passengers is a test of Merchant skill. For each successful roll, determine the number of each type available as follows:

High Passage: Roll 1d/2 for the number of passengers.

Middle Passage: Roll 1d for the number of passengers.

Low Passage: Roll 2d-3 for the number of passengers. See p. 108.

For each successful Merchant roll, determine the tonnage of each type available as follows:

Mail: If the ship is fitted with weaponry and carries a gunner, and the starport is Class II or worse, 1 ton of mail is available.

Freight: Roll 1d to find the number of lots of freight available.

For each lot, roll 4d-4 to find its size in tons. The ship must accept or reject each lot in its entirety. Carrying just part of a lot is not allowed.

Speculative Cargo: Determine the number of tons of speculative cargo in the same way as freight.

REVENUE

Merchant ships earn money according to the *Merchant Ship Revenues* table (see sidebar), except for speculative cargo. Speculative cargoes may involve either a profit or loss for the ship, as determined below.

For the speculative cargo as a whole, determine the profit/loss as a test of Merchant skill. Roll once per lot of speculative cargo. On a success, the cargo was sold at a profit; on a failure the cargo was sold at a loss. Profit and loss are both determined by rolling $1d/2 \times$ Cr1,000 per ton of speculative cargo.

Interstellar Mapping

Normal space is three-dimensional, but jumpspace maps in *Traveller* are two-dimensional for simplicity. Game Masters who wish to represent space as three-dimensional in their campaigns are free to do so in any way they see fit.

This map shows the Regina subsector, one of 16 subsectors in the Spinward Marches sector. Regina is the sector capital, and the region is a hub for trade with the Vargr to coreward and the Zhodani to spinward.

Planetary Locations: The Imperium refers to planets and systems by the name of the main or inhabited world, followed by sector and subsector. For instance, the world Dentus on the map below is formally Dentus (Spinward Marches/Regina).

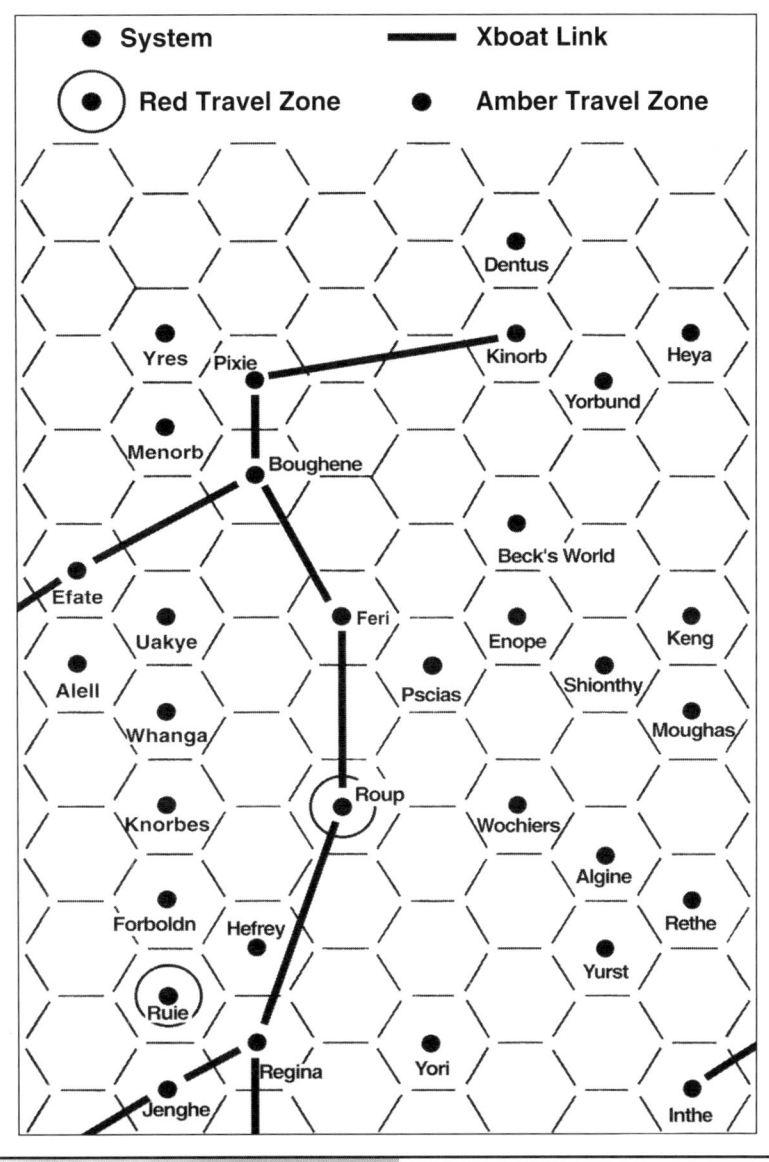

- ● System
- ⊙ Red Travel Zone
- ── Xboat Link
- ● Amber Travel Zone

Dentus

Yres · Pixie · Kinorb · Heya

Yorbund

Menorb · Boughene

Beck's World

Efate

Uakye · Feri · Enope · Keng

Alell · Pscias · Shionthy

Whanga · Moughas

Roup

Knorbes · Wochiers

Algine

Forboldn · Hefrey · Rethe

Yurst

Ruie

Regina · Yori

Jenghe · Inthe

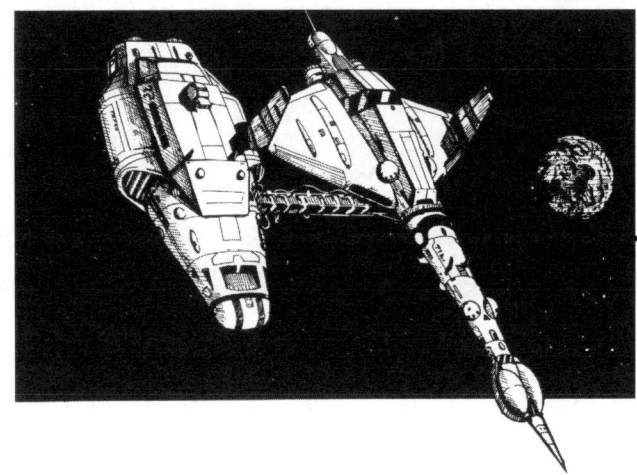

PLANETS

Thousands of world descriptions have been created for *Traveller* and hundreds for *GURPS Space.* These tables convert the two systems. For more detail about exotic and poisonous atmospheres, strange and unusual governments, the physics of star systems, and so on, see *GURPS Traveller: First In.*

STARPORT EQUIVALENTS

Traveller	GURPS Space	Traveller	GURPS Space
A	Class V	D	Class II
B	Class IV	E	Class I
C	Class III	X	Class 0

See p. S122 for descriptions.

PLANETARY SIZE EQUIVALENTS

The *Traveller* UPP (Universal Planetary Profile) code corresponds exactly with its diameter in thousands of miles, with "A" indicating 10,000 miles and "0" an asteroid belt. Planetary diameter may be used to generate values for gravity if density is known. *Traveller* usually assumes Earth-like densities (5.5 Earth, 5.2 Venus, 4 Mars, 3.3 Luna). Very low densities (under 2) are most likely in huge gas giants like Jupiter, Saturn, Uranus, and Neptune.

To get gravity, use the formula: Diameter (in miles) × Density × 0.0000229 = gravity, where 1 = Earth gravity. Rules for gravity effects are found on pp. S71-73 and CII133-135, 140-144.

GOVERNMENT EQUIVALENTS

Traveller UPP government codes correspond with the following *GURPS* government descriptions:

	Traveller	GURPS
0	No government/family	Anarchy or Clan/Tribal
1	Company/corporation	Corporate state
2	Participatory democracy	Athenian democracy
3	Self-perpetuating oligarchy	Oligarchy, caste, or meritocracy
4	Representative democracy	Representative democracy
5	Feudal technocracy	Technocracy or cybercracy
6	Captive government	Colony, subjugated, or military government
7	Balkanization	Multiple societies
8	Civil-service bureaucracy	Bureaucracy
9	Impersonal bureaucracy	Bureaucracy
A	Charismatic dictator	Dictatorship
B	Non-charismatic dictator	Dictatorship
C	Charismatic oligarchy	Oligarchy
D	Religious dictatorship	Theocracy

See pp. CII185-186 for descriptions of *GURPS* governments.

ATMOSPHERE EQUIVALENTS

	Traveller UPP Code	GURPS Space
0	No atmosphere	None, vacuum
1	Trace	Trace oxygen-nitrogen
2	Very thin, tainted	Very thin oxygen-nitrogen, polluted
3	Very thin	Very thin oxygen-nitrogen
4	Thin, tainted	Thin oxygen-nitrogen, polluted
5	Thin	Thin oxygen-nitrogen
6	Standard	Standard oxygen-nitrogen
7	Standard, tainted	Standard oxygen-nitrogen, polluted
8	Dense	Dense oxygen-nitrogen
9	Dense, tainted	Dense oxygen-nitrogen, polluted
A	Exotic	Thin, standard, or dense reducing or exotic
B	Corrosive	Thin, standard, or dense corrosive
C	Insidious	As above, but highly corrosive gasses such as fluorine

See pp. S108-109. *GURPS* rules for handling alien atmosphere types are found on pp. S74-75 and pp. CII136-137.

LAW LEVEL EQUIVALENTS

Traveller UPPs rate government restrictions on personal freedoms, especially the right to carry weapons, on a scale of 0 (none) to 9+ (very heavy). In *GURPS* this corresponds with Control Ratings as follows:

Traveller Law Level	GURPS Control Rating
0	0 (anarchy)
1	1 (very free)
2	1 (very free)
3	2 (free)
4	2 (free)
5	3 (moderated)
6	4 (controlled)
7	4 (controlled)
8	5 (repressive)
9 and up	6 (total control)

HYDROGRAPHIC PERCENTAGE

The *Traveller* UPP rates surface water in 10% increments. This corresponds exactly to the surface water percentages used in *GURPS Space* (p. S110).

POPULATION EQUIVALENTS

Traveller UPPs record population exponentially: 0 is none, 1 is tens, 2 is hundreds, 3 is thousands, 9 is billions, A (10) is tens of billions, etc. *GURPS* uses the same system (see p. S117).

TECH LEVEL EQUIVALENTS

See sidebar on p. 107.

CHAPTER SIX

Character Conversions

Intelligence Vs. Education

Traveller drew a distinction between intelligence, which was a raw talent, and education, which represented formal schooling or training. This reflected the notion of the original designers that intelligence and education are not necessarily linked; it is possible for a person to be highly educated, but not very intelligent, and vice versa. The *GURPS* IQ attribute is a composite attribute that represents many things, including a certain amount of education (see p. CI7 for details).

Traveller had four main versions: ***Classic Traveller, MegaTraveller, Traveller: the New Era,*** and ***Traveller (4th Edition).*** This chapter converts characters from all four. All four versions of ***Traveller*** featured semi-random character generation, which means that a typical group of characters converted to ***GURPS*** will end up with vastly different point totals. Game Masters may ignore this, or may allow the "shortchanged" players to make arguments for ***GURPS*** advantages that weren't part of their character's ***Traveller*** stats.

As in all conversions, GMs should bend the rules to retain character concept or playability. These are rough guidelines, to be fine-tuned as needed.

STATISTICS

All four ***Traveller*** versions generated six personal characteristics. ***Classic Traveller (CT), MegaTraveller (MT),*** and ***Traveller 4th Edition (T4)*** used Strength, Dexterity, Endurance, Intelligence, Education, and Social Standing. ***Traveller: the New Era (TNE)*** used Strength, Agility, Constitution, Intelligence, Education, and Charisma. TNE retained Social Standing, but as a secondary attribute.

These convert to *GURPS* as follows:

GURPS Attribute	based upon this Traveller Characteristic
ST	Strength*
DX	Dexterity or *TNE*'s Agility*
IQ	(Intelligence + Education)/2*
HT	Endurance or *TNE*'s Constitution*
Charisma	Charisma*
Status	Social Standing

* If *TNE* character, add +1 to Characteristic or result of IQ formula.

For ST, DX, IQ, and HT, use the following conversion table:

Trav	GURPS	Trav	GURPS	Trav	GURPS	Trav	GURPS
1	6	5	9	9	12	D	15
2	7	6	9	A	13	E	16
3	8	7	10	B	13	F	17*
4	8	8	11	C	14		

* For NPCs, *Traveller*'s F represents an attribute anywhere from 17 to *GURPS'* mundane ceiling of 20. For PCs, the minimal 17 should be reward enough.

For Charisma or Status, use:

Trav	GURPS	Trav	GURPS	Trav	GURPS	Trav	GURPS
1	-4*	5	-1*	9	1	D	4
2	-3*	6	0	A	1	E	5
3	-2*	7	0	B	2	F	6
4	-1*	8	0	C	3		

* A *TNE* character who converts to *GURPS* with "negative" Charisma should take Odious Personal Habits, negative Appearance, and similar disadvantages that sum to the reaction penalty indicated by the table.

GMG '98

SKILLS

Converting skills from the *Traveller* systems to *GURPS* involves more interpretation than calculation.

The *Traveller* systems varied among themselves – and with *GURPS* – in how skill levels were applied to game mechanics. More importantly, *Traveller* skill systems were usually less "detailed" than *GURPS*. A commando-trained mercenary in *Traveller* might list 10 skills. An equivalent template in *GURPS Traveller* requires roughly 30. Background knowledge, familiarities, and secondary skills that were assumed in *Traveller* are spelled out in *GURPS*.

Traveller skill levels were single digits generally ranging from 0 (familiarity) to 5 (expertise). To convert a *Traveller* skill level to a *GURPS* skill, give 1 character point for level 0, 2 for level 1, 4 for level 2, and 8 for level 3. For each subsequent level, add 8 more points to a *physical* skill or two more to a *mental* skill. These points must be applied to the equivalent *GURPS* skill or skills.

For each skill converted, give the character an *equal* number of character points to be spent on "secondary" skills appropriate to his background or that skill! Up to 8 of these points could be spent to increase the original skill if the controlling attribute is less than 12. In some cases, these points can be spent on advantages, martial-arts maneuvers, etc.

Example: The player of an Army veteran first determines his DX is 9 and IQ 11. He then converts the character's Combat Rifleman-2 into 4 points of Guns (Light automatic), or a skill of 12. He has 4 more points for complementary skills. At DX 9, he could use the points to increase to Guns (Light automatic)-13, but decides against it. He also thinks about boosting his Guns (Rifle) default a little, since Combat Rifleman included single-shot firing, but decides he can live with the less-than-exact conversion. Instead, he puts 2 points in Armoury (Small arms) and 2 in Savoir-Faire (Military).

SKILL COMPARISON TABLES

The following tables convert *Traveller* skill names to equivalent *GURPS* skill names. Some *Traveller* skills convert to one of several *GURPS* skills. Some convert to a mix of several *GURPS* skills. The player may choose how he allocates points in these cases.

Jack-of-All-Trades

Traveller has a special skill called Jack-of-all-Trades, giving low proficiency in skills the character *doesn't* have. To convert it, use this advantage:

Jack-of-All-Trades 10 points/level

This advantage reflects an unusual breadth of talent and versatility. Each level grants +1 to all skill defaults from attributes (but not other skills), to a maximum of +3 for 30 points. It has no effect on skills without a default, and modified default level may never equal or exceed the level that ½ point would purchase. Jack-of-All-Trades does not make *learned* skills any cheaper.

Default skill usage remains restricted as per the sidebar on p. B44.

Traveller	GURPS	Traveller	GURPS
Acrobatics (TNE)	Acrobatics	Armory (T4)	Armoury/TL (type)
Act/Bluff (TNE)	Acting	Art (T4)	Artist or other (Sculpting, etc.)
Acting (T4)	Acting	Artillery (T4)	Gunner/TL (type)
Admin (MT)	Administration	Artisan (MT)	Artist or other (Sculpting, etc.)
Admin/Legal (TNE)	Administration and/or Law	Assault Rifle (MT)	Guns/TL (Light automatic)
Administration (CT)	Administration	Astrogation (TNE, T4)	Astrogation/TL
Advanced Combat Rifle (MT)	Guns/TL (Light automatic)	Athletics (T4)	Running, with aspects of Sport (type)
Air/Raft (CT)	Piloting (Contragravity)		
Animal Handling (MT)	Animal Handling	ATV (CT)	Driving (Heavy wheeled)
Archaic Artillery (TNE)	Gunner/TL (type)	ATV, Tracked (MT)	Driving (Tracked)
Archaic Weapons (MT)	Black Powder Weapons/TL (type)	ATV, Wheeled (MT)	Driving (Heavy wheeled)
		Autocannon (MT)	Gunner/TL (Machine gun)
Archeology (T4)	Archeology	Autogun (TNE)	Gunner/TL (Cannon, possibly machine gun)
Archery (TNE)	Bow		
Armed Martial Arts (TNE)		Automatic Pistol (CT)	Guns/TL (Pistol)
Club	Broadsword or Axe/Mace	Automatic Rifle (CT)	Guns/TL (Light automatic)
Large Blade	Broadsword	Autorifle (MT)	Guns/TL (Light automatic)
Polearm	Polearm	Axe (MT)	Axe/Mace
Small Blade	Knife	Axe, Battle (MT)	Axe/Mace

Traveller	GURPS
Carbine (CT, MT)	Guns/TL (Rifle)
Carousing (MT, TNE, T4)	Carousing
Carpenter (TNE)	Carpentry
Chemistry (MT, TNE, T4)	Chemistry/TL
Climbing (TNE)	Climbing
Combat Engineer (TNE)	Engineer/TL (Combat)
Combat Engineering (MT)	Engineer/TL (Combat)
Combat Rifleman (MT)	Guns/TL (Light automatic)
Communications (MT, T4, TNE)	Electronics Operations/TL (Communications)
Computer (CT, MT, T4)	Computer Operation/TL and Computer Programming/TL
Computer Tech (TNE)	Computer Operation/TL and Computer Programming/TL
Construction (TNE)	Engineer/TL (Civil)
Craftsman (T4)	Woodworking, Sculpture, etc., as appropriate
Criminology (T4)	Criminology/TL
Crossbow (MT)	Crossbow
Cudgel (CT, MT)	Broadsword
Cutlass (CT, MT)	Broadsword
Dagger (CT, MT)	Knife
Dance (TNE, T4)	Dancing
Demolition (MT, T4)	Demolition/TL
Diplomacy (T4)	Diplomacy
Disguise (MT, T4, TNE)	Disguise
Early Firearms (MT, TNE)	Black Powder Weapons/TL (type)
Electronics (CT, MT, T4)	Electronics/TL (type)
Electronics Tech (TNE)	Electronics/TL (type)
Energy Artillery (TNE)	Gunner/TL (type)
Energy Weapon (Pistol) (TNE)	Beam Weapons/TL (type)
Energy Weapon (Rifle) (TNE)	Beam Weapons/TL (type)
Energy Weapons (MT)	Beam Weapons/TL (type)
Engineering (CT, MT, T4)	Engineer/TL (Vehicles)
Environment Combat (T4)	Free Fall/TL
Environment Suit (TNE)	Vacc Suit/TL
Equestrian (MT, T4)	Riding (type)
Excavation (TNE)	Engineer/TL (Mining or Civil)
FA Gunnery (MT)	Gunner/TL (type)
Farming (TNE)	Agronomy/TL
Fast Talk (T4)	Fast-Talk
Fencing (T4)	Fencing
First Aid (T4)	First Aid/TL
Fleet Tactics (MT)	Strategy (Space)
Foil (CT, MT)	Fencing
Forensic (MT, T4)	Forensics/TL
Forgery (CT, MT, TNE, T4)	Forgery/TL
Forward Observer (CT, MT, TNE, T4)	Forward Observer /TL
Fusion Gun (MT)	Beam Weapons/TL (Plasma blaster)
Gambling (CT, MT, TNE, T4)	Gambling
Gauss Rifle (MT)	Guns/TL (Light automatic)
Genetics (MT, TNE)	Genetics/TL
Geology (TNE, T4)	Geology/TL

Traveller	GURPS
Axe, Hand (MT)	Axe/Mace
Bargain (TNE)	Merchant
Battle Dress (MT, T4)	Battlesuit/TL
Bayonet (CT, MT)	Spear
Biology (MT, TNE, T4)	Botany/TL, Zoology/TL, etc.
Blade (CT, MT)	Shortsword
Blade, Long (T4)	Broadsword
Blade, Large (MT)	Broadsword
Blade, Short (T4)	Shortsword
Blade, Small (MT)	Shortsword
Blowgun (MT)	Blowpipe
Body Pistol (CT, MT)	Guns/TL (Pistol)
Bola (MT)	Bolas
Boomerang (MT)	Throwing Stick
Bow Combat (CT, T4)	Bow or Crossbow
Brawling (CT, MT, T4)	Brawling
Bribery (CT, MT, TNE, T4)	Streetwise or Fast-Talk
Broadsword (CT, MT)	Two-Handed Sword
Broker (MT, T4)	Merchant
Camouflage (T4)	Camouflage

Traveller	GURPS	Traveller	GURPS
Grav Belt (MT, TNE)	Piloting (Contragravity)	Mechanical (CT, MT)	Mechanic/TL (type)
Grav Craft (T4)	Piloting (Contragravity)	Mechanics (T4)	Mechanic/TL (type)
Grav Vehicle (CT, MT)	Piloting (Contragravity)	Medical (CT, T4)	Physician/TL, Diagnosis/TL, and Surgery/TL
Gravitics (MT, TNE, T4)	Electronics/TL (Contragravity)	Medical, Diagnosis (TNE)	Diagnosis/TL
Grenade Launcher (MT, TNE)	Guns/TL (Grenade launcher)	Medical, Surgery (TNE)	Surgery/TL
Ground Craft (T4)	Driving (type)	Medical, Trauma Aid (TNE)	First Aid/TL
Ground Vehicle Tracked (TNE)	Driving (Tracked)	Melee Combat (T4)	Brawling
Ground Vehicle Wheeled (TNE)	Driving (type)	Meson Guns (MT)	Gunner/TL (Meson)
Guard/Hunting Beasts (MT, TNE)	Animal Handling	Metallurgy (TNE)	Metallurgy/TL
Gunnery (CT, T4)	Gunner/TL (type)	Meteorology (TNE)	Meteorology/TL
Gunnery, Missiles (TNE)	Gunner/TL (Missiles)	Mortars & Howitzers (MT)	Gunner/TL (Mortar and/or Cannon)
Gunnery, Energy Weapon (TNE)	Gunner/TL (type)		
Gunnery, Grav Weapon (TNE)	Gunner/TL (Gravitic)	Muscle Transport, Skates (TNE)	Skating
Halberd (CT, MT)	Polearm	Muscle Transport, Skis (TNE)	Skiing
Handgun (MT)	Guns/TL (Pistol)	Muscle Transport, Wheels (TNE)	Teamster or Bicycling
Heavy Artillery (TNE)	Gunner/TL (type)	Music (T4)	Singing and/or Musical Composition
Heavy Guns (TNE)	Gunner/TL (type)		
Heavy Weapons (T4)	Gunner/TL (type)	Musical Instrument (TNE)	Musical Instrument (type)
Helicopter (CT, MT, T4)	Piloting (Helicopter)	Music, Composition (TNE)	Musical Composition
Herding (MT)	Agronomy/TL		
High Energy Weapons (MT)	Beam Weapons/TL (type)		
High-G Environment (MT, TNE)	Improved G-Tolerance		
History (MT, TNE, T4)	History		
Hovercraft (CT, MT, TNE)	Driving (Hovercraft)		
Hunting (MT)	Tracking		
Instruction (MT, TNE, T4)	Teaching		
Interrogation (MT, TNE, T4)	Interrogation		
Interview (MT, TNE)	Interrogation		
Intimidation (T4)	Intimidation		
Intrusion (MT, TNE, T4)	Lockpicking/TL		
Investigation (T4, TNE)	Criminology/TL		
Jet Aircraft (CT), Jet Plane (T4)	Piloting (High-performance airplane)		
Jet-propelled aircraft (MT)	Piloting (High-performance airplane)		
Jeweler (TNE)	Jeweler/TL		
Language (TNE, T4)	Language (type)		
Large Watercraft (CT)	Powerboat or Seamanship		
Laser Carbine (CT, MT)	Beam Weapons/TL (Lasers)		
Laser Pistol (MT)	Beam Weapons/TL (Lasers)		
Laser Rifle (CT, MT)	Beam Weapons/TL (Lasers)		
Laser Weapons (MT)	Beam Weapons/TL (Lasers)		
Law (T4)	Law		
Leader (CT, MT)	Leadership		
Leadership (TNE, T4)	Leadership		
Legal (MT)	Law		
Liaison (MT, TNE)	Savoir-Faire		
Light Assault Gun (MT)	Guns/TL (Light automatic)		
Lighter-than-air Craft (MT)	Pilot (type)		
Linguistics (MT, T4)	Linguistics		
Machinegun (MT)	Guns/TL (Machine gun)		
Machinist (TNE)	Blacksmith/TL		
Map (TNE)	Cartography		
Marketing (TNE)	Merchant		
Mason (TNE)	Masonry		
Mass Drivers (MT)	Gunner/TL (Electromag)		
Mechanic (TNE)	Mechanic/TL (type)		

Traveller	GURPS	Traveller	GURPS
Music, Keyboard (TNE)	Musical Instrument (type)	Pilot, Rotary Wing (TNE)	Piloting (Helicopter)
Music, Other (TNE)	Musical Instrument (type)	Pistol (MT, T4)	Guns/TL (Pistol)
Music, Percussion (TNE)	Musical Instrument (type)	Plasma Gun (MT)	Beam Weapons/TL
Music, Strings (TNE)	Musical Instrument (type)		(Plasma blaster)
Music, Wind (TNE)	Musical Instrument (type)	Polearm (MT)	Polearm
Naval Architect (MT)	Shipbuilding/TL (Starship)	Prop Plane (T4)	Piloting (Light airplane,
Navigation (MT, TNE, T4)	Navigation/TL		possibly ultralight)
Navigator (CT)	Navigation/TL	Propeller Aircraft (CT, MT)	Piloting (Light airplane,
Neural Pistol (MT)	Beam Weapons/TL (Neural)		possibly heavy airplane)
Neural Rifle (MT)	Beam Weapons/TL (Neural)	Prospecting (MT)	Prospecting
Observation (TNE)	Tracking	Psionicology (T4)	Psionics/TL
Painting (TNE)	Painting	Psychology (TNE, T4)	Psychology/TL (race)
Parachute (TNE)	Parachuting	RCV Operations (TNE)	Piloting (type)
Persuasion (MT, TNE)	Fast-Talk	Recon (MT, T4)	Tracking and/or Stealth
Philosophy (T4)	Philosophy (type)	Recruiting (MT, TNE)	Fast-Talk
Physics (MT, TNE, T4)	Physics/TL	Research (T4, TNE)	Research
Pickpocket (TNE)	Pickpocket	Revolver (CT, MT)	Guns/TL (Pistol)
Pike (CT, MT)	Polearm	Riding (TNE)	Riding (type)
Pilot (CT, MT, T4)	Piloting (Starship)	Rifle (MT, T4)	Guns/TL (Rifle)
Pilot, Airship (TNE)	Piloting (Lighter-than-air)	Rifleman (MT)	Guns/TL (Light automatic)
Pilot, Fixed Wing (TNE)	Piloting (Heavy, high-performance, or light airplane)	Robot Ops (MT)	Artificial Intelligence/TL and Mechanic/TL (Robotics)
Pilot, Glider (TNE)	Piloting (Glider)	Robotics (MT, TNE, T4)	Artificial Intelligence/TL and Mechanic/TL (Robotics)
Pilot, Interface/Grav (TNE)	Piloting (Contragravity)	Science (MT)	GM and player's choice(s)

Traveller	GURPS
Screens (MT)	Electronics Operations/TL (Force shields)
Screens, Black Globe (TNE)	Electronics Operations/TL (Force shields)
Screens, Meson Screens (TNE)	Electronics Operations/TL (Force shields)
Screens, Nuclear Dampers (TNE)	Electronics Operations/TL (Force shields)
Screens, Sandcaster (TNE)	Gunner/TL (Sandcaster)
Sculpture (TNE)	Sculpting
Sensor Ops (MT), Sensors (TNE, T4)	Electronics Operations/TL (Sensors)
Service (TNE)	Savoir-Faire (Servant)
Ship Tactics (MT)	Tactics
Ship's Boat (CT, MT, T4)	Piloting (Spaceship)
Ship's Engineering (TNE)	Engineer/TL (Vehicles)
Shotgun (CT, T4)	Guns/TL (Shotgun)
Sling (MT)	Sling
Slug Weapon, Pistol (TNE)	Guns/TL (Pistol)
Slug Weapon, Rifle (TNE)	Guns/TL (Rifle)
Small Watercraft (CT)	Boating
Snub Pistol (MT)	Guns/TL (Pistol)
Song (TNE)	Singing
Spear (CT, MT)	Spear
Spinal Weapons (MT)	Gunner/TL (Particle beam)
Starship Architecture (TNE)	Shipbuilding/TL (Starship)
Stealth (MT, TNE, T4)	Stealth
Steward (CT, MT)	Savoir-Faire (Servant)
Streetwise (CT, MT, TNE, T4)	Streetwise
Submachinegun (CT, MT, T4)	Guns/TL (Light automatic)
Submersible (CT)	Seamanship
Survey (MT, TNE, T4)	Astrography
Survival (MT, TNE, T4)	Survival (type)
Swimming (TNE)	Swimming
Sword (CT, MT)	Broadsword
Tac Missile (TNE)	Gunner/TL (Missile)
Tactics (CT, T4)	Tactics
Tactics, Fleet (TNE)	Strategy (Space)
Tactics, Ground (TNE)	Tactics
Tactics, Ship (TNE)	Tactics

Traveller	GURPS
Throwing (T4)	Throwing or Thrown Weapon
Thrown Weapon (TNE)	Throwing or Thrown Weapon
Tracked Vehicle (CT)	Driving (Tracked)
Tracking (TNE)	Tracking
Trader (MT, T4)	Merchant
Turret Weapons (MT)	Gunner/TL (type)
Unarmed Martial Arts (TNE)	Karate or Judo, etc.
Vacc Suit (CT, MT, T4)	Vacc Suit/TL
Vehicle (MT)	Driving (type)
VRF Gauss Gun (MT)	Gunner/TL (Machine gun)
Watercraft (T4)	Boating, Seamanship/TL, or Powerboat/TL
Watercraft, Large (MT, TNE)	Seamanship/TL
Watercraft, Small (MT, TNE)	Powerboat/TL
Wheeled Vehicle (CT)	Driving (type)
Writing (T4)	Writing
Xenobiology (TNE)	Xenobiology
Zero-G Combat (CT)	Free Fall/TL
Zero-G Environment (MT, TNE)	Free Fall/TL
Zero-G Ops (MT)	Free Fall/TL
Zero-G Weapons (CT)	Guns/TL (Gyroc)

Advantages, Disadvantages, and Quirks

These three features of *GURPS* character creation have little direct correspondence in *Traveller*. Status can be determined from *Traveller* stats, of course, and Wealth judged based on the character's Status and fiscal position at conversion. Controlling interest in a ship is handled with the Ship Patron rules on pp. 84-85 or Ship Owner on p. T:FT101. The *TNE* system covered Charisma, Contacts, and Patrons, but for other *Traveller* systems these will have to be estimated.

Other advantages, disadvantages, and quirks can be given based on the character's concept. Certainly an experienced Marine could have Combat Reflexes. GMs might allow more advantages for low-attribute, low-skill conversions than those with high attributes and/or skills.

Starships

This appendix describes some of the most common ships in the Imperium. Each class is rated in displacement tons (also called dtons), but with masses given in standard tons. Displacement tons measure *size* (500 cf per dton). The masses listed measure *weight* (2,000 pounds per ton).

See *Modular Starship Design*, pp. 149-162, for an explanation of ship statistics. See *Crew Requirements*, pp. 149-150, for the skills required at each crew position.

Prices are given with any weaponry listed in the writeup, but without any ship's vehicles, ammo, fuel, or computer programs.

The EMass (empty mass) listed assumes only fuel is carried. The LMass (loaded mass) assumes standard ship's vehicles, 5 tons per cargo space, and fuel.

Listed Accel is based on LMass. To calculate different Accels: divide LMass by (EMass plus cargo, extra weapons, and vehicles carried), then multiply by the listed Accel.

SULIEMAN-CLASS
100-TON SCOUT/COURIER (TL10)

Commonly used for survey, reconnaissance, courier, and liaison duties, the *Sulieman* class is one of the most commonly encountered vessels in interstellar space. Selected retirees from the Imperial Interstellar Scout Service (IISS) are granted the long-term use of a Scout/Courier (see *Ship Patrons*, pp. 84-85).

The ex-scout may use the vessel for any legal purpose, and many engage in small-scale speculative trade. The ship really isn't suited for passenger service, but it's not unkown.

The large number of such vessels in existence has given rise to a number of rumors: The most common of these is that Scouts are often used for espionage. The large number of sheep means that a goat or two might be concealed among them, the thinking goes.

The spacedock usually houses an air/raft.

■ **Crew:** Pilot, co-pilot, and engineer are the most common arrangement. An exceptional person might fill all slots and operate the vessel alone, but few people have all the requisite skills (see *Crew Requirements*, pp. 149-150).

■ **Design:** 100-ton SL Hull, DR 200, Basic Stealth, Basic Emissions Cloaking, Heavy Compartmentalization. *Modules:* 1 Basic Bridge, 1 Engineering, 20 Maneuver, 3 Jump, 20 Fuel, 1 Space Dock, 4 Staterooms, 1 Utility, 2 Fuel Processors, 1 Turret, 12.5 Cargo (+3 in Turret).

■ **Statistics:** EMass 268, LMass 346, Cost MCr26.4, HP 15,000. Size Modifier: +8.

■ **Performance:** Accel 2.3 Gs, Jump 2, Air Speed 2,357.

SULIEMAN II-CLASS 100-TON SEEKER (TL 10)

The *Sulieman II*-class seeker is a common IISS modification of the *Sulieman,* used for mineral surveys and similar duties. Crew requirements are the same.

The spacedock usually houses an air/raft.

■ **Design:** 100-ton SL Hull, DR 200, Basic Stealth, Basic Emissions Cloaking, Heavy Compartmentalization. *Modules:* 1 Basic Bridge, 1 Engineering, 20 Maneuver, 3 Jump, 20 Fuel, 1 SpaceDock, 2 Staterooms, 1 Utility, 2 Fuel Processors, 1 Turret, 20.5 Cargo (+3 in Turret).

■ **Statistics:** EMass 263, LMass 382, Cost MCr26.4, HP: 15,000. Size Modifier: +8.

■ **Performance:** Accel 2.1 Gs, Jump 2, Air Speed 2,357.

100-TON *SULIEMAN*-CLASS SCOUT/COURIER

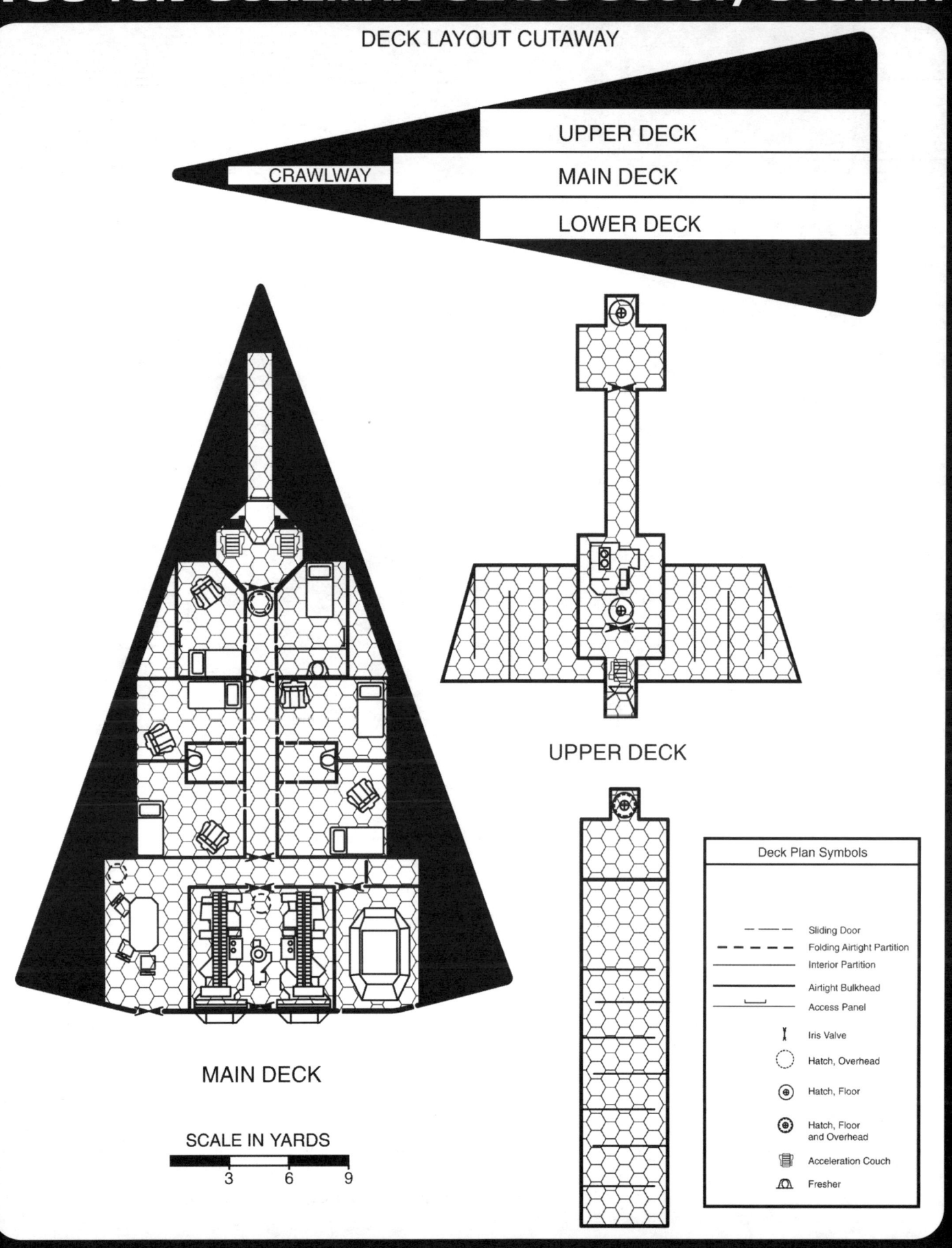

DECK LAYOUT CUTAWAY

UPPER DECK

CRAWLWAY   MAIN DECK

LOWER DECK

UPPER DECK

MAIN DECK

SCALE IN YARDS

3   6   9

Deck Plan Symbols

– – –	Sliding Door
– – –	Folding Airtight Partition
———	Interior Partition
———	Airtight Bulkhead
⌐_⌐	Access Panel
⅄	Iris Valve
◌	Hatch, Overhead
⊕	Hatch, Floor
◉	Hatch, Floor and Overhead
▤	Acceleration Couch
⋒	Fresher

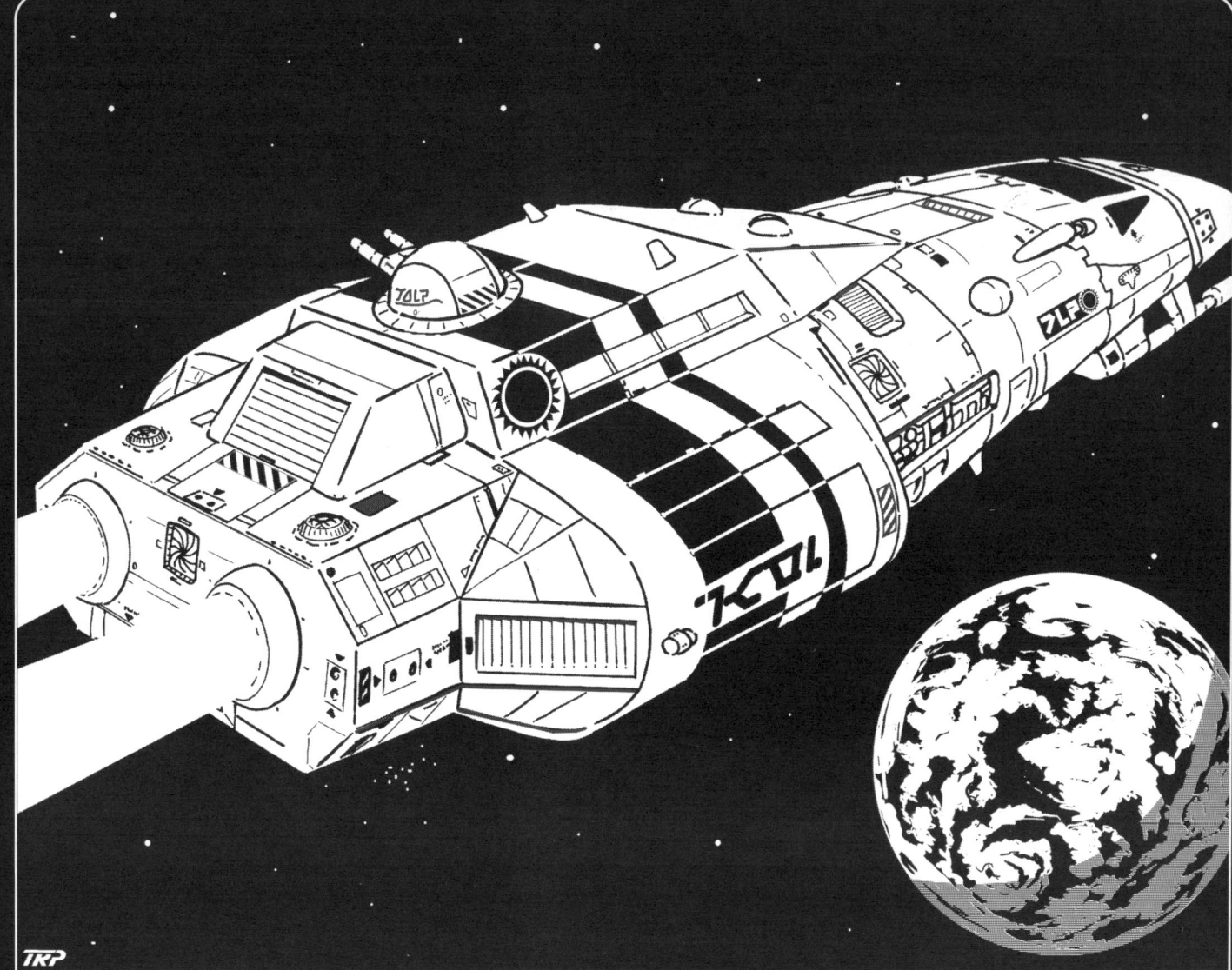

BEOWULF-CLASS 200-TON
FREE TRADER (TL10)

The *Beowulf* class is the most common design of Free Trader, at least in the frontier regions of the Imperium and the surrounding client states. Huge megacorporate transports dominate mercantile service in the Imperial core regions. These little freighters fill the irregular and small-lot needs of the less habitated fringes, while keeping overhead and crew administration needs to a minimum.

Numerous formal variants, and a myriad of individual modifications, mean that the deck plan layout presented is subject to considerable change.

The *Beowulf's* most serious limitation is that it is only capable of jump-1, meaning that it is restricted to the "mains," as the stretches of J-1 linked star systems are called.

Captains often omit the air/raft and use the spacedock for additional cargo.

■ **Crew:** Captain/pilot, navigator, sensor/commo operator, steward, and two engineers. One of the crew will serve double duty as a pilot for the enclosed air/raft if carried aboard.

■ **Design:** 200-ton SL Hull, DR 100. *Modules:* 1 Basic Bridge, 1 Engineering, 16 Maneuver, 4 Jump, 20 Fuel, 5 Low Berths (capacity 20), 10 Staterooms, 1 Spacedock (up to 250 cf air/raft), 1 Utility, 2 Fuel Processors, 2 Turrets, 68 Cargo (+6 in Turrets).

■ **Statistics:** EMass 257, LMass 598, Cost MCr28.9, HP: 22,500. Size Modifier: +8.

■ **Performance:** Accel 1.1 Gs, Jump 1, Air Speed 1,700.

200-TON BEOWULF-CLASS FREE TRADER

This deck plan is of a formal variant that includes an air/raft dock (replacing 1 space of cargo).

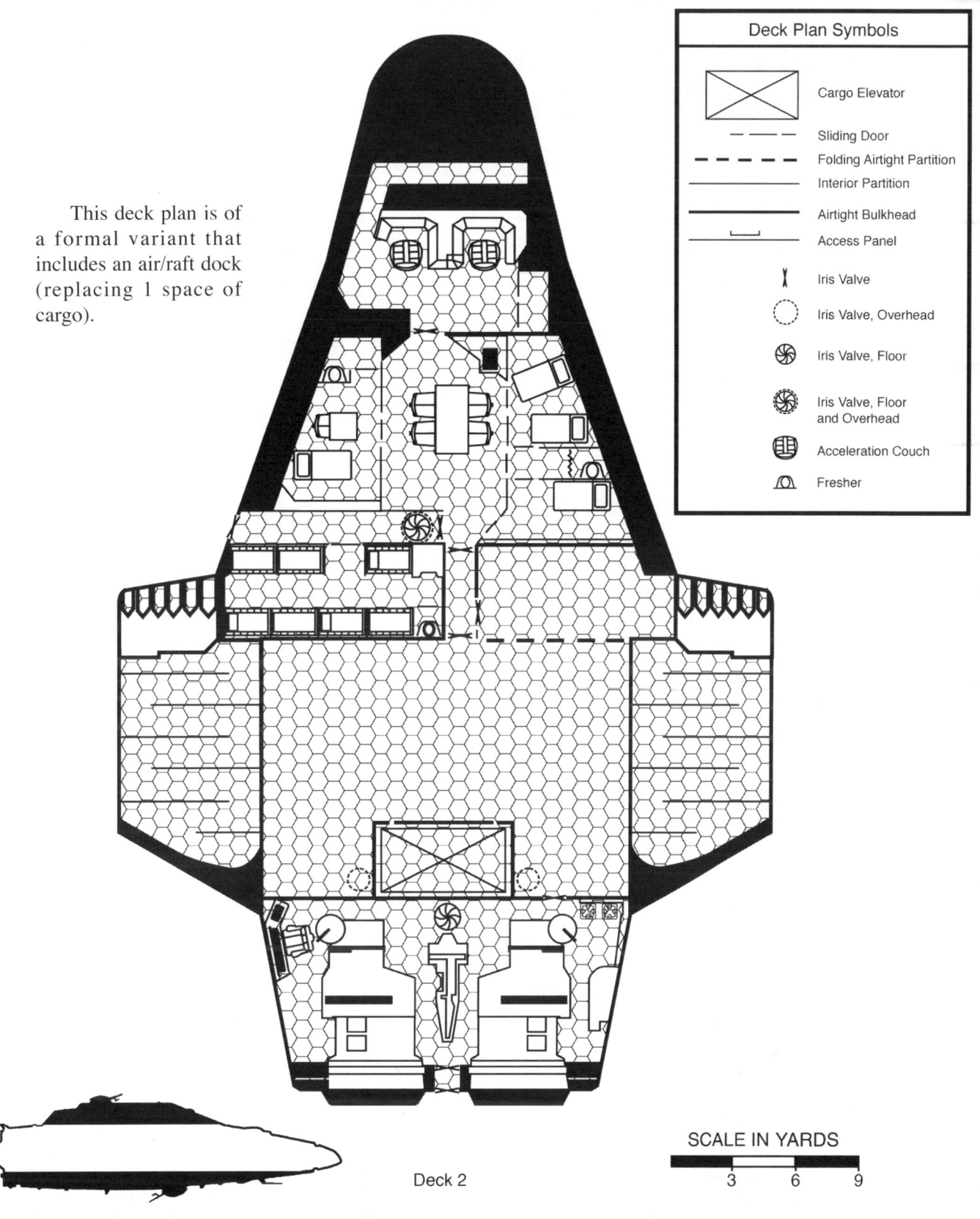

Deck Plan Symbols

- Cargo Elevator
- Sliding Door
- Folding Airtight Partition
- Interior Partition
- Airtight Bulkhead
- Access Panel
- Iris Valve
- Iris Valve, Overhead
- Iris Valve, Floor
- Iris Valve, Floor and Overhead
- Acceleration Couch
- Fresher

Deck 2

SCALE IN YARDS

3   6   9

BEOWULF-CLASS
200-TON FREE TRADER

MAIN DECK ON P. 133

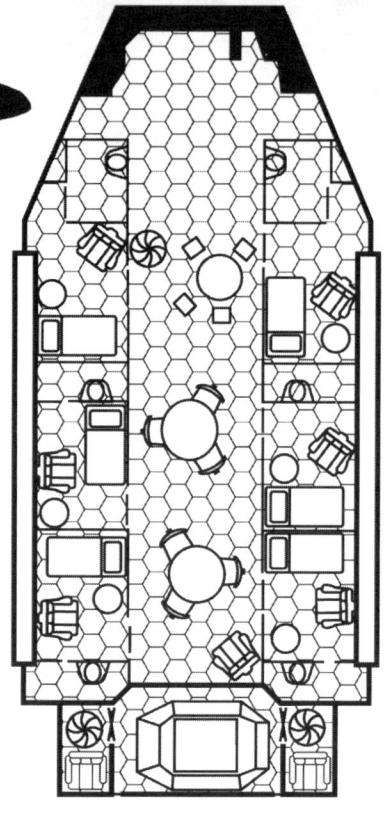

Deck 1

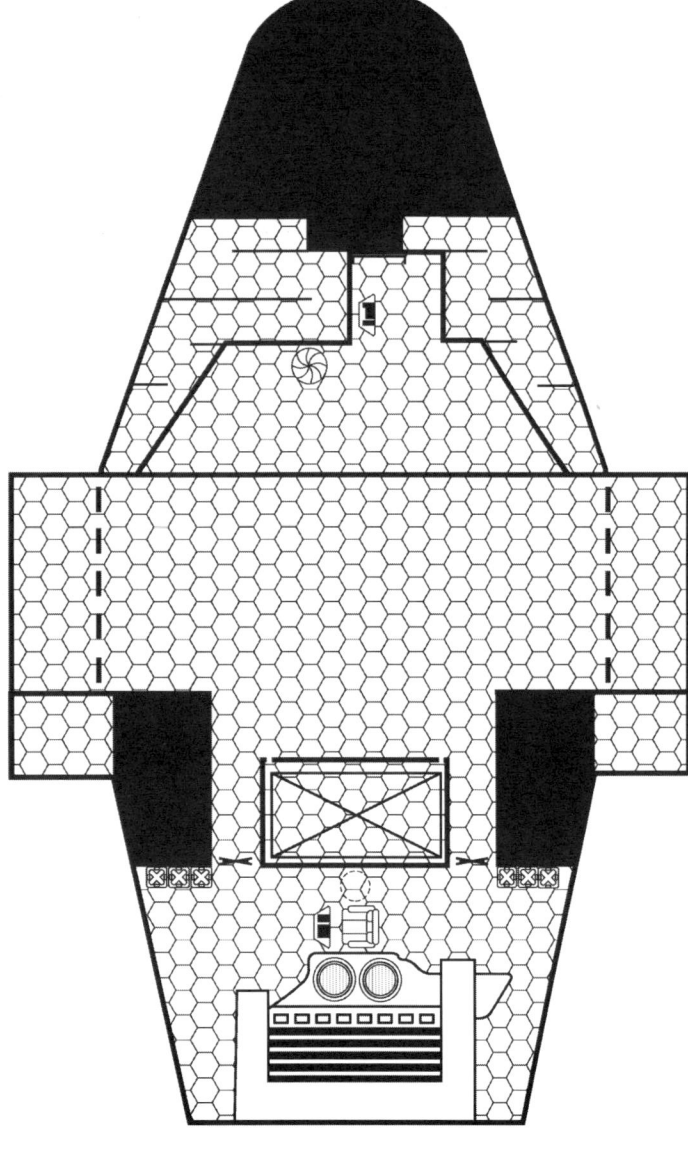

Deck 3

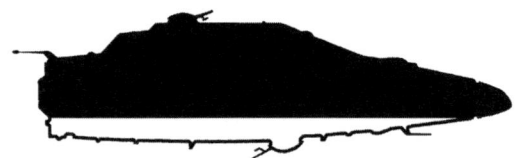

Deck Plan Symbols

Cargo Elevator	
Sliding Door	
Folding Airtight Partition	
Interior Partition	
Airtight Bulkhead	
Access Panel	
Iris Valve	
Iris Valve, Overhead	
Iris Valve, Floor	
Iris Valve, Floor and Overhead	
Acceleration Couch	
Fresher	

EMPRESS MARAVA-CLASS
200-TON FAR TRADER (TL10)

Far Traders earn their name with their jump-2 capability. With "longer legs" than the somewhat more common Free Trader, the Far Traders can service routes their brethren can't reach.

The increased jump and fuel requirements mean that cargo capacity and stateroom numbers must suffer, but in some areas no other vessel will do the job as well. A common practice is to hire a steward with some medical training in place of installing a sickbay, and to help ensure the survival of low-berth passengers. As with the Free Trader, custom refittings are common.

The 48-point Ship Patron cost cited on p. T:FT100 assumes an air/raft is carried, one turret is armed, and the ship profit/upkeep arrangement evens out to 0 points.

■ **Crew:** Captain/pilot, navigator, sensor/commo operator, steward, and two engineers. One of the crew doubles as air/raft pilot. The steward should have Electronics Operation (Medical)-10+ if low passengers carried.

■ **Design:** 200-ton SL Hull, DR 100. *Modules:* 1 Basic Bridge, 1 Engineering, 15 Maneuver, 6 Jump, 40 Fuel, 3 Low Berths (capacity 12), 1 SpaceDock (holds up to 250 cf air/raft), 10 Staterooms, 1 Utility, 2 Turrets, 1 Fuel Processor, 49 cargo (+6 in Turrets).

■ **Statistics:** EMass 283, LMass 559, Cost MCr36.8, HP: 22,500. Size Modifier: +8.

■ **Performance:** Accel 1.1 Gs, Jump 2, Air Speed 1,646.

VANDERBILT-CLASS
200-TON YACHT (TL10)

This particular class represents a typical yacht used by planetary nobles, corporate officials, and interstellar diplomats. Externally, however, this design and the *Lady of Shallot* class (below) are nearly identical.

Two of the staterooms are merged to form a suite for the owner. Two more are merged to form a lounge area. Six are for guests, and five house the crew (four at double occupancy, plus a single-occupancy berth for the captain). The five tons of cargo space allow the owner to travel as light as the wealthy usually travel.

The two stewards double as small-craft crew, flying the ship's boat or air/raft carried aboard. If the yacht is armed, one or more of the crew double as gunners during emergencies. Bodyguards, assistants, and assorted other members of an owner's retinue are carried as passengers, often doubling up on staterooms and thereby increasing overall occupancy.

As luxury items, yachts often are embellished with expensive decor and trappings, substantially increasing their cost with features that aren't reflected in the ship's performance. These same fittings sometimes get ripped out and sold by less savory second owners, who find the vessel's harmless appearance and jump-3 capability useful for disguising illicit functions and getting away afterward respectively.

- **Crew:** Captain/pilot), navigator, sensor/commo operator, two stewards, two medics, and two engineers.
- **Design:** 200-ton USL Hull, DR 100. *Modules:* 1 Basic Bridge, 1 Engineering, 12 Maneuver, 8 Jump, 60 Fuel, 15 Spacedock, 15 Staterooms, 1 Sickbay, 1 Utility, 1 Vehicle Bay (30-ton Ship's Boat), 2 Turrets, 1 Fuel Processor, 5 Cargo (+6 in Turrets).
- **Statistics:** EMass 313, LMass 439, Cost MCr44.1, HP: 22,500. Size Modifier: +8.
- **Performance:** Accel 1.1 Gs, Jump 3.

LADY OF SHALLOT-CLASS
200-TON YACHT (TL12)

This represents a higher-tech and more-expensive yacht used by Imperial nobles, extremely high-level corporate officials, and upper-level Imperial diplomats. *Ladies of Shallot* are not so commonly encountered as the other starships detailed in this section. For that reason – and given the nature of their average occupant – the arrival of one of these yachts in a star system never fails to draw attention.

The *Lady of Shallot* class actually houses fewer people than the *Vanderbilt* class, but uses the space for a slightly larger manuever drive that – given its higher TL – more than triples performance. Similar to the *Vanderbilt*, two staterooms are merged to form a suite for the owner. Two more are merged to form a lounge. Five are for guests, and five house the crew (four at double-occupancy plus one single-occupancy berth for the captain). The two stewards double as small-craft crew, and one or more of the crew double as gunners if weapons are installed. (One mildly unhinged Imperial noble had the turrets on his yacht loaded with specially modified

sandcasters that discharged 10-mile-long party streamers . . .) The owner's entourage usually must still double-occupy staterooms; even though the boss has more Status, the help doesn't.

Wildly expensive custom trappings are even more common on *Ladies of Shallot*, with some examples having cost their owners 10 times the list price. Unlike the *Vanderbilt,* these yachts rarely see more secretive duties; they're simply too conspicuous and attract too much interest.

- **Crew:** Captain/pilot, navigator, sensor/commo operator, two stewards, two medics, and two engineers.
- **Design:** 200-ton USL Hull, DR 100. *Modules:* 1 Basic Bridge, 1 Engineering, 15 Maneuver, 8 Jump, 60 Fuel, 15 Spacedock, 14 Staterooms, 1 Sickbay, 1 Utility, 1 Vehicle Bay (30-ton Ship's Boat), 2 Turrets, 1 Fuel Processor, 6 Cargo (+6 in Turrets).
- **Statistics:** EMass 266, LMass 397, Cost MCr49.9, HP: 22,500. Size Modifier: +8.
- **Performance:** Accel 3.8 Gs, Jump 3.

ANIMAL-CLASS 200-TON
SAFARI SHIP (TL10)

Safari ships are used for hunting or photographic expeditions, depending on the predilections of the owner and the laws of the local world.

The main distinguishing feature of this vessel is the presence of a trophy room/lounge, looking out through a large viewing window (protected by a sliding shutter) onto whatever planetary vista presents itself. Of the 11 staterooms, two are merged to form a suite for the owner, and two more are merged to form the trophy room/lounge. Three are set aside for guests of the owner, and four for the crew (at double occupancy). An air/raft is carried to convey the hunting/photographic party. The steward usually serves as its operator.

■ **Crew:** Captain/pilot, navigator, sensor/commo operator, two medics, two engineers, and a steward.

■ **Design:** 200-ton SL Hull, DR 100. *Modules:* 1 Basic Bridge, 1 Engineering, 11 Maneuver, 6 Jump, 40 Fuel, 15 Spacedock, 11 Staterooms, 1 Sickbay, 1 Utility, 1 Vehicle Bay (30-ton Ship's Boat), 1 Turret, 1 Fuel Processor, 5 Cargo (+3 in Turret).

■ **Statistics:** EMass 262, LMass 373, Cost MCr35.5, HP: 22,500. Size Modifier: +8.

■ **Performance:** Accel 1.2 Gs, Jump 2, Air Speed 1,445.

RAMPART-CLASS FIGHTER (TL12)

The *Rampart*-class fighter series (introduced during the Fifth Frontier War) is the most recent fighter design adopted by the Imperial Navy, and can operate either from a planetary surface or from a larger vessel in space. A number of variants are produced, but almost all are in service only with the Imperial military or megacorporations – very few have made it to private mercenary organizations.

Note that a single-purpose fighter will attract official interest where a similarly armed freighter would not.

■ **Crew:** Pilot.

■ **Design:** 10-ton SL Hull, DR 1,175, Radical Stealth Cloaking, Radical Emissions Cloaking, 2 hull-mounted Lasers. *Modules:* 1 hardened Cockpit Bridge, 5 Maneuver.

■ **Statistics:** EMass 90, LMass 90, Cost: MCr10.8, HP: 3,000. Size Modifier: +6.

■ **Performance:** Accel 5.5 Gs, Air Speed: 4,330.

IRAMDA-CLASS FIGHTER (TL10)

This aging warhorse is now almost completely replaced in front-line service by the *Rampart*-class. It is now relegated to secondary duties, such as rear-area planetary defense, scouting, customs patrol, and piracy suppression.

The *Iramda*-class is the fighter most commonly encountered in mercenary organizations.

As with the *Rampart*, non-megacorporate or bonded-mercenary private owners may face official inquiry as to why they need a boat with no non-combat utility.

■ **Crew:** Pilot.

■ **Design:** 10-ton SL Hull, DR 200, Basic Stealth Cloaking, Basic Emissions Cloaking, 1 hull-mounted Laser. *Modules:* 1 Cockpit Bridge, 6 Maneuver.

■ **Statistics:** EMass 57, LMass 57, Cost: MCr5.1, HP: 3,000. Size Modifier: +6.

■ **Performance:** Accel 4.2 Gs, Air Speed: 3,000.

10-TON LAUNCH (TL10)

The 10-ton Launch is the smallest surface-interface craft commonly encountered, and is used where small loads or a few passengers need to be transferred from one ship to another or to/from a planetary surface.

While this configuration offers a mix of passenger and cargo service, many Launches simply cater to one or the other payload, with a maximum of 72 passengers or 3,000 cubic feet of cargo. Generally, 24 long-term passengers require 1 cargo space to shuttle their luggage.

Outwardly, the 10-ton Launch and 10-ton Lifeboat appear very similar.

■ **Crew:** Pilot, engineer, and steward if passengers are carried.
■ **Design:** 10-ton SL Hull, DR 100. *Modules:* 1 Cockpit Bridge, 1 Maneuver, 3 Passenger Couches (occupancy 36), 3 Cargo.
■ **Statistics:** EMass 22, LMass 37, Cost: MCr3.3, HP: 3,000. Size Modifier: +6.
■ **Performance:** Accel 1.1 Gs. Air Speed 1,225.

10-TON LIFEBOAT (TL10)

Smaller vessels rely on rescue balls or conventional small craft in emergencies, but larger starships are equipped with some form of long-term lifeboat. This example can carry up to 12 individuals in its passenger couches and a further 40 in low berths. With the low berths full, couches empty, and power consumption set to minimum (a distress beacon broadcasting on a timer; minimal power to the low berths and computer; no life support), lifeboats can and do keep passengers alive for centuries. This design has no airlock, so cannot take on more passengers while in vacuum or harmful atmospheric conditions unless everyone already aboard is inside rescue balls, vacc suits, or low berths.

■ **Crew:** Pilot; autopilot only if life-support lacking.
■ **Design:** 10-ton SL Hull, DR 100. *Modules:* 1 Cockpit Bridge, 1 Maneuver, 10 Low Berths (capacity 40), 1 Passenger Couch (capacity 12).
■ **Statistics:** EMass 41, LMass 41, Cost: MCr5.3, HP: 3,000. Size Modifier: +6.
■ **Performance:** Accel 1 G. Air Speed 1,225.

800-TON *BROADSWORD*-CLASS MERCENARY CRUISER [TL10]

The *Broadsword*-class mercenary cruiser can be encountered throughout the Imperial fringes. It is easily the most common transport for small, independent military units.

The starship's jump-3 allows it to reach the fringe worlds where trouble most often flares, while the impressive Accel allows the owner to fill its cargo hold with superheavy AFVs (should he enjoy the luxury of affording that sort of equipment) and still manage decent transit times.

Broadswords generally carry a crew of nine, with the owner-aboard serving as captain, and a troop contingent of 31. The ship features a double stateroom for the owner-captain. The leader of the mercenary troop – who traditionally holds the rank of (army or marine) captain – enjoys single occupancy. Everyone else double-bunks. In the event that a separate owner and captain are aboard, requiring that another single-occupant berth be created, some unlucky troopers will be triple-bunking.

The design is not streamlined, relying upon a standard air/raft and two modular cutters (p. 142) for orbit-to-ground transport. Two stubby silos attached to the spherical hull house a module-fitted cutter each and a spare module each. The fit is tight; switching modules requires the cutter to leave the cruiser, offload its module in space, re-enter the cruiser, and attach the new module. The process generally takes 37 minutes.

The spacedock usually holds an air/raft.

■ **Crew:** Captain, pilot, navigator, sensor/commo operator, two medics, three engineers, and eight gunners. The gunnery needs are almost invariably supplied by the ship's troop contingent, reducing ship's crew to nine.
■ **Design:** 800-ton USL Hull, DR 100, 4 Turrets with 3 Lasers each, 2 Turrets with 3 Missile Racks each, 2 Turrets with 3 Sandcasters each. *Modules:* 1 Basic Bridge, 1 Engineering, 175 Maneuver, 32 Jump, 240 Fuel, 1 Spacedock, 22 Staterooms, 1 Sickbay, 2 Utilities, 2 Vehicle Bays (1 50-ton Modular Cutter (p. 142) and 1 spare 30-ton Module each), 1 Fuel Processor, 80.5 Cargo.
■ **Statistics:** EMass 1,613, LMass 2,280, Cost MCr188.8, HP: 60,000. Size Modifier: +10.
■ **Performance:** Accel 3 Gs, Jump 3.

20-ton Gig (TL10)

The Gig is primarily designed for cargo, but can carry up to 24 passengers for a duration of 24 hours or less.

- **Crew:** Pilot, engineer, and steward if passengers are carried.
- **Design:** 20-ton SL Hull, DR 100. *Modules:* 1 Basic Bridge, 1 Engineering, 4 Maneuver, 2 Passenger Couches (capacity 24), 6.5 Cargo.
- **Statistics:** EMass 45, LMass 78, Cost: MCr5.7, HP: 4,500. Size Modifier: +6.
- **Performance:** Accel 2.1 Gs, Air Speed 2,000.

30-ton Ship's Boat (TL10)

The Ship's Boat is a smaller, more affordable surface-interface craft. Up to 96 passengers can be carried for durations of up to 24 hours. Passenger payload can be doubled if couches are fitted into the cargo space.

- **Crew:** Pilot, engineer, and steward.
- **Design:** 30-ton SL Hull, DR 100. *Modules:* 1 Basic Bridge, 1 Engineering, 4 Manuever, 8 Passenger Couches (capacity 96), 8.5 Cargo.
- **Statistics:** EMass 55, LMass 97, Cost: MCr6.3, HP: 6,000. Size Modifier: +7.
- **Performance:** Accel 1.7 Gs, Air Speed 1,732.

40-ton Fuel Skimmer (TL10)

This vessel was designed to skim and process jump fuel for large unstreamlined starships, military fleets, or deep-space installations.

In appearance, it differs from the 40-ton Pinnace only in minor details.

- **Crew:** Pilot and engineer.
- **Design:** 40-ton SL Hull, DR 100. *Modules:* 1 Basic Bridge, 1 Engineering, 11 Maneuver, 2 Fuel Processors, 15 Fuel, 0.5 Cargo.
- **Statistics:** EMass 102, LMass 104, Cost: MCr11.1, HP: 7,500. Size Modifier: +7.
- **Performance:** Accel 4.2 Gs, Air Speed 2,569.

40-ton Pinnace (TL10)

This particular design empha- sizes speed over some other considerations, and is used for planetary interface work by large unstreamlined vessels. Up to 96 passengers can be carried for durations up to 24 hours.

- **Crew:** Pilot, engineer, and two stewards.
- **Design:** 40-ton SL Hull, DR 100. *Modules:* 1 Basic Bridge, 1 Engineering, 16 Maneuver, 8 Passenger Couches (capacity 96), 1 Utility, 3.5 Cargo.
- **Statistics:** EMass 113, LMass 130, Cost: MCr8.7, HP: 7,500. Size Modifier: +7.
- **Performance:** Accel 4.9 Gs, Air Speed 3,098.

100-ton Shuttle (TL10)

This shuttle is designed for orbital work or inter- planetary voyages taking less than 24 hours. Up to 240 passengers are carried, but life support does not permit lengthy trips.

More than half of the available hull tonnage in these boats is taken up by cargo space and passenger couches that can be stripped out, leaving a large amount of room for custom needs. For that reason, these vessels often are encountered in one-of-a-kind configurations. Belters often strip out the passenger couches and haul ore with them.

- **Crew:** Pilot, co-pilot, engineer, and five stewards.
- **Design:** 100-ton SL Hull, DR 200. *Modules:* 1 Basic Bridge, 1 Engineering, 30 Maneuver, 20 Passenger Couches (capacity 240), 1 Utility, 25.5 Cargo.
- **Statistics:** EMass 247, LMass 375, Cost: MCr13.4, HP: 15,000. Size Modifier: +8.
- **Performance:** Accel 3.2 Gs, Air Speed 3,000.

100-ton Interplanetary Shuttle (TL10)

This shuttle is used for in-system travel and is fitted out to carry 12 passengers and four crew for trips last- ing days or weeks. Armed versions are also manufac- tured, equipped with one triple turret and adding an additional crewmember with Gunner skill.

Not as customizable as its cousin, the Interplanetary mostly sees modification by local militaries. More than one fleet has stripped the staterooms out and used the vessel as a fast fuel transport in a crisis. The shuttle also can serve admirably in rapidly deploying troops from orbit.

- **Crew:** Pilot, co-pilot, engineer, and Steward.
- **Design:** 100-ton SL Hull, DR 200. *Modules:* 1 Basic Bridge, 1 Engineering, 17 Maneuver, 14 Staterooms, 1 Utility, 2.5Cargo.
- **Statistics:** EMass 226, LMass 238, Cost: MCr10, HP: 15,000. Size Modifier: +8.
- **Performance:** Accel 2.9 Gs, Air Speed 2,258.

50-ton Modular Cutter (TL 10)

This vessel was developed for use during the Third Frontier War, but design was not completed before the end of that conflict. The 50-ton modular cutter was designed originally by Ling-Standard Products, but proved to be such a useful design that the firm discovered it could not produce enough to satisfy demand, and licensed production to other companies. Such was its penetration in the market that today the word "cutter" is hardly ever used to refer to anything but this particular design of small craft, and often "modular cutter" is assumed.

Originally intended as a utility vessel for support of military operations, the cutter is designed in two parts, a 20-ton hull section and a 30-ton module section. The modules are readily switched out, either in space or inside a hangar. This takes an average of 15 minutes under normal conditions.

The modules themselves are available separately, and separate prices are given below. Some modules were designed to be used only in conjunction with the hull section; others were intended to be operated either joined with or separated from the hull.

All modules can be linked to each other, and are often deployed in deep space or on a planetary surface as components of bases or stations. The variety of modules designed and constructed over the years is large, and only a few will be described here.

Performance statistics are given for the cutter with various modules fitted, and for the hull section alone (since it will often be maneuvered by itself after it has dropped off a module).

50-ton Modular Cutter, Hull Section without Module

- **Crew:** Pilot, co-pilot, and engineer.
- **Design:** 20-ton SL hull, DR 100. *Modules*: 1 Basic Bridge, 1 Engineering, 12 Maneuver, 0.5 Cargo.
- **Statistics:** EMass 72, LMass 74, Cost MCr6.8, HP: 4,500. Size Modifier: +6.
- **Performance:** Accel 2 Gs, Air Speed 1,200. Without a module, the cutter hull is limited to 2 Gs acceleration, because the frame is not able to withstand the strain of further acceleration without the bracing effect of a module. In an atmosphere, it is limited to 1,200 mph top speed.

50-ton Modular Cutter with Passenger Module:
This module is not intended for use separately from the hull, as it provides life support for trips of 24 hours or less duration. The main purpose of this module is the transfer of passengers and cargo from ship to ship, ship to world surface, or the reverse.

Both hull and module sections have airlocks.

- **Design:** 30-ton SL Hull, DR 100. *Modules*: 1 Engineering, 4 Passenger Couches (capacity 48), 19.5 Cargo.
- **Crew:** Standard for cutter, plus steward for module.
- **Statistics:** *(Cutter and Module):* EMass 102 (*Module alone:* 30), LMass 199 (*Module alone:* 125), Cost MCr8.2 (*Module alone:* MCr1.4), HP: 6,000. Size Modifier: +7.
- **Performance:** Accel 2.4 Gs, Air Speed 2,353.

50-ton Modular Cutter with Fuel Skimmer: With this module, the cutter becomes a fuel skimmer for a larger craft. The two fuel-processing modules can refine a total of 16 jump-fuel modules per hour, or the entire load in 1 hour, 22.5 minutes.

- **Design:** 30-ton SL Hull, DR 100. *Modules*: 2 Fuel Processors, 22 Fuel.
- **Crew:** As hull section.
- **Statistics:** EMass 126 (*Module alone:* 55), LMass 129 (*Module alone:* 55.), Cost: MCr12.8 (*Module alone:* MCr6), HP: 6,000. Size Modifier: +7.
- **Performance:** Accel 3.7 Gs, Air Speed 2,353.

50-ton Modular Cutter with ATV Cradle: This module allows the cutter to transport a single ATV (either wheeled or tracked) to or from a world's surface as needed. No airlock is provided, and no provision is made for moving in and out of the ATV while in flight. If the ATV is not sealed, any passengers carried in it must wear vacc suits. Passengers are seldom carried in ATVs while in transit because few have artificial gravity or G-compensators.

■ **Design:** 30-ton SL Hull, DR 100. *Modules*: 14 Spacedock, 10 Cargo.

■ **Crew:** As hull section.

■ **Statistics:** EMass 97 (*Module alone:* 25). LMass with wheeled ATV 180 (*Module alone:* 106), with tracked ATV 169 (*Module alone:* 95). Cost : MCr7.6 (*Module alone:* Cr765,000). HP: 6,000. Size Modifier: +7.

■ **Performance:** Accel 2.9 Gs with tracked ATV, 2.7 Gs with wheeled ATV, Air Speed 2,353.

50-ton Modular Cutter with Weapons Pod: The module was intended to provide a defensive weapon for an orbital or deep-space installation, although it has been used as a fighter and a close-support ground-attack vessel as well (note that its lack of significant armor means that it is not well suited to the latter two uses). The turret is a standard model and can be fitted with lasers, missile racks, or sandcasters as desired (a mixture is common).

■ **Design:** 30-ton SL Hull, DR 100. *Modules*: 1 Cockpit Bridge, 1 Turret with 3 Lasers, 22 Cargo.

■ **Crew:** As hull section, plus Gunner. Substituting missiles or sandcasters for lasers will change the mass and cost. Cargo space is provided for extra missiles or sand canisters, as desired. An airlock is provided in both hull and module sections.

■ **Statistics:** EMass 141 (*Module alone:* 70), LMass 254 (*Module alone:* 180), Cost: MCr13.3 (*Module alone:* MCr6.5), HP: 6,000. Size Modifier: +7.

■ **Performance:** Accel 1.9 Gs (but 3.4 Gs if cargo spaces emptied in preparation for a fight!), Air Speed 2,353.

50-ton Modular Cutter with Quarters Module: This module is designed to provide shelter for a surface or deep-space station or base, as well as other purposes. At double occupancy, the module can support 10 inhabitants for an indefinite period of time (provided food and other perishables are occasionally replenished). Used with a cutter hull, it can provide long-duration sublight transport. An airlock is provided in both the hull and module sections.

■ **Design:** 30-ton SL Hull, DR 100. *Modules*: 1 Engineering, 5 Staterooms, 1 Utility, 2 Cargo.

■ **Crew:** As hull section.

■ **Statistics:** EMass 123 (*Module alone:* 52), LMass 136 (*Module alone:* 62), Cost: MCr8.3 (*Module alone:* MCr1.4), HP: 6,000. Size Modifier: +7.

■ **Performance:** Accel 3.5 Gs, Air Speed 2,353.

50-ton Modular Cutter with Lab Module: This module provides lab facilities for a station or base, and can be deployed on a world's surface or in deep space. An airlock is provided in both the hull and module sections. Three staterooms for the lab technicians are included (six can be accommodated with double occupancy).

■ **Design:** 30-ton SL Hull, DR 100. *Modules*: 1 Engineering, 2 Laboratories, 3 Staterooms, 1 Utility, 6 Cargo.

■ **Crew:** As hull section, plus three to six laboratory personnel.

■ **Statistics:** EMass 138 (*Module alone:* 67), LMass 171 (*Module alone:* 97), Cost: MCr10.2 (*Module alone:* MCr3.4), HP: 6,000. Size Modifier: +7.

■ **Performance:** Accel 2.8 Gs, Air Speed 2,353.

50-ton Modular Cutter with Medical/Surgical Module: This module provides medical facilities for a station or base, and can be deployed on a world's surface or in deep space. It can also be used as a portable emergency hospital for disaster relief, rescue operations, and so on. An airlock is provided in both the hull and module sections. Quarters exist for three, six with double occupancy.

■ **Design:** 30-ton SL Hull, DR 100. *Modules*: 1 Engineering, 3 Staterooms, 2 Sickbays, 1 Utility, 8 Cargo.

■ **Crew:** As hull section, plus three medical personnel.

■ **Statistics:** EMass 120 (*Module alone:* 48), LMass 162 (*Module alone:* 88), Cost: MCr8.5 (*Module alone:* MCr1.7), HP: 6,000. Size Modifier: +7.

■ **Performance:** Accel 3 Gs, Air Speed 2,353.

50-ton Modular Cutter with Fighter Module: This pod was designed to be joined with other cutter modules as part of a base facility, but can also be used in conjunction with the cutter hull. The module provides a vehicle bay for a single 10-ton fighter (in this case, a TL10 *Iramda*-class, but others can be used) and quarters for the crew, for the defense of the station or base to which it is attached. Used with a cutter hull, it provides a deep-space "rest stop" for fighter crews, extending their operational duration.

■ **Design:** 30-ton SL Hull, DR 100. *Modules*: 1 Engineering, 2 Staterooms, 1 Utility, 1 Vehicle Bay (for 10-ton Fighter), 3.5 Cargo.

■ **Crew:** As hull section. Quarters for two.

■ **Statistics:** EMass 116 (*Module alone:* 45), LMass 196 (*Module alone:* 122), Cost: MCr8.2 (*Module alone:* MCr1.4), HP: 6,000. Size Modifier: +7.

■ **Performance:** Accel 2.4 Gs, Air Speed 2,353.

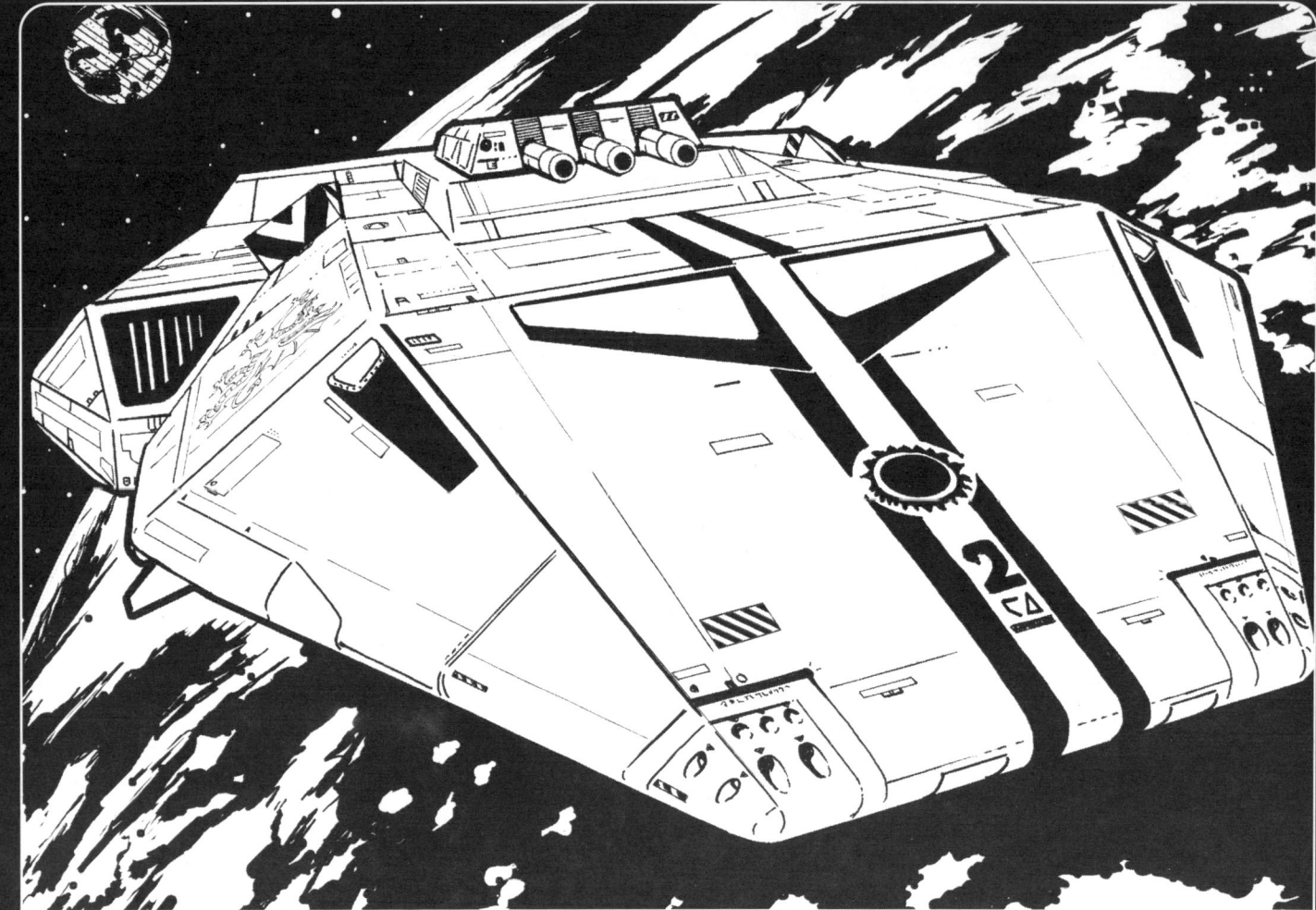

DRAGON-CLASS 400-TON SYSTEM DEFENSE BOAT (TL10)

The *Dragon*-class SDB is found in local defense squadrons throughout the Imperium. These vessels are used for customs inspections, piracy suppression, system defense, and whatever else a local government might need done. A few are still found in the Imperial Navy, but they have largely been replaced by more modern craft. *Dragon*-class boats have a variety of armament configurations, but the most common is two laser turrets (each housing triple 360-MJ lasers) and two missile turrets (each with triple launchers). Sandcasters are sometimes fitted in place of one or more missile racks or lasers. Note that there are only six staterooms for use by 12 crewmembers, necessitating a procedure called hotbunking, where several crew use the same bed at different times, meaning that the bed is always occupied (except during general quarters) and water must be strictly rationed. Because of this, and the lack of other crew amenities, the *Dragon*-class SDBs are given the nickname "Pig Boat" in many services.

- ■ **Crew:** Captain (pilot and navigator), second officer (sensors and commo), five engineers, and four gunners.

- ■ **Design:** 400-ton SL Hull, DR 1,011, 2 Turrets with 3 Lasers each, 2 Turrets with 3 Missile Racks each, Radical Stealth, Radical Emission Cloaking, Heavy Compartmentalization. *Modules*: 1 hardened Basic Bridge, 1 Engineering, 284 Maneuver, 6 Staterooms, 1 Utility, 3.5 Cargo.

- ■ **Statistics:** EMass 2,639, LMass 2,657, Cost: MCr120.1, HP: 37,500. Size Modifier: +9.

- ■ **Performance:** Accel 4.3 Gs, Air Speed 5,497.

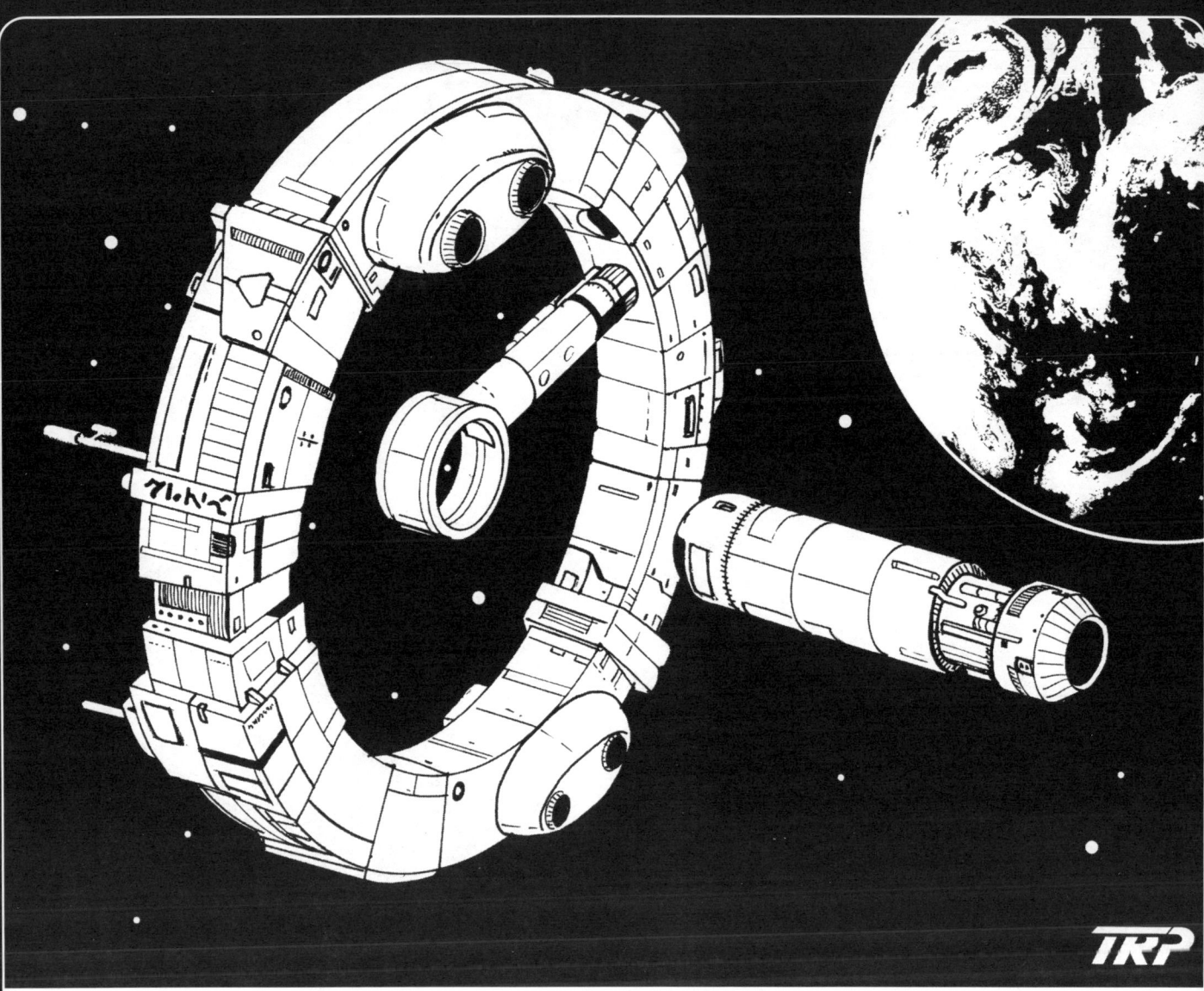

KUGASHIN-CLASS 400-TON LAB SHIP (TL10)

This vessel is used by government (both Imperial and others) and private-research organizations. The equipment in the labs varies with the mission of the vessel. Laboratory ships are not normally armed unless they expect to be operating in dangerous areas, in which case one or more of the crew will have gunner training in addition to their other skills. The fuel skimmer is used to obtain fuel in frontier areas, and the skimmer crew often pilots the two air/rafts with which the ship is normally equipped (other small craft may be assigned depending on the vessel's mission).

■ **Crew:** Captain, pilot, navigator, sensors operator, commo operator, two medics, two engineers, 10 scientists/lab techs, small-craft pilot, and small-craft engineer.

■ **Design:** 400-ton USL Hull, DR 100. *Modules*: 1 Basic Bridge, 1 Engineering, 28 Maneuver, 12 Jump, 80 Fuel, 1 LowBerth, 100 SpaceDock (capacity 50 tons), 20 Staterooms, 1 Sickbay, 1 Utility, 1 Vehicle Bay (40-ton Fuel Skimmer), 10 Lab, 1 Turret, 31 Cargo (+3 inTurret).

■ **Statistics:** EMass 578, LMass 944, Cost: MCr72.8, HP: 37,500. Size Modifier: +9.

■ **Performance:** Accel 1.2 Gs, Jump 2.

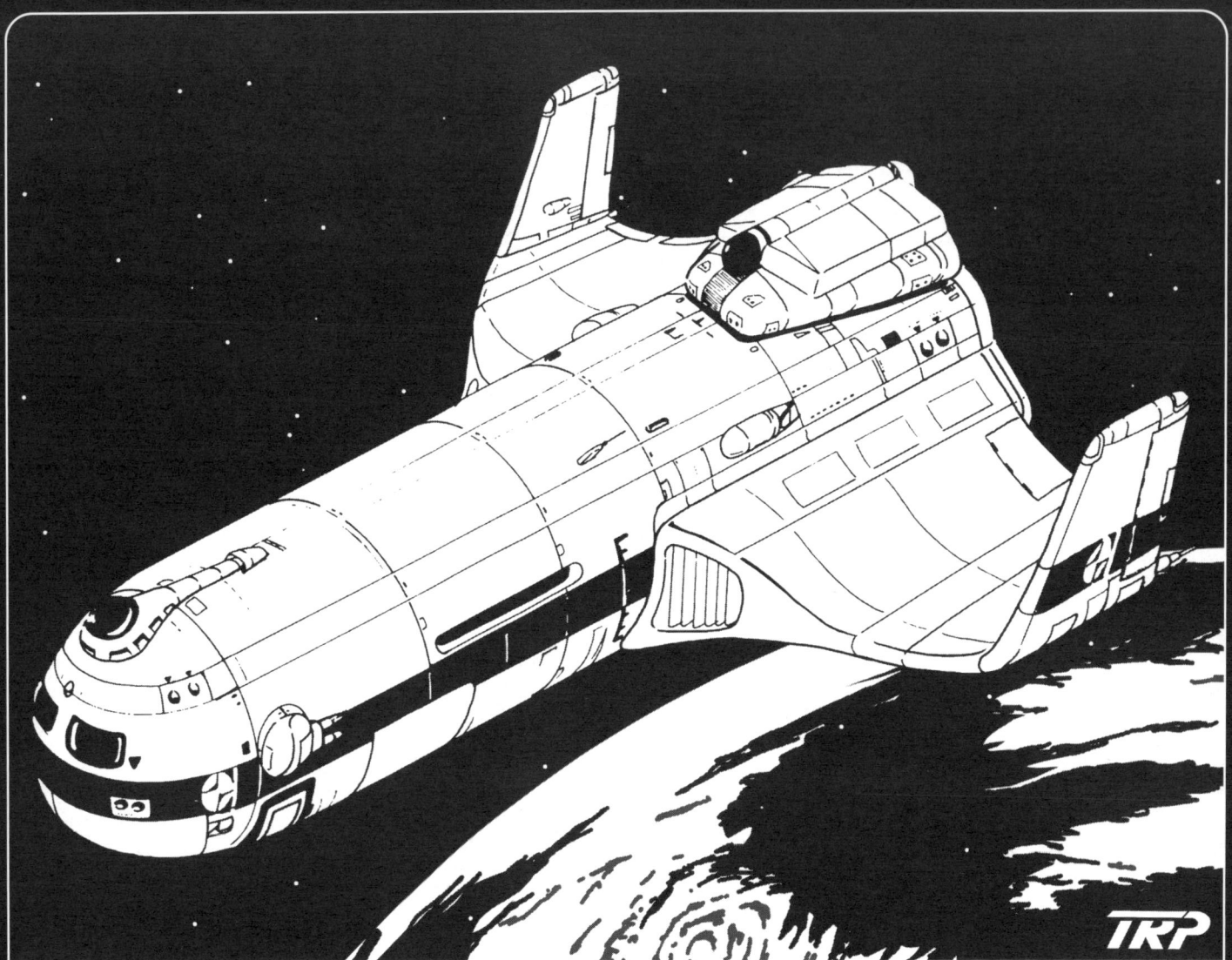

AKKIGISH-CLASS 400-TON SUBSIDIZED MERCHANT (TL10)

Subsidized Merchants are usually found operating a set route where part of the operating expenses are met by an outside party in return for some guarantee (usually a courier contract or a regular shipment/passenger contract of some kind).

Usually a part of the hold or one or more passenger cabins will be reserved for the use of the subsidizer, and the ship required to service a set and scheduled route.

A 10-ton Lifeboat may be substituted for the launch if desired. Members of the crew will be cross-trained as small-craft crew for operating the Launch or Lifeboat.

The 72-point Ship Patron cost on p. T:FT100 assumes an unarmed ship carrying its Launch, with -5 points for owner profit-taking/upkeep.

- ■ **Crew:** Captain, pilot, navigator, sensors operator, communications operator, steward, two medics, and two engineers.

- ■ **Design:** 400-ton SL Hull, DR 100. *Modules*: 1 Basic Bridge, 1 Engineering, 34 Maneuver, 8 Jump, 40 Fuel, 2 Low Berths (capacity 8), 13 Staterooms, 1 Sickbay, 1 Utility, 1 Vehicle Bay (10-ton Launch), 4 Turrets, 165 Cargo (+12 in Turrets).

- ■ **Statistics:** EMass 430, LMass 1,277, Cost: MCr47.4, HP: 37,500. Size Modifier: +9.

- ■ **Performance:** Accel 1.1 Gs, Jump 1, Air Speed 1,902.

ATV, Tracked (TL7)

Scouts on low-tech worlds, mercenaries skirting Imperial intervention, and others often avoid conspicious grav vehicles. This vehicle fills the bill. Its huge cargo capacity makes it ideal to carry supplies for a base camp. With 400 cf of empty space, there is plenty of room for customization. On some worlds these are armed against the fauna, and on others they are fitted with turrets (or pop turrets) and used as APCs.

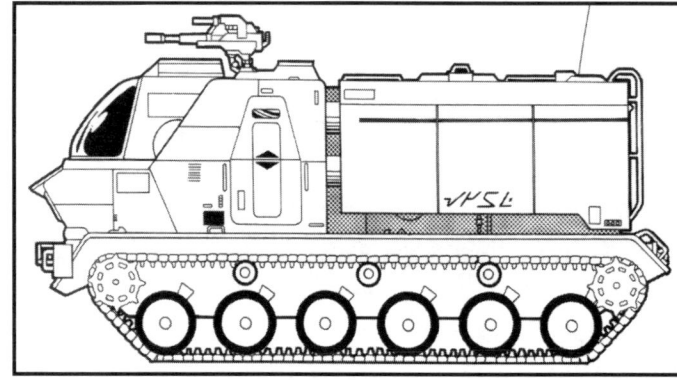

- **Subassemblies:** Tracks.
- **Body Features:** None.
- **Propulsion:** 500-kW tracked drivetrain (HP 72).
- **Instruments and Electronics:** Very-long-range radio (3000 mi., HP 15, 0.1 kW); sensitive receive-only RDF (10× range, HP 1, 0.001 kW); passive infrared (2 mi., Scan 13, HP 3, neg. power); navigation instruments (3 HP, neg. power); GPS (1 HP, neg. power).
- **Miscellaneous:** Full fire suppresion (HP 15); environmental control for six (HP 4, 1.5 kW).
- **Controls:** Mechanical. Crew stations: Roomy. "Driver" operates manuever controls.
- **Accommodations:** Five roomy crew stations. One bunk.
- **Power System:** 520-kW gas turbine (HP 47, 31.2 gph); 1,000-gallon standard tank (HP 169, 32 hrs.); 10,000kJ advanced battery (HP 4).
- **Access, Cargo, and Empty Space:** 63.2 cf access space. 1,200 cf cargo space (12 tons). 401.172 cf empty space.
- **Volume:** Body 2,187.5 cf. Tracks 1,312.5 cf.
- **Surface Area:** Body 1,011 sf. Tracks 719 sf.
- **Structure:** Standard heavy.
- **Hit Points:** Body 3,033. Tracks 1,079 each.
- **Armor:** Body PD 4, DR 100 expensive composite. Tracks PD 4, DR 20 standard composite.
- **Surface Features:** Waterproof.

- **Vision:** Vision slits only.
- **Statistics:** Empty weight 39,041 lbs. Usual internal payload 31,200 lbs. Loaded weight 70,241 lbs. (35.12 tons). Volume 3,500 cf. Size modifier +6. Price Cr481,245. Structural HT 12.
- **Ground Performance:** Top speed 45. gAccel 3 mph/s. gDecel 20 mph/s. gMR 0.125. gSR 6. Off-road speed 36. Very low ground pressure.
- **Water Performance:** Top speed 4. wAccel 0.3. wMR 0.1. wSR 5. wDecel 10. Draft 2.7 feet.

Passenger Option:

Add: 25 roomy seats.

Change: 31-person environmental control (HP 13, 7.75 kW). Cargo 200 cf and 4,000 lbs. Empty space 398.6 cf. Empty weight 40,166 lbs. Internal payload 16,000 lbs. Loaded weight 56,166 lbs. Top ground speed 51 mph. gAccel 4.5. Off-road speed 41. Top water speed 5 mph. Draft 2.5 feet.

Air/Raft, Open Topped (TL12)

This is a sturdy, high-tech grav vehicle, using contragravity for lift and thrusters for propulsion. It has an open top and cargo bed. It can carry four people and up to four tons of cargo. Its nuclear power unit runs it for 10 years. This vehicle (and its close topped cousin) is one of the most commonly produced TL12 vehicles within the Imperium, and innumerable variants are produced.

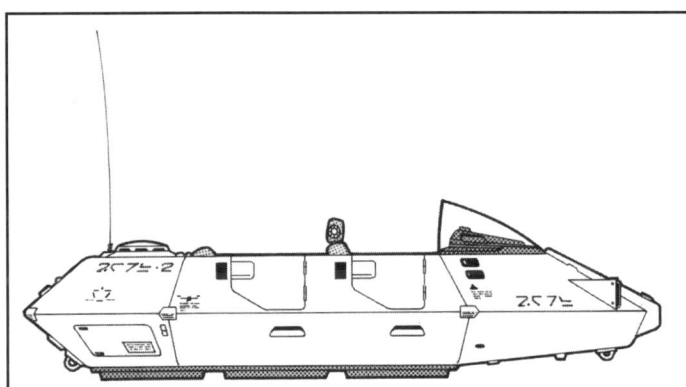

- **Subassemblies:** None.
- **Body Features:** None.
- **Propulsion:** Reactionless thruster (TL11), 800 lbs. thrust (40 lbs., 0.8 cf, Cr800, 40 kW).
- **Aerostatic Lift:** Four CG units each rated at 4,000 lbs. (48 lbs., 0.96 cf, 16 kW, Cr2,080).
- **Instruments and Electronics:** Long-range radio communicator (50,000 mi., 2.5 lbs., 0.05 cf, Cr150, 0.04 kW); low-res imaging radar (20 mi., no targeting, 5 lbs., 0.1 cf, Cr6,250, 5 kW); PESA (5 mi., 2.5 lbs., 0.05 cf, Cr10,000); terrain-following radar (1.25 lbs., 0.025 cf, Cr500, 0.25 kW); small computer (0.5 lbs., 0.01 cf, Cr250, Complexity 6).
- **Controls:** Computerized (Cr1,000). Crew stations: One roomy exposed. "Pilot" operates manuever controls.
- **Accommodations:** One roomy exposed crew station (40 lbs., 20 cf, Cr100). Three roomy exposed seats (120 lbs., 60 cf, Cr300). Short occupancy.
- **Power Systems:** 61.29 kW nuclear power unit (21.4 lbs., 0.214 cf, Cr20,000).
- **Access, Cargo, and Empty Space:** 1.014 cf access space. 160 cf open cargo space. 1.777 cf empty space.
- **Volume:** 165 cf.
- **Surface Area:** 200 sf.
- **Structure:** Heavy frame, cheap materials (600 lbs., Cr10,000).
- **Hit Points:** 600.
- **Armor:** PD 4, DR 28 cheap metal overall (560 lbs., Cr560) protects body (but not exposed seats or cargo from all angles).
- **Surface Features:** None.
- **Vision:** Good.
- **Statistics:** Weight 1,441.15 lbs. Usual payload 8,800 lbs. Loaded weight 10,241.15 lbs. (5.1 tons). Volume 165 cf. Size modifier +3. Price Cr51,960. Structural HT 12.
- **Air Performance:** Aerial motive thrust 800 lbs. Aerodynamic drag 140. Aerial top speed 160 mph. aAccel 2 mph/s. aMR 5. aSR 4. aDecel 20 mph/s.
- **Space Performance:** sAccel 0.08 Gs. Most air/rafts *can* reach orbit (this one would require vacc suits be worn), but are rarely used for such.

GROUND CAR (TL6)

The ground car is a typical passenger motor vehicle suitable for road travel on low-tech worlds. This particular design is typical of a wide variety of variations produced on countless worlds. Luxury, sports, utility, exploratory, scientific, commercial, paramilitary, and military versions are manufactured. The version here is for use in standard atmospheres; special fixtures may be needed for non-standard atmospheres.

Obviously, the basic performance, cost, and features available on the typical ground car on a given world can vary immensely with tech level. The TL6 version shown here, while found in many places around the Imperial frontiers, likely will be non-existent on a TL12 world.

- **Subassemblies:** Standard wheels (four).
- **Body Features:** None.
- **Propulsion:** 100-kW wheeled drivetrain (240 lbs., 4.8 cf, Cr960).
- **Instruments and Electronics:** Headlights.
- **Miscellaneous:** None.
- **Controls:** Mechanical. Crew stations: roomy. "Driver" operates maneuver controls.
- **Accommodations:** One roomy crew station (40 lbs., 40 cf, Cr100), four normal seats (120 lbs., 120 cf, Cr400).
- **Power Systems:** 100-kW standard gasoline engine (630 lbs., 12.6 cf, Cr1,260, 4.5 gph); 18-gallon standard fuel tank (27 lbs., 2.7 cf, Cr36) filled with gasoline (108 lbs., Fire 12).
- **Access, Cargo, and Empty Space:** 17.4 cf access space. 40 cf cargo space. No empty space.

- **Volumes:** Body 280 cf. Wheels 28 cf.
- **Surface Area:** Body 300 sf. Wheels 60 sf.
- **Structure:** Light frame, cheap materials (2,160 lbs., Cr900).
- **Hit Points:** Body 225. Each wheel 23.
- **Armor:** PD 3, DR 5 cheap metal overall (1,260 lbs., Cr1,260).
- **Vision:** Good.
- **Statistics:** Empty weight 4,625 lbs. Usual internal payload 2,000 lbs. Loaded weight 6,625 lbs. (3.31 tons). Volume 308 cf. Size modifier +4. Cost Cr5,016. Structural HT 12.
- **Ground Performance:** Top speed 90 mph. gAccel 4 mph/s. gDecel 10 mph/s. gMR 0.75. gSR 4. Off-road speed 15. High ground pressure.

ATV, WHEELED (TL8)

This eight-wheeled transport is suitable for use on the most hostile of worlds. It is capable of extended operations in nearly any environment. Three variants are standard and commonly found almost everywhere.

- **Subassemblies:** Off-road wheels (8).
- **Body Features:** Sealed body.
- **Propulsion:** 500-kW all-wheel drivetrain (HP 36).
- **Instruments and Electronics:** Very-long-range radio (10,000 mi., HP 10, 0.1 kW); very sensitive receive-only radio direction finder (100 × reception, HP 3, 0.0005kW); thermograph (2 mi., Scan 13, HP 1, neg. power); navigation instruments (HP 3, neg. power); global positioning system (HP 1, neg. power); active/passive sonar (2 mi., no-targeting, Scan 13/15, HP 7, neg. power); 4 AESAs (2 mi. each, no targeting, Scan 13, HP 1 each, neg. power); minicomputer (Complexity 3, HP 5, neg. power); 5 × terminals (HP 28 each, neg. power).
- **Miscellaneous:** Full fire-suppression system (HP 15); two-man airlock (HP 129).
- **Controls:** Computerized. Crew stations: five roomy. "Driver" operates maneuver controls. "Radio operator" operates communications equipment. Two "radar operators" operate sensors. "Computer operator" operates computer.
- **Accommodations:** Long term, 5 roomy crew stations, 5 bunks, TL8 full life system for 10 persons (HP 254, 100 kW), 500 man-days provisions, 10 crashwebs.
- **Power System:** 600-kW nuclear power unit (HP 81); 2.16-million kJ rechargeable energy bank (HP 11, will run life support for six hours).
- **Access, Cargo, and Empty Space:** 130 cf access space. 1,600 cf cargo space. 0.1607 cf empty space.

- **Volume:** Body 2,916.7 cf. Wheels 583.3 cf.
- **Surface Area:** Body 1,500 sf. Wheels 500 sf.
- **Structure:** Heavy standard frame.
- **Hit Points:** Body 4,500. Each wheel 375.
- **Armor:** Body PD 4, DR 50 expensive metal. Wheels PD 4, DR 25 expensive metal.
- **Surface Features:** Sealed.
- **Vision:** Viewports only.
- **Statistics:** Empty weight 61,382 lbs. Usual internal payload 33,000 lbs. Loaded weight 94,382 lbs. (47.191 tons). Volume 3,500 cf. Size modifier +6. Cost MCr1.456. Structural HT 12.
- **Ground Performance:** Top speed 52. gAccel2.8. gDecel 20. gMR 0.75. gSR 5. Off-road speed 13 mph. Ground pressure high.
- **Water Performance:** Floats. Drag 2,073. Top speed 5. wAccel 0.2. wMR 0.25. wSR 6. wDecel 10. Draft 3 ft.

Science Lab Option:

Adds: Science lab (HP 600, 3 kW)

Changes: Cargo 600 cf. Empty weight 81,382 lbs. Payload 13,000 lbs. Cost MCr2.456.

Passenger Option:

Add: 15 roomy seats.

Change: Cargo 505 cf. 750-kW nuclear power unit (HP 436). Full life support for 25 (HP 450, 250 kW). Empty weight 70,682 lbs. Payload 14,100 lbs. Loaded weight 84,782 lbs.

Ground Performance: Top speed 55 mph. Off-road speed 14 mph.

Water Performance: Drag 1,930.

Modular Starship Design

Spacecraft are built and sold at shipyards across known space. *GURPS Vehicles* offers a complete design system suitable for all types of vehicles (including starships), but it is also time-consuming and complex. To make *GURPS Traveller* more accessible, this section is a modular design system enabling ships to be assembled from standard-sized hulls and components.

These hulls and modules were all created using *GURPS Vehicles*, so experienced GMs may use that book to design their own modules or to create custom-built designs.

Terminology

Vessel: Any spacecraft.

Hull Class: The Imperium customarily rates vessels in "displacement tons," each representing the volume occupied by a ton of liquid hydrogen. This can cause confusion – since tonnage references to all non-hull components indicate mass or weight, not volume – but is entrenched in tradition. To avoid confusing these terms, these rules usually will call displacement tons "spaces." A "space" is assumed to be 500 cubic feet (this is an approximation that simplifies design).

Ship: A vessel of 100 tons or larger.

Small Craft: A vessel of fewer than 100 tons.

Starship: Any ship with a jump drive.

Non-starship: A vessel lacking a jump drive.

Ton: For vessels and vessel hulls, 500 cubic feet of volume. For all else, 2,000 pounds.

cf: *GURPS* abbreviation for "cubic foot."

kW: A kilowatt; kJ is kilojoule or kilowatt-second (kWS); a thousand kW is a megawatt (MW); a thousand kilojoules is a megajoule (MJ) also known as a megawatt-second (MWS).

Tech Levels

This simplified design system allows vessels to be built at two distinct tech levels, TL10 and TL12.

TL10 vessels are often used by merchant lines, independent traders, and planetary and subsector navies. Many TL7-9 worlds also use TL10 designs, ordering them (and spare parts and service) from shipyards elsewhere in their sector, just like Third World nations today order ships from Europe, Russia, or the United States.

TL12 vessels represent the cutting edge of naval architecture. The Imperial Navy is equipped at TL12, with TL10-11 vessels in service in backwater areas. Shipping lines and corporations use TL12 vessels as fast couriers or liners.

When designing the vessel, do not install components higher than the vessel's TL without good reason (e.g., a TL10 hull that was upgraded with TL12 electronics and weapons).

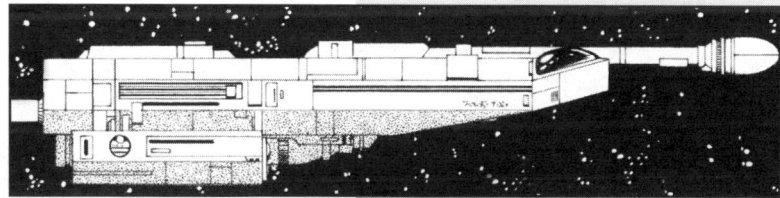

Crew Requirements

The *Module Table* (p. 155) lists starship crew needs. Here's an explanation:

Cockpit: A pilot and sometimes a co-pilot. Pilot should have Piloting (Spaceship), Electronics Operation (Sensors, and Communications would be wise), and Gunner for any weapons he plans to use. On military vessels he should have Tactics as well. The co-pilot needs the same skills, or to provide any the pilot lacks.

Basic Bridge: Standard crew includes a captain, pilot, navigator, sensors officer/operator, and commo officer/operator.

The captain requires Leadership, and Tactics is essential on a military vessel and wise on any ship. The pilot needs Piloting (Starship), the navigator Astrogation, the sensors operator Electronics Operation (Sensors), and the commo operator Electronics Operation (Communications).

Bridge crews are often smaller, with one person handling multiple tasks.

Command Bridge: As above, often augmented by one to three extra commo/sensor operators, a computer officer with Computer Operations and Computer Programming, and a screens officer with Electronics Operation (Force shields) if a meson screen or damper is installed.

Sickbay: One or two medics with Diagnosis, Physician, and Surgery. The first module requires two medics; additional sickbays may have fewer as long as there is at least one per module.

Engineering, M-drive, and J-drive: Fractional requirements are listed for M-drive and J-drive modules; e.g., 1/60 means one engineer per 60 modules. Total up these requirements to determine the number needed. Round fractions down, but vessels of 200+ tons generally have a minimum of one engineer!

Continued on next page . . .

Crew Requirements

[Continued]

Engineers need Engineering (Vehicles) and Mechanic (M-drive, J-drive, and Power Reactor). Large crews of engineers can split up the Mechanic specializations.

Small crafts' engineers are usually carried aboard the mother vessel or base.

Labs: 1-2 scientists per lab module.

Ship's Vehicles: Air/rafts and small craft require Piloting (Contragravity) and (Spaceship) respectively.

Weapons: One gunner for each turret, with Gunner (Laser, Missile, and/or Sandcaster) as appropriate. One or two per bay with Gunner (Missile, P-Beam, or Meson). A gunner or pilot on the bridge operates any hull-mounted weapons.

Cargo: Large merchants may have a cargo master with Freight Handling and Merchant. On small vessels, the captain handles purchases.

Staterooms: Paying passengers require a steward with Savoir-Faire (Servant), plus at least one additional per full 50 middle or 20 high passengers carried.

Stewards should have First-Aid on ships without sickbays, and Electronics Operation (Medical)-10+ if overseeing low berths.

Passenger Couches: A steward with Savoir-Faire (Servant) is required for each 48 passengers carried in couches, unless the trip duration is under 2 hours.

DESIGN SEQUENCE

The next several pages provide a step-by-step spacecraft design process. Calculations are simple and can be easily done on scrap paper. A calculator is useful but not absolutely essential.

Step 1: Design the hull and record its characteristics.
Step 2: Designate turrets and/or bays.
Step 3: Select armor tonnage. Calculate its cost, DR, and PD.
Step 4: Seal hull and consider adding sensor-masking features.
Step 5: Fill all internal spaces with component modules.
Step 6: Add turret and bay weapons (optional).
Step 7: Calculate basic statistics.
Step 8: Calculate performance.
Step 9: Finalize design.

As design choices are made, keep a running total of the vessel's mass (in tons) and cost (in millions of credits, or megacredits). All masses are in tons, all costs in megacredits (MCr).

STEP 1 – HULL DESIGN

Decide whether the vessel is streamlined or unstreamlined. *Streamlined* vessels are sleek lifting bodies (often needle, wedge, or disk shaped) and may fly within a planetary atmosphere. *Unstreamlined* vessels cannot enter atmosphere. Cylindrical, spherical, and "patchwork" hulls usually fall in this category.

Select a standard hull tonnage from those listed on the following table:

HULL TABLE

Hull Tonnage	Volume (cf)	Hull Area	TL10 Mass	TL12 Mass	Hull Cost (in MCr)	Size Modifier
10	5,000	2,000	2	1	0.1/0.24	+6
20	10,000	3,000	3	1.5	0.15/0.36	+6
30	15,000	4,000	4	2	0.2/0.48	+7
40	20,000	5,000	5	2.5	0.25/0.6	+7
50	25,000	6,500	6.5	3.25	0.325/0.78	+7
80	40,000	8,000	8	4	0.4/0.96	+8
100	50,000	10,000	10	5	0.5/1.2	+8
200	100,000	15,000	15	7.5	0.75/1.8	+8
400	200,000	25,000	25	12.5	1.25/3.0	+9
600	300,000	30,000	30	15	1.5/3.6	+9
800	400,000	40,000	40	20	2.0/4.8	+10
1,200	600,000	50,000	50	25	2.5/6.0	+10
2,000	1,000,000	60,000	60	30	3.0/7.2	+10
3,000	1,500,000	80,000	80	40	4.0/9.6	+11
4,000	2,000,000	90,000	90	45	4.5/10.8	+11
5,000	2,500,000	110,000	110	55	5.5/13.2	+11
10,000	5,000,000	170,000	170	85	8.5/20.4	+12
15,000	7,500,000	230,000	230	115	11.5/27.6	+12
20,000	10,000,000	280,000	280	140	14/33.6	+12
30,000	15,000,000	360,000	360	180	18/43.2	+14
50,000	25,000,000	510,000	510	255	25.5/61.2	+14
100,000	50,000,000	810,000	810	405	40.5/97.2	+15

Record hull mass (varies by TL), hull cost (the costs given are for non-streamlined/streamlined vessels), and size modifier (see p. B201). Hull areas and volume are for reference and will figure in later calculations.

Calculate the vessel's *internal spaces*. An unstreamlined vessel has spaces equal to its hull tonnage. A streamlined vessel has spaces equal to 0.8 × hull tonnage. Internal spaces will be used up by equipment and other options. Keep a running total of how many remain; when they are all gone, nothing else can be installed in the vessel.

Step 2 – Turrets and Bays

Turrets are standard mounts for shipboard weapons. A ship can have one turret per 100 tons, or it can have fewer or none at all. A small craft may have one or no turret.

Bays are large weapon mounts. A ship can install one bay for every 10 turrets *not* installed. For example, a 10,000-ton ship may have up to 100 turrets, but could instead have installed 80 turrets and two bays.

Decide how many turrets and/or bays the vessel has. Their mass and cost are shown below. As with the hull, mass varies by TL and cost varies depending on whether the hull was streamlined or not.

TURRET AND BAY TABLE

Type	Mass TL10	Mass TL12	Cost (MCr)	Internal Spaces
Bay	6.5	3.25	0.325/0.78	10
Turret	0.825	0.425	0.0406/0.0966	1

Interior Facilities

Vessel interiors generally have these details in common:

Partitions are light wall panels used to separate facilities such as individual staterooms, galleys, and offices. They aren't airtight. DR 8 and 40 hit points. *Bulkheads* are armored walls used to separate major airtight compartments. An internal bulkhead has DR 50 and 250 hit points; an external bulkhead has the vessel's armor DR.

Doors are sliding panels set in partition walls. They are not airtight, and open or close at the touch of a stud (takes one second if power is on). Stateroom doors come with electronic locks in various styles (voiceprint, keypad, card, etc.), but these are for privacy only – use Lockpicking skill (or a crowbar) to break in; locks can also be overridden or changed from the bridge. A door has DR 4 and 10 hit points. A locked door can also be forced open by brute strength. Make a ST-4 roll; repeated attempts cost 1 fatigue each.

Iris valves are powered portals set in bulkheads, at either end of airlocks and in vertical shafts. An iris valve resembles the aperture of a camera: a series of metal plates that slide into place to block an opening. It is opened or closed by depressing a stud next to the valve, provided the vessel has power. Any iris valve can also be locked from the bridge. A closed valve is airtight; as long as a vessel has power, iris valves will shut automatically when interior pressure nearby drops, preventing a single hull leak from decompressing the vessel. It takes iris valves one second to shut – an object like a metal bar that is jammed in a valve as it closes will prevent closure, allowing it to be reopened with ease. Otherwise, once fully shut they are difficult to force open: Roll as with doors, but against ST-6. Iris valves are tough: DR 50 and 100 hit points.

Hatches are hinged, pressure-tight metal doors that are placed at some locations secured by pins operated by a handwheel on the door. They take five seconds to open and are not powered or controlled by the ship's bridge. Hatches are intended as damage-control devices to restrict atmosphere loss in the case of a hull breach. Thus, there is normally no provision for locking hatches, but a crowbar inserted into the handwheel will jam one shut from that side requiring the destruction of the hatch to open it. Nothing prevents a character from installing locks on any given hatch, but these cost extra. Hatches can be found in floors, decks, or bulkheads, often in engineering or spacedock areas. They are typically used to provide alternative routes for damage-control teams in the event of power loss that seals iris valves. Hatches are DR 50 and 250 hit points.

See p. B125 for rules on breaking down walls and similar inanimate objects.

Turrets and bays take up internal space. Each turret uses up one internal space. Each bay uses up 10 internal spaces.

Turrets come with a roomy built-in crew station (seat and console) with computer terminal and a Heads-Up Display/Weapon Aiming Computer (HUDWAC). Bays don't – but these crew stations are built into the actual weapons that are installed in the bay.

STEP 3 – ARMOR

Vessels are armored to protect against cosmic rays, micrometeors, and enemy weapons.

Surface Area: Calculate the vessel's total surface area. This is the number shown in the "area" column on the *Hull Table* (p. 151) plus the surface area of all turrets and bays. Each turret has an area of 800. Each bay has an area of 6,500.

Armor Mass: Decide how many tons of armor the vessel will carry. Most civilian vessels have 0.5 to two tons of armor times their hull tonnage. Warships usually have 0.5 to five tons times their hull tonnage. The more mass a vessel has, the slower it accelerates.

Armor Cost: Multiply armor mass by MCr0.012 to get cost.

Armor Damage Resistance: Calculate armor DR:

If TL10 armor, DR = (armor mass × 20,000) / surface area.

If TL12 armor, DR = (armor mass × 50,000) / surface area.

Optionally, rather than assigning armor mass and calculating DR from it, choose a DR first, then calculate mass. To do so, multiply the DR by 0.00005 at TL10 or 0.00002 at TL12 and then by hull area. This gives the armor's mass; calculate cost as above.

Optionally, armor for the turrets/bays may be calculated separately from hull armor. Turrets and bays are often designed with lighter armor than the hull itself. For a fast way to design this, just add *half* the turret or bay's area to the vessel's area, and then afterward it can be assumed to have half the DR the hull has.

Passive Defense (PD): Armor PD depends on DR, as follows: 1 if DR 1, 2 if DR 2-4, 3 if DR 5-15, 4 if DR 16+. Almost all vessels have PD 4.

STEP 4 – OTHER SURFACE FEATURES

Sealed: Vessels must be sealed. Multiply total surface area by MCr0.00001 to get the price of sealing the hull against vacuum.

Sensor Masking: Usually only warships use sensor-masking. A vessel may optionally be given *stealth* making it harder to detect by active sensors (like radar) and/or *emission cloaking* to mask it from passive sensors (like infrared). Each type comes in two levels, "basic" and "radical."

Sensor Masking Feature	Mass (tons)	Cost (MCr)
Basic Stealth or Emission Cloaking	0.00025	0.000075
Radical Stealth or Emission Cloaking	0.0005	0.00075

Mass and cost are each equal to the vessel's total surface area times the number shown on the table above. A vessel may not have both basic and radical versions of the same feature.

Basic emission cloaking subtracts (TL-4) from rolls to determine the success of passive sensor scans, while basic stealth subtracts from active sensor scans. Radical cloaking or radical stealth will double this penalty; i.e., -2 × (TL-4).

STEP 5 – COMPONENT MODULES

A component module is a set of spacecraft components that are grouped together, such as a bridge or maneuver drive.

All modules are rated for the internal space they take up in the vessel (spaces), their mass (tons) and cost (MCr). Select precisely the number of modules that fills the vessel's internal space.

Bridge: The vessel's control, navigation, sensor, and communication systems. All ships require one bridge module, and larger vessels sometimes have a second auxiliary bridge. Two types of bridge module are available. A "basic bridge" is typical of ordinary ships. Some ships (especially those with tonnage over 1,000) will install a larger and better-equipped "command bridge." See *Bridge Systems* (pp. 160-162) for each type's capabilities.

Engineering: All ships require a single engineering module. It has a fusion reactor core (the base "startup" weight, cost, and volume for a fusion reactor), full fire-suppression system, and a six-person airlock. Included with the airlock is an inflatable 100′-long passage tube (armored to DR 20) that can be deployed in 30 minutes to connect two airlocks for passenger boarding.

Cockpit/Systems: A cockpit/systems module is used on small craft instead of the bridge and engineering modules. It provides control, navigation, avionics, and fusion-power startup, plus a one-person airlock and two man-days limited life support.

Hold: Each hold module has space for 500 cubic feet (18.5 cubic yards) of cargo. Multiple hold modules may represent a single large hold or a number of smaller holds. Holds in ½-space increments (250 cf) may also be installed.

Jump Drive: A ship requires a jump drive if it's to make interstellar jumps. Each module includes the jump-drive machinery and fusion-power components to power it. Decide on the ship's jump-drive number to a maximum of jump-3 at TL10 or jump-6 at TL12. The number of J-drive modules required is then:

number of j-drive modules = 0.01 × hull tons × (jump number+1)

Jump Fuel: These modules consist of an ultralight self-sealing tank that stores the liquid hydrogen fuel used by the jump drive. A ship with j-drive requires a number of fuel modules equal to:

number of jump-fuel modules = 0.1 × hull tons × jump number

Low Berth: A low-berth module contains four cryonic freeze capsules, each capable of holding one person in suspended animation ("low passage") plus fusion-power components. See p. 108, and pp. UT103, S66, or BT115 for detailed rules.

Maneuver Drive: An M-drive is a reactionless thruster that produces thrust without fuel or reaction mass. Each module has a reactionless thruster that produces 40 tons of thrust at TL10 or 100 tons at TL12 and a slice of fusion-reactor power to run it. Install as many M-drive modules as desired. A vessel's acceleration (in gravities) equals thrust divided by its total mass. As a result, it can be desirable to install the M-drive last so that you can estimate the total mass of the vessel (or make use of a computer spreadsheet to recalculate the thrust and Gs for each different configuration).

Passenger Couch: This module is only available for small craft. It incorporates 12 roomy seats and limited life support (lasts 12 man-days) plus the necessary fusion-power components to operate the life-support system.

Creating Deckplans

Ship designs can be used to create deck plans to facilitate boarding actions, hijackings, and other adventures.

Hexgrid Deck Plans: GURPS uses a 1-yard hexagonal grid for maps. Assuming headroom of about 8-9 feet and some room under the decks, a "space" in a module can be represented by six squares or four hexes (GM's option). If a square grid is used, GMs will have to improvise movement: multiply diagonal movement costs/distances by 1.5.

Existing Deck Plans: Original *Traveller* ship plans use a 1.5m (5′) or 2m (6′) square grid. GMs using them should multiply movement costs and ranges by 1.5 (2 to move/shoot diagonally).

GURPS Vehicles Conversions

All structures and components were built using the **GURPS Vehicles** rules, with these exceptions:

1) Reactionless thruster technology is far more advanced. Accordingly, TL10 standard thrusters appear at TL8, TL10 super thrusters appear at TL9, TL11 standard thrusters appear at TL10. TL11 super thrusters are unchanged, while TL13 "mega thrusters" remain TL13.

2) The jump drive. It works differently than existing **GURPS** jump engines, because its performance is based on transporting a specific *volume* rather than mass and because it consumes hydrogen.

3) Final weight in pounds and cost in dollars were converted to tons and millions of credits (rounding off). Outputs listed are given in megawatts (1,000 kW), megawatt-seconds, and megajoules (1,000 kJ) to save space.

Sickbay: A sickbay consists of an operating table, a diagnostic table, either two (TL10) or three (TL12) automeds, a computer terminal, and sufficient fusion-power components to run them. Ships should have one sickbay per 120 staterooms, rounding up. See p. UT94 or S66 for medical-equipment statistics.

Spacedock Hangar: An airlock hangar bay designed to house smaller vessels within the ship. Its doors or landing-pad elevators open into space, but the hangar bay is sealed off and can be evacuated or filled with air. Each module provides hangar space for 250 cubic feet (½ ton) of vessel; decide if multiple modules form one large or several smaller hangars.

Stateroom: Living quarters and total life support suitable for one or two people: bed, chair/desk, closet, and "fresher" unit (toilet, sink, and shower) plus an intercom and controls for light, heat, and gravity (0-3 G). Install enough staterooms for the estimated crew and passengers – crew or middle-passage passengers often endure double occupancy; high passage passengers and (some) officers should have a room of their own. Staterooms are not available on small craft unless the craft is designed with bridge and engineering modules, not a cockpit/systems module.

Utility: An artificial gravity generator that can vary gravity from 0 to 3 G. It also includes an airlock. Install one per 500 spaces, rounding up. Small craft normally omit utility modules.

Meson Screen (TL12): A meson screen disrupts incoming high-energy mesons. The module includes a screen generator and fusion-power components. The vessel's DR *vs. meson guns only* is 20.8 *million* times the number of meson screen modules divided by its total surface area.

Nuclear Damper (TL12): A nuclear damper focuses a field that subtly interferes with the strong nuclear force causing nuclear warheads to fail to detonate. A spacecraft damper field protects a 10-mile radius, increased by +5 miles each time the number of modules installed is doubled.

Vehicle Bay: A vehicle bay is custom-designed to snugly hold a single, specific small craft (e.g., "30-ton ship's boat"). It is not usable for other sorts of vehicle. It takes up 21 spaces per 20 tons of vessel stowed.

Lab Module: A laboratory dedicated to one scientific skill (e.g., Geology) as well as room for one or two scientists to work. For larger teams, multiple labs are a necessity! It gives +2 to skill in situations where the lab equipment would be beneficial; the GM can also rule a lab is required for a task – it gives no bonus but work would be impossible without it.

Fuel Processor: Purifies raw fuel (skimmed from a gas-giant atmosphere or from another source), turning it into refined fuel. Each module can process eight jump-fuel modules full of raw gas-giant atmosphere every hour. The module also includes necessary fusion-power components.

MODULE TABLE

Type of Module	Spaces	Mass	Cost (MCr)	Crew
Cockpit Bridge				
TL10	1	4.9	2.5	1-2
TL12	1	4.7	2.3	1-2
Basic Bridge				
TL10	2.5	8.6	4.0	1-5
TL12	2.5	7.3	3.1	1-5
Command Bridge				
TL10	5	20.9	9.6	1-10
TL12	5	19.2	8.8	1-10
Engineering				
TL10	1	4	0.32	0-1
TL12	1	3.6	0.16	0-1
Hold	1	0	0	0
Maneuver Drive				
TL10	1	3.4	0.16	1/60
TL12	1	4	0.65	1/100
Jump Drive				
TL10	1	4	3.1	1/25
TL12	1	4	3.05	1/100
Jump Fuel	1	1.3	0.16	0
Low-Berth (4 tubes)	0.5	2	0.22	0
Passenger (12 seats)				
TL10	1	0.54	0.075	0
TL12	1	0.54	0.073	0
Spacedock	1	1*	0.005*	–
Stateroom (1-2 occupants)				
TL10	4	2.4	0.012	0
TL12	4	2.0	0.012	0
Sickbay				
TL10	1	0.75	0.16	1
TL12	1	0.85	0.21	1
Utility				
TL10	1	11.5	0.30	0
TL12	1	11.5	0.25	0
Meson Screen (TL12)	1	5	2.258	0
Nuclear Damper (TL12)	1	10	4	0
Fuel Processor	1	1.1	0.85	0
Lab	2	10	1	1-2
Vehicle Bay	1.05**	0.5*	.003*	0

* Mass and cost are paid only once, regardless of the number of modules making up the spacedock hangar or vehicle bay – it mainly represents the mass and cost of the hangar doors and air pump.

** Multiplied by hull tonnage of vessel carried.

Notes: When estimating performance, spacedock mass should include the vessels that normally dock there, while cargo mass should assume five tons of mass per cargo module as an average load.

All bridge/cockpit computers can be "hardened" (fiber-optic backup) to resist radiation for an additional 0.15 tons and MCr0.04 (cockpit), 0.375 tons and MCr0.6 (in basic bridge), or 3 tons and MCr6 (command bridge).

Crew is the suggested number of crew per module. See *Crew Requirements* sidebar on pp. 149-150 for details of crew requirements.

Creating Non-Standard Hulls

You can use *GURPS Vehicles* to extend the hull table to include non-standard hull designs. Standardized hulls were built as vehicle bodies in multiples of 500 cubic feet using TL10 and TL12 medium frames and standard materials. Streamlined hulls used the lifting body and "very good" streamlining features.

Armor: The armor formula assumes "expensive metal" armor, and converts numbers to tons and MCr. Other armor types are possible, as described in *Vehicles.*

Subassemblies: Turrets and bays are both turret subassemblies using medium frames and standard materials. Bays are limited rotation, turrets are full rotation.

Basic landing legs for soft vertical takeoffs/landings are subsumed in streamlining. To keep things simple, we've omitted proper wheels/skids, since all ships are vectored-thrust designs.

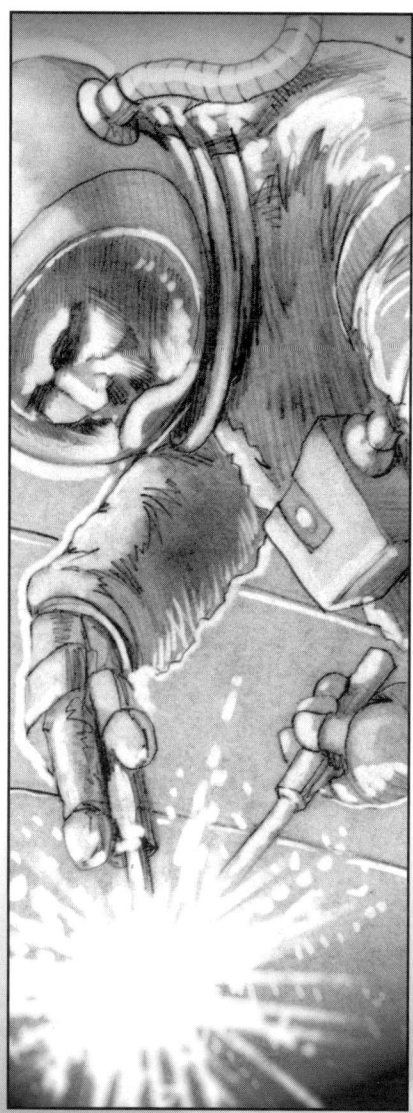

Design Your Own Modules!

Modules were built in multiples of 500 cubic feet with extra "empty space" being added to round them out as necessary. Weights were calculated in pounds, then rounded to the nearest 0.1 ton.

All modules are collections of components assembled from those in *GURPS Vehicles*. This book can be used to design new modules or modify existing ones.

To design a new module, decide on its TL and then select which components (see p. VE12) are built into it. Make sure that the total volume of all components is a multiple of 500 cf. If it doesn't match, add extra empty space to it.

If any of the components in the module require power, make sure that one of the components includes the necessary power systems. Use either rechargeable power cells or fusion reactors (or at TL13+, antimatter reactors). When installing fusion or antimatter power systems, only include the weight, volume, and cost per kilowatt, plus the volume of "long-term" access space. The base weight, volume, and cost, and the reactor-core cost, is included in the engineering module that every vessel requires.

The same rule applies to TL9-10 life support. Add any incremental requirements, but the base costs have already been tallied.

Component modules do not have any structural weight or cost – they should not be thought of as actual homogenous systems (like the modular sockets on p. VE72), but rather as sets of components some of which might be scattered throughout a vessel. Component modules simply bundle related features for ease in accounting during vehicle design. (Power plant slices actually within turrets and bays represent the necessary power conduit connections.)

Turrets are semi-recessed in hull (hence the restriction on volume); thus, even in craft with Very Good streamlining weapons take up volume/50 cf rather than volume/20 cf.

STEP 6 – BAY AND TURRET ARMAMENT

Each turret a vessel possesses has room for up to three turret weapons to be plugged into it. Each bay has room for a single bay weapon. Armament need not be specified when a vessel is designed, as shipyards can leave turrets or bays empty for the owner to later customize. Merchant ships in safe subsectors or on a tight budget may have empty turrets or mount only one or two rather than the full three weapons. (Crew often find creative uses for the unused 500-1,000 cf, such as illicit liquor stills.)

Fixed-Mount Weapons: Instead of a turret or bay, weapons can be built directly into the hull. A hull-mounted weapon takes up space just as if it were a component module. If a turret-sized weapon, it is fired from the bridge/cockpit crew stations (often by the pilot). Hull-mounted weapons are assumed to be installed in casemate swivel-mounts that enable them to fire directly forward and 45 degrees to either side. The spaces occupied by fixed mount weapons count against the number of turrets that can be included: up to three spaces of fixed-mount weapons are allowed for every turret not installed.

Spinal Mounts: Spinal mounts are huge weapons built into the centerline of the vessel. A ship can only have one spinal mount. They are hull mounted, but are limited to firing directly forward, and are aimed by pointing the ship.

If weapons are to be fitted, select from these standardized designs:

ARMAMENT TABLE

Weapon	Spaces	Mass	Cost
Turret Weapons			
Missile Rack	1	13	0.0175
Turret Laser (TL10)	1	8.3	0.82
Turret Laser (TL12)	1	7.8	0.68
Sandcaster	1	5	0.25
Bay Weapons			
Missile Bay	10	618.8	0.85
Particle Beam Bay (TL10)	10	467	23.21
Meson Gun Bay (TL12)	10	467	21.04
Spinal Mount			
Spinal P-Beam (TL10)	1,513	15,126	1,035
Spinal Meson Gun (TL12)	1,512	15,119	939

Add each weapon's mass and cost to the running total of vessel mass and cost. Turret weapons may occupy a turret space (three to a turret) or take up space in the hull. Bay weapons may occupy an entire bay or take up space in the hull. Spinal mounts always take up hull space. Note that the same missile launchers and sandcasters are used at both TL10 and TL12.

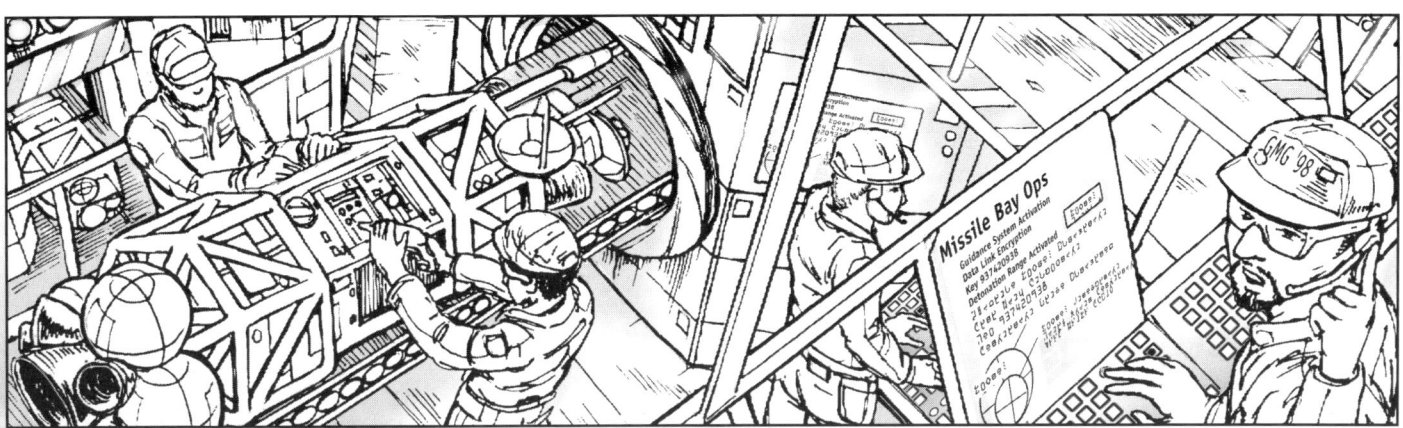

Turret Weapons

Missile Rack: A launch tube rated to fire 250mm 300-pound (0.15 ton) missiles. The system also includes a 50,000-mile-range laser communicator used to control operator-guided missiles. Magazine space sufficient for 77 standard 0.15-ton space-interceptor missiles is included.

Sandcaster: A unique defensive weapon that launches clouds of ablative crystals (nicknamed "sand") into the projected paths of enemy laser fire. Unlike prismatic aerosols used in ground combat, sand clouds are thick enough to ablate X-ray laser beams. Space for 200 120-lb. sand canisters is included.

Turret Laser, 250-MJ (TL10): This system consists of an X-ray laser (250-MJ output, cyclic rate ½, extreme range), a power cell that stores enough energy (667 MW) to fire one shot, and fusion-reactor components that generate the 11.1 MW required to fully recharge that power cell every 60 seconds. The X-ray laser is fully stabilized and installed in a universal mount (if in a turret) or casemate (if in hull). Turrets can fire in all directions, the casemate forward.

Turret Laser, 405-MJ (TL12): The previous weapon's replacement at TL12, cheaper but more powerful. The system is an X-ray laser (405-MJ output, cyclic rate ½, compact, extreme range), a 1,080-MWS power cell and fusion-reactor components generating 18 MW to permit one shot every 60 seconds. The X-ray laser is fully stabilized and installed in a universal mount (if in a turret) or casemate (if in hull). Turrets can fire in all directions, the casemate forward.

Bay Weapons

Bay weapons available are listed below. Besides the weapon, power supply and any ammunition, each also includes a pair of roomy crew stations for two gunners (though the weapon can be fired by only one person), a computer terminal, and a HUDWAC.

Missile Bay: A weapons bay housing 50 launch tubes and laser coms (each the same as the missile rack's), plus space for 3,800 standard 0.15-ton missiles.

Particle Beam Bay (TL10): This weapon accelerates hydrogen nuclei to relativistic velocities, strips them of their charge and fires them. P-beams are shorter ranged but more powerful than turret lasers, and sandcasters don't affect them. The bay houses a 12,810-MJ neutral particle beam (cyclic rate ½, extreme range option), a power cell storing 25,620 MWS (enough for one shot), and fusion-reactor components generating 427 MW (recharging the power cell every 60 seconds).

Meson Gun Bay (TL12): Meson guns use nuclear dampers and particle-beam technology to generate and aim a beam of high-energy mesons (subatomic particles that carry nuclear force). Mesons pass harmlessly through normal matter, but soon decay explosively in a storm of other energetic particles – but with precise calculation a meson beam may be created and aimed so this explosion occurs inside an enemy vessel. The bay includes a 12,810-MJ meson gun (extreme-range option), a power cell storing 25,620 MWS energy (one shot), and sufficient fusion-reactor components to generate 427 MW, recharging it every 60 seconds.

Spinal Weapons

Particle Beam (TL10): This is a 569,500 MJ neutral particle accelerator (cyclic rate ½, extreme range option) installed in a fully stabilized mount, powered by a 1.139 million MWS rechargeable energy bank and 18,983.3 MW fusion reactor.

Spinal Meson Gun (TL12): A meson gun of similar characteristics to the spinal particle beam.

Jump Drives in GURPS Vehicles

If building a ship using the modular system, just plug in the requisite number of jump drive modules. However, if you want to install a *Traveller* jump drive in a ship built entirely with *GURPS Vehicles*, here's how to do it.

First, decide on the intended jump number – how many parsecs the ship can jump. This cannot exceed a maximum of jump-2 at TL9, jump-3 at TL10, jump-4 at TL11, or jump-6 at TL12+.

Then assign the drive a "jump capacity" normally equal to the desired (jump number+1) × anticipated volume of the vessel.

Weight is jump capacity × 0.12 lbs.

Volume is jump drive weight/50 cf. As ships spend a week in jump, add "long term" access space equal to 2 × volume.

Cost is jump drive's weight × Cr500.

Power required is jump capacity × 0.2 kW, which must be provided continuously throughout the week in jump or the ship is lost (either dropping out of jump space or destroyed).

As well as using energy, a jump consumes gallons of hydrogen equal to displacement tons (which is body volume in cf/500) × 333.3 × the length of the jump in parsecs (round up to nearest parsec). Fuel tanks are usually ultralight and self-sealing.

To function, the jump capacity must be at least twice the volume of the ship. Once the ship's volume is known, its actual jump number can be calculated as: Jump number = (jump capacity/volume) - 1, limited by the TL maximums above. Jump capacities larger than a ship's jump number are useful for towing non-starships.

The ship must be at least 100 displacement tons.

BEAM WEAPONS COMBAT TABLE

Name	Type	Acc	SS	Damage	1/2D Range	Max Range	RoF	FP
Laser, 250-MJ	Imp.	32	30	5d×50 (2)	17,045*	51,135*	1/60	3
Laser, 405-MJ	Imp.	33	30	5d×100 (2)	26,022*	78,068*	1/60	7
P-Beam bay	Imp.	33	30	6d×1,000	14,630*	43,890*	1/60	63
Meson Gun bay	Exp.	30	30	6d×1,000 (!)	14,630*	43,890*	1/60	63 (!)
Spinal P-Beam	Imp.	36	30	7d×3,000	97,600*	292,800*	1/60	424
Spinal Meson Gun	Exp.	36	30	7d×3,000 (!)	97,600*	292,800*	1/60	424 (!)

(2) after damage means DR protects at half normal.
(!) after damage means that armor DR is ignored. In the *GURPS Space* system, meson guns ignore armor DF.
*Range is in *miles*. In a planetary atmosphere divide laser ranges by 100 and particle beam ranges by 50.
FP = firepower, used for *GURPS Space* abstract combat.

Sandcaster rules are found in the Space Combat appendix. If using *GURPS Space* rules, each adds +1 DF vs. lasers or missiles; each time the number of sandcasters doubles, add another +1.

SIM-10 Missile (TL10)

A standard TL10 space-interceptor missile.

Features: Very good streamlining.

Propulsion: 1,800 lbs. vectored thrust (135 lbs., 2.7 cf, 90 kW, Cr2,700).

Armament: 250mm "small" HEAT warhead self-destruct device (15.625 lbs., 0.3125 cf, Cr468.75).

Communications: Laser communicator, receive-only, very long range (1 million mi., 50 lbs., 1 cf, Cr625, 0.16 kW).

Sensors and navigation: None – guided by controlling ship.

Computer: Hardened robot brain small computer (1.5 lbs., 0.03 cf, Cr1,250, Complexity 4).

Power: Rechargeable power cell stores 324,576 kWS (18.17 lbs., 0.1817 cf, Cr1,817), good for one hour of operation.

Body: 6 cf (including 0.4875 cf empty space). Area: 20 sf. Medium frame, very expensive materials, very good streamlining, robotic (20 lbs., Cr20,000, 30 hit points).

Armor: PD 4, DR 40 advanced metal (50 lbs., Cr1,000).

Surface Features: Basic Stealth and Emission Cloaking (20 lbs., Cr3,000.)

Statistics: Volume 6 cf. Weight: 310.295 lbs. (0.15 tons). Price: Cr30,860.75. HT: 12 (30 hit points). Size Modifier: +0. Space acceleration: 6 Gs (for one hour).

Standard Missiles

If using the **Vehicles** space combat system, standard missiles maneuver like spacecraft under the direction of the firing gunner. In a 20-minute combat round a missile rack can fire and control one missile or a missile bay as many as 50.

The standard missile has basic emission and stealth cloaking and 6-G acceleration (TL10) or 10 G (TL12) for 60 minutes (three space combat rounds). When a missile ends its turn in a target vessel's hex, it may detonate, typically an explosive shaped charge doing 6d×60 (10) at TL10 or 6d×80 (10) at TL12. Missiles have Size Modifier +0, DR 40 (TL10) or DR 120 (TL12), and 30 HPs. (If using the **GURPS Space** combat system, treat as "medium explosive missile" with FP 3 at TL10 or 5 at TL12.) See sidebar for missile costs and exact statistics.

STEP 7 – STATISTICS

Total Empty Mass: Total the mass of hull, turrets/bays, armor, surface features, chosen modules, and weapons. This is the vessel's empty mass.

Total Loaded Mass: This is equal to empty mass plus these additions:

■ The weight of cargo carried. Assume 5 tons per space of cargo hold (i.e., about 20 lbs./cf) unless you desire to recalculate every time these vary.

■ The mass of vessels carried in spacedocks.

Total Cost: Add together hull, turret/bay, streamlining, armor, surface features, module, and weapon costs to get the vessel's cost. This does not include the cost of carried vehicles.

Hit Points: Record hit points for the hull and each bay or turret. A hull, bay, or turret's hit points are its area × 1.5. Standard turrets have 1,200 HP. Standard bays have 9,750 HP.

STEP 8 – PERFORMANCE

Space Acceleration is measured in gravities (G) and determines how rapidly the vessel can accelerate or decelerate. To find space acceleration, add up the thrust in tons: This is 40 per TL10 M-drive or 100 per TL12 M-drive. Divide by the ship's *weight* in tons (*not* displacement tons). The result is the ship's space acceleration (sAccel) in G. Accelerations in the 1 G to 6 G range are typi-

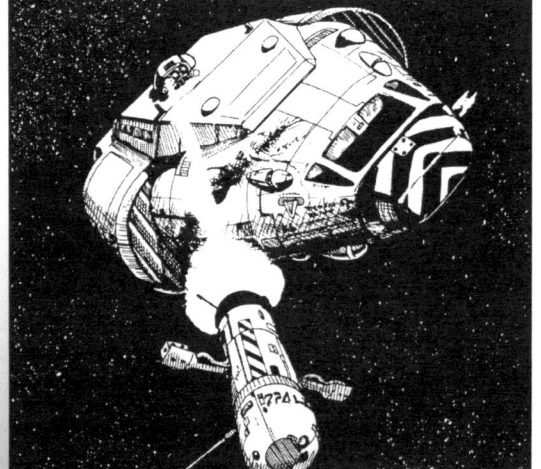

cal of *Traveller* vessels – at least 1 G is a good idea, to enable liftoff from a standard planetary surface without atmosphere. Designers may wish to tweak their designs (often by carefully manipulating armor mass) to give results that yield "round" numbers.

Jump Number: This is the distance a starship can jump measured in parsecs. See the description of the J-drive and jump-fuel modules for the requirements needed to jump.

Air Speed: This is the top speed in mph a streamlined vessel can fly at and still maneuver while within a planetary atmosphere. (Vessels going to and from orbit may reach higher straight-line speeds in the upper atmosphere.) To calculate it, first determine its drag: total surface area/5. Then divide thrust by drag. Multiply that by 15 million, and find the square root of the product to get air speed. Thus:

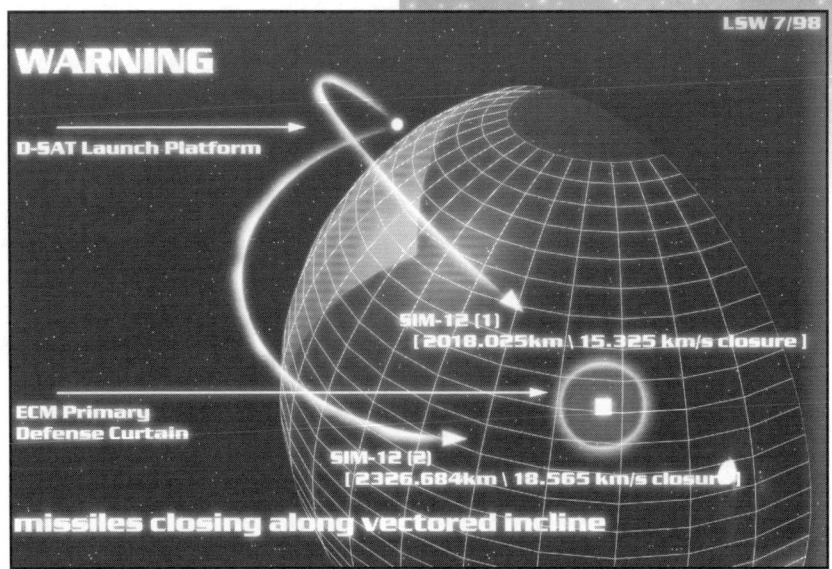

$$\text{mph} = \text{square root } [(\text{thrust/drag}) \times 15 \text{ million}]$$

Calculate other useful aerial-performance statistics with *GURPS Vehicles*.

STEP 9 – FINALIZATION

The vessel design is now complete. A new class of vessel is assigned a descriptive name like "mercenary cruiser" or "fast merchant" that abbreviates to a letter code (see *Ship Codes*, p. 160). Ship designs are usually also given a *class name* for the first vessel of its type to fly. Later vessels generally follow the same theme; e.g., all mercenary cruisers in the *Broadsword* class are named after archaic hand weapons.

Fitting Out: Vessels may require these additional expenditures not included in their cost:

■ Computer programs (p. 161).
■ Missiles (standard missile costs Cr31,955 at TL10, Cr22,050 at TL12).
■ Sand canisters (replacement cost Cr400).
■ Fuel (refined hydrogen at Cr350 per fuel-tank module).
■ Spares and maintenance: assumed at 0.1% of total cost of vessel per year.
■ Berthing costs: To land or dock at a ground port or orbital facility, plus berthing for up to six days, costs Cr100 per displacement ton. It costs the same to stay docked for each additional week or fraction thereof.

ADVANCED DESIGN OPTIONS

Compartmentalization: Vessels are already divided into airtight compartments with interior walls and pressure doors. For extra weight and cost, vehicles can have "heavy" compartmentalization (masses 10% of hull mass) or "total" compartmentalization (masses 20% of hull mass). Either type costs MCr0.01 per ton of weight added.

Variable-Mass Performance: GMs may wish to calculate multiple sets of performance figures for ships whose mass can change dramatically; e.g., for example with near-empty vs. full cargo holds, tanks, or hangar decks, or with/without drop tanks.

This can make flight operations more complex; e.g., a Free Trader might take off from a planet with empty fuel tanks to save mass, refuelling at a gas giant, ice asteroid, or space station.

SIM-12 Missile (TL12)

A TL12 space-interceptor missile.

Features: Very good streamlining.

Propulsion: 3,000 lbs. vectored thrust (90 lbs., 1.8 cf, 150 kW, Cr9,000).

Armament: 250mm "modest" HEAT warhead self-destruct device (31.25 lbs., 0.625 cf, Cr937.5).

Communications: Laser communicator, receive-only, very long range (1 million mi., 50 lbs., 1 cf, Cr625, 0.16 kW).

Sensors and navigation: None – guided by controlling ship.

Computer: Hardened robot brain small computer (1.5 lbs., 0.03 cf, Cr1,250, Complexity 6).

Power: Rechargeable power cell stores 540,576 kWS (20 lbs., 0.2 cf, Cr2,000), good for one hour of operation.

Body: 6 cf (including 0.93 cf empty space). Area: 20 sf. Medium frame, standard materials, robotic, very good streamlining (20 lbs., Cr4,000, 30 hit points).

Armor: PD 4, DR 120 advanced metal (60 lbs., Cr1,200).

Surface Features: Basic Stealth and Emission Cloaking (20 lbs., Cr3,000).

Statistics: Volume 6 cf, Weight: 292.75 lbs. (0.15 ton). Price: Cr22,012.5. HT: 12 (30 hit points). Size Modifier: +0. Space acceleration: 10 Gs (for one hour).

After-Market Mods

Traveller has a healthy tradition of user modifications to an existing ship. *GURPS Vehicles* purists will note that adding components with increased power needs effectively makes the core power system larger after it's been built! Instead, consider the power "slice" of an after-market module to be a more robust cooling system or somesuch for the existing reactor. Just as a TL7 car enthusiast might have his existing engine bored out, a TL10 ex-scout will find a way to power a laser or three in that once-empty turret of his . . .

Ship Codes

T he Imperium assigns one- or two-letter codes to ship designs for their intended function, either a single primary letter or a primary followed by a qualifier. Some examples:

Primary		Qualifier
A	Merchant	Armored
B	Battle	Battle, Boat
C	Cruiser	Cruiser
	or Carrier	or Close
D	Destroyer	Destroyer
E	Escort	Escort
F	Frigate	Fast
	or Fighter	or Fleet
G	Gig, Refinery	Gunner
H	–	Heavy
I, J	Intruder	–
K	Pinnace	–
L	Corvette, Lab	Leader, Light
M	Merchant	Missile
N	–	Non-standard
P	Planetoid	Provincial
Q	Auxiliary	Decoy
R	Liner	Raider
S	Scout, Station	Strike
T	Tanker, Tender	Troop, Transport
U	–	Unpowered
V	–	Vehicle
W	Barge	–
X	Express	–
Y	Yacht	Shuttle, Cutter
Z	–	Experimental

STARSHIP OPERATIONS

This section explains the operation and care of a *GURPS Traveller* starship.

BRIDGE SYSTEMS

The heart of a bridge is its crew stations. A cockpit has one or two crew stations, a basic bridge has five such stations, while a command bridge has 10. Each is a seat facing a console with a computer terminal and various multi-function displays that can be reconfigured to enable any station to perform any bridge crew function – pilot, navigator, communications officer, gunner, sensor operator, and so on.

Communications

As well as seats and consoles, a cockpit or bridge has various "avionic" systems, such as communicators.

Radio: A basic multi-frequency broadcast communicator capable of sending and receiving radio signals over great distances. Transmissions may be scrambled (encrypted), but if continuous will be received by all radios within range. A cockpit has one radio, a basic bridge two, a command bridge 10.

Lasercom: A tight-beam directional communicator using a modulated laser beam. Only another lasercom can receive its signal and only if directly in the path of the pencil-thin beam. This makes transmissions secure, but it can only talk to one vessel at a time, and it must be focused on the recipient: no broadband "Free Trader *Beowulf*, Calling Anyone" SOS . . . Laser signals are blocked by solid objects, smoke or prism clouds. and sandcasters. A cockpit or basic bridge has one, a command bridge four.

Meson Communicator: This system uses a modulated beam of mesons for communication. It functions like a lasercom, but is not blocked by solid objects, smoke or prism clouds, etc. Only another meson communicator can receive its signal. Basic bridges at TL12 and both TL10 and TL12 command bridges have meson communicators.

IFF-Transponder: This sends out an automatic identification code (via communicator). Civilian systems are factory-sealed – they can be turned on or off, but the signal can't be altered; military systems can be reprogrammed to give false identities. Of course, a ship that claimed to be a 100-ton scout but appears on radar as a 50,000-ton vessel would attract suspicion, but if it claimed to be a bulk transport . . . Cockpits/system have one IFF, bridges include two to provide one backup.

COMMUNICATION RANGE TABLE

Module	— Communication Ranges —		
	Radio	Laser	Meson
TL10			
Cockpit/Systems	0.5 mil.	1 mil.	none
Basic Bridge	5 mil.	10 mil.	none
Command Bridge	5 mil.	10 mil.	0.1 mil.
TL12			
Cockpit/Systems	0.5 mil.	1 mil.	none
Basic Bridge	5 mil.	10 mil.	0.02 mil.
Command Bridge	5 mil.	10 mil.	0.2 mil.

Communicator ranges are in *millions* of miles.

Sensors

Bridge and cockpit/system module avionics generally consist of four standard sensor types: PESA, AESA, radscanner, and radar/laser detector.

MODULAR STARSHIP DESIGN

Passive Electromagnetic Sensor Array (PESA): This is an array of infrared thermal imaging and low-light telescopic sensors. A PESA gives the bridge crew a visual picture of objects within its sensor range. The PESA is mounted in a small pop turret that can extend out to scan a 360-degree arc.

Radscanner: This is a multi-function energy scanner that can detect and scan for various types of radiation, such as radio, neutrino, or radar emissions. It can detect the neutrinos emitted by fusion-power plants – this is a good way to tell a scoutship from a dreadnought . . . It is capable of detecting radiation from all directions simultaneously.

Active Electromagnetic Sensor Array (AESA): A multi-mode sensor that works as a radar, imaging radar, and ladar. In radar mode it detects objects within its range, although they only appear as "blips" with inexact size and shape. In imaging radar or ladar mode, it has only half its range but better resolution: Objects appear as actual silhouettes permitting identification of known vessels and exact determination of size.

In any mode it will also function as a rangefinder, feeding targeting data to weapons consoles and giving +2 to hit detected objects. It's mounted in the same pop turret as the PESA.

Advanced Radar/Laser Detector: This sensor can detect and locate any operating radar or ladar sensor (such as an AESA) within twice that sensor's range. For this reason any vessel wanting to avoid detection will often turn off their active sensors and rely solely on their passive PESA sensor arrays. All bridges include two of these for redundancy.

SENSOR RANGE TABLE

— Sensor Range in Miles —

Module	PESA	AESA	Radscanner
TL10			
Cockpit	10,000	50,000	1,000
Basic	20,000	100,000	2,000
Command	50,000	150,000	4,000
TL12			
Cockpit	20,000	70,000	2,000
Basic	30,000	150,000	10,000
Command	100,000	200,000	30,000

Sensor ranges quoted above are averages for detecting a man-sized object, such as a person in a vacc suit or a missile. Big ships can typically be detected at 5-20 × these ranges, but actual ranges may vary greatly in various situations – see the *Space Combat* table of modifers on p. 173.

In atmosphere, PESA and AESA sensors (but not radscanners) have one-tenth this range.

Computers

Each bridge or cockpit system incorporates *three* computers: a trio of microframes in the cockpit, mainframes in the basic bridge, and macroframe "super computers" in the command bridge. The computer's Complexity is shown at right.

COMPUTER TABLE

	Complexity	
Module	TL10	TL12
Cockpit	6	8
Basic	7	9
Command	8	10

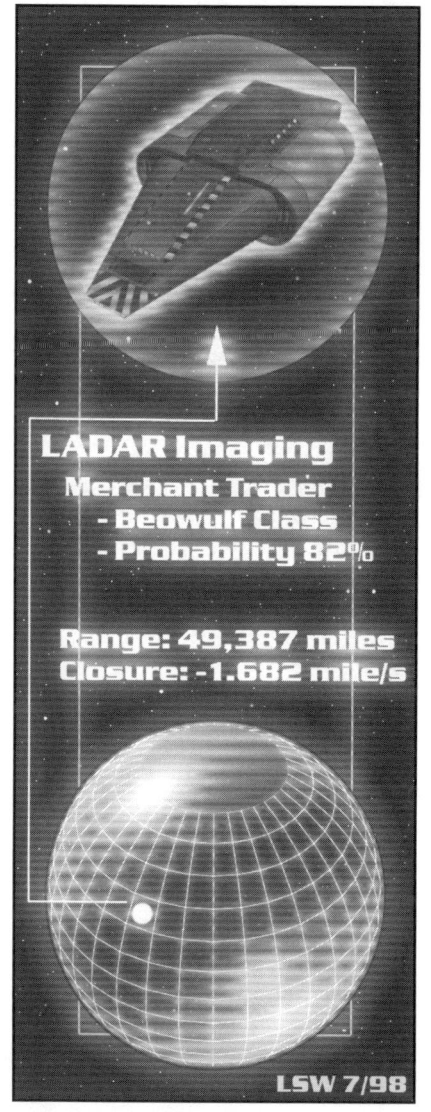

LADAR Imaging
Merchant Trader
- Beowulf Class
- Probability 82%

Range: 49,387 miles
Closure: -1.682 mile/s

LSW 7/98

Any cockpit, bridge, sickbay, turret, or bay incorporates computer terminals that can access the computers.

Using Computers

Every computer has a Complexity rating which governs the software it can run and how fast it will run. Each +1 Complexity represents an order-of-magnitude performance increase.

A computer needs programs, which also have Complexity ratings. A computer of a given TL and Complexity can't run higher-TL or higher-Complexity programs. The number of programs that can run concurrently is based on computer Complexity: two programs of its own Complexity, 20 of Complexity-1, 200 of Complexity-2, etc. They can be mixed; e.g., one at Complexity, nine more at Complexity-1, and 100 more at Complexity-3. Switching a program takes only a few seconds. Programs vital for space operations include:

Astrogation: Needed to make an interstellar jump. Complexity equals jump distance+1. Costs Cr10,000 × jump number.

Datalink: Used to share realtime data with other computers, sensors, missiles, etc. Complexity 1, Cr400.

Damage Control: Monitors systems status, +2 to rolls to repair ship damage. Complexity 2, Cr2,000. Also requires ship blueprints (1 gigabyte and Cr1,000 per ship).

Gunner: In conjunction with a Targeting program, it lets the computer act as a gunner with skill-12. Complexity 4, Cr45,000, double cost and +1 Complexity per +1 added to skill. The bonus to skill is not cumulative with a Targeting program – use the *lower* of the Targeting or Gunner program bonus.

Library Data: An encyclopedia program containing detailed non-classified information on the Imperium. Not always up-to-date for all worlds, but licensed owners can often download supplementary data at local starports. 100 gigs, Cr100,000.

Targeting: Predicts target positions and helps aim weaponry adding a bonus to a gunner's skill equal to its Complexity+1. Costs Cr1,000 for Complexity 1 program, doubling per +1 Complexity increase. One needed per human or computer gunner. Due to the long ranges at which spacecraft engage their opponents, a targeting program giving a +7 to +10 bonus is *strongly* recommended for all armed spacecraft!

More programs can be found on pp. UT33 and VE63.

Power Plant

The standard shipboard power plant at TL9-12 is a fusion reactor. Its supply of internal hydrogen fuel is sufficient to operate it for 200 years without refuelling under ideal conditions, but without annual checkups in a major shipyard it can cease functioning – a ship that misjumps ending up years away from home (by sublight speeds) may have trouble returning.

Fusion reactors are fairly safe: If an operating reactor was destroyed, steam and high-energy plasma might wreck and irradiate the engine room, and this might cause a steam explosion, but there wouldn't be a nuclear blast.

Atlas Corp. AC135 Weapon Bay

Sigma Systems STU47b Turret

LSW 7/98

Other Ship Systems

Navigation Electronics: Bridge and cockpit modules each include precision navigation and inertial-navigation systems (one in a cockpit, a pair on basic and command bridges).

Flight Recorder: All cockpit and bridge modules include a tough "black box" flight recorder (like those on modern aircraft) that records voice transmissions and instrument readouts. One is in a cockpit/systems module or basic bridge, a pair in a command bridge.

Fire Suppression System: Vessels are normally fitted with automatic fire and explosion extinguishers that use non-toxic inert gas to smother fires within microseconds. One fire-suppression system is in each bridge, cockpit/systems, and engineering module.

Space Combat

This system resolves space actions on a hexagonal grid using counters or miniatures, much like the *Advanced Combat System* does personal combat. It's intended for vessels created with the *GURPS Traveller* modular system, but is also usable with other *Vehicles*-built spacecraft. It is derived from the system in *GURPS Vehicles* but makes several changes in scale and modifiers to better reflect the high-gee, long-ranged space battles of *Traveller.* GMs should feel free to use it in non-*Traveller* campaigns where ships have multi-G thrusts and weapons have ranges in the tens of thousands of miles.

Blank hexgrids may be photocopied from the *GURPS Basic Set.* GMs will have to devise their own counters.

Scale and Definitions

Space battles are fought in 20-minute combat rounds. One map hex is about 10,000 miles. Each spacecraft counter represents a single vessel or a salvo of missiles. A velocity of one hex per round is a speed of about 30,000 mph. "Acceleration" is measured in Gravities (G). For tactical combat purposes (not long-distance travel) round accelerations over 1 G to the nearest full Gravity.

Any unqualified use of the term "spacecraft" can be assumed to encompass ships, small craft, and missiles.

Preparation

In addition to a hexagonal grid map, each spacecraft requires two counters: a "spacecraft counter" (or miniature) representing the vessel's location and a "vector counter" marking its future position. Both should be distinct, but marked with the same ID.

Just like characters, spacecraft and vector counters must be placed on the map so they are fully inside a hex. Spacecraft must always face a particular hex side (although facing can be ignored if the ship has no fixed weapons). Facing of vector counters is unimportant.

The GM should prepare statistics of the spacecraft involved and their most important crew (captain, pilot, gunners, engineers, sensor and commo operators). As gunnery skills are subject to large modifiers due to the systems or weapons used, the GM can save time by calculating an "adjusted gunner skill" for each gunner, human, or computer controlling beam weapons:

Adjusted Gunner Skill is Gunner base skill modified as follows:

+ Weapon's Accuracy (up to Gunner skill level). As all standard-design weapons have Acc 30+, this means the bonus is generally limited to an effective doubling of gunner skill.

+ Weapon's RoF bonus. This is +7 for standard weapons, which are all RoF 1/60. For *Vehicles*-built weapons that have different RoFs, refer to the *RoF Bonus Table,* p. 174.

+ Targeting program's Complexity+1. (Do not add this bonus if the weapon already has a computer Gunnery program.)

Thus, for standard weapons, adjusted gunner skill simplifies as: (Gunner skill × 2) + 7 + Targeting program bonus.

Setting Up

The GM should only set up a map and counters if space actions are a possibility (or he wants players to think they are). While deep-space encounters are possible, most action occurs within 100 planetary diameters of a world, as ships head to and from the world and the safe jump distance. For example, if the world was 8,000 miles in diameter, encounters might occur anywhere from orbit to 800,000 miles out: 1 to 80 hexes away.

If space action seems imminent, the GM should first place any planets, moons, or other large bodies on the map (see *Celestial Bodies,* p. 170). Different planets will be tens of thousands of hexes apart, but a planet/moon system may fit on the map – e.g., Luna's average distance from Earth is 24 hexes.

ing by, and captains won't start getting antsy until a vessel passes within a half-light second or so (7-9 hexes). Likewise, if players are planning nefarious activity of their own, an enemy won't usually pay much attention to them until they get within that distance. In an actual war zone, or in frontier systems, any contact might be suspicious. The GM may wish to start checking for detection within a light second or two (e.g., 18-37 hexes range). On the other hand, if an enemy vessel was hiding behind a planet, asteroid, or moon, the combat could begin at only a few hexes range as it suddenly appeared within line of sight.

If it's a set-piece battle or a random encounter, the GM should take care to place ships with converging vectors, while if it's a chase, place the quarry in the middle of the map and the pursuers at one end, bearing in mind that the pursuer will be unable to catch up unless he possesses a faster ship or missiles. Care should also be taken when placing things that can't maneuver (or can't maneuver much) in the context of the game; i.e., stations, satellites, or low-acceleration ships.

The GM secretly decides on the location and course of NPC spacecraft, then, before revealing the location of any vessels, asks players to provide him with the same information for their vessels. Based on this, the GM should place friendly, neutral, and hostile spacecraft (except any carried aboard ships) on the map. (The GM may sometimes wish to keep some unspotted craft "off the map" to surprise players, especially stationary vessels hidden on or behind worlds.) In a duel between players, they should secretly record their general formation ("ship #1 in the lead, ship #2 two hexes to the right . . .") and vector length (in hexes).

Place each spacecraft's counter where the spacecraft is, and its vector counter where the spacecraft will be next round if it does not maneuver. The position of the vector counter is its course, while the distance from the spacecraft to its vector counter is its velocity. Thus, a stationary spacecraft has its vector counter in the same hex it occupies, one moving at one hex per round (30,000 mph) toward a planet would have a vector counter in the adjacent hex closest to the planet, and so on. Relatively low velocities (1-5 hexes/round) are most playable, as vessels that move too fast will take a long time to turn about.

How far apart should spacecraft begin on the map? That depends on the situation. In a system with a busy starport (V to III), there's usually a fair bit of traffic pass-

SEQUENCE OF ACTION

Play proceeds through this sequence each round. There are no individual turns per se: Detection is checked for all spacecraft, then maneuvers are made for all spacecraft, and so on.

1. Detection and Communication.
2. Maneuver.
3. Movement.
4. Direct Fire.
5. Collision and Point Defense.
6. Launch/Docking.
7. Damage Control.

If one spacecraft has yet to spot another, the unaware crew may not take previously unplanned actions until events such as hostile fire or detection alert them. The GM should go through the Sequence of Action each round, checking to see if unaware vessels have detected opponents (phase 2) and moving the spacecraft (phase 3). Once a crew becomes aware of a potential threat (or target!) it can begin to maneuver, fire, etc. Until then, though, a ship should continue on its pre-planned course. Eventually, all spacecraft will either spot one another, reach their destinations, or drift apart and go their separate ways.

1. Detection and Communication

Each space combat round, check to see if spacecraft detect previously unnoticed objects. Large objects like planets, stars, or moons are automatically spotted. GMs may require sensor rolls to find smaller bodies like asteroids, if they aren't on charts.

At the start of this phase, the GM should secretly decide whether NPC spacecraft are using active sensors (such as AESAs) or sending out radio broadcasts, then ask players to reveal if their own spacecraft are "going active" or broadcasting. If using an AESA, specify whether using it as a radar or ladar.

After these decisions are made, the GM should check for detection – there are several ways in which another object can be detected or deliberately announce its presence. Detection depends on picking up communicator or transponder transmissions, enemy fire, or active sensor emissions with radscanners – or upon use of PESA or AESA sensors to locate other craft.

All three types of sensor can be used in a single round. If a ship has multiple sensors of the same type (e.g., extra bridges) only check detection for the sensor with the highest combined operator skill and scan rating in that category.

If a single sensor operator tries to use more than one sensor type in a round, he rolls at -2 per extra sensor he's using.

While successful detection with any sensor type alerts a vessel to an opponent's presence, beam-weapon fire is only allowed against vessels detected with targeting sensors. AESA or PESA are targeting sensors; radscanners are not. (Missiles can still be maneuvered to attack targets detected only by radscanners.) Detecting a vessel with one sensor type doesn't mean detection with the others, but gives a bonus to do so on *later* rounds (see *Sensor Modifier Tables*, pp. 172-173).

Radscanners

Cockpit and bridge modules include radscanners. They are normally used in space as radar/radio/laser/particle detectors. If the ship was hit by laser or particle-beam weapons fire on the previous turn, its radscanners automatically detect the firer's position. Otherwise, a radscanner can check for detection if an undetected object is broadcasting on radio, using transponders, or has "gone active" with an AESA or other active sensor.

To determine if a transponder, radio broadcast, or active sensor use has been detected, roll vs. the sensor operator's Electronics Operation (Sensors) skill, adding appropriate modifiers from the *Sensor Modifiers Table* (pp. 172-173). Failure means the object's emissions went unnoticed (or were overlooked against the general radio noise in a system).

Success means the emitting object is detected: Its location is known, along with information on the type and strength of emission it was broadcasting (radio, active sensor, transponder, etc.). The detecting ship is now alerted.

If a detected object has a broadcasting transponder, that signal also provides the vessel's name, registry, and traffic-control information (ship class, identity number, origin, and destination); e.g., "Type-R merchant *Gyro Zorina,* ID #17960327DY5, Rhylanor registry, inbound Hefry to Regina."

At very close (0 hex) range, radscanners can also provide information on whether target power plants are functioning, etc.

"improve the picture." If so, ignore any results that would lower the degree of detection achieved.

Any objects that a spacecraft launches after it has been detected are spotted automatically. Thus, if a spacecraft that has been identified fires missiles, they are identified as they launch.

Active Electromagnetic Sensor Arrays (AESA)

Ships with a standard-design cockpit or bridge module incorporate an array of radar and ladar sensors known as AESA. An AESA provides precise ranging information, but its use emits electromagnetic radiation that will usually give away the vessel's position, so wary vessels often leave it turned off.

An AESA can only be used if the decision was made to "go active" at the start of this phase. An AESA also improves the chance of hitting targets with direct fire; even if an enemy has already been detected, this is an advantage to "going active."

Use the same procedure as for PESA systems, but use the AESA scan ratings and skill modifiers instead (see *Sensor Modifier Table,* p. 172-173). Also, if using an active sensor as search radar rather than ladar, treat "detection and identification" as merely "detection and recognition."

2. MANEUVER PHASE

In this phase, all spacecraft with working M-drives may maneuver. Spacecraft maneuver in order of lowest to highest acceleration (in gravities); spacecraft of equal acceleration maneuver in order of highest to lowest Size Modifier. Break ties with a quick contest of Tactics skill between the respective captains. The spacecraft's pilot (or controlling gunner, for a missile) decides how the spacecraft will maneuver.

On its turn to maneuver, a spacecraft may change facing and/or accelerate. A spacecraft may change facing so it faces any hex-side. Acceleration is performed by moving its *vector counter* a number of hexes *in any direction* to a maximum of the spacecraft's acceleration. Round acceleration to the nearest G for this purpose.

Slow Acceleration: If a spacecraft has an acceleration substantially under one G, it will not accelerate every round. It requires (1/G) rounds to make a one-hex vector change (round down). For example, a spacecraft capable of 0.3 G accelerates every 1/0.3 = 3.33 rounds, rounded off to every three rounds.

Endurance and Missiles: A spacecraft with a fusion power plant and reactionless thruster M-drive has no fuel restrictions. However, the power cells that energize standard missiles store energy for only three rounds; GMs may wish to use a die next to missile counters to keep track of their remaining power. Other craft built with

Passive Electromagnetic Sensor Arrays (PESA)

All standard-design spacecraft incorporate an array of thermal-imaging, passive-radiation, and visual-detection systems, collectively called a PESA. If an undetected object is within sensor range (and not hidden behind a celestial body), the GM should make detection rolls to see if the PESA has detected it.

Roll against the sensor operator's Electronics Operation (Sensors) skill, adding appropriate modifiers from the *Sensor Modifiers Table* (pp. 172-173). Failure means the object is not detected, but another try may be made next round.

Success by 0-2 means *detection.* The object's existence has been discovered, alerting the spacecraft to its location and course.

Success by 3-4 means *detection and recognition.* The object is detected, and its general shape resolves as a fuzzy image.

Success by 5+ means *detection and identification.* The object appears "on screen" as an actual image.

Once detection is achieved, it is retained unless something occurs that would interrupt a direct line of sight between the vessels, such as a ship moving behind a planet. If only detection or recognition was achieved, on later rounds further attempts at detection may be made to

GURPS Vehicles may be limited in the number of rounds of operation and/or acceleration before running out of fuel or energy.

Control of Missiles: Standard shipboard missiles are drones remotely piloted by their gunner. The missile can only maneuver if in sensor *and* communicator range of its launcher. A single gunner (one per turret, two per bay) can control one missile per communicator dedicated to this purpose. Standard missiles use laser communicators. One laser communicator is built into each missile rack and 50 into each missile bay. If a gunner has to drop a missile because he can't control all the ones he has, he may "reacquire" it on a later round. Missiles can be (and often are) pre-programmed to self-destruct after a certain number of rounds uncontrolled.

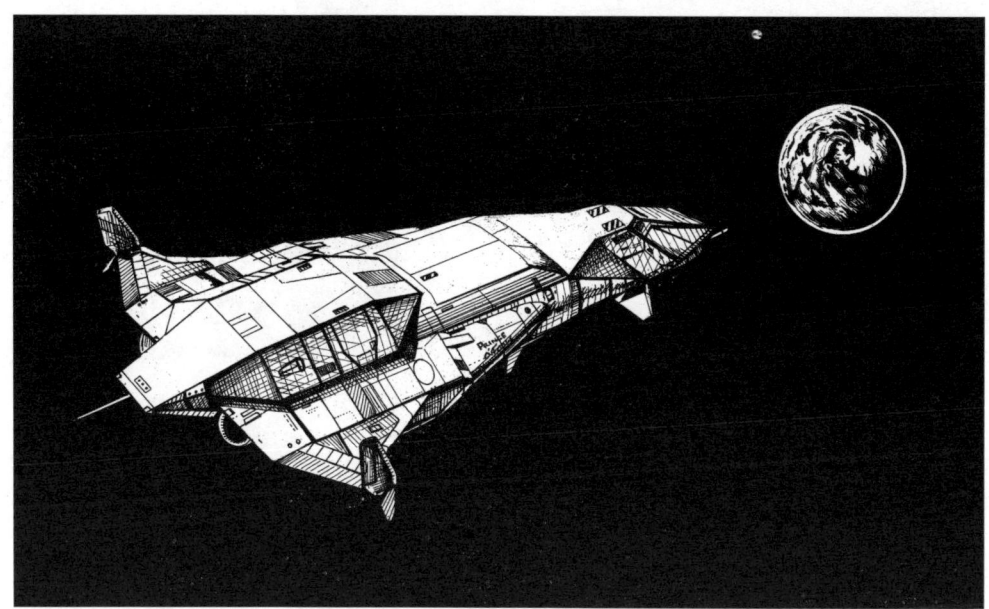

3. MOVEMENT PHASE

Spacecraft can move in any order – it doesn't matter. For each spacecraft, the GM or a player should do the following:

1. Put a marker (e.g., a small coin or die) in the spacecraft's hex as a placeholder.

2. Move the spacecraft into the same hex as its vector counter.

3. Visualize a line between the placeholder and the spacecraft's current hex and move the vector counter a number of hexes along that line equal to the distance from the placeholder's hex to the spacecraft's hex.

(In other words, the spacecraft moves into the same place as its vector counter, and the vector counter is moved to a new location along the same projected course. In this way, a spacecraft that does not otherwise accelerate will continue to move each round in the same direction. Facing has no effect on movement – all that matters is the vector counter's location.)

4. If a spacecraft passes close to a world, it may be affected by gravity. The hexes adjacent to worlds are gravity hexes – see *Celestial Bodies* (p. 170). Imagine a line from the placeholder's hex to the spacecraft's hex – this is the spacecraft's course. For each gravity hex that this line passes through, visualize an arrow from that gravity hex pointing to the planet and move the *vector counter* one hex in that arrow's direction.

5. After gravity effects, if any, are resolved, remove the placeholder marker and go on to the next spaceship's movement.

Some other special factors may influence movement.

Collisions: If a spacecraft's course intersects a planet-sized celestial body, the spacecraft may either crash into it or land – see *Celestial Bodies* on p. 170. However, any number of spacecraft may safely occupy or pass through the same hex containing small bodies like asteroids or other spacecraft.

Vector Adjustment: Spacecraft moving at very high velocities may move off the map. If this seems likely, the GM should simply move all spacecraft, planet, and vector counters a fixed number of hexes in an appropriate direction. (If necessary, record locations of planets or ships that "disappear" off map.) Another possibility, of course, is to lay down a second mapsheet.

Ramming: After *all* spacecraft have completed their movement, a spacecraft that has other spacecraft (or other things) in its hex may attempt to ram. This is the way standard missiles attack. Ramming must be declared at the end of the movement phase by the craft's pilot (or missile's gunner); the target of a ram may cooperate or attempt to evade the ram, or even announce that it is ramming a different vessel. The actual results of ramming are resolved in the *collision* phase, but the decision must be made now, as a vessel closing to ram becomes easier to hit. A spacecraft may only try to ram a single target each round.

See *Celestial Bodies* (p. 170) for more on landing and takeoff.

4. DIRECT FIRE PHASE

Direct fire is fire performed using beam or gun weapons such as lasers. Spacecraft perform direct fire one at a time. All fire is considered simultaneous – resolve attacks sequentially, but actual damage should not be applied until the end of the phase.

When it's a spacecraft's turn to fire, resolve fire one gunner at a time – that character decides whether to shoot and whom to shoot at. Also in this phase, a gunner controlling sand-casters should indicate the spacecraft the 'caster will be protecting against – this protection continues until the gunner's turn to act on the *next* round. (See *Using Sandcasters* on p. 172 for more information.)

A single gunner can fire the weapons in his turret or bay; the gunner must be in the crew station in his turret or bay to control its weapons. Other hull-mounted weapons can be fired by a single gunner from a bridge crew station. A Gunner program running on the spacecraft's computer can replace a single gunner. A single gunner can only fire at one target per round.

Each weapon may only attack once (regardless of its actual rate of fire) – in a space combat round, weapons are firing multiple carefully aimed tracking shots over the 20-minute period. Thus, while a standard weapon has a RoF of $1/60$ (one shot per minute), for playability only one attack is allowed per weapon, to prevent the game degenerating into dozens of rolls. Higher RoF weapons get a bonus to hit, rather than multiple attacks.

Use this procedure for each weapon that is being fired:

First, the gunner chooses the target. Missiles *can* be targeted in this phase. A weapon can fire on any target the gunner's spacecraft has detected with a targeting sensor that is within his weapon's maximum range and arc of fire. Ranges in hexes are shown on the *Space Weapons Table.* Weapons in bays/turrets may fire in any direction. Weapons in hull mounts can fire at any targets in front of the spacecraft – use the normal "arc of vision" (p. B115). Weapons in spinal mounts can fire at targets in the spacecraft's hex and in a row of three hexes wide extending from its three front hexes straight forward out to maximum range.

Second, determine the modified Gunner skill of the firing character (or program) using the *Gunner Skill Modifiers Table* (p. 173), then roll against modified skill to determine if the hit occurred. In the 20-minute combat rounds, an attack roll scores a number of hits on its target equal to half the margin of success (minimum one hit). Thus, success by 0-3 scores one hit, success by 4-5 scores two hits, and so on.

Third, spacecraft with at least 0.1 G thrust can Dodge: roll vs. (Piloting skill + thrust in G - ship Size Modifier)/2, rounded down. Modifiers: +1 if pilot has Combat Reflexes; + ship PD (4 usually, 0 vs. meson gun). Ramming craft cannot Dodge point-defense fire.

For each hit not dodged, determine hit location. If the target spacecraft lacks bays or turrets, the attack hits the hull. Otherwise, roll 1d: On a 1-2, it hit a turret or bay of the attacker's choice. On a 3-6, the attack hits the hull.

For each hit, roll the weapon's damage dice (see *Space Weapons Table* on p. 173). Damage is halved beyond the $1/2$D range. Subtract target DR (modified by armor divisor). Sandcasters offer extra DR against lasers (see *Using Sandcasters,* p. 172). Meson screens (p. 154) sometimes give DR against meson guns (see *Meson Guns and Meson Screens,* p. 171). If damage penetrates armor and screens, subtract it from the hit points of the hull, turret, or bay location that was struck. On a critical hit, the attacker may choose to do double damage or have defenses protect at one-tenth DR.

Damage Effects

Damage effects are calculated immediately but do not "take effect" until the end of the direct fire phase – thus, everyone has a chance to fire before being killed or crippled.

A hull ("body"), turret, or bay reduced to 0 or fewer hits is "disabled." One reduced to -5 × its original hit points is "destroyed." The effects are described below:

Hull Disabled: The spacecraft is crippled, out of power, and leaking any air. A crippled vessel continues to move, but cannot maneuver, jump, or use shipboard systems like sensors, computers, communicators, or weapons. Piloted spacecraft (such as lifeboats or fighters) can still be launched.

Hull Destroyed: The spacecraft loses structural integrity. At the GM's discretion it may break up or even explode. Occupants may be killed, trapped in wreckage, or escape depending on the situation. GMs may require a successful Vacc Suit roll to survive.

Turret or Bay Disabled: Weapons and other systems built into that turret or bay no longer function.

Turret or Bay Destroyed: As above, but no repairs possible; systems must be replaced at full cost. Crew members take 5d damage each (personal DR does not protect).

More specific damage effects, such as disabled drives, may occur. Each time cumulative damage to a ship or smallcraft hull reaches a multiple of 10% of the spacecraft's original hit points, roll 3d on the *Major Damage Table* (see p. 174) and apply the result on the table to the spacecraft. This simplifies the **GURPS Vehicles** advanced-damage system, but gives more flavorful results with **GURPS Traveller**-designed vessels.

5. COLLISION AND POINT DEFENSE PHASE

If a spacecraft attempted to ram its target and was not destroyed by enemy fire, resolve the ram attempt as described here. If multiple spacecraft are ramming each other in the same hex resolve them in order of highest to lowest acceleration, then lowest to highest Size Modifier, breaking ties with a Quick Contest of Tactics.

After a ram is announced, the target spacecraft may attempt to use point-defense fire as a "last chance." Fire is allowed even if the weapon fired during the direct fire phase. Point-defense fire is resolved exactly like normal direct fire against a target at 0 hex range, except that weapons receive a bonus to hit due to the closing range and much simpler target solution.

Each beam weapon can only fire *once* in the point-defense phase. If its gunner scores multiple hits (see p. 168) he may divide those hits among different targets (for example, several incoming missiles) rather than hitting the same target more than once, as long as these other targets are craft that are no harder to hit than his first target. This means a single beam may, on average, stop two or three missiles. Sandcasters may be fired as point-defense weapons: Treat them as TL10 turret lasers for this purpose against missiles. A hit destroys a single missile, but has no effect on larger vessels.

If both spacecraft cooperate in ramming each other, the attempt succeeds automatically. Otherwise it is a Quick Contest of Piloting skill between rammer and the evading target. Missiles use their controlling Gunner's skill, with a -1 per 3 hexes range from *controlling spacecraft* to the target. Add the target Size Modifier to rammer skill; a craft with a higher acceleration adds half the difference in G to skill (round down).

If the rammer loses or ties, it fails to hit the target. If this occurs, nothing happens: it remains in the current hex. If the rammer wins, both spacecraft collide.

A collision inflicts crushing damage on both spacecraft equal to the relative velocity times the lower of the two craft's hull hit points times 20d (5) – that is, armor protecting at $\frac{1}{5}$ DR. As both craft will be in the same hex, relative velocity is the distance between their respective vector counters. For a standard missile with 30 hit points, this simplifies to 6d×100 (5) × relative velocity. A missile's gunner may choose to detonate the warhead's shaped-charge warhead *instead* of doing impact damage. This is more effective if relative velocity is 0-1. Standard missiles use shaped-charge warheads doing 6d×60 (10) damage at TL10 or 6d×80 (10) at TL12 – the (10) means armor protects at one-tenth DR.

Ramming an asteroid, planet, or moon won't do damage on a planetary scale, but can devastate an area – aside from warhead effects, assume anything nearby takes explosive concussion damage from the impact based on one-tenth the collision damage.

6. LAUNCH/DOCKING PHASE

In this phase spacecraft may launch missiles and other craft in order of lowest to highest captain initiative.

A missile rack can launch one missile and a missile bay can launch up to 50 (subject to remaining ammunition). A spacedock or vehicle bay can launch any number of vessels carried in it or initiate docking and recovery operations with any number of vessels per bay, but not both at once.

Newly launched spacecraft are placed in the launching vessel's hex; place their vector counter in the same hex as the launching spacecraft's vector counter. The launch mechanism of missile bays or racks may impart an additional 1-G acceleration as it launches – if desired, place the missile's vector counter in any adjacent hex.

Docking: A spacecraft can dock with another (link airlocks using passage tubes) if both have matched courses. One of the docking spacecraft must be capable of maneuver; the other must either cooperate, or be crippled and unable to maneuver. Safe docking requires precise maneuvering and takes a complete round. Neither craft may maneuver in the *next* space combat round's maneuver phase, and the docking maneuver is not completed until the beginning of the next round's docking phase. Docked spacecraft can maneuver while docked provided that they continue to match courses and don't exceed 1 G acceleration. Undocking is faster: It takes a single phase and does not restrict maneuver.

Recovery: A spacecraft can recover smaller craft into a spacedock or vehicle bay if it meets the above docking requirements and the smaller craft can fit aboard. The smaller spacecraft is taken aboard at the beginning of the next round's launch/docking phase.

Matching Courses: Two spacecraft have matched courses if both occupy the same hex *and* both their vector counters also occupy a single hex.

Emergency Docking and Recovery: A docking or recovery operation can be performed more quickly. The maneuvering craft makes a Piloting skill roll. If the roll succeeds, the docking or recovery occurs in a single round – there's no restriction on maneuver next round. If it fails, the two craft collide, each taking dice of damage equal to 1/10 the smaller spacecraft's hit points (this is equivalent to a collision at about 20 mph).

7. DAMAGE CONTROL PHASE

In this phase, engineers can attempt to repair damage to their spacecraft.

An engineer can repair either hull damage, damage to a specific subassembly (a turret or bay), or a single major system (such as the M-drive) that was damaged or knocked out by a roll on the *Major Damage Table*. Spacecraft with multiple engineers can divide them into teams working on the same or different areas. Assigning them is usually the responsibility of the chief engineer.

Disabled hulls or subassemblies can be repaired, but destroyed ones can't – they must be replaced in a shipyard.

To determine the success of repair attempts, roll against the engineer's Mechanic or Engineering skill. Modifiers: -2 if working on a disabled hull or subassembly. If a team is working under a chief engineer's direction, all may add +1 to skill if the chief engineer makes a successful Leadership roll.

If a single engineer is making repairs, a number of hit points of damage are regained equal to the margin of success. For a team, use their average skill but multiply the margin of success by the number of engineers to get hit points repaired.

If repairing a hull or subassembly, reduce its accumulated damage by the hit points repaired. If disabled it begins to function again after being raised above 0 hit points. When repairing a system knocked out by Major Damage rolls, assume that getting it working requires accumulating hit points' worth of repairs equal to 10% of the hull's original hit points.

A critical success doubles the hit points repaired. On a critical failure, roll 1d: On a 1-3, there is an accident; a plasma or hydrogen leak, a fire, or a collapsing weakened structure does 5d damage to an engineer. On a 4-6, there is a setback (someone cut the wrong cable or turned on a circuit breaker before it was ready) and the area being repaired suffers 1d damage multiplied by the number of engineers in that team.

Rushed Repairs: Engineers can rush ahead on repairs, ignoring safety procedures, performing dangerous jury-rigs, and so on. Multiply the number of HPs repaired by 5,

but any failure is a critical failure, and on a critical failure roll three times for effects.

CELESTIAL BODIES

While most of space is empty, the valuable parts aren't. Many engagements will take place around planets and other strategic objectives.

Worlds

These are planets and moons whose diameter is 1,000 miles or greater. Typical inhabited world sizes are 10,000 miles or less and so comfortably fit in a single hex (Earth is 8,000 miles across). Worlds should be represented on the map either by drawing a circle or placing an appropriate counter in a hex.

Line of Sight: A world blocks line of sight past it: A spacecraft may use PESA and AESA sensors, laser communications and direct fire (except with meson guns) into but not through a world hex.

Gravity: The six hexes adjacent to a world with a surface gravity of 0.25 G or more are its "gravity hexes." They affect spacecraft passing through them, as described in the *Movement* rules. The world's hex itself is *not* a gravity hex. If the world's surface gravity is over 0.5 G, gravity effects are mandatory. Otherwise, the pilot may decide whether to pass close enough to the world for them to take effect. (If he passes through more than one of a world's gravity hexes, then if one takes effect, all must take effect.)

High Orbit: A spacecraft which moves one hex in the movement phase directly from a gravity hex to an adjacent gravity hex is in orbit. The spacecraft's movement should carry it around the planet without any further acceleration being required.

Low Orbit: A stationary spacecraft in a world's hex is assumed to be in low orbit.

Takeoff: A spacecraft on a world's surface may leave that world by accelerating into an adjacent hex, and on future rounds, leave the planet's gravity hexes or enter orbit.

Landing: A streamlined spacecraft can land on a world by moving onto it at one hex speed; it can also land if it occupies the hex and is at zero speed. Entering a world hex at higher speeds destroys the spacecraft. Attempting a landing also destroys the spacecraft if the world has more than a trace atmosphere and the craft is unstreamlined.

Large Bodies

Large bodies such as stars and gas giants will take up multiple hexes. Represent such bodies as a circle of (diameter/10,000) hexes across. A large body's gravity hexes are represented by a larger circle with a diameter four times the square root of the planet's mass (in Earth masses).

Don't worry about aligning a big planet on the hex grid; it won't fit. Just draw a circle for the given diameter, and if the 1-G gravity well is larger, a second circle for it.

Large bodies will also block line of sight as per worlds. Realistic gravity and orbital mechanics for large bodies are beyond the scope of this system. GMs can apply gravity effects as per the ordinary world rules, except that the gravity zone may be a number of hexes deep, rather than just the six adjacent hexes.

Landing on a gas giant is fatal, but vessels with DR 100+ armor can enter or move through a gas-giant hex if it keeps its velocity below one hex/round. The vessel is assumed to be flying through or hovering in its upper atmosphere.

Moving into a star will destroy any spacecraft.

Small Bodies

This includes asteroids (a few yards to several miles across) and small moons or planets up to 1,000 miles in diameter. In the 10,000-mile-hex scale, such bodies do not affect detection or fire unless a ship is in the hex and deliberately keeping the asteroid between it and another spacecraft.

Ships may freely pass through hexes containing small bodies. Even an asteroid belt is fairly thinly spread: In a dense asteroid belt there would only be one small asteroid every hex.

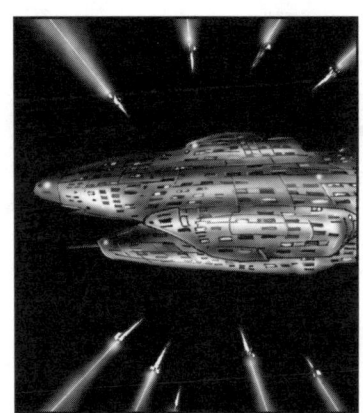

MISCELLANEOUS SITUATIONS

The following rules elaborate on various aspects of space combat.

Anti-Missile Fire

Standard missiles have DR 40 (TL10) or DR 120 (TL12) and can withstand 30 hits each. A single laser or particle beam hit is enough to destroy a missile, so feel free not to bother rolling damage if using ordinary turret or bay weapons.

Communications

Radio communications must be declared in the detection phase; otherwise, spacecraft can communicate freely back and forth with radio, laser, and meson communications as described in the *Starship Operations* rules. These give communication range in millions of miles; one million miles = 100 hexes. Note that communications are limited by lightspeed. Light travels 18.6 hexes per second or 22,320 hexes per combat turn.

Friendly ships in communication using datalink programs can share sensor data, giving a bonus to their friend's detection chances.

Standard missiles must remain within communication range to be controlled. In most cases, this is not a problem, but a missile behind a planet (for example) cannot maneuver or attack.

Broadcast communications may be picked up by anyone in range, but the *content* of scrambled transmissions will not be understood unless decoded (see Cryptanalysis skill, p. B245).

Crew Positions and Skill Rolls

Smaller vessels often have the same crewman performing multiple roles. If a crew member is filling multiple positions during a particular space combat round, he will suffer a -2 penalty on all skill rolls for each extra task he is performing.

Actions counted as tasks are: piloting; fire of one weapon or set of linked identical weapons (except sandcasters) at the same target; controlling one missile or a salvo; acting as a sensor operator; damage control; complex communications (GM's option, e.g., coordinating a squadron or tracking a signal); meson screen operation. A ship with more than two crew engaged in the above tasks should also have one captain who does nothing but give orders – if not, the GM can apply an extra -1 penalty to everyone's skill rolls!

Jump

A starship with an operating jump drive and enough fuel may prep for a jump in the Maneuver Phase. The ship may not maneuver while jumping. It will then jump at the start of its next round's maneuver phase. A safe jump (entry or exit) requires a distance from a body of at least hundred diameters. Thus, starships may jump in or out safely from (planetary diameter in miles/100) hexes. See p. 121 for the skill rolls needed to perform a safe and accurate jump. Ships jumping *in* appear during the maneuver phase. They retain whatever vector they had when they went into jump.

Meson Guns and Meson Screens

Meson gun hits ignore the target's damage resistance, unless the target has a meson screen. *Meson screens* must be carefully focused to deflect meson gun fire. Whenever a spacecraft is hit by a meson gun, the screen operator must make an Electronics Operation (Force Field) roll.

A critical success means the screen provides its full DR against the attack. Success by 4 or more means it provides half DR. Success by 0-3 means it provides 10% DR. Failure means it provides no DR. Critical failure means it malfunctions and cannot be used next round. To get it back on line requires a successful Electronics Operation (Force shields) roll, one try per round.

Missile Salvos

Big ships sometimes fire many missiles at a time. It can be convenient to represent these by single counters each representing multiple missiles from a single bay or turret – just record that a given set of missile and vector counter represents *n* number of missiles, and reduce *n* if the missiles take hits.

If a very large salvo of missiles attempts to ram the same spacecraft, GMs may wish to make contests of skills for *groups* of 3, 5, 10, or more missiles rather than rolling individually for each attack.

Likewise, GMs can simplify damage by rolling once per group and multiplying both damage and DR by the number of missiles.

Planetary Defense Fire

TL8+ planets with large populations and/or good starports often have planetary defenses. Ground-based lasers and particle beams cannot penetrate a planetary atmosphere and still carry enough energy to hit high orbital targets, so static planetary defenses generally take one of two forms: ground-based missile launchers, or a number of armed "orbital platforms" (built as ships with no drives), or meson guns buried deep underground. Such "deep meson guns" are immune to most attacks except other meson guns, sabotage, or destruction of their orbital or surface sensors.

GMs can assume that surface starport installations have sensors at least as capable as those of a command bridge (type V-IV starport) or basic bridge (type III or II starport).

Using Sandcasters

In the Direct Fire Phase, a turret's sandcasters can be targeted vs. a single enemy vessel (or a group of vessels in *very* tight formation). A sandcaster adds DR 400 to its ship's armor DR vs. all laser fire originating from the targeted vessel. Multiple sandcasters can combine to protect against laser fire from a single vessel, but each extra 'caster only adds an additional +50 DR. X-ray laser fire halves sandcaster DR just like ordinary armor, so against standard shipboard lasers it's DR 200 + DR 25 per extra sandcaster.

Selective, Pinpoint, and Battery Fire

A gunner can choose to selectively target individual turrets or bay subassemblies. A standard turret has a Size Modifier of +5, a bay has +7 – use these modifiers instead of the spacecraft's Size Modifier when firing. A successful hit means that hit location is not rolled for – instead, that turret or bay is hit.

A gunner using a direct-fire weapon can attempt to use "pinpoint marksmanship" vs. a weak spot (e.g., hatches, weapon tubes, turret rings, etc.) in the target's armor. This is extremely difficult: Roll to hit at -6 *and do not add the Size Modifier to the roll.* DR protects at half normal, cumulative with other armor divisors.

To simplify big-ship battles, GMs can require identical laser-equipped turrets be grouped into fairly even "batteries" of up to 30 lasers each. Each battery fires as one weapon (roll to hit only once). Calculate "adjusted battery skill" just as you would adjusted Gunner skill, except use the average of individual Gunner skills, and find RoF bonus by adding all RoFs together and using the RoF Bonus table (p. 174) to find the new bonus. E.g., if five turrets each with three RoF $1/60$ lasers fired as a 15-laser battery, they would be treated as one RoF $(15 \times 1/60) = $ RoF $15/60$ = RoF $1/4$ weapon; while it would only fire once rather than 15 times, the usual +4 RoF bonus would become a +8.

Transponders

Civilian ships are legally required to activate transponders broadcasting their location and identity. Transponders can be unplugged, but naval patrols reserve the right to fire on ships detected that are not operating transponders. (Usual peacetime procedure is to order it to cut its velocity and stand to for boarding, but in troubled regions or in sensitive areas such as around restricted naval depots, patrols may not be that patient.)

It may take weeks to check registry, while origin and destination information are only as accurate as the navigator who entered them.

SPACE WEAPONS TABLE

Weapon	RoF	1/2 D	Max	Acc	Damage
360-MJ Laser	1/60	2	6	32	5d×50 (2)
405-MJ Laser	1/60	3	8	33	5d×100 (2)
Particle Beam Bay	1/60	1	4	30	6d×1,000
Meson Gun Bay	1/60	1	4	30	6d×1,000 (!)
Spinal P-Beam	1/60	5	15	36	7d×3,000
Spinal Meson Gun	1/60	5	15	36	7d×3,000 (!)

Ranges are in 10,000-mile hexes. (2) means armor DR is halved; (!) means armor DR but not meson-screen DR is ignored.

SPACE RANGE TABLE

Hexes	Modifier	Hexes	Modifier
0	-39	11-15	-48
1	-41	16-20	-49
2	-43	21-30	-50
3	-44	31-45	-51
4	-45	46-70	-52
5-7	-46	71-100	-53
8-10	-47	etc.	etc.

SENSOR MODIFIERS

Scan Values Table

Type	—PESA— TL10	TL12	—AESA— TL10	TL12	—Radscan— TL10	TL12
Cockpit/System	35	37	39	40	29	31
Basic bridge	37	38	41	42	31	35
Command bridge	39	41	42	43	32	38

Scan Modifiers

Sensor: Add value from *Scan Values Table*, above.

Skill: Add Electronics Operations (Sensors) skill level.

Range: Count the range in hexes from the sensing spacecraft to its target. Look this number up on the *Space Range Table*, above, and subtract the corresponding modifier.

Prior Detection: Object detected on prior round by other sensor type or by ally sharing information through datalink: +4.

AESA only:
■ Object's Size Modifier.
■ Object has basic stealth: -(TL-4).
■ Object has radical stealth: -2 × (TL-4).
■ Object in same hex or adjacent to planet or moon: -4.
■ Object or sensor within planetary atmosphere (more than Trace): -6.
■ AESA used as ladar: -2.

PESA only:
■ Object's Size Modifier.
■ Object in same hex or adjacent to planet or moon: -2.
■ Object silhouetted against a star: -4.
■ Object or sensor within planetary atmosphere (more than Trace): -6.
■ Object has basic emission cloaking: -(TL-4)/2, round down.*
■ Object has radical emission cloaking: -(TL-4).*

* Emission Cloaking doubles (to the same effectiveness as stealth) if the object is in a planetary atmosphere, including a gas giant. In space, emission cloaking is less effective, as the vehicle is always going to be "hotter" than surrounding space.

Radscanner only:
■ Object using active sensors: + the Scan value of the active sensor (e.g., AESA) that the object is using (see *Scan Values Table*, above) but *minus* the TL of that active sensor. If the active sensor is used as a ladar, use the Scan value - (TL+2).
■ Object is using transponder or broadcasting wideband radio signals: +40. Note – if the object is also using active sensors, use the higher of the two modifiers; don't add them together.

GUNNERY MODIFIERS

Use augmented Gunner skill (the sum of Gunner skill, Acc bonus up to a limit of base Gunner skill, RoF bonus, and targeting program) with these additional modifiers:

Target Size: Add the Size Modifier of the target. (Standard missiles are +0). If using pinpoint marksmanship (p. 172) use a -6 penalty instead of Size Modifier.

Range Modifier: Add the range in hexes from the firing spacecraft to its target, counting the firing hex. The result is linear Range in hexes. Look this up in the "Hexes" column on the *Space Range Table*, above. Read the number to the right ("Modifier" column) to get the range modifier applied to the gunner's skill.

Active Sensors: +2 if target is within sensor range and detected with active sensors.

Point Defense Fire: +10.

Firing beyond ½D range does not reduce Accuracy to 0; as ships are firing over a 20-minute round using fully stabilized beam weapons in the vacuum of space, there is no sudden Acc loss.

Note there is no modifier for target velocity: Over space combat ranges, gross course changes are predictable enough that speed itself isn't a major factor, while relative velocity is factored into engagement times, as ships with high velocities will flash past each other for only a few rounds of firing.

MAJOR DAMAGE TABLE

3 – Fuel tank shattered; half of fuel capacity lost.

4 – 1d passengers injured; 5d damage each, ignore DR.*

5 – J-drive knocked out.

6 – Cargo damaged; a quarter of all cargo carried is lost.

7 – One computer knocked out (standard bridges have three).

8 – 1d crew are injured; 5d damage each, ignore DR.*

9 – Power loss; halve Gs and jump number.

10 – Weapon: one turret, bay or other weapon disabled.

11 – No special effect unless damage caused by particle beam or meson gun; then one non-hardened computer is knocked out.

12 – Fuel tank shattered; half of fuel capacity lost.

13 – 1d passengers injured; 5d damage each, ignore DR.*

14 – M-drive acceleration halved (round down).

15 – Cargo damaged (see above).

16 – Bridge (or cockpit) knocked out.

17 – 1d crew are injured; 5d damage each, ignore DR.*

18 – Power plant knocked out; ship crippled.

* Add an extra 1d casualties *per full 50 people* aboard; e.g., if 50-99 passengers were left, 2d would be hit. The GM chooses or rolls to see who is hit. Rather than roll damage for NPCs, GMs can assume each hit disables or kills. Add +1 per die of damage (or use explosive decompression rules) for anyone not suited up!

GURPS VEHICLES-DESIGNED SPACECRAFT

These rules are designed for use with spacecraft built using the **GURPS Traveller** design system. Ships constructed with **Vehicles** may have additional systems or design choices – if so, just add the appropriate rules from **Vehicles**. Here are a few guidelines on issues not addressed in **Vehicles**:

Partial or Unstabilized Mounts: If a vessel is given partially stabilized weapons, Acc halves (round down) at ½D range; if unstabilized weapons, Acc goes to zero past ½D range.

Ships Without Vectored Thrust Engines: These can only accelerate (move their vector counter) in the direction they are facing, and may not add a G-bonus to Dodge. They may still change facing at the start of the maneuver phase, before accelerating.

Higher or Lower RoF: In a space-combat round, weapons are assumed to be firing multiple carefully aimed tracking shots over the 20-minute period, and taking time to aim between each shot. All standard turret and bay weapons fire with an effective RoF ⅟60 (including time to recharge power cells), giving a bonus of +4. In the 20-minute scale, higher or lower RoF provides a modifier to adjusted skill as follows:

ROF BONUS TABLE

RoF and Bonus	RoF and Bonus	RoF and Bonus
⅟600.........+4	⅛ ....+10	8 ....+16
⅟300 .... +5	¼ ....+11	15 ....+17
⅟150 ....+6	½ ....+12	30 ....+18
⅟60 ....+7	1 ....+13	and so on . . .
⅟30 ....+8	2 ....+14	
⅟15 ....+9	4 ....+15	

Values that fall between these numbers use the lower bonus. When calculating RoF for **GURPS Vehicles** weapon that use power cells, base it on sustained RoF over a 20-minute period. If a weapon can fire four shots, but then takes a minute to recharge its power cells, its sustained RoF would be ⅟15 rather than 4.

Guns: On a 10,000-mile scale, guns, including railguns, will only be able to hit maneuvering targets within a 0-hex range. Against stationary targets (e.g., derelicts, planets), they have unlimited ranges, but suffer normal range modifiers to hit.